A BOND OF BROKEN GLASS

THE SEVERED REALMS

T.A. LAWRENCE

To Rachel Bobo,
For finally making me understand how some girls can become instant best
friends

ALONDRIA

MYSTRAL

DWELLEN

Verni Forest

Kobii Mountains

The Bluffs

Wyndham

Adreean Sea

AVELEA

FORGOTTEN ISLE

Edii Gulf

Evaen

The Hills

Nettlewood

Rivre

CHARSHON

Meranthi

Sea of Lythos

NAENDEN

Talens

Grythos Channel

LAEI

PROLOGUE

The parasite had worn many bodies over the centuries.

The frantic girl who shuffled into Madame LeFleur's Cosmetics Boutique: Your One-Stop Shop for All Things Alluring would be her next.

The pyrite bell dangling above the shop entrance jingled, alerting the Madame to the girl's arrival. The shop owner jerked, spilling her last bottle of LeFleur's Specialty Vanishing Ink across the counter, causing it to soak into the previously pristine wood and drip onto the floor.

The ink did not vanish as advertised.

Madame LeFleur spun the bottle to hide its label lest her lone customer take notice. But the young girl wasn't paying attention. Instead, she lingered by a shelf of products that claimed to alleviate sudden bursts of heat in aging women.

The shop owner narrowed her eyes. She hadn't been expecting a customer tonight. In fact, she'd closed up an hour early for a handful of reasons.

One, Prince Evander's ball was to be held at Othian Castle tonight. As the Madame's business model revolved around preying upon the insecurities and groundless hopes of women wishing to make themselves prettier than nature had blessed them with the capability of being, it made no sense to keep the shop open past sundown.

Every human girl in the city of Othian would attend the ball, vying for the chance to snag the handsome fae prince. The Madame estimated not one of them would chance spending fewer than three hours preparing their skin with fragrant oils, arranging their hair in ornate braids, and stuffing their corsets with her bestselling LeFleur's Miracle Endowment Enhancer—which was really just dyed cotton and the Madame's most lucrative idea yet.

It didn't matter how much the entire kingdom detested the Heir to the Throne of Dwellen.

The opportunity to become a princess had presented itself, and there wasn't a woman in Dwellen who wouldn't grasp at it.

Except, perhaps, for Ellie Payne. If all went according to plan, the parasite would be seeking her out later.

In the past few hours, the traffic in the shop had dwindled to almost nothing, and the Madame had purchased too expensive a porcelain tub and too exotic a collection of foreign soaps not to be soaking in lavender bubbles. All for the sake of a stray sale here and there.

At least, that was what the Madame told herself.

Then there was the real reason—one from which the parasite lurking in the corners of the Madame's consciousness derived no small amount of satisfaction.

Tonight was a full moon, and the Madame was superstitious about this heavenly occurrence above all others. All her neighbors knew as much.

Rather, everyone *thought* they knew as much.

That was the thing about humans, the parasite mused; they always assumed they knew more than they did.

The parasite, of course, knew perfectly well that Madame LeFleur's superstitions regarding the monthly celestial event were more than well-founded, the parasite herself having planted the gnarled roots by which these superstitions fed.

Madame LeFleur paid little attention to the girl as she tried and

2

failed to wipe the spilled non-vanishing ink with a nearby terrycloth. "Silly me, forgetting to lock up. We're closed, dearie."

If the parasite could have rolled her eyes, she would have. Madame LeFleur had the irksome habit of floundering about, using the same sort of language one might hear from an elderly woman whose only concerns were that of who had accidentally dyed their hair blue recently when attempting to go silver-plated, or whose grandchild had disgraced their family by eloping with a farmhand.

The parasite knew better than to be fooled by her host's carefully crafted facade.

Underneath the cheery disposition and altogether silly demeanor, the Madame's mind was sharp as an adder's fang.

Madame LeFleur was like many living beings in this strange and wonderful realm, disguising deadly venom under an array of vibrant colors.

That was part of the reason the parasite had picked Madame LeFleur. Typically, the parasite went for weaker-minded hosts, ones whose consciousnesses were more readily overcome. But with each body, each mind, came a price, and the parasite had grown weary of inhabiting the unintelligent.

Madame LeFleur sometimes used brains in the many potions she concocted—the ones that actually worked, the ones she sold in the underground market rather than the watered down briarseed oil she bottled in cheap crystal and peddled to desperate women. The parasite had now witnessed quite the assortment of brains. Lizard brains, rat brains, human brains. It fascinated the parasite to observe the differences—the smooth silky film that coated the outer layer of the rodents' brains versus the cascading folds and the plunging shadows that carved texture into the human brains.

The parasite sometimes wished Madame LeFleur could use that glinting scalpel of hers to slice out the brains of the parasite's previous human hosts; she was fairly certain what she would find: a glaring absence of hills and valleys cresting the wet, juicy membranes.

But the parasite's previous hosts would all be decayed beyond recognition by this point. Most of them had returned to dust and were likely being chewed up by livestock at this very moment, so the parasite could only dream of such things.

"Did you hear me, child?" Madame LeFleur asked, her pitch heightening in what most would have mistaken for agitation when the girl remained planted in front of the counter. "We're closed."

Madame LeFleur finally looked up from her incessant scrubbing, allowing the parasite to get a good look at the girl through the Madame's eyes.

Plain and unadorned as a mouse's tail, the girl was the kind who often fell prey to the beauty elixirs the Madame fashioned from the leftover lard that sloshed off her morning bacon.

That was, of course, all the Madame noticed about her.

The Madame couldn't sense what the parasite could.

Desperation, raw and crude and completely unrefined, emanated from the girl, radiating from her soul and pulsing in noxious waves.

The parasite could get drunk on that sort of energy.

"I..." The girl's gaze flitted back toward the door, and the parasite's hope threatened to wither. No, the girl couldn't leave now. Not when the parasite had endured so many unsuitable women with unsuitable auras today. Not when she'd almost given up hope of finding anyone fit for her intentions. But then the girl's back straightened, and she plastered a look of determination on that unremarkable face of hers and said, "I'm told you sell potions that alter one's appearance."

Predictable, the parasite thought. But useful all the same.

"You're a bit too late for that, I'm afraid." Madame LeFleur lowered her spectacles, as she often did when she was looking to get a particular thrill from asserting her dominance—disguised as disapproval, of course—upon a youngster. "Sold out of those a week ago, the hour the prince announced he'd be throwing a ball."

The girl frowned, which didn't help to soften her less desirable features. Tethered to the Madame for now, the parasite had only recently become able to discriminate the slight differences between the faces of the humans. The variation in their features was so slim already, and the Madame had never been all that good at it. It was as if the Madame could see faces as a whole—pretty or, more importantly, ugly—but her brain couldn't quite grasp onto the details. The parasite was almost positive this had not been the case in previous hosts, and it often had her wondering what sort of pattern the curves on the Madame's brain made.

Perhaps one day the parasite would find out.

"Surely you have something." The girl tapped her fingers against the counter, the beat off-kilter with the dripping of the spilled ink still slowly splattering the floor.

The Madame shook her head, her curls bouncing against her ears. "Nothing at all."

It seemed that whatever courage or insanity it had taken the girl to come here expired as her shoulders deflated and she turned to go.

No, no, no. The parasite tried to remember the position of the sun a few moments ago when the Madame had glanced out the window, for the Madame kept scrubbing, and the window was nowhere in sight. The parasite was certain it had been just about to slip over the horizon, and if that was the case, she needed only a few more moments...

If only she could be free of the shackles that bound her, the magical barrier between the Madame's faculties and her own...

"But dearie?" the Madame asked just as the girl reached the door. The parasite wasn't sure that she'd ever felt relief, not like her human hosts did, but the weight that pulled away from her consciousness when the girl turned back around was a striking replica.

"Yes?"

The curiosity in Madame's brain warred with the anxiety welling in her stomach.

Once again, the parasite was thankful to her past self for her choice of host.

As far as the Madame was concerned, curiosity would always win.

"I must ask, why are you not attending the ball?"

The plain girl swallowed and bit her lip, embarrassment flushing her cheeks. "I thought I might, but I'm no fool. There's no use going like this." She gestured to herself as if that explained everything.

In the Madame's opinion, it did.

Something pungent wafted through the Madame's consciousness. The parasite fought back the sudden urge to recoil. Over the years, she'd come to recognize the useless emotion, but its scent never failed to make her queasy.

Pity was the most unpleasant of human emotions. It smelled like rotting flowers and settled in the Madame's stomach about as well as soured milk.

The Madame sighed. "Well, perhaps I might have something stored in the back. But have your payment ready. It'll cost you forty coppers and I haven't time for you to be finagling through your coin purse. I really don't have time to be doing this at all."

The girl nodded and rummaged through her coin purse while the Madame slipped behind a red velvet curtain into the storeroom and did some rummaging herself.

The parasite never understood why the Madame did this, if not for the sale. She was a clever human—about as clever as they came. And during the full moon, her hands could craft poisons specific enough to kill only the intended target, leaving buyers free to distribute the poison into entire vats of wine rather than a specific glass, without threat of murdering an entire party. She could brew love potions that needn't be drunk, only inhaled, and the victim would fancy themselves obsessed with the original wearer of the scent. That was the parasite's gift to the Madame, another reason she'd chosen her above all others.

The parasite had been around for a long time. Long enough to have gotten good at knowing just what kind of gift a host might manifest.

It was all in their aura, which the parasite could taste in the air as potential candidates soiled it with their breath, with their fears and hopes and dreams. Sometimes it was a skill—one they were already predisposed toward—and all the parasite did was enhance that skill.

Other times, it was a desire.

And from the sweet, intoxicating desperation sluicing off the plain girl in sheets, the parasite had a sneaking suspicion of how the girl's gift might manifest were the parasite to take her on as a host.

It was the kind of potential gift the parasite had been sniffing for all week, ever since the Madame had heard the news.

Did you hear? The prince is throwing a ball. He intends to take a human as a wife!

Oh, the parasite had heard all right.

And better yet...

He's hosting it the night of the full moon. Isn't that romantic?

These humans of Dwellen and their fascination with the moon. It was part of the reason the parasite had migrated here.

In fact...

I was just dreaming of you, sweet friend, the parasite thought as the sun slipped over the horizon and the crest of the moon took its place. It didn't matter that the storeroom contained no windows. The parasite didn't need to glance outside to know what shift had just occurred.

Cool, intoxicating pleasure washed over Madame LeFleur's body, and when she stepped out from behind the curtain, the hands into which the girl pressed forty copper coins no longer belonged to Madame LeFleur.

SLIPPING from Madame LeFleur's fingertips into the plain girl's body was as easy as letting go. As simple as the thudding of Madame LeFleur's dead body against the cold ground.

That had a tendency to happen when the parasite abandoned a host.

She wasn't entirely sure why, but she liked to imagine that when she joined herself to a human, she slipped her ethereal tendrils into the crevices of their brain, caressing the silky membrane and attaching herself to them so deeply that when she eventually rent herself from them, she ripped out a chunk of their mind in the process.

The parasite's eldest sibling hadn't cared for her habit of discarding her hosts before their life came to a natural end. That was how the parasite had gotten into this mess to begin with.

7

Still, she had no regrets as she stared down at Madame LeFleur's pale face.

For starters, the plain girl's brain actually possessed the capability of processing the Madame's facial features. Her empty eyes were the color of moss and she had a mole on her upper lip. Her skin was pale rather than tanned.

But one could never tell in pale-skinned humans whether that was a byproduct of their complexion or just being dead.

The parasite would miss certain aspects of her former host, of course. She doubted she'd ever find a mind like hers. One that, when enhanced, proved there was nothing quite impossible as far as chemistry was concerned.

It had been an enjoyable pastime. But pastimes were aptly named. The opportunity to achieve something greater had shuffled through the shop doors, and the parasite wasn't keen on missing out on it.

The parasite stretched out her new host's limbs like a cat might unsheathe its claws as it woke from a nap in the sun.

And like a cat, it was time to go strolling in the moonlight.

The parasite stumbled to the door, grabbing first at the counter, then at shelves, to steady herself. It was always a bit of a pain—getting used to a new body, the lankiness or stoutness of the new host's limbs, the length of their stride, even the rate of their breath as their lungs coordinated with the rest of their body.

The plain girl was of average build. But that wasn't surprising, since the girl was practically average in everything. Not ugly. Not pretty.

Totally unremarkable, just as the Madame had thought.

But the parasite had known better.

She shook the girl's head—*her* head now. What was she thinking, trying to get used to this body? The only reason she'd wanted her was to do, well, this...

It didn't take long for the parasite to locate the source of the girl's utmost desire. In fact, it practically leapt out at her, and the parasite had to focus a bit to grasp onto it. It was a bit like trying to contain a fish with wet hands. It flailed and wriggled, but this wasn't the parasite's first utmost desire wrangling, and she soon overcame it. Channeled it until it flowed through her, melded with her.

It stung at first, hot and sharp and potent. A bit like taking a brand straight from the fire and delving it into the ribcage.

The parasite reveled in it. Allowed it to consume her.

What they made together was remarkable.

The girl's legs lengthened, muscles bulking around her slender thighs. Her hips were next, and the parasite cried out in masochistic delight as the girl's hipbone splintered. It expanded and readjusted, the bone and muscles knitting themselves back together, a smooth layer of fat coating the edges, forming curves the parasite couldn't have painted better herself.

The girl's breasts followed. Then her face, her eyes widening, her nose shrinking, her cheekbones lifting. Where lifeless locks had once been, silky ashen hair took its place, cascading over the girl's slender shoulders in gentle waves.

The blotches on her forearms faded, the blemishes smoothed over and replaced with skin as delicate and pale as Madame LeFleur's prized porcelain tub.

To be someone different was what the girl had wanted.

Different, indeed, the parasite thought as she reached the door. As soon her fingers touched the handle, an idea plucked at the parasite's mind. Before leaving, she fetched a vial from the storage closet behind the thick curtain. Painted mandrakes decorated the vial, and the parasite used her new, full lips to smile as she tucked it into the girl's coin purse.

Then she slipped out of Madame LeFleur's shop and into the tender embrace of the moonlight.

MOONLIGHT HAD ALWAYS BEEN a touchy subject for the parasite, and for good reason. It was the force that both bound her and freed her.

When the parasite's bleeding soul of an eldest brother had learned what she'd been up to, how many hosts she'd discarded in her quest for adventure, he'd gotten it into his head to punish her.

9

Punishing a being as ancient as the parasite turned out to be quite the ordeal, so he'd used moonlight to bind the curse.

And cursed she was.

While her siblings had been left free to work their magic anytime they wanted, so long as their hosts allowed it, her brother had harnessed the energy of the full moon to bind her power to it.

Only when the full moon crested the horizon could the parasite draw upon her power, and even then she didn't get the *full* full moon. Only until it apexed in the sky.

Her brother hadn't left her much to work with, though she supposed that, if he could have, he would have locked her power away entirely.

That had been many moons ago.

Her siblings had gotten what was coming to them in the end. When the fae slipped into this realm at the heels of one of their runaway children, it hadn't taken long for them to hunt down the parasite's siblings. It hadn't taken long for the fae to consume them.

None of her siblings had bothered to unbind her in the years prior to the fae's arrival. Other than her eldest brother, they hadn't even known what crime she'd committed to be condemned to such a cruel imprisonment. They hadn't cared. Her eldest brother had commanded them to have nothing to do with her, and they obeyed.

That was just as well, because her banishment had meant that she'd been kingdoms away when the fae consumed her siblings.

Good riddance.

She hoped they'd fractured into mindless, half-life shadows by now, their very sense of being eaten up by how many times they'd been split and severed and passed onto the fae's offspring.

The parasite found herself skipping down the streets of Othian at the very thought.

THE GARMENTS the plain girl had come into the shop wearing would not do. They were clean and well-kept, certainly not rags, but on the parasite's new masterpiece of a body, they might as well have been.

It was a good thing the tailor down the street also held fast to silly superstitions about the full moon and had closed up early. Madame LeFleur had visited him only last week to be measured for a new gown—a frilly pink monstrosity that now sat on display in the shop window, waiting to be picked up.

There were qualities of Madame LeFleur's that the parasite would miss.

Her affinity for frills was not one of them.

In a past life, the parasite had taken the form of a petty thief, so although the plain girl possessed no such muscle memory, the parasite wrestled with the lock using a set of hairpins from the girl's pockets.

The door hardly creaked as it opened. Madame LeFleur had mentioned the off-putting noise to the tailor during her last visit, and he must have heeded her advice to have it oiled.

It didn't take long for the parasite to find the dress. She'd spotted it last week through Madame LeFleur's eyes, a shimmering blue gown that sparkled like the view one could catch of the night sky a few miles out from the distracting lights of the city.

It was as if the tailor had made it with the parasite in mind.

That was why she'd been so delighted when he'd complained to the Madame that he'd wasted his time and resources making it. The lady of the court who'd paid for it had apparently done so without her wealthy parents' knowledge, stealing their coin with the intent to commission the sort of gown that would never catch her parents' approval.

It wasn't exactly proper.

The neckline plunged almost to the belly button, the waist was practically sheer, and the slit that cleaved the fitted skirt snaked almost up to the hip.

It was perfect.

Before the tailor woke, it would be gone.

The PARASITE SLUNK through the shadows, mindful of the wafting lilt of music that originated in the towering castle. This was the perfect night for sneaking around the city, for everyone who would typically be out and about had gone to the ball, and everyone who would typically stay in had gone to bed early, muttering about how they had better stay ahead of the noise lest they never be able to fall asleep.

While the dress itself was perfect, the plain girl's sturdy boots would not do. And the parasite couldn't very well show up at the ball with bare feet.

Thankfully, she knew a girl.

Well, Madame LeFleur had known a girl, the parasite supposed.

It was a bit of a detour to get to the modest cottage where Ellie Payne lived with her parents. She was a frequenter of Madame LeFleur's shop, though she never bought anything.

The Madame had always thought Ellie Payne beautiful, though it had frustrated her host to no end that she couldn't pinpoint Ellie's exact features. But her flawless deep brown skin and perfect black ringlets had the other girls in the shop tripping over each other in a demand to know what products she used, and that was enough proof for the Madame.

To the Madame's ever-present frustration, the products never came from her shop.

No, Ellie Payne was too practical a person to bother with the Madame's magical remedies, claiming she preferred the natural products she could purchase from a shop down the street.

The Madame had always suspected that this had not been entirely true, and that Ellie Payne had simply been onto the fact that half of the Madame's storefront was a sham.

Although Ellie Payne had never entered the store as a customer, she occasionally bought trinkets, probably hoping to butter up the Madame. What the girl really wanted was to sell her glassware. At an exorbitant prince, the Madame had always thought.

The parasite had never agreed.

Ellie Payne had a talent. The intricate designs she fashioned out of glass might have had the parasite wondering if one of her siblings inhabited Miss Payne, had they not been gobbled up by the fae centuries ago.

There was no telling what the girl and parasite could make together.

The parasite couldn't count the times that she'd almost done it—slipped from the Madame's thick fingers into Ellie Payne's smooth and slender ones, just to get a taste of what they could achieve.

But the parasite had little need for glassblowing, and Ellie Payne didn't exactly emit the aura of a woman easily controlled. Madame LeFleur's mind might have been sharp, but it could never have been described as strong.

Thus Ellie Payne had been regrettably disqualified.

Still, the girl had her uses. She had held a fondness for the Madame and often ranted to the woman about the hours of labor she invested in her work.

For over a year, she'd been trying her hand at making glass slippers.

Glass slippers, the Madame had scoffed internally many a time. The parasite herself didn't think it possible. A shoe made of glass would never hold under the weight of the wearer, after all.

But just this morning, Ellie had come bursting through the shop door, declaring that she'd done it. She'd created the perfect set of glass slippers.

Her only regret was that she hadn't perfected the design in time for the ball—at least, not to produce multiples and sell them to princess-hopefuls and their mothers, who would have been more than eager to throw heaps of cash at the chance of arming their daughters with something to help them stand out.

The upstairs window of the cottage flickered. Good, the girl wasn't out working in her father's shop like she tended to do all hours of the night. She must not have gone to the ball either. Though this didn't come as a surprise, the parasite was still glad about it. No need to chance Ellie noticing the glass slippers at the ball and accusing the parasite of thievery.

It took no time at all to pick the lock on the workshop behind the house. Even less to find the metal box in the back of the shed, in which a pair of glass shoes were rather poorly hidden.

They glittered in the glow of the dying cinders Ellie Payne had left in the furnace.

THE GLASS SLIPPERS did not fit the plain girl's feet, and though the parasite waited to change into them until she arrived at the castle, even the stroll up the palace steps had already rubbed blisters into her soles.

No matter. The Prince of Dwellen would not be looking at her feet, anyway.

The parasite had spent the entirety of her walk constructing an identity for herself—one the prince would not soon forget.

She only had a few hours before the moon reached its apex, and she needed the impression to linger on the prince's heart for an entire mooncycle. Or at least until she could determine how to free herself from its curse.

The memorable story came to her with little effort. Ellie Payne's talent served as an inspiration in more ways than one, and it was a simple task to construct a tale surrounding the shoes.

Gifted by a faerie who had watched over her since she was a child. Crafted to fit her and only her.

Yes, that would do.

Yet another detail to hammer the concept into his fae brain with its many folds—*this girl is special; she even has special shoes to prove it.*

The name proved more difficult. It needed to be different, memorable, but not so unfamiliar it would slip from his mind.

The parasite thought of the dying embers of Ellie Payne's furnace, of the remarkable woman whose confidence she would soon channel, whose artwork would aid her rise to power.

Then the parasite smiled.

Though she was late to the ball, that only seemed to serve as an advantage. She had no trouble slipping in as most all the guests had already shuffled through the doors and now waited inside for their Crown Prince.

The parasite huffed. Funny how two weeks ago every human

Madame LeFleur had come in contact with had despised the Crown Prince; now they'd all stuffed themselves into the massive ballroom, hoping to hand their daughters over to him in marriage.

Humans can be amusing sometimes, the parasite conceded.

The parasite practiced a demure yet seductive smile, getting used to the feel of it on this unfamiliar face, then stepped onto the ballroom floor.

And so, a mystery woman with no name stole the first dance with the Crown Prince. And the next, and the next.

When she slipped away at midnight, all she left behind was a glittering glass slipper.

She had called herself Cinderella.

CHAPTER 1

ELLIE

ontrary to popular belief—rather, the belief of a certain prince prone to decisions made in haste and under the influence of copious amounts of flattery—there were plenty of human women in the kingdom of Dwellen whose feet were the same size. Maybe that was why my parents and I thought the entire ordeal was so hilarious.

At first.

A crisp morning breeze wafted into my family's breakfast room through the nearest window, rays of light warping as they bent through the amateur etchings I'd carved into the glass with my mother's favorite kitchen knife when I was nine.

My mother had eventually forgiven me.

The knife had not.

I sat at our hand-engraved mahogany table, the scent of coffee and pastries and eggs sneaking in from the adjacent kitchen. It was my favorite place to read the daily paper. Partially because the cherubs my mother had painted onto the blue wallpaper always looked as if they were reading over my shoulder. Partially because my father often *did* read over my shoulder, a disapproving huff escaping from his mouth every time he happened across a juicy piece of gossip.

My father always insisted there was no reason to stay caught up on current events. After all, there was little our family could do to change what was going on in the entire kingdom. Our responsibility was to the residents of our city. We could make a difference to them, he always reminded me. Who else would blow the glass to form the windows that kept the citizens of Othian from freezing to death in the winter, while still allowing them to enjoy the beauty of snow-capped mountains and rooftops from safely within their heated homes?

At that, I was always quick to remind him that plenty of our neighbors coveted our business and would happily take up the charge in the event of our untimely demise.

Most of the time, I'd catch an amused tone hidden within his grunt.

I had a feeling that the discussion of today's paper would be no exception to our daily ritual.

Little did I know it would derail our ritual entirely.

"Oh, he didn't!" I gaped in feigned terror, as all proper young ladies are taught to do from a young age when they've learned of something delightfully appalling. "Papa, you'll never guess what the prince has done now."

I reared back, cackling, as all proper young ladies are taught *not* to do.

Mama strolled into the dining room from the kitchen balancing a tray, atop which she had perched three piping hot bowls of oats. My mother had a way of somehow looking radiant even as sweat from the stove pooled on her brow, her apron crinkled in the places she'd wiped her hands all morning. "Let me guess, rather than offering his hand in marriage to one of the women falling all over him at the ball, he's run off and eloped with a servant."

I admired my work as my mother set the bowls down before us. The terrycloth pattern in the glass bowls caught the light and tossed it in every direction imaginable.

Papa offered a disapproving scowl at my latest creation. "Pretty fancy for a bowl that holds oats." The corners of his lips twitched, his tell for *I might be impressed if my brain wasn't calculating exactly how much of my material you used to fashion such an impractical item.*

"Perhaps. But by the time I've sold thousands of them, they'll be holding caviar," I teased.

Mama yanked the paper from my hand. Her mouth pursed as she quickly scanned the article. "And to think he'll be our king someday."

Her words dampened the lighthearted mood at the table. While Prince Evander was Heir to the Throne of Dwellen, that had only been a recent development. His elder brother, Prince Jerad, the original heir to the fae King of Dwellen, had died in a tragic accident only last year, shaking the entire kingdom. And probably its future.

Prince Jerad had been the responsible one of the two sons.

Papa raised a brow, wrinkling his forehead. "Do you two ladies intend to torture me by withholding information?"

This brought a sly smile to my mother's lips. "I thought you had no interest in politics, dear."

"That may be true. But I have even less interest in being excluded from breakfast conversation."

Mama and I laughed, and she tossed the paper onto the table.

The Prince's Ongoing Search for His Mystery Woman: Will a Shoe Tell All?

My father groaned as he brought his glass spectacles to his face, resting them on his crooked nose. I grinned, proud that he was using them. Papa liked to pretend that he disapproved of my work, but no practiced scowl or lecture regarding my duties to the people of Dwellen, to his business, could ever fool me. He called me his little entrepreneur, always as if it were a cursed thing, but never without a twinkle in his eyes.

"I thought you said this wretched ball was supposed to help the prince find a bride, not lose one," he grumbled.

A laugh escaped my throat. "And I thought you said you hoped he'd fail in that endeavor."

He grunted. "I just hate to see a human end up on the wrong side of a fae bargain."

"Is there a right side?" I asked. Humans rarely intermarried with the fae, even in Dwellen, where fae-human relations were amiable compared to the rest of Alondria.

Apparently, there was something about entering a covenant that would suffocate you if you broke it that had most humans reconsidering their undying love for the immortals.

My father placed the paper down on the table and sighed. "Exactly."

"Oh, I don't know." I scooped up a bite of hot oats, my stomach growling in anticipation as the sugary goodness slipped down my throat. "The Queen of Naenden seems happy, from all I've read."

My mother shook her head. "Ellie, must you wear on your father's heart?"

My father's eyes twinkled. "I'm afraid she gets it honest, my dear. Besides, I know better than to be concerned. My Ellie wasn't among those girls who pampered themselves up at the chance to throw their lives away for some immortal child parading as a qualified heir to the throne."

It was true. I'd been forced to swallow my fit of laughter when the palace couriers had visited our cottage a month ago with news that the Crown Prince of Dwellen was to host a ball come the next mooncycle. The intention of the event had been clear in the invitation: the prince was in want of a wife.

Rather, *the king* was in want of his son being in want of a wife.

It hadn't been all that strange that the prince was throwing a ball to solve his bachelorhood, which I figured had much more to do with the new social pressures to become a qualified heir to the throne than a desire to conform to the "subtle snare of monogamy," as he often referred to marriage.

What struck me as odd was that I, a human, should be invited.

As it turned out, *only* human women had been invited. Apparently having a human bride was all the rage in fae social circles ever since the King of Naenden had fallen in love with a human woman (for the second time, people seemed eager to forget).

I'd promptly declined the invitation, of course, claiming duty to my aging parents as an appropriate excuse. Never mind that my parents were healthier than most humans half their age.

The invitation hadn't been *that* specific.

In truth, I hadn't the faintest desire to attend. The same morning of the courier's visit, I'd received my first official order for decorative plates from an innkeeper in town, and the sum he'd offered had been sizable. Missing a ball where I might have had to pretend to actually like the immature prince had been a small price to pay for the thrill that had raced through my veins at the weight of the bulging money purse the innkeeper had handed me just yesterday.

It wasn't as though my family was poor. At least, not in my lifetime. My parents came from modest means, but my father had been talented and my mother supportive, and now most of the windows in Othian were supplied by my father.

And me, of course, though most everyone seemed to forget that.

But that was about to change.

The thrill of the money in my palms had stoked an ember in me, one I was desperate to fan. *I* had made that money. Not my father. Someone had found my work beautiful enough to spend quite a bit of money on it, and that was the high I was eager to chase. Not the hand of some prince who would likely take on a dozen mistresses as soon as the honeymoon was over.

Mama's words broke me from my trance. "Well, it seems the woman the prince set his sights on wasn't so naïve, either. According to the paper, she danced with the prince all night, so much so that none of the other girls had a chance to even speak with him. Then she ran off around midnight."

I downed the rest of my oats. "Serves him right. I bet that's the first time he's ever had a woman reject him."

Mama scowled. "If that is the case, he doesn't seem to be taking the hint. He's got an entire platoon of his father's guard out searching for her. And all they've got to identify her is a shoe."

This sparked my attention, and I remembered I hadn't finished the article before getting into this conversation. What a ridiculous notion

—that the prince's current object of adoration was so entirely unique, even her shoes would fit only her feet.

I snorted. "What do you bet that there's a thousand women out there trying to sand their feet down just to fit into it?"

My father took a sip of his coffee. "Well, they're going to have a difficult time making it stretch, considering it's glass."

I choked on my oats. "It's *what?*"

My father's deep chuckle echoed through the room. "Ridiculous, right? Glass slippers." He rolled his eyes. "Even you haven't thought of such a thing, and you're always trying to invent new ways to fashion glass into objects it was never intended to be."

My mother handed me a goblet of water, which I attempted to slurp once my chest had stopped spasming from inhaling the oats. "Mind if I take another look at that?"

Papa shrugged and handed me the paper, which I searched over and over for any further description of the glass slippers. I found none, however, and eventually gave up. "I'm going to get started early this morning." The newspaper crumpled in my shaking hands as I placed it back on the table.

"You sure? You haven't even had your coffee yet." My father frowned, but it was Mama who placed the back of her hand on my forehead and said, "You're not ill, are you?"

One would have thought that my leaving the breakfast table before my first cup of coffee was the sign of an international incident.

I nodded and shook Mama's hand off. "I'm sure." Then I bolted from the room as quickly as I could manage without raising more suspicion.

The dewy grass soaked my morning silk slippers as I traipsed across our yard in my robe. The sun was just beginning to rise over the grassy hillside, and Mama's chickens clucked as they scampered through the grass.

It wasn't until I reached our workshop, a large wooden shed that looked lopsided from all the additions Papa had built over the years, that I realized I had forgotten to grab the key from my room. I almost turned around to fetch it, but a sinking sensation thudded in my stomach. The large wooden door stood before me, taunting me. I reached out a trembling hand and pushed.

The door opened.

My lungs must have fallen out of my ribcage.

Someone had been here. Someone had broken in.

I turned the knob of the gas lamp next to the entrance and a flame appeared, lighting the workshop. Relief flooded my bones as hundreds of glass windows glittered back at me in the firelight. I leaned my hand against the entryway to steady myself. Whoever had broken in hadn't touched father's windows. At least, if they had taken any, it hadn't been enough for me to notice. Not enough to crash our business.

But the windows weren't what had me traipsing out here in my slippers.

I wove my way through the wooden tables where my father and I had neatly organized our creations and made my way to the back of the shop, where a single furnace and blow pipe served as *my* shop. My workspace—after-hours, of course—once I'd fulfilled all my regular orders.

It was here that I'd spent what probably equated to months of my life laboring over the fancy glass plates I'd made with the local inn in mind. Where I'd practiced on our bowls. A few panes of glass, covered by burlap, leaned against the back wall. Underneath were my first attempts at painting glass, and though they were so messy and simplistic that I vowed never to show them to anyone, I still kept them.

If the intruder had looked under the burlap, they must have agreed with my embarrassment, because they hadn't bothered to take them.

So far, nothing seemed out of place. I clutched my chest and tried to calm myself. If there really had been an intruder, surely some of our equipment would have gone missing, and I hadn't noticed anything out of place. Maybe there hadn't been an intruder at all. I'd been working long hours into the night all this past week trying to get the innkeeper's order fulfilled. Yesterday, I'd allowed myself a break from work, as it was the weekend. Father had rested, too. Perhaps I'd simply forgotten to lock the workshop door.

That would be a problem in its own way, of course. Papa would be displeased at my irresponsibility. Maybe even forbid me from working after hours until I learned my lesson. Though I knew it hurt him to discipline me, he'd always been a boulder of will in that regard, reminding me the Fates had entrusted him with the duty of raising not just a child, but a woman who would take over his business one day and needed to learn responsibility.

But all that would be fine, just as long as the shoes were still here.

I leaned down and pulled a metal box out from under my workstation.

The box was too light.

My heart sank.

I knew before I opened it that my shoes, my glorious creation, the glass slippers that had taken two years to perfect, were gone.

Tears crowded my eyelids, and I tossed the empty box aside. It clattered on the floor and the lid fell aside, only rubbing in the truth as the box lay gaping and empty on the ground.

My dreams shattered, every single one of them. Decorative plates and bowls had only ever been a means to an end. The shoes had been my real prize, the beautiful creation that would have become synonymous with my name. The shoes that would have launched my career.

Now the shoes were going to be famous, all right. And every glassblower in the kingdom was going to have a head start on recreating them.

I could practically hear the glass melting all around the kingdom, the glassblowers who'd been at work since before I sat down for breakfast.

The door creaked, and I bolted to my feet.

My mother's voice whispered through the room. "Ellie? There are people here to see you."

I squinted the tears from my eyes. "People? Who...?"

My mother stepped into the workshop, the rising sun silhouetting her sturdy frame. She creased her eyebrows as I wiped the dirt from my morning robe. "What's wrong, Elynore?"

I swallowed the burning lump in my throat. "It's nothing."

I crossed the room and went to sidestep her, but she blocked my path and set that familiar glare on me. "Don't insult me. I'm your mother. I know when my child is hurting."

My mother had a sense for these sorts of things, it was true. She'd probably even guessed that I'd been working on something special, but she hadn't pressed me about it. I almost never showed my creations to my parents until they were finished, and even then, there was a proper way to present art.

The crimson satin cushion I'd bought for showcasing the shoes wasn't finished yet. I was supposed to pick it up from the seamstress tomorrow.

A tear slid down my cheek, and her face softened as she wrapped me in a hug. "Tell you about it later?"

She kissed my forehead and nodded before releasing me from her embrace. Then she wiped the tears from my cheek with her thumb, rough from all her gardening, cooking, and tending the chickens.

She scrutinized my robe, specifically my sleeves, the edges singed from years of forgetting to roll them up as I brought my projects to the fire. Her nose turned upward, a smile curving at her full lips. "You might consider changing for our guests."

CHAPTER 2

ELLIE

I'd had to dab paint on the skin beneath my blotchy eyelids to hide the swelling my tears had caused. By the time the redness in the whites of my eyes had faded and I'd changed into an outfit more suitable for company—an ivy-green house dress with a flaring skirt and a cinched waist, I was fairly certain our guests, whoever they were, had been waiting at least half an hour.

It didn't matter, though. I could only hope the delay would serve to shorten our visit. After all, I had much to do today, including submitting a petition to the Palace Guard to open an investigation regarding my stolen property. Unlikely as it was that the Guard would agree that my property was valuable enough to lift a pen, much less open up a proper investigation, I had to do something. I had to try.

I took one last glance in the mirror, less than satisfied with my paint, which was doing a poor job of obscuring my distress, but pleased with my appearance all the same. My mother had gifted me her beauty—brown eyes, wide but sharp; strong cheekbones that paired well with my curved jaw; and her warm, deep brown complexion.

I applied another coat of paint under my eyes, all the same.

My heels clanked down our glazed cherry wood stairway as I descended into the parlor.

I came to a stop when my heels clicked against checkered tile.

"Ah, Miss Payne."

The bored voice sounded familiar, though I didn't think it was one of our neighbors. When I turned the curve of our winding staircase, I realized why.

It was the same courier who had delivered my invitation to the ball. The same who I was fairly certain heard me burst into a fit of unrestrained giggles as soon as I'd shut the door. Two soldiers accompanied him, each in a royal indigo uniform bedecked with large silver buttons.

The courier wore similar colors, but on a velvet robe that ballooned out at his feet and sleeves. I wondered if he recognized how ridiculous he looked. Even felt a twinge of pity for the faerie. His skin was pale as eggshells and thinner than a human's, so much so that I would have been able to tell he was faerie even if the pointed tips of his ears hadn't protruded from underneath his velvet cap. My parents stood on either side of the guards, amused expressions tempered under solemnly tight lips. I wondered what was so funny, yet inappropriate to express.

"Welcome." I curtsied as I reached the bottom of the stairs. "Might I ask what brings you to—" All sense of propriety fled me as my gaze halted on the object in the courier's hand. He held a box made of dark chestnut wood. There was no lid, leaving the contents visible. Inside was a red velvet cushion, atop which sat a shoe.

My shoe.

Light danced in the intricate heel of the glass slipper, as if to taunt me. Like it was bragging that it had been out dancing without me, and this was what I got for trapping it inside a dark metal box.

"Where did you get that?" Fire rushed to my cheeks as I reached for the glittering slipper. The courier yanked it back just before my fingertips could graze the clear glass.

"Miss Payne, this is a possession of the Prince of Dwellen and is not to be handled lightly."

"That's not the prince's. It's mine," I snapped. The courier and the guards tensed, even as I drew my hand back. Confusion flickered over my father's face, and my mother's for a moment, before her perceptive eyes scanned the familiar pattern in the heel and widened in realization.

"Ah, yes. As it was Miss Lightfoot's next door, and Miss Balfour's next door to her." The courier rolled his eyes, and the two guards fought back snickers. "Let us simply pray that you are the unique one among them and that you refrain from wasting our time and the precious skin on your feet by attempting to shove them into this poor, abused slipper."

"Fine." I shrugged. "Let me try it on. Unless the criminal who stole them from me stretched out the glass, I imagine it still fits. Considering I made them from a mold of my foot." I sauntered over to a woven chair in the parlor and whipped my skirts up, tossing my house shoes across the room with a flick of my ankles.

Exasperation flooded my mother's face at the unladylike gesture, but my father had to clamp a hand over his mouth to suppress his laughter. Clearly he thought my antics were just that, an attempt to get a good laugh out of him at the expense of the courier's embarrassment. I could only imagine the anger that would flood his face once he realized I wasn't bluffing. That someone really had broken in and stolen years' worth of work, just to leave one of my precious shoes at that stupid ball—in an attempt to run away from a prince who apparently couldn't take no for an answer.

The courier sighed. "Very well." He kneeled and placed the wooden box gently on the black-checkered tile next to my feet. When he pulled the shoe from the box, the heel sparkled in the chandelier light above us, and my eyes met my father's. The sight of the intricate pattern on the shoe wiped the amusement from his face, and this time he stifled a gasp rather than a chuckle.

My mother clamped a hand around his wrist and squeezed, no doubt a warning for him to keep calm.

The courier brought the shoe to my foot and slipped it over my toes and onto my heel. When he brought his hands away, the shoe stayed glued to my foot.

As if it had been made for me.

Imagine that.

"Well, now that that's settled." I wrenched the shoe off my foot and gripped it tightly, just in case the courier got it into his mind to take it back. "I would like my other shoe now. Please," I added with a saccharine grin.

The courier's jaw dropped as he slowly rose to his feet. He exchanged confused looks with the guards, who both raised their palms in a "don't look at me" kind of expression.

The courier cleared his throat. "Miss Payne, I'm afraid there has been a misunderstanding. By all eyewitness reports, you are not the woman with whom the prince danced last eve."

By all reports. I snorted. That could only mean one thing. In the city of Othian, fashion came and went within the span of a butterfly's lifespan. Last season, having skin the deepest hues of brown had been all the rage. At least half a dozen painters in the art district had approached me, inquiring about whether I would pose for a portrait.

Now, the more veins one could count beneath a woman's translucent skin, the better. The people who'd had the foresight to get into the parasol industry were doing quite well for themselves. There'd been a mass exodus in the cobbling, forgery, and baking industries so their owners could open parasol shops.

My father and I hadn't been so inclined, knowing the fashion pendulum would swoop in the opposite direction before the season adjourned.

That wasn't even the most ridiculous of Othian's ever-revolving fashion trends. A significant portion of Othian's human population had developed an obsession with the fae. One couldn't take a trip to the city center without passing a male whose ears were bandaged over, recovering from a recent procedure that would leave his previously rounded ears whittled into crisp points. Since the popularity of the Queen of Naenden had surged, some had gone as far as having an eye plucked out in her honor—and she wasn't even fae.

"And by that, you mean that the woman the prince danced with had skin as pale as the flickering moonlight, and hair to match, I assume?" I waved my hand, flicking my slippered foot, marking how nicely the floral pattern on the heel had turned out.

"Miss—"

"The thing is, I never claimed to be the one with whom the prince danced. I only claimed that these shoes belong to me. Which they do, clearly. If you need further proof, my father and I would be more than happy to show you our workshop. I'll show you the mold I used to make them, if you so desire."

"Indeed." My father's voice boomed. "I'd be pleased to escort you there myself." Though the tight-lipped expression on my father's face indicated the opposite.

A crease formed between where the courier's eyebrows might have been if he were human or high fae. "You admit it then, that you are not the woman who danced with the prince last eve?"

My mother stepped between me and the courier, towering over the thin fae. "Admit? Admit to what? Are you accusing my daughter of a crime?"

"No, of course not," the courier muttered. "I meant to only—agh. Chrisington, the decree, please."

The guard to the courier's left removed a tightly rolled piece of parchment from his coat and handed it to the courier, who pulled the indigo string that secured the paper until it unraveled. His eyes darted across the page as the crease above his brow furrowed deeper into his skull. His lips muttered something unintelligible as he searched the smooth paper.

In the end, he rolled up the parchment, taking his time securing the string that kept it tightly wound.

Then he closed his pale eyelids and inhaled.

In that moment, I realized how weary he looked, and I wondered what foolishness the prince had subjected him to in his years of running errands for the spoiled heir. "Very well. Miss Payne, you are to come with me."

"Pardon me?" my parents chimed.

The courier extended his hand for the slipper, but my mother didn't budge from between us. "Why must she go with you?"

My father advanced and stood by her side, completely blocking the courier from my view. My heart raced. Moments ago, I had been so furious that someone had stolen my craftsmanship to wear to a silly ball, that I'd been glad to defy the scrawny courier. But now, as my parents stood between me and the spokesman of the palace, I wondered if I had made a mistake.

Though the King of Dwellen was not known for being unnecessarily cruel to humans, like some of the other rulers in Alondria, I didn't know how he would take to a human family defying his messenger.

When my parents discovered my mother's pregnancy, they'd escaped from Charshon, where humans continued to be abused and mistreated, in the hopes of bringing their daughter into a world where she could thrive. When they'd arrived, they'd found Dwellen to be a less pristine version of the faerietale they'd been sold. But still. The fae here did not openly oppress humans, and the king had upheld a long-standing policy of including humans in his host of advisors.

That didn't mean the fae king took kindly to those who transgressed his orders. Would any of the king's human advisors bat an eye if the crown stripped my father of his business license?

I doubted it.

"Mama, Papa, it's alright. I'll go with him." I stepped out from behind their tensed frames.

"Elynore," Mama said, but I cut her off.

"Really. I need to submit a plea for an investigation for my other shoe, anyway. And to open a request for a patent. This way I won't even have to wait in line," I added, flashing them what was apparently a pretty unconvincing attempt at a light-hearted grin, considering the way their faces hardened.

The courier closed his eyes, and I couldn't tell whether the expression betrayed relief at not having to fight my parents, or disgust at a human woman's intention to request a patent, but I didn't care. All that mattered right now was making sure my parents didn't risk falling onto the king's bad side.

Before either of them could protest, I wrapped them up in a hug and kissed them both on the cheek, careful not to let my fingers slip from the slipper's heel. "I love you both. This will all be resolved shortly. Just you wait."

Then I turned and walked out the front door, intentionally beating the courier and the guards to it. I couldn't have them escorting me and getting it into their heads that I wasn't doing this completely of my own volition.

Outside our cottage was a velvet blue coach, attached to which were two starlight white horses.

Footsteps shuffled behind me, and I propelled myself into the coach before the guard could offer me his hand. I settled myself onto the pleasantly comfy seats, still frazzled at how my day had certainly not gone as expected, but feeling optimistic. Surely the prince would happily give me my other slipper back once he realized the woman he probably thought was his fated mate was actually a thief, and that he must have misheard the call of the Fates.

This could actually turn out for the best, really. The glass style would surely come into fashion now that a drawing of the shoes was all over the papers, promoted by the prince himself. And once everyone recognized me as the designer... My heart pounded with excitement.

The courier climbed into the coach, followed by the first guard. When the second guard attempted to join us, the courier held out his palm. "Wait. You'll need to stay behind and gather her things. I'll send another coach to fetch you once we arrive at the palace."

Those words snapped me from my inner daydream of fame and glory and self-made fortune.

"Wait. Why does he need to fetch my things? The castle is less than half an hour away by coach, and it's still morning. I know I'm fond of my clothes, but I don't change my outfit that often."

The guard who had situated himself to my left laughed. "You really think we're escorting you to the castle so you can get a patent on your shoes?"

"I—" My hands trembled, causing the slipper to shake in my sweaty palms.

What was this?

There had been a misunderstanding, of course, but surely the prince wouldn't punish me for claiming the shoes his missing lover had stolen from me. I scooted toward the coat door, but the guard rested a firm, threatening grip on my shoulder.

"Miss Payne," the courier drawled, leaning forward so that his hot breath wet my face, making me cringe, "as much as I regret this to be the case, you, my dear, are now the prince's betrothed."

CHAPTER 3

EVANDER

*B*reakfast with the royal family—my family—was typically conducted in long stretches of silence punctuated by my precious mother's occasional attempts at prompting conversation between my father and me.

Most mornings, I found the silence agonizing.

Today?

What I would have given for my father to ignore my existence.

"My dear Evangeline, do you imagine the envoy has caught up with our son's future bride yet?"

Okay, so he was *technically* still ignoring me, talking about me instead of to me as if I hadn't been sitting at his right hand for the past half hour.

My mother's ageless face lit up; she must have considered this progress.

Great.

"I don't imagine she could have gone far," my mother said, her rosy cheeks rounding in delight. "That would defeat the purpose of playing hard to get."

My mother reached for my hand and beamed at me.

Playing hard to get.

I couldn't help the grin that tugged on the edges of my lips. Leave it to my mother to spin the fact that my betrothed quite literally ran away from me into the romantic beginnings of a faerietale.

To most, it might have seemed like the end.

I knew better.

Apparently, so did my mother.

"Hard to get?" my father drawled, cruel amusement flickering on his lips, though his gray eyes remained untouched. "Yes, I'm sure that's exactly what it is."

Something about his tone suggested otherwise.

Shocker.

I leaned back in my chair, placing my hands behind my head and interlocking my fingers, mirroring that amused confidence of his in my smirk.

This was the game we played, he and I. Who could show their hatred for the other the most without ever coming out and saying so?

If my mother hadn't been sitting across from me, I might have volleyed back something like, *What, Father? Are you jealous that you missed out on the chance to pursue my dear mother when you bought her from her father in Avelea? Do you regret missing out on the chase?*

But, alas, I'd sooner pick my teeth with wasp stingers than embarrass my mother like that.

So instead I went with, "What, Your Majesty? Am I sensing regret that the heir to your throne will have human blood running through their veins? Was it not you who commanded me to select a human bride in the first place?"

My father dabbed his lips with his napkin, his piercing gray eyes glinting like a double-edged sword as he folded his napkin and placed it over his finished plate. "It is not the human blood I regret, son."

The barbs in his words pierced deeper than just my skin.

My only regret is that the bloodline runs through you, and not your brother.

Yeah, well, he wasn't the only one.

My smirk didn't falter, though. I'd had two hundred years of this to perfect it.

Besides, my father was at a distinct disadvantage this morning. Most days, the sting of his words would have lingered longer, but most days, I hadn't just danced the night away with the most dazzling woman in all of Alondria.

He'd meant it as a punishment, forcing me to select a bride from the humans. While our human citizens assumed it was a demonstration of goodwill toward them, I knew better.

My father had done it to shame me. It didn't matter that my father maintained the facade of caring for his human citizens, that he both appointed and catered to the human ambassadors to keep the humans well-fed and blissfully apathetic. It didn't matter how popular it had become for the fae to select a bride from among the humans since the King of Naenden had done it and succeeded. My father knew it was simply a fad, one that would fade in a few short years, and that then I'd be stuck with a wife who would wither away in less than a century.

Then, there was the other reason.

He also wanted an heir to the throne, and heirs were much easier to produce with human women. While most fae females found conception elusive, only occurring after decades or even centuries of trying, human women could produce several offspring within their short time under the sun.

At first, this had puzzled me. It seemed out of character for my father, who turned his sharp nose up at the humans (unbeknownst to them), to accept a half-fae as an heir.

But then I'd realized.

He simply hated me *that* much. Even an heir soiled with human blood would be a better alternative to his disappointment of a son ruling in his place. While it wasn't common by any means, it wasn't unheard of for a Dwellen king to name his grandchild as heir in place of his child.

Joke was on him; I never wanted the throne, anyway. Not when Jerad had been such a perfect, obvious choice, deserving of every bit of respect and adoration the Dwellen people had bestowed upon him.

My chest clenched at the thought of my brother.

The ball was meant to be a punishment. Of that much, I was sure.

Meant to shackle me to a new bride as well, as my father disapproved of my nightly company. My father assumed the worst of me in almost every regard, except in the cases in which assuming the best of me could be twisted into a punishment of some sort and used against me.

I was a lot of things by his standards—a whore, a partier, a drunkard.

But I wasn't a cheat.

And he'd shackle me to a human woman I had no interest in, just to deprive me of my pleasures for a few decades.

Well, the joke was on him in that area, too.

I'd known it as soon as Cinderella waltzed up to the front of the crowd like the rest of them didn't exist.

I'd given every dance to her.

Every part of me would come later.

She'd been dazzling, her porcelain skin glowing in the lantern light, her dark blue dress hugging her every curve, sparkling like a beacon.

There was no looking anywhere else.

I hadn't decided yet that she'd be my wife.

The papers thought me a lovesick prince, falling for her at first sight.

Let them think what they wanted.

I'd wanted her the moment I'd laid eyes on her. But that wasn't why I'd proposed. I'd expected her to swoon as I pressed my lips to her palm.

She'd only met my hungry stare with an appetite to match.

When I'd swept her onto the dance floor, she'd hadn't melted in my arms like I'd expected. She hadn't batted her eyes in an outrageous display of faux meekness, nor had she slipped a thousand innuendos into the conversation, lest I miss the hint that she wanted in my bed.

No, Cinderella had simply talked to me, and not like I was a prince. Not once did she mention that awful word—*heir*.

Three dances later, and the music lulled. I'd drawn her into my chest, enraptured by her scent. Lilac and rosebuds. I'd never been the type to believe in mating bonds. The concept that the Fates preor-

37

dained a perfect match for each fae had always seemed a bit too sentimental for me.

But then I'd scented her, and something in me *snapped*. Not in the
sort of snapping that breaks. The sort that binds objects together in
perfect unison.

I couldn't think of another way to describe it but Fated. I knew
then that hers was the only head I wanted resting against my shoulder, hers the only scent to settle into my clothes.

And then she'd asked me a question. The same question I'd been
waiting a year for a woman to ask.

I couldn't think of it here, not in front of my father, who would
surely sense it and find some way to use it against me.

So instead I remembered what she'd said later that night.

Give me something romantic. Something I won't forget.

By the time the night was over, I'd leaned in and whispered a question into her ear.

She'd just grinned up at me, dazzling me with that perfect smile of
hers.

"Of course," she'd said, and the words were a melody in my ears.

But then the clock had struck midnight, and she'd blushed, a
frantic look overcoming her face. "I mustn't stay. I must go, but I vow
to return to you."

I'd shaken my head, confused, but still grinning. "You're going to
leave right after agreeing to spend your life with me?"

"I promise myself to you, Prince Evander of Dwellen," she'd said,
just as her hands slipped from mine and she disappeared into the
crowd.

I'd been so dazed, so confused, it had taken me a moment to come
to my senses, to go after her.

When I finally had the wherewithal to cut through the crowd
searching for her, she was gone.

The guards had found a glass slipper on the palace steps later that
night. A slipper crafted by the faerie who'd watched over Cinderella
since she was only a girl. A slipper crafted for her, and her alone.

Give me something romantic. Something I won't forget.

So I had.

And now that something romantic was making its way through Othian, ready to find my betrothed and bring her back to me.

Honestly, I'd been shocked my father had agreed to the idea, and the ease with which he'd granted my request still made my stomach churn a bit.

He probably thought he was still punishing me somehow. Even though his plans had gone awry, and I'd actually found a woman I was more than eager to bind myself to, he surely thought he'd won in the end.

She was human, after all.

Her life would be a blink in my existence, but if I loved her, the sting of her loss would last much longer.

But even fae died.

My brother's face flashed before my memory, and I shut it out.

When my mother and father left the table, I stayed, mostly because it irritated my father when I postponed my princely duties by extending mealtimes. Indeed, he scowled at me as he dismissed himself, but my mother touched my hand absentmindedly on her way out.

Not moments after they departed, a breathy, labored voice shook through the hall. "Your Majesty, Your Highness."

I waved him in. "It's just me, Orvall."

The courier looked relieved not to be facing my father, but he didn't enter. Instead, he plastered an unconvincing grin on his face.

"We have located the prince's betrothed."

CHAPTER 4

ELLIE

The doors to the king's breakfasting room were plated with silver, etched with intricate patterns from which I soon had to avert my eyes, lest my vision double.

I hardly heard the courier announce my presence as he poked his head into the breakfasting chambers, presumably speaking to the royal family. My ears were still buzzing from the absurdity of his claim—that I, Ellie Payne, had somehow unwittingly betrothed myself to the Prince of Dwellen.

Someone inside the breakfasting room coughed. A moment later, the sound of a chair scraping across the floor screeched in my ears.

"We present the Crown Prince's Betrothed." The courier coughed slightly as his voice gave out toward the end, and the doors swung open.

I had always thought our house ornate, furnished with every luxury a human might desire, all funded by my father's thriving business.

That, apparently, was not the case.

Or perhaps there lay a chasm between every luxury a human might desire and every luxury fae royalty might desire.

The walls were painted blue, just like our breakfasting room—it was the current fashion, after all. But instead of my mother's hand-painted cherubs, silver leaf textured the walls, swirling and pivoting until they formed the scene of a great battle, a host of winged fae swooping from the clouds, reaping judgment upon the humans below.

It was as terrifying as it was breathtaking.

When the prince heard the courier's announcement that not only had they found his betrothed, but that she was here, the prince seemed to freeze. "My love," he said, gaining momentum and craning his neck to get a glimpse of me over the courier's shoulder. "You asked for something roman—"

I stepped out from behind the courier.

The prince's jaw dropped as he caught sight of me. Me, who probably looked like a hot mess as I'd only done the minimum to get ready this morning for our guests, who I had had no idea would present me to the Crown Prince of Dwellen. As his betrothed. I might have laughed at the ridiculous sight of Prince Evander fumbling to reclaim a calm expression as he took in the sight of me.

Me. Not whomever he had danced the night away with last night.

"Who is this?" He glared at the courier, clearly still in shock. "I told you to bring me Cinderella."

I barely stifled a scoff, and only managed to do so by clearing my throat. Cinderella? What kind of a name was Cinderella?

A thief's name, I supposed.

Perhaps thieves donned stage names, much like courtesans.

"This, Your Highness, is your Betrothed. The one whose foot the glass slipper fit." The courier could have audibly sighed his voice sounded so defeated. As unpleasant as the faerie was, I couldn't help but feel sorry for him. How many other pointless tasks had Prince Evander sent him on?

"I have a name, you know," I said. "Not that you need bother to remember it, as I'll be leaving shortly. But you may address me as either Miss Payne or Ellie during our exchange."

"Our exchange?" The prince's eyebrows narrowed as his gaze settled on the glass slipper, which now clung to my sweaty palms. "By

Alondria, Orvall. Could you please explain to me why you've brought me a petty swindler while I've been agonizing over my lost love?"

I might have been offended, had I not been too busy snorting. "Your *lost* love? Really? Because I heard she fled the premises."

The prince gritted his teeth.

"I wouldn't do that too often if I were you," I said. "Detracts from the pretty face." It was true. When it came to his reputation with women, the prince had clearly been assisted by his looks. His sea-green eyes gleamed, contrasting with his tanned skin, which almost seemed to blend in with his coppery-brown hair. Pointed ears poked through his slightly shaggy haircut, which, from all I knew about the King of Dwellen, I was sure his father detested. To top it all off, he somehow pulled off possessing a muscular build on a lean frame, and I couldn't help but wonder if there was some fae glamour at work here.

No one looked that good.

"Orvall, retrieve the slipper from this human and see her out," the prince seethed.

I gripped the slipper tighter, but neither the courier nor the guards made a move for it.

The prince's unfairly rugged jaw bulged. "Did you mishear me?"

The courier—Orvall—sighed, which I now suspected was just his default response to existing. "How I wish I had, Your Highness." He held out a hand, in which the guard placed the small rolled-up sheet of paper. "But we are unable to throw the woman out, for she is, indeed, your Betrothed."

The prince's tanned face drained of color, which amused me greatly. I considered telling him not to worry about it, that he had gotten lucky and mistakenly proposed to the one woman in the city who had no desire to take advantage of such a mistake. But, then again, who knew how often this spoiled brat had actually had to face any consequences for his actions? Why not make him sweat a little?

"That's not possible," the prince said, though his voice had lost its grit.

"I'm afraid it is not only possible, but happening, Your Highness."

The courier shifted on his feet, causing his puffy robes to billow like blobs on the floor. "The slipper fit the foot of Miss Payne."

The prince nodded toward the slipper in my hand. "Put it on."

"You could say *please*, you know."

"Put it on, *please*." The way he said the word made it sound like he was being forced to swallow lye. His throat even bobbed a little.

I shrugged and leaned over, balancing on one foot as I slipped the shoe on the other. "See? It fits."

"That's not possible."

"Are you in the habit of denying things that occur in your very presence, *Your Highness?*"

The prince shook his head, something like disbelief mingled with horror flickering in his wild sea-green eyes. Wow, he really was getting worked up about this, wasn't he? Though I supposed for a male who was used to getting whatever he wanted immediately, this whole situation must have come as a shock. "Those slippers belong to Cinderella. Her faerie godmother gifted them to her. They're enchanted to only fit her feet, and her feet alone."

I brushed him off. "Oh, good. So the future princess of Dwellen is both a thief and a liar. Excellent."

"Don't call her that," he snapped.

"Oh? And what word do the fae use to describe someone who takes objects that aren't theirs and tells untruths?"

The prince bristled, jerking his head toward the slipper. "How did you get the shoes to fit? Are you a witch?"

I couldn't help it. The laugh slipped out before I could grasp hold of it. "What?"

"Did you convince your own faerie godmother to bewitch your feet, then?"

I was pretty sure I'd lost all function in my jaw. The prince had broken it. "Why would I have a faerie godmother?"

The prince's eyes swept over me, and a lopsided grin appeared on his face. "I do wonder why the faerie godmothers would have decided to skip over you, with that delightfully amiable personality of yours."

43

I drew up my brow. "Is this your strategy every time a woman lacks interest in you, Your Highness? Insult her temperament?"

"Wouldn't know. This is a novel experience for me." I couldn't decide what made me more uncomfortable—the way his tongue seemed to relish the word *experience*, or the way his wink sent my stomach nosediving into a flurry of cartwheels.

Nauseous cartwheels. Obviously not the other kind.

"The shoes fit because I made them. Not with magic. With my hands, and a blow pipe, and some sand, and a mold I crafted from my foot."

"Is that so?" The prince crossed his arms, a gesture that should have made him look juvenile. Instead it highlighted the deep fissures between the muscles of his bare forearms, exposed by his rolled sleeves.

He was exceedingly attractive, which I found rather annoying. Spoiled brats should come with sniveling noses and bloated pouts, not looking like they were the prototype the Fates consulted when creating sentient beings.

He glanced over at the courier, who shrugged. "I am afraid she speaks the truth, Your Highness. Miss Payne and her father own a glassmaking business in town. Whether your Cinderella bought them from her for the ball or stole them, as this woman insists, we have yet to prove. But this we know: the shoe fits."

The prince's taut arms went limp. His footsteps echoed through the large breakfast hall as he paced back and forth on the marble tile. As he ran his hands through his already messy hair, I couldn't help but notice how his shirt tugged at his shoulders and biceps. It was unfair, really, that such an attractive exterior should be wasted on the likes of someone who thought all humans had faerie godmothers tucked away in our pockets.

The courier and the guard went silent, and when the prince turned to face us again, I realized his hands were trembling, and his eyes had widened in panic.

This I did not find satisfying. Sure, I had intended to make the guy sweat a little, but at this rate, I wondered if he would break down into a panic attack. As someone who had never witnessed her father as much as shed a tear, I was not ready for the emotional awkwardness of witnessing the fae Crown Prince, Heir to the Throne of Dwellen, cry.

Why was he panicking, anyway? He was the Crown Prince of Dwellen, for Fates' sake. He was immortal. Fae. He could do anything he wanted.

As long as he hadn't struck a bargain, that is.

"Oh." The realization dawned on me. The shoe. The scroll of paper the courier kept referencing. "You extended a bargain, didn't you?" If there was anything my parents had instilled within me since infancy, it was how dangerous it was for humans to make bargains with fae, beings who had become expert deceivers over the centuries, driven by the inability to lie outright. The magic fae used to seal bargains was a tricky one that would kill any party who broke the terms of the bargain. Of course, he was panicking. The slipper must have been enchanted with a bargain. The fae prince had vowed to marry the woman whose foot fit the slipper, thinking it would only fit Cinderella because of the thief's silly lie. If I accepted the terms of his bargain, he would be stuck married to me, and if he tried to violate the marriage by divorcing me, he would die.

The prince's eyes locked on mine, and where I expected to see pleading, all I found was a numb resignation.

He really thought I'd do it. He thought I'd trap him in a marriage, just for the glory of being a princess. Now that I considered it, I figured he would have been right, had the shoe fit either of my neighbors. The thought perforated my conscience a bit. As much as the prince deserved a poor result from rashly throwing his life away over a silly grand gesture, I couldn't help but feel for his helplessness. Clearly, he thought he loved this Cinderella girl, regardless of the fact that he didn't seem to realize Cinderella had to be a stage name. Who was I to make him suffer any longer, thinking he could never marry her?

Never mind the fact that she ran away from him, my mind interjected.

Well, I figured that was all the more reason to get away from him as quickly as possible.

"Don't fret, Your Highness. I have no intention of accepting the terms of your bargain. All I want is my other slipper, and a legal patent protecting its design. Then I'll happily be on my way. I'll even wish you luck in finding Dwellen's future princess."

The courier groaned. Prince Evander looked me over, and I had to fight the urge to squirm as he locked those piercing green eyes on mine.

"You didn't tell her, did you?"

"Tell me what?"

Something like grim satisfaction snaked at the edges of his lips, and I got the dreadful feeling he was sinking. And he was the type to derive satisfaction from pulling others down with him.

"That you, my dearly betrothed, accepted the terms of my bargain as soon as you put on that slipper."

CHAPTER 5

ELLIE

*S*omewhere between the prince's mouth and my rounded ears, there must have been a glamour cast, a prank that convinced my mind that the prince had really said what I thought he'd said.

What did he mean that I'd agreed to a fae bargain simply by donning a pair of shoes? Not even a pair! One shoe!

"No. Um. No. I agreed to nothing. All I did was put on a slipper. My slipper, mind you." I meant to sound confident, assured, but all I managed was to sound like I was taste-testing the prince's claim, hoping to catch a counterfeit. This could not be happening. Sure, I had been warned since childhood that the fae could be tricky, that they had deceived plenty of foolish humans into sly bargains that rarely ended well. For the humans, at least.

But I hadn't made a bargain.

I hadn't agreed to anything, actually.

Suddenly, the silver-leafed mural on the wall seemed to spin, the metallic brushstrokes swirling, throwing me off balance and churning my stomach, threatening to reveal my breakfast all over the Crown Prince's shoes.

"I'm afraid—"

"Fates above, do you ever use another phrase?" I ran my palm over my face, snapping at Orvall, my voice shaking like an acrobat who'd just learned the net had been pulled out from beneath them for the crowd's amusement.

Orvall bristled and, upon regaining his composure, continued on in the same drawling voice, like he was about to recite the selection of teas available for breakfast rather than the terms that would, for all intents and purposes, ruin my life. "I have reviewed the bargain drawn up by Your Highness, and it is clearly written so that the act of fitting one's foot into the slipper is to accept the terms of the bargain, which, in this case, is to be betrothed to the prince himself."

I ripped the paper from the courier's hands, and he squelched. "Surely that's not all it says."

MY DEAREST LOVE.

In a few hours' time, you have captured my heart. What a small sacrifice it is to offer my vows to you as well. I offer my hand in marriage. You asked for something romantic, so here it is. I've enchanted this slipper with the highest of fae bargains—a betrothal bond. By the authority of common Fae law, should you place this slipper upon your foot and accept my proposal, the enchantment will bind our souls together in a bond neither of us may break. Here is my vow to you: Come the Vernal Moon, I shall be your husband, if only you'll become my wife. I will await your answer with bated breath.

BATED BREATH. If only the prince would hold it instead.

I wound the paper back into its roll, knotting the leather tie around my life sentence.

Orvall cleared his throat, reaching for the decree. "Miss Payne—"

"You." I jabbed the decree into the courier's chest. "You didn't read this to me before you made me try on the shoe." Try as I might to contain it, my voice went shrill at the end of my sentence. That was it. I'd officially lost all composure.

Oh, well. What did composure matter anymore now that I had

unwittingly signed the rest of my life away?

"Miss Payne, you did not fit the description. It was natural to assume—"

"Yeah, well, you assumed incorrectly, didn't you?" the prince interjected.

"And you!" I turned my paper weapon upon the prince's Fates-chiseled face. "I'm not sure whether to hate you or pity you for being such an idiot. Who does this?" I demanded, waving the paper in the air for emphasis. "What kind of lovesick fool writes a bargain with so few stipulations? I don't even *look like her*. Oh, but apparently only one human woman in all of Alondria could be special enough to have such *delicate* feet."

Prince Evander closed his sea-green eyes and rubbed his temples. "In my defense, Cinderella told me they were enchanted."

I huffed, annoyed that this male had the gall to avert his gaze from the woman whose life he'd just ruined. "I think you forfeited the right to defend yourself when you composed a fae bargain and were too lazy to deliver it yourself."

The prince threw up his hands. "Oh, don't act like you don't benefit from this. We both know you're the one who stands to gain in this misunderstanding. You? You get to be Princess of Dwellen. What more could you have asked for from your petty human life? Me? I'm stuck cuffed to a human for the next fifty years, while the woman I love grows old."

I allowed my lips to curve into a pleasant grin, one with which my eyes did not partake. When I spoke, my voice was practically saccharine. "Ah, my apologies for ruining the five to ten happy years you would have spent together before she got cellulite and wrinkles and you had to endure the dreadful inconvenience of hunting down a mistress."

Prince Evander ground his teeth and scraped his palms against his eyelids, as if he could wipe the sleep from his eyes, blink a few times, and look up a moment later to find that I'd been an apparition. When he deigned to look at me again, a serene, crazed expression had overcome his face. "Oh, and how delighted my father will be about all this."

49

"Your father?" I scoffed. "You just made a bargain to marry the wrong woman and you're worried about what your father will think?"

"My father happens to be the king. It tends to make disagreements a tad more complicated. Not that you would know."

"Right, because how could my tiny human mind comprehend—"

He didn't seem to hear me, or, if he did, he had no qualms about interrupting me as he paced. "Oh, he's just going to revel in this." He grabbed the scroll, taking his turn to shake it.

I went to yank it back, but he held it above my reach, like I was a child. I seethed. "Aren't you two hundred years old? And your daddy still has to sign your bargains?"

His jaw bulged. "It's supposed to protect royalty from making rash decisions."

I let out a laugh, though the bitterness in it poisoned my throat, leaving a foul taste behind. "Glad that system is in place. Can you imagine what might have happened if we didn't have an infallible system to protect us?"

"Orvall, would you get her out of here, please? I can't think while her voice is grating my ears."

"Yes, Your Highness."

I seethed as the courier grabbed my wrist, though more gently than I had expected, and led me toward the door.

"Oh, and Miss Payne," the prince added, "I'm going to need that slipper back. If I'm going to be stuck with you for the rest of my life, I'd appreciate it if I had something to remember her by."

"Of course." I smirked and reached out as if to hand him the slipper. His arm extended, smugness tugging his lips upward. Something told me this coddled prince wasn't exactly used to losing. It was my turn to smile, and when he caught my expression, his smirk faltered. "On second thought... it's mine. I can do what I want with it." In a moment of fury, my finger relaxed.

Time slowed as the shoe slipped across my fingertips.

Glass shattered on the marble tile.

"There," I seethed. "Something to remember her by."

CHAPTER 6

EVANDER

*H*ate was typically an emotion I reserved for my father.

I figured in this case, I could make an exception.

My beloved betrothed strode through the door, the shards of my broken dreams littering the floor, and had the gall to smirk at me on the way out.

"Fates, Andy. How did you manage to find the one woman in the kingdom who's not dying to crawl into your bed?"

I didn't have to turn around to recognize the voice. The only other living being in this castle who ever spoke to me with such adoration in their voice was my mother, and she was certainly not the kind to bring up women and my bed in the same sentence.

Plus, no one else called me Andy. Probably because everyone else who knew me well enough to address me by name was centuries older than me and had always possessed the acumen to pronounce my name correctly.

Blaise ducked out from behind a decorative suit of armor, an ancient relic of the time humans ruled Alondria. A hole gaped in the armor's chest, a reminder that such an era had long passed.

She strolled up to me, a cocky grin plastered on her face, and made like she was considering propping her elbow on my shoulder. That would never happen, of course. Blaise wasn't what I'd consider tall, even by human standards, and I towered over her. Instead, her bony elbow poked into my arm.

"Are you trying to stab me?" I asked, eyeing her elbow.

"I would, but I'm afraid your betrothed might resent me if I beat her to it."

I grimaced, which didn't gain me an ounce of sympathy in Blaise's brown eyes. Her gaze had always possessed this sharp and knowing quality, and I could tell she intended to make me explain myself, even though she usually knew what I was up to before I did.

"I didn't find her," I explained, "which you would know if you bothered to show up at the ball last night."

I shot a disapproving look down my nose, but it glanced right off of her.

Blaise was used to disapproving looks. She was about the laziest servant in the entirety of Dwellen, and given her competitive nature, I imagined that was just the reputation she strove for.

"Why in Alondria would I attend a ball where no one bothered to invite any men?"

"I was there, wasn't I?" I teased.

She worked her tongue like she was trying to get a bitter taste out of her mouth, and I laughed.

Blaise was the closest thing I'd ever had to a sister. Well, a sister I liked. There was Olwen, of course, my younger sister. But as soon as my father had tried to marry her off to a wealthy duke, she'd run off and trapped herself in a tower made entirely of vines.

Of the three of us siblings, she'd always been the prodigy when it came to magic.

Don't get me wrong—I didn't blame Olwen. I wouldn't have wanted to marry the oily duke either. But Olwen could take care of herself, and as we didn't exactly get along, I couldn't say I missed her presence in the castle.

But Blaise? I'd loved her since the moment her family attended court over sixteen years ago. She was hardly a toddler then, but she'd had this keenness to her gaze that struck me. She'd been clever and mischievous and totally unreproved for it.

She was human, her father serving as the king's mediator to the humans of Dwellen.

When Blaise was twelve, her father had fallen ill and died. Her mother had passed before I met her, and the rest of her family, quite frankly, could eat porcupine feces for all I cared, so she had no one. In a rare act of something resembling kindness, my father had taken her on as a servant, so at least her needs could be provided for.

Right. Again, resembling kindness. Not actual kindness.

If it had been just me entreating him to take care of her, I was fairly certain Blaise would be begging for scraps in a foreign kingdom right now, but Jerad had also taken a liking to her and had persuaded my father with his ardent requests.

That being said, Blaise's father had never taught her to as much as lift a finger, and she rarely did more than the minimum required to keep the head maid from screaming at her, if she bothered with doing that much at all.

She really was a horrible servant.

But a sister? She was pretty stinking good at that.

"So, what *were* you doing when you were supposed to be attending the ball?" I asked, more than eager to steer the conversation away from my current predicament. I was pretty sure Blaise already knew the crap I'd gotten myself into, but if I didn't distract her, she'd force me to admit it out loud just so she could mock me as I squirmed in embarrassment.

She didn't miss a beat before she said, "Making out with Gregor in the pasture behind his pa's house."

I didn't bother to fight back a gag, to which she raised an eyebrow of faux offense. Gregor was the youngest son of the human farmer who supplied at least half of the castle's produce, and he wasn't the sort I had in mind for Blaise.

I had no idea whether Blaise was pretty. She must have been, with

53

all the suitors that weaseled their way past guards and into the castle to get to her. But when I looked at Blaise, I couldn't see past the little girl I used to scoop into my arms, the child who I'd pretend not to see during our games of hide-and-seek, even though she'd always choose the suits of armor as her hiding spots.

The long black hair that she kept in a messy braid, the big brown eyes and the disarming grin? They were all just stretched out versions of the adorable child I'd grown to love.

Unfortunately, the entire city of post-pubescent boys didn't seem to see her that way. She had them entranced with that boisterous laugh of hers, had them working for her smile like it was the last sack of grain during a famine.

"Remind me to have him whipped," I grumbled, trying and failing to shove the image of the pimply farmhand's hands all over Blaise out of my mind. Permanently.

She scoffed. "You wouldn't dare."

I craned my neck in challenge. "You sure about that? Isn't Gregor considerably older than you, anyway?" *And immature, and constantly spouting out lies to get attention,* I didn't add.

She rolled her big brown eyes. "I'm eighteen, Andy. All my peers have been married for at least two years and are already on their second pregnancy."

She laced every word with venom, like a life married off young, a child in the arms and another on the way was a nightmare that other women her age didn't know they were trapped in.

I wondered sometimes if she really felt that way, if she was glad for the life she'd escaped through her misfortune.

I wondered if maybe she told herself that to dull the ache.

Her peers, she called them—the girls with whom she used to toss pebbles into the pond, hoping the number of ripples would determine the names of their future husbands.

"Well, aren't you going to go after your future bride?" She waved her hand toward the excessively ornate doors out of which Ellie had just stomped.

54

I let out an agitated breath. "I'd rather not."

"Remind me why, exactly, you picked her."

I let my eyes roll over to Blaise slowly and deliberately. "You act like you weren't hiding behind that suit of armor during the entire conversation."

She shrugged, her eyes lighting with mischief. "But I wanted to hear your side of the story."

She looped her arm into mine and dragged me toward the doors. "Oh, come on," she said as I protested, digging my feet into the ground like a pouting child. "I won't make you talk to her. But I've been out all night, and I won't be able to stay awake for your tragic tale if I don't get some coffee in me."

THE KITCHEN WAS PROBABLY Blaise's favorite place in the entire castle, if not the entire world, and if she was shirking her responsibilities, this was likely where you could find her.

Unless it was her day to clean the kitchens, in which case your best bet was to search for a pair of boots sticking out from underneath the garden shrubs.

"So, let's get this straight..." Blaise shoved a pecan tart into her mouth, pocketing it in her cheeks as she twiddled her thumbs. "You, Prince Evander Thornwall, Heir to the Throne of Dwellen and suitor of many a courtesan, fell in love with a mysterious stranger, a human woman, quite literally at first sight."

I picked the last pecan tart from her plate, and she pouted. "It wasn't at first sight. We danced and talked all night."

Before I could bring the tart to my mouth, she grabbed it from me and licked it.

I grimaced. "You're disgusting."

"And you're glossing over some important details," she said, as if this were far greater a crime than infecting the last pecan tart with her saliva. "Also, it totally counts as love at first sight if it's the first time you meet someone."

"I'm afraid you're wrong about that, young lady. It only counts if you love them the instant you lay eyes upon them."

"Would you say that you've seen her a second time yet?"

I didn't answer, which Blaise took as response enough. "I'll take that as a no. Now, I know my education was cut tragically short, but I'm pretty sure if it comes before second, that makes it the first."

"So you're going to drag me down to the kitchens, make me smell the pecan tarts, not even let me taste one, then tell me how wrong I am?"

She nodded. "Pretty much." But then her face softened, as it so rarely did. "I'm sorry it didn't work out the way you wanted."

I swallowed. I knew almost every one of Blaise's maneuvers. Earnest was not one she plucked out very often.

"It's really my own fault," I said. It had been stupid to convince my father to let me place a bargain onto those shoes. He'd known that, and that's exactly why he'd let me do it.

Not to mention the fact that Cinderella had been lying when she told me the shoes were glamoured to fit only her. As a fae incapable of lying, it was the one thing that made me wary about most humans, the one power they boasted over us.

But then again, she probably just came from a lowly family and worried I would have cast her to the side if I'd realized she had no name and no money.

Could I blame her?

"Your fault or not, it still stinks," Blaise said.

"Yeah."

"You wanna tell me what you loved about her?"

Her voice was so gentle, so soft, it sounded unnatural. I furrowed my eyebrows, then took the back of my palm and placed it over her brow. "Are you feeling ill?"

"No, it's just that I've never seen you really care about any of them before. It makes me worried, that's all."

I cocked my head, puzzled. "You know I'm never going to let anyone take your place, right?"

At that, Blaise jerked out from underneath my hand and pushed it away, grumbling. "You're coddling. It's overbearing."

"Fine," I said, unable to help but smile at her reaction to my sap. "To be honest, I didn't think she was any different from the rest at first. But she was gorgeous, and I thought, who better to dance the night away with than the most stunning woman in the room? But when we danced, it was almost like... almost like she knew me."

Blaise looked about ready to gag with revulsion, which kept me from mentioning the tiny detail about me being pretty sure a mating bond had snapped into place, but she motioned for me to continue.

"I don't know, Blaise. Ever since Jerad..." I trailed off, still unable to say the words, as if they would somehow make what had happened a reality, rather than the nightmare I'd been trapped in for the past year. Blaise reached her hand across the counter and took mine in hers. Her hand was cold and trembling. For the first time today, I noticed the dark circles underneath her eyes.

My subjects were none the wiser, but my late-night rendezvous had only increased in frequency since the accident.

For her, that's when the late night rendezvous had begun.

"I miss him too," she whispered.

I cleared my throat. I could hardly get a word out about Jerad, much less admit out loud how much I missed him. How empty this eternal life felt without him. "All the women I've met since..." I took a breath, and Blaise squeezed my hand. "They're always so quick to bring up that I'm the heir. What a glorious kingdom I'm going to run when it's my turn to take the throne."

Blaise nodded, understanding creasing her pale forehead.

"She didn't bring it up. Not once." My throat went dry. "She just told me she was sorry. That she knew what it was to...to lose someone very dear. To have a life thrust upon her that wasn't the one she'd envisioned for herself."

Silver lined Blaise's brown eyes before the tears began to spill down her sleep-deprived, sunken cheeks.

"We should both get to bed." Dying inside from the pain in her expression, I tousled her raven-black hair. "Some of us were up all night and are in desperate need of a nap."

She swallowed and nodded, pushing herself off the kitchen counters. As we left, her eyes narrowed in question. "What'd you say her name was?"

"Cinderella."

"You know that has to be a stage name, right?"

CHAPTER 7

ELLIE

J had to admit, I'd half expected Orvall to send me to the dungeons for that little act of defiance I'd pulled back in the prince's presence. So when he brought me to a cozy suite with a soft bed and a smoldering fireplace instead, I tried to act pleasantly surprised.

You know, as pleasantly surprised as one can be when they've accidentally sworn their life away to a twelve-year-old in an immortally twenty-five-year-old body.

"I suggest you rest," Orvall said as I examined the room. "There is parchment on the desk should you wish to write your family."

I nodded, the motion more a reflex than anything. I mostly wanted him and the guard to get out. Thankfully, they cleared their throats and shuffled away, shutting the door behind me. I watched the door handle as they did, noticing just the subtlest of jerks in the wood.

Subtle enough to be caused by a key in a lock.

Great.

So it seemed I was a prisoner, after all.

What did they think I was going to do? Run away? I'd come here willingly.

All at once, the injustice of it all overtook me, and I collapsed onto the soft silver pillows on the bed. Salty tears soaked the pillowcases and burned my cheeks as I sobbed, hoping that no one outside was listening. How weak they would think I was. Just a little girl, barely an adult by human standards, weeping into my pillows like a schoolchild.

But the embarrassment only fueled my tears, and I sobbed harder. Just this morning, I had woken to the belief that today would be different—I would finally present my shoes to the world and strike the deal that would launch my business into success. That my work would be profitable, something that would truly make my father proud, not simply amused.

My father. My throat tightened at the thought of him.

Would I even see him again? I had no idea what betrothal entailed for the prince. If he was as rash as everyone said he was, as he had already proven himself to be, what lengths would he go to in order to free himself of this betrothal? Would he kill me just to end the bargain? Would that even work, or would the fae curse that forbade fae from lying keep him from sabotaging the bargain with foul play? I didn't have high hopes in that regard. The fae boasted a reputation for being ruthless when it came to finding loopholes.

That was it. Either I would be made a reluctant princess, or I was going to die. If that happened, Papa would probably die inside too. Mother would keep him as healthy as she could. She'd put on a strong face for him, but in the end she would crumple.

And there was nothing I could do about it.

By the time I awakened, the sun drooped low in the sky, its rays shimmering through my window which, from the looks of it, had been supplied by none other than yours truly. If I squinted, I could make out the brand in the lower right-hand corner, the curves in the glass that spelled my initials.

E.P.

There might have been a time when I would have been ecstatic about discovering my initials inside the castle walls.

Today was not that day.

It must have been late afternoon already, and I marveled at what a capable sedative shock made, forcing me to sleep for so long in the middle of the day. My eyes were puffy and tired, but the cry and nap seemed to have drained some of the tension that had built up in my chest. Now that my head felt clearer, I examined my room.

Indigo wallpaper with swirling silver patterns that matched the color of the sheets on my bed overlaid the walls. There was a desk in the corner, the one that I remembered contained parchment that I should probably use to write to my family. The door to my right had been left ajar, and it led into a spacious bath with a large silver bathtub. I'd have to indulge in that before I was inevitably assassinated.

Or moved to the prince's quarters.

My cheeks heated at the very idea, but I banished the silly notion. My parents might have shared a room, but that likely was not standard practice among nobility. I couldn't imagine Prince Evander sharing anything with anybody.

Except for perhaps his bed.

My cheeks burned this time, and I tried, with great difficulty, not to think of that, either.

A white-oak vanity perched on the wall directly across from the bed, and I ignored my reflection as I walked past it. I had no desire to see how disheveled I must look after a long afternoon of napping and crying and sniffling and snotting all over my pillows.

I had to do something, though. I was wide wake from my fitful nap, and I wanted nothing more than to pace, but my room wasn't quite spacious enough for it. So instead, I wrote to my family.

Dear Mama and Papa,

It seems my stay at the palace will be longer than I intended. Apparently, our beloved prince enchanted my slippers with a bargain that I accidentally agreed to when I put them on. I must stay at the palace while we try to work out an exception to the bargain, but I hope to see you shortly.

Love,

Ellie

. . .

I SCRIBBLED ON THE PAPER, the foolishness of what I was writing becoming more pronounced with each word. I'd send it anyway, because I couldn't bear for my parents to have no idea what had happened to me or why I hadn't returned home. But the notion that there was an exception to a fae bargain wouldn't fool them. If anyone was going to find a loophole, it was always going to be the fae, not the human.

Though, I had to admit, at least the fae I'd made a bargain with had an incentive to find a loophole.

It was then that I remembered that a perfectly reasonable exception would be to kill me.

I groaned and folded the letter before stuffing it into an envelope and addressing it.

Not long after, I heard a knock at my door.

I responded out of reflex. "Come in." Though I quickly remembered that this was a silly thing to tell someone when I was locked inside a room to which they most likely had the key.

The door creaked open, and in peeked a slight girl dressed in servants' attire. Her hair straddled the line between blonde and brunette. She'd pulled it into a lifeless bun at the nape of her neck, the shape of which did nothing to frame her thin jawline. Her pale-white cheeks were sallow, and she looked as if she hadn't seen the sun since childhood. My gut reaction was to check her forehead for a fever, but guilt immediately usurped that instinct when I realized sickly was simply how the girl looked.

"Lady Payne? May I come in?"

"It's Miss Payne. Or just Ellie, really. And yes." I wasn't sure why I was worrying about what I wanted to be called when the prince was probably going to have me killed soon. If his molasses mind ever made it around to that solution, that was.

"Not to argue with you, ma'am, but I do believe you've been promoted to a lady now that you're betrothed to the prince. I'm to be your lady's maid." The girl walked in and curtsied. "Along with a servant named Blaise, although she's nowhere to be found."

Was it my imagination, or did I sense a twinge of bitterness in the girl's voice, along with an "as usual," muttered under her breath?

Oh, well. I supposed it would frustrate me to no end if I was supposed to be sharing duties with a partner who never pulled their weight. Though I'd most likely be happier doing it all myself. "What's your name?"

"Imogen, my lady."

"Imogen, would you mind delivering this to my parents?" I asked, handing her the envelope. She took it and slipped it into one of the many pockets in her drab dress.

"I'd be happy to. Is there anything else I might get you?"

"No, thank you," I said, though, in reality, I was really quite thirsty. I simply felt bad asking it of her, but then I remembered I couldn't exactly leave the room myself.

"Maybe some water?" I asked.

"Of course." She scuttled out of the room, locked the door behind her, and was back within a few minutes with a glass. I pondered whether I could overpower her the next time she unlocked my room, but I had no idea how I was going to make it out of the palace once I made it into the hallway.

Instead, I gulped down my water as Imogen shifted on her feet, rocking back and forth slightly. "Pardon, milady. But the other servants are saying that even though you're the prince's betrothed, you weren't the one to dance with him last night at the ball."

She bit her lip and picked at the hem of her sleeves. I supposed this was probably a very improper question to ask of a lady, and I wasn't sure how to take it. On one hand, Imogen could be taking advantage of the fact that I wasn't a lady and didn't understand the proper etiquette between a servant and a lady. On the other hand, it wasn't a question I would have found rude yesterday.

"No, I wasn't. This is all some misunderstanding."

"But the shoe did fit your foot?"

"Only because I made it. I used a mold from my own foot to shape

63

the glass."

"Oh." Imogen went quiet and bit her lip, then asked, "Did you know the shoe was enchanted?"

"No." I straightened in my chair, feeling a bit antsy now. She seemed sweet enough, but I wasn't typically fond of nosy people.

She frowned, something like concern furrowing in her brow. "Then this must be quite a shock to you. Being betrothed to someone you don't know."

The comment took me aback. "You mean, you don't assume that I'm groveling after the prince and just thrilled with my luck?"

Imogen smiled weakly and blushed. "I might have assumed so at first. Fae females and women are always pining after the prince. They forget I'm around sometimes to hear them gossip," she explained, but then she motioned to my eyes, which were probably still red with tears. "But I can see that you're different. I'm sorry you've found yourself in a situation you have little control over."

My heart warmed a bit. At least someone here didn't think I should be jumping up and down in glee at being the forced betrothed of Prince Evander.

"Do you think there is any way out of it?" she asked.

My curiosity piqued. "Is there a way out of a fae bargain?"

She rubbed her thumb and forefinger together. "Sometimes. Rarely, but sometimes. Occasionally, when a bargain is written, another fae cosigns it, and if they're really careful about how they word it, that fae can end the bargain on behalf of the other fae…and humans…who actually made the bargain. But that doesn't happen very often," she said, her voice shaking, as if she were afraid of getting my hopes up.

Her words struck a chord in my mind, and the cusp of an idea took shape. But I couldn't let it fully form. Not at the chance that it would crush my spirits when the idea didn't end up working.

"Thank you, Imogen," I said. She blushed again, then curtsied before leaving the room.

When the key clicked in the lock, I couldn't help but wonder if my Fate had been sealed with it.

CHAPTER 8

ELLIE

Consistent with his reputation, it took the Prince of Dwellen less than a day to seek me out in my chambers.

In fact, he appeared that evening, just after the last streak of pink faded from the sky, following the sun over the edge of the horizon.

"I have an idea." Prince Evander strode into my room halfway into me telling him it was alright to come in, thinking I was inviting in Imogen.

I wasn't convinced the prince had yet come to the inevitable conclusion that the easiest way out of this bargain would be to kill me, but I wasn't keen on taking my chances either. I jolted to my feet and grabbed the lamp stand on my bedside table. It wasn't much, but it was heavy, crafted of wrought iron, and the detailing at the base looked intricate enough to do some damage. If I could land a solid blow on the prince's head—or elsewhere, if the prince's actions deemed such a scandal necessary—perhaps I could buy enough time to escape.

The prince's sea-green eyes brightened as he scanned the lamp stand, the corners of his lips twitching in amusement. "You know if you bludgeon me with that, you'll be charged with treason, right?"

"Well, better a treasonist than dead," I said, clutching the lamp stand tighter.

"Pretty sure that's not a word."

"You knew what I meant."

He rolled his eyes, picking at a stray piece of fuzz on his shoulder, as if that were more worthy of his attention than the woman wielding a potential murder weapon. "Relax. I'm not going to kill you."

"How am I supposed to believe that?"

He shrugged, flicking the piece of lint at me. It hit my nose, and I had to stifle a sneeze. "I suppose you don't have to. But we have a long conversation ahead of us, and I figure your puny human arms are going to tire of supporting double their weight in wrought iron at some point."

Not quite ready to relinquish my grip on the lamp stand, even if it was only a false sense of security that it provided, I continued, "You could make it easier for me and give me a reason to trust you."

"Fine." Faster than I could blink, he'd closed the distance between us. He reached around my body, pinning my waist with his firm arms as he plucked something from the bed behind me. I tensed, and a wicked grin spread across his striking face, the flame from the lamp stand reflecting in his vivid eyes. "I could suffocate you with this fluffy pillow you've drooled all over and blame it on a jealous ex." He flourished the pillow in question before tossing it and its incriminating drool stain onto the bed.

Dread consumed me, and his gaze swept downward, his pointed ears twitching as if he could sense my heart hammering against my ribcage. He leaned closer, pinching the wick of the candle and stealing the flame's last breath between the pads of his fingertips.

The room went dark, his violent green eyes banishing the shadows, reflecting the silver glow of the barely waning moon that peered through my window.

"Tell me, Miss Payne. Is this the kind of story you'd like to read about? One you'd be inclined to believe?"

His gaze landed on my neck, to where my pulse pounded at the divot in my skin. I wondered then if there were things we didn't know about the fae, things they'd kept hidden over the centuries, distracting us with their unparalleled beauty and their fancy balls and their coveted immortality.

But then the wick on the lamp stand flickered with new life, and a flame doused the room in light once more.

Prince Evander tore his brilliant eyes away from my pulse, and that carefree nature settled over him once again as he laughed. "Relax. I'm just messing with you. Even if I wasn't, my father wouldn't believe me, anyway. Any attempt to frame your murder on someone else, he'd trace back to me immediately. In fact, if you ever decide to exact revenge against me, save yourself some time and fake your own death. He'll blame me for your *innocent* life and ruin me, I assure you."

As he stepped away, I let out a breath, much louder than I intended to, and the edge of his lips quirked. Then, mostly because he was right —my arm was getting tired, and there wasn't much I could do if an immortal fae wanted me dead anyway—I laid the lamp on the table.

"Good. Now we can talk without distractions." He sauntered over to the bed and plopped atop it, sprawling his legs out and propping the back of his head in his hands. "Care to join me?" His eyes flickered with the mischief of the sea, egging its prey into its treacherous waves. The look, and all it insinuated, had the muscles in my back tensing until I must have looked as stiff as the cedar bedposts that supported my mattress.

"No, thank you. I prefer to keep my dignity intact."

"Your loss." He shrugged, ruffling the bedsheets in the process. "Your mattress is comfy. Perhaps when we're married, we can move it up to my suite."

Heat flooded my cheeks, and I did my best to hide the trembling in my voice. "Yes, and then you can move to a mat on the floor."

"Suit yourself. You'll be missing out, though."

"That's my hope and prayer."

Quick as a fox, he swung his legs over the side of the bed and leaned forward. "And why, might I ask, are you so intent on rejecting me?"

"Do you always throw yourself at women who've made it clear that they despise you?"

The insult didn't land as I'd intended, and his green eyes sparkled. "You haven't seen me throw myself at you yet."

He sprang from the bed and landed right in front of me, his face a breath away from mine. He craned his neck down so that his nose almost rested against my forehead. My breath caught, and for a moment I froze, my heart pounding.

"Would you like to see me throw myself at you?" he whispered, his breath a gentle caress against my skin.

My heart thudded against my chest, an unwanted warmth pooling in my belly.

A wicked grin tugged at his mouth, revealing a dimple on his left cheek. He leaned in, his lips...

Fates above, he really was going to kiss me.

Shocked by the prince's audacity, I shoved his chest, propelling myself backward. "What do you think you're doing?"

That dimple was still on full display, highlighting his cocky smirk. "Just a little test, that's all."

"A test?" I asked, unable to tamp down the scoff in my voice. Not that I was trying too hard.

Prince Evander flicked his eyes back toward me, and that assessing look took on a judgmental tint where the hunger had once been. "For all I know, you planted the shoes on Cinderella and fed her that lie about the shoes only fitting her feet, all the while intending to trick me into a bargain. Which I maintain works out fairly well for you. I had to be sure you were the honest sort of human. There aren't many of you out there."

I crossed my arms as if I could smother the phantom warmth of his hands on my waist if I just squeezed myself hard enough. "Oh, I'm sure there's a reason you fae are cursed with the inability to lie. You were probably lying in excess before some greater force punished you all for it. It's not as if you lack the skills to deceive. In fact, fae probably have more talent in that area than humans."

"Only of necessity, of course," he said. "I needed to know that you weren't the type to play hard to get. That you weren't secretly delighted with our misunderstanding."

I tried to ignore the prick of hurt pride that punctured my gut at the admission that the prince hadn't actually wanted me. Instead, I thought back to what he had said, about making sure I was being honest about not desiring him. Had his entire ruse of trying to seduce me really been to make sure I really didn't want to be married to him?

He couldn't be lying. That wasn't possible for the fae. But it did reinforce the lessons that my father had taught me from a young age. *The fae will go to great lengths to omit the truth, or give you just a sliver of it. That way, nothing they say is an outright lie. Never mistake such for the full truth.*

"And what good does that do you, to be so sure I don't secretly want you? Surely you're not so bored as to find such a thing interesting," I said, picking at my fingernails in distaste.

He grinned, though his eyes didn't partake. That didn't make it any less disarming. "Because, my dearly betrothed, I needed to be sure that you and I are on the same team."

"Did tricking me into pledging my marriage to you not do that already?"

"Not quite," he said. "Actually, I'd like for you to help me get out of it."

This caught me off guard, though I wasn't sure why. Of course the prince would want out of the bargain, possibly even more desperately than I did. For me, the problem with the bargain was that I had lost my dream. That thrill of the feeling of hard-earned coin in my hand. That rush. As a princess, I'd likely not be allowed to do such menial tasks as glassblowing. Instead, I'd be forced into the company of the fae nobility, whom I wasn't exactly eager to befriend.

But for the prince, he'd lost the chance to marry a girl he loved. Well, a girl he thought he loved; I still wasn't ever going to be convinced it was possible to truly fall in love with someone after meeting for only a handful of hours. What my parents had was love.

What the prince had for this woman was probably just an accelerated form of lust. Even so, in his mind, he *thought* he was in love. And from the little I knew about love, even the perception of it could make one desperate.

But I had dreamed of love, too, hadn't I? My parents weren't like our neighbors, trying to shove their daughter into marriage like it was a business transaction. Maybe that was why they'd never discouraged me from my ambitions. Because a woman who had her own money could choose to marry for love. That was what my parents had done. Except in their case, they'd done so without means. And they had instilled in me the importance of doing the same.

But now, if the prince and I found no way to break the bargain, any hopes of marrying a man for the sake of affection would be swept away. For though I was sure the Crown would tolerate a host of the prince's mistresses, there would be a pair of heads to pay should I ever be caught with a man in my bed.

I might not have wasted my life away dreaming of love, but now that the possibility had escaped my grasp, I found myself clutching at it.

I swallowed, finding I'd rather singe off my prints with my blow-torch than say what I was about to say. "It seems we're partners then. Actually, I've been thinking—"

"Great," he said, clapping his hands together as he sat up. "In fact, I already have an idea. You see, my—"

"Father," I said, crossing my arms.

"By Alondria, aren't you clever?" He beamed, actually beamed, and I resented the way the air in my lungs went thin at the sight of it. "You know, maybe we should get married after all. You're already finishing my sentences."

"That's only because you rudely interrupted me. Otherwise, I would have already said it."

"Fine, fine. Tell me your plan, Miss Payne."

I straightened my back and clasped my hands together in front of me. "Your bargain had to be cosigned by your father, the king."

The prince rubbed his temples. "Oh, and how I begged for him to sign it. To bless our marriage. Looking back, he would've never agreed to something so..." He fumbled for the right word.

"Rash?" I offered.

The prince flashed a grin. "Spontaneous. He never would have agreed to something so spontaneous, unless it was some sick way of teaching me a lesson. But there's a reason I'm not technically supposed to enter a bargain without a cosigner."

"I can't imagine why that would be."

"And now who's interrupting?"

I flitted my hand at him. "Go on."

"In fae society, betrothals are binding, as we consider them a bargain. I understand that humans may propose and go on to end the relationship without much consequence," he said.

I considered that, biting my lip. "Well, there is the matter of the ring. I suppose that's our way of saying that we mean it. Pouring a lot of money into it, I mean."

He snickered. "I assure you, in the case of a failed engagement, the man will pawn the ring off or recycle it for the next woman."

"Unless the woman keeps it," I countered.

"And you claim that the fae are cruel."

"You were saying?"

"As my father is the cosigner, he is the only one who can annul the bargain."

So there it was: confirmation that the solution to our betrothal truly did lie with the king. Hope rose in my chest, but I tried to dampen it, lest I find myself disappointed. "Doesn't that defeat the purpose of the can't-lie-can't-break-a-bargain-curse?"

"Oh, not nearly as much as we would like for it to," he said, leaning against the bedpost. "If I had it my way, I would be free to lie as I wished."

I raised a brow. "So you wouldn't have to admit to your mistresses that they're not as unique to receiving your attention as they might think?"

He pointed a knowing finger at me. "My thoughts exactly."

"If your father has the power to reverse the bargain, why are you sitting here talking to me instead of him?"

He let out a wry laugh, one that sent tingles across the back of my neck. "If I'm the one to ask my father to reverse it, he'll simply laugh in my face and force us to marry tomorrow."

My heart sank. Surely the king wouldn't be so foolish as to force his heir to marry someone unfit for the Crown. Not that I thought I'd do a worse job at being a princess or a queen than whoever this woman was who couldn't even handle holding onto the shoes she had stolen. But still. I hadn't exactly been trained in royal affairs. "But you have to try. Surely there's some way to convince him."

"Why do you think I'm here? Because I felt like hearing your unfounded assumptions about what an undesirable bedmate I am? No, Miss Payne. You'll be the one who convinces him."

"Me? Why me?"

"Because he'll like you."

"More than his own son?"

The prince swallowed. "Shouldn't be that difficult. The bar is set abysmally low."

Something plucked at my heart at that statement. As much as I found the prince to be a vile pig and his suitors blinded to his stench by his good looks, something about the idea that a male, even a fae male, could feel so despised by his own father twisted at my insides. My father and I argued from time to time, sure. But not once in my life could I remember doubting his love for me. Deep down I knew that, were I to go sell myself to the local brothel, he'd liquidate his entire business just to get me back.

For the prince to think that his father would prefer me, a human stranger, to him, the only son he had left... I couldn't fathom it.

"What would you have me do?" I asked.

"We're to dine with my parents this evening. I'm to introduce you. I wish you to woo my father." He must have seen the way my nose crinkled in disgust, because he laughed. "Oh, not like that. Don't worry, my dearly betrothed. My father might despise his own son, but he adores my mother and has never been one to allow his eyes to wander. I simply ask that you charm him with your...erm...deter-mined personality. Then, when dinner concludes, ask him to free you of your miserable fate."

"And you think that will work?" I tried not to sound skeptical and failed miserably.

"Of course it will work. You'll find conversation between the two of you easy. All you have to do is commiserate about how you've been unfairly matched with an idiot who is unfit to rule the kingdom, and you'll be instant best friends, I assure you. By the time dinner is over, he'll see that you're much too clever of a woman to be stuck with someone as simple-minded as his son. He'll feel pity for you, since he's also stuck with me, in his own way. By dessert, you'll be back with your parents doing…whatever it is that delights your mortal heart, I assure you."

I chewed my lip. "You're sure it will work?"

"I know my father. It'll work. Just play up the glassblowing entrepreneur thing. He'll like that. He thinks I'm entitled," he said, rising from the bed and strolling to the door. When he turned around to face me, I tried to catch a glimmer of sadness in his eyes, but all I could find was that self-possessed mask of a smirk. "I'd tell you to wear something pretty tonight, but I figure that would just offend you."

CHAPTER 9

ELLIE

"When Evander was sulking about his accidental betrothed, he forgot to mention you were a goddess."

Blaise, my other lady's maid, the one with whom Imogen had been agitated for skirting her duties, leaned against my bedpost.

She and Imogen had arrived at my quarters to help me ready myself for dinner, but the latter had left to retrieve my gown, which the tailor had only just finished due to the late notice.

Blaise lingered behind, claiming she would start on my paint, though she hadn't yet made a move for the ornate wooden palette that rested top of the white oak vanity.

After a heavy internal debate regarding whether to inquire about Blaise's religious beliefs—she'd mentioned a goddess rather than the Fates—or about her casual nature with Evander, I settled on the latter. "You call him by his given name?"

Blaise shrugged, a common mannerism though it came so naturally to her, she made it look as if she'd invented it. "Not usually. Most of the time I call him Andy, but I thought I'd be considerate and not leave you wondering who I was talking about."

"Ah." Andy. How endearing.

I fought the urge to roll my eyes and determined that I'd probably need to do my own paint if I didn't want to end up looking like a circus clown tonight.

My guess was that *Andy* rarely befriended his female servants out of a good-natured desire to understand the viewpoints of the working class, and as the prince's betrothed, I wasn't keen on letting one of his bedmates near my eyes with something long and pokey.

I reached for the palette and brush, but Blaise abandoned her sedentary station beside my bedpost and waved me away from the paint.

"I can do it myself. I've been doing it myself my entire life," I protested.

Blaise shrugged, taking the brush and opening the palette anyway. "Usually I'd take you up on the offer to do my work for me, but this is the only part of this promotion I've actually been looking forward to."

When she lifted the lid, I couldn't help but note that the palette differed from any I'd bought in town. Where most of the paints I'd purchased included a variety of shades that needed to be hand mixed to match one's skin tone, this palette contained only one shade—a sickly gray that I'd only ever seen on faeries and light-skinned humans...who happened to be dead.

She really was intending to ruin my paint.

Blaise smirked, reading my expression. "Relax. I thought it looked disgusting the first time I saw it, too. But it's some sort of special faerie paint." I must have not looked like I believed her, because she dipped the brush in the paint and swiped it across her own cheek. The paint instantly melded with Blaise's pale white skin, cloaking any blemishes and highlighting the cool undertones so that her face retained a delicate shimmer. "See?"

"You'd think that would have found its way into the human markets by now," I said, nodding toward the paint.

Blaise made an exaggerated swoop of her neck. "Yes, but can you imagine the lines? Besides, I think they have to boil human kidneys to make it, so I can see how that might impact sales."

I jerked back from the brush she was bringing to my forehead, but Blaise only laughed. "Kidding."

She applied the paint all over, but before I could catch a glance of myself in the mirror to be certain it didn't look as though I was wearing a nighttime clay mask, she swiveled my chair to face away from the mirror.

"It's more fun if you wait until the end. More dramatic that way," she explained with a flourish of her hands.

I wiggled uncomfortably in my chair, but she went back to work, applying paint from a different palette to my eyelids, biting her protruding tongue as she concentrated. "This part is more fun," she explained, nodding toward the eyelid paint. "I guess even faerie magic hasn't figured out how to experiment with this many hues yet. I hope they don't figure it out."

I couldn't help the smile that tugged at my lips. While my first impression of Blaise was that she was a jealous lover of the prince's, she seemed earnest, and while she certainly wasn't demure and sweet like Imogen, I could appreciate her frankness. That, and the way she spoke about the paint like it was art. It reminded me of my glass, and it had my hands aching for something to do, something to create.

"How long have you been a lady's maid?" I asked, not sure what topics to broach. My family had never employed any servants. That was more of an "old money" thing in Dwellen, but I was pretty sure decorum stated they weren't supposed to talk much about themselves.

Something gave me the impression that Blaise didn't give a frog's butt about decorum.

"About..." She glanced intently up at the looming grandfather clock in the corner of my room. "Twenty-six hours now."

"Oh," I said, unable to hide my surprise.

"I've served in the palace since I was a child." Blaise opened her mouth, as if to say more, but then she shook her head, moving on to what I assumed was something considerably less personal. "But before the ball, Andy decided to promote me to lady's maid, so I could attend to whoever he picked to be his wife at the ball."

There it was. That pet name again.

"I think he meant for it to be a promotion, but really, I'm still

76

required to complete all my other tasks, so it's more of a nuisance than anything."

I waited for the aftertaste of her words to sting like bile, to turn bitter in the air, but they didn't. Blaise went on applying my paint, and if she was aware of how her words could be interpreted as resentful, she didn't show it on her face.

"But it could be much worse," she said.

I had a difficult time believing that. "How so?"

"Andy has awful taste in women. I was prepared to spend the rest of my existence waiting hand and foot on a princess who expects rose petals garnishing her iced water and for her baths to be heated to the exact temperature of Paradise Cove at sundown on Summer Solstice."

My laugh came forth so abruptly, it sent Blaise's careful brush-strokes off-course. Her brown eyes went wide, and she clamped her hand over her mouth to stifle the giggles. When I attempted to turn toward the mirror to examine the damage, she grabbed me by the shoulder and shook her head. "It's better if you don't look. Trust me."

BY THE TIME Imogen returned with the gown, Blaise had declared that she'd be leaving servitude to explore her options as a cosmetologist, given what she'd accomplished with my face as the canvas—which she still wouldn't allow me to sneak a glance at.

"You look stunning," Imogen whispered in a breathy voice, though I couldn't help but notice the way her lips pursed when she glanced back and forth between Blaise and me.

Both maids helped me into my gown, and when Blaise finally spun me around to look at myself in the mirror, I practically gasped.

"I think you're right about that career change, Blaise," I whispered, catching sight of her smug grin as I examined my reflection in the mirror.

I HAD TO ADMIT. The gown wasn't exactly unflattering.

My family had never wanted for fine clothing, at least not since I was old enough to remember. But our wealth hadn't changed the fact that most of our neighbors still considered us a working-class family. It hadn't mattered that my father had accrued his wealth from the business of practically every house in town, that we'd had enough money to buy our beautiful cottage on two acres of land within the city limits. Father had earned his money, rather than inheriting it, which meant while our neighbors had been careful to be polite, we had always lived on the outskirts of fine society.

I had never attended a dinner party, a ball, or any other gathering that would require me to wear a gown this fine.

Not that my family could have afforded a gown this fine.

The gown was a deep cobalt blue, the color of the slivers of sky that outlined the glow of the stars at night. And stars were an appropriate description, for the entire dress was embedded with tiny gemstones that sparkled in the chandelier light. When I moved, the skirt of the dress moved beyond me, fluttering and swaying as if it had its own life about it. The dress had a scooped neck that brushed the edges of my shoulders before descending in a small "v" that skirted just below my shoulder blades.

"This is..." I couldn't find the words for the beauty of the garment that hugged my waist. Or for how I looked in it. With my curls pulled back into a low braided updo, a string of pearls crowning my head, and a matching set of a necklace and earrings, I looked, well, regal.

Blaise had been precise with my eyes, lining each with a dash of kohl, enhancing their round shape with a sharpness I quite enjoyed.

"The prince picked it out himself." Imogen's quiet comment caught me off guard, which she apparently picked up on because she quickly explained, "He originally intended it for the young woman from the ball, but..." She cleared her throat.

Blaise crossed her arms and huffed. "Well, that taints it a bit, doesn't it?"

"You never know. You might have liked her, Blaise. The two of you might have been the best of friends." I caught the reflection of her half-open mouth in an amused smirk and returned the expression.

She picked at her nails. "Like I said, Andy has poor taste."

I couldn't help but pick up on something else in the mirror—Imogen shifting ever so slightly on her feet.

"I have to admit, though," I said, running my hand over the cinched waist of the dress, "I would have expected a gown the prince picked out to have less material around the bosom."

Blaise gagged and made as if she were shoving her finger down her throat. That did little to distract me from the longing that deepened Imogen's fiery eyes as she gazed hungrily at the gown.

She caught me staring at her, and a warmth overcame her features so quickly, it had me wondering if I'd simply imagined the bitterness I'd sensed rolling off of her.

Discomfort settled over me as I couldn't help but compare us side-by-side. Imogen's servant's dress was black and lacked any frills or splendor. In fact, it barely fit her and seemed to hang off of her slender body as if it had originally been the object of a much larger maid.

A hand-me-down, probably.

I wondered what family situation Imogen came from, for her to choose employment as a servant. As much as living in Othian proved a better living situation for humans than most of Alondria, it didn't stop humans from looking down their noses upon their own. Most men in Othian didn't seek out employed females as their brides.

For me, that had never been an issue, for I'd always intended to use my self-employment as a weeding-out factor for eligible bachelors, as well as a reason not to have to marry anyone at all, should I find no one to my liking.

Which, let's be honest, seemed likely.

But was this how Imogen had felt when she took this job? Had she longed for the financial freedom to choose whatever life she wished for herself? Or did her situation come from a place of poverty? I couldn't help but feel self-conscious in the ornate gown, now that I wondered whether the ill-fitting maid's dress was the nicest piece of apparel that Imogen owned.

I decided that, on the highly likely chance this plan didn't work, and I somehow became Princess of Dwellen, I'd find Imogen something nicer to wear. And make sure she was being paid well, too.

Imogen took a courteous bow. "You're all set, my lady."

Blaise locked her arm through mine, surveying me up and down. Then she grinned. "You might just leave Andy at a loss for words."

In what was quickly escalating into an unbecoming habit, I noted Imogen's reaction to the pet name.

Her jittering fingers clenched.

CHAPTER 10

ELLIE

Both Imogen and Blaise escorted me to the dining hall, which really was, as the name suggested, a hall and not a room at all. It stretched the length of three of my family's house, and a crystal table acted as its centerpiece. Silver lamp stands supported the tiniest of candles, whose light scattered across the room, dispersed through the intricate cuts in the crystal table. In fact, every object in the room seemed to be intent on reflecting light every which way.

Including me, I realized, as my form cast not a shadow upon the floor, but a dazzling array of colorful specks of light.

As we were the first to arrive, Imogen and Blaise escorted me to my seat, but Imogen stopped me with her hand before I sat down. "No one sits before the king arrives," she explained.

"So I'm just supposed to stand here?" I asked, annoyed.

"If you wish to make a good impression, yes," she whispered, her eyes wide, as if to heavily suggest that I should at least *try* to make a good impression.

Blaise just rolled her eyes.

As much as Blaise was starting to grow on me, Imogen was right. My and the prince's plan hinged on winning the favor of the king. So I stood, a gentle hand upon one of the silver-plated chairs, just as Imogen instructed.

It wasn't long before the prince strolled in and stood behind the chair immediately across the table from me. His eyes grazed what seemed to be every inch of the fabric of my dress, and not for the first time tonight, I found myself thankful that the gown was fairly conservative.

Not that it likely mattered to the prince. He'd had two centuries to train his mind to identify the curves in a potato sack.

"Hm," he said, the corner of his mouth twisting. An assessment of surprised approval that made my skin crawl with irritation.

"What? Did your mystery woman tell you that her faerie godmother bewitched all the dresses in the kingdom to only look good on her?"

That wiped that wretched grin off his face and plastered it right onto mine.

"Ah, it seems a voice of reason has entered my son's life," said a strong, hearty voice behind me. I jolted in place, which, judging by his not-so-subtle wink, seemed to amuse the prince.

"Good evening, Father." Prince Evander nodded in deference as the king appeared at the head of the table. The motion was so jolted, so unnatural, it had me wondering if this was the first occasion the prince had attempted a gesture of respect. "May I introduce Miss Ellie...I mean...erm..."

"Elynore."

"Right, Miss Elynore Payne, my betrothed."

The king's eyes settled on me, and he offered me an approving nod before silently dismissing Blaise and Imogen with a wave of his hand. The king was just as handsome as his son, and hardly looked five years older, which I found immensely unsettling. The fae's magic kept them from aging as quickly as humans, making them, for all intents and purposes, immortal. At least, that was what we all assumed, since no one had yet to document a fae who died of natural causes. Still, when the prince had described his father, I'd imagined someone older. Someone with frown lines.

Instead, the king appeared to be hardly pushing thirty in human years, though I wondered if without his carefully trimmed beard he'd look even younger. His hair was blond, his skin lightly tanned, much like his son's, but his eyes were a deep gray, a wall of steel that might have guarded millennia's worth of pain.

Ah, there it was.

The signs of age.

The tired, exasperated aura. I wondered if it exuded from him all the time, or if it was selective to encounters with his son.

"Welcome, Miss Payne. Or shall I say Lady Payne, now that my son has promoted you? My condolences for your loss."

I fought the tug of amusement that pulled at my lips, but I avoided looking in the prince's direction.

"Marken," a deep, female voice said, full of disappointment. "Must you speak so unkindly of our son?"

A fair-skinned female fae, the Queen of Dwellen, apparently, appeared beside her husband, her hair pulled back into an austere knot that almost had her looking older than her son.

Almost.

It made me a bit queasy recalling that she had birthed him.

Fae were strange.

Off the queen's shoulders hung a silver dress that complemented her hair, so light it was almost white, and I wondered if that was from age, if it was natural, or if it was one of the fae glamours I'd heard about. Her face was dainty, and she looked to be about twenty, barely older than me. Except when her gaze fell upon her son. The flood of warmth that swelled in her eyes would have betrayed their relationship even if her words had not.

One couldn't fake that look. That kind of love.

She took the chair between the king and their son, leaving me at the king's right hand. Nerves made my arms jitter, as this didn't seem the proper way to do things at all. But then the king and his wife and son sat in unison, and I found myself the odd one out.

The prince stifled a laugh, and I plopped myself down in my chair. The clatter of my chair legs scraping the marble floors echoed across the hall. This sent the prince into a choking fit, and I shot a glare in his direction.

"My son is quite the charmer," the king said, turning to me. "At least, until he's opened his mouth. He seems to have figured a way around that, though, when it comes to females."

A sly smile broke across Prince Evander's face, but it didn't meet his eyes. "I'm not so sure about that, Father. They seem to like my mouth just fine."

The queen coughed into her napkin, which did nothing to mask the mortification staining her pale cheeks, but it seemed embarrassing one female at the table wasn't enough. Because Evander flicked those stunning sea-foam eyes toward me and said, "Isn't that right, Miss Payne?"

I shrugged, then against every sound piece of judgment my parents had ever offered me, said, "I've kissed better."

This, of course, wasn't remotely true. I'd never kissed anyone in my life. But as I was the only one at the table who possessed the capacity to lie, I considered it my duty as a human to take advantage of that fact.

The prince's eyes shuttered, which I might have found more satisfying if they weren't examining my mouth with such intensity that I couldn't help but wonder if he was searching for evidence of whether my statement was true.

"Your table is fine, Lady Queen," I managed to comment, despite the immortal child across the table from me staring at my mouth as if it were a map to his next expedition. I fought back a shudder at the thought. "The intricacy of the design…I would love to know the name of the craftsman."

The prince snorted. "Are you in the market for a dining table, then?"

"No. But I'd love to learn to make them."

The queen raised her eyebrows, more out of curiosity than judgment. "It's the work of an Avelean craftsman by the name of Boeuk. We pay him handsomely for his skills."

"You mean to convince us that a human woman is interested in craftsmanship?"

My blood went hot from the king's condescension, but when I turned to face him, I found no such thing. Only curiosity. In fact, his mouth rose at the edges as if he were pleased.

"I…" I swallowed, disarmed by the fae king's genuine interest. "I do. I mean, I am. My father supplies most of the glass windows in the city. He's trained me as his apprentice since I was a child. But my interests extend past windows. I wish to create art, clothing, jewelry. Even to stain the windows that we sell. There's something about using glass as a canvas…the way it allows the sunlight to pass through the paint… It's… Well, it's breathtaking."

"Breathtaking, indeed." The king smirked as he took a sip from his goblet. "And how, might I ask, did you come to be the unfortunate soul who is now bound to my son?"

Across from me, I thought I sensed the prince shift in his chair, but I dared not look at him now.

When my answer found itself lodged in my throat, Evander cleared his throat. "She crafted the glass slippers worn by the woman with whom I danced at the ball."

The king smiled from behind his goblet, his grin eerily ancient, too calculating to match the youth of his face. "The woman who had the good sense to run before it was too late, you mean?"

Evander opened his mouth, then shut it and swallowed. His father raised a brow, as if he weren't used to his son reining in his disrespect. Apparently Evander wasn't used to it either, because his throat bobbed, and his voice went dry as he spoke. "She informed me she was required to leave by midnight. She wouldn't have taken off so quickly, only she was having so much fun, she lost track of time."

"Evander," the queen said, resting a thickly bejeweled hand upon his arm. "It's impolite to speak of other women in front of your betrothed."

"Mother," Evander said, grasping the queen's hand with such gentleness, even I was tempted to find it endearing. "Lady Payne is just as confused as I am about this situation we find ourselves in. I'm certain she doesn't mind."

"Speaking of this mystery woman of Evander's..." The king turned toward me. "You must have met her, haven't you? If you're the one who crafted her shoes? Surely you recall this young woman's name, something we could use to identify her, since she bought her shoes from you." His dark eyes glinted with vengeance, with an invitation.

Play this game with me? his eyes seemed to say.

I couldn't help but accept.

CHAPTER 11

ELLIE

I took a sip from my goblet and chanced a glance at
Evander. His jaw had gone rigid, but his eyes pleaded with
me. Was it real, or just part of his plan? He was the one who had told
me to bond with his father over our shared disregard for the prince's
lack of sense. Besides, I needed this. I had no desire to be stuck with a
lazy rake for the rest of my life. No riches in the world could undo
what my parents had placed inside my heart. I wouldn't be muted and
tamed for the sake of propriety. For the sake of a good match.

No, I would make my own way in this world.

And I would marry for love.

So I played my part, answering the king's inquiry regarding
whether I remembered anything about the prince's mystery woman.
"Perhaps I could, had she bothered to pay. Or even notify me of her
intentions to take my shoes for herself."

My words landed, and the king's eyes flickered with amusement as
the prince squeezed his eyes shut and created a fist with his hands.
Decent acting on his part, I had to admit.

He almost had me convinced it bothered him that I had slipped
this tidbit of information.

"Should I call for the second course?" The queen straightened in her seat. "Marken, Evander, I know how you love the flanveise. I asked Collins to prepare it tonight."

This moved me a bit—the queen's equally desperate and hopeless attempts to unite the two people she loved the most. I wondered if things had been different before Prince Jerad had passed, if he had been the glue that held the family together. Other than the fact that the entire kingdom rested on their combined shoulders, that is. The memory of the late prince's death only swayed me further toward pitying the queen. What must it feel like to have your older son ripped away from you, leaving your family fractured, your soul desperate to suture the two remaining pieces of your heart?

"I've never had flanveise. Is that a fae dish?" I asked, hoping to steer the conversation away from the prince's folly, even just for a moment, if it might spare the queen some pain.

The wrinkles between her perfectly plucked brows softened a bit, and though her smile was effortful, it seemed eager and genuine. "Oh, you've never had flanveise? Well, of course you wouldn't have. I forget it is customarily not a human dish. You'll be delighted, I'm sure. Stanton!" she called, to which a servant rushed forward. "We're ready for the flanveise now."

The servant nodded and shuffled off, leaving the table in silence. Before I could insert my voice into the awkwardness by asking about how a flanveise is prepared, the king spoke, his voice dripping with insult. "So, Evander. Do you happen to be cursed with poor luck, or were all the eligible young women at the ball too boring for your tastes, leading you to seek out a petty thief?"

"I was not aware that she was a thief."

"Did you not approach me, begging for me to cosign a bargain? One that would bond you to the woman who had stolen your heart?"

Heat rushed to my cheeks on Prince Evander's account. Sure, he was an idiot. He deserved to be taunted. I just found myself wishing it was coming from my mouth, the mouth of a complete stranger, not his father's.

But apparently Evander was used to it, because he transitioned to the next topic without missing a beat. "Perhaps if the lovely Miss

Payne had been in attendance, I would have had the chance to dance with someone more admirable." Even in his compliment, he sneered, and I found myself sneering right back.

"Perhaps so," his father said before looking at me. "Why is it you declined my son's invitation to the ball?"

The queen answered for me, twirling her gloved thumbs. "I am sure she had prior obligations, didn't you, dear?"

The king was not convinced. "Obligations that were more important than a royal invitation?"

Suddenly, my pity for Evander dissipated, and I found myself wishing the king's attention might return to berating his son with humiliating questions.

"Perhaps she has elderly or sickly parents. And perhaps it is none of our business." The queen offered me an amiable grin. An *I-want-to-be-your-friend, it's-us-against-them, it's-up-to-us-to-bring-them-together* kind of smile. She was dazzling, and the genuineness of her gesture warmed me, but as I glanced back and forth between Evander and his father, I couldn't help but notice the prince's cold stare, not directed at his father, but at me. Like he was trying to send me a message.

It took one look at the king to recognize why.

He had been fishing for bait. For salt to pour upon his son's wound.

And I was going to give it to him. Even if the aftermath ricocheted and took out the gentle queen.

I mustered what I thought was a pretty convincing smirk, considering my reluctance. "I did claim elderly parents on my invitation, yes. But, truth be told, I had no desire to flirt with a male with a list of bedmates behind him that could probably span the length of this table."

Evander tensed and muttered another, "By Alondria," but his reaction was subtle in comparison to his mother's. The queen flushed crimson, her jaw clenching. "Excuse me," she said, pushing her chair from the table and fleeing with such haste that she carried her napkin with her.

My stomach churned as the delicate female rushed away.

The king stifled a chuckle with his napkin. If it bothered him that I'd humiliated his wife, he didn't let it show. "And how could I blame you?"

Evander cleared his throat. "Well, that seems to be my cue. I'm sure the two of you have plenty you'd like to discuss at my expense. Good evening to you both." As he stood to leave, his green eyes lingered on mine for a moment, and where I expected a nod of approval, an assurance that this was the time to make my request of the king, I found only hurt and embarrassment.

Confused, I swallowed as he walked away.

"You must think me a poor excuse for a father," the king said, wrenching me from my thoughts.

"Oh, I—" But I couldn't think of a response. Was Evander wrong about his father's disregard for him? Did the king feel remorse for the cruel words he constantly directed toward his youngest son?

"Say no more," he said. "You need not offer me pity or craft excuses on my behalf. I'm aware I've done badly with him. You're a woman who speaks your mind plainly, and I don't wish for you to dull your words simply because of our respective positions. But I will have you know that your opinion of me would have been greater had you met my oldest."

My heart sank. The king wasn't expressing remorse for how he treated Evander. He was concerned about his reputation for being able to raise a suitable heir.

Not knowing how else to respond, I went with the obvious. "I am sure you have all suffered immeasurable loss."

"Indeed," he sighed, setting his fork upon his plate, just as the servant arrived with the flanveise, which looked to be some sort of chocolate custard garnished with—Fates, surely those weren't pixie wings.

"Leave it for Miss Payne," the king ordered the servant. "I am retiring early."

"Wait." The plea burst out of me as he rose. But then I swallowed, because it occurred to me how inappropriate it was for me, a commoner, to make demands of the king.

The king who had been king since before my grandparents were born.

"I'm listening," he said, though the stillness that had settled over his face conveyed the opposite.

I nodded, squaring my shoulders, as if making myself bigger would somehow make my request more important. I supposed that was how the world tended to work, anyway. "I am under the impression that, as the cosigner of the prince's bargain, you also have the right to annul it."

The king clasped his hands together, his face lined with curiosity.

"Your Majesty, surely you of all people understand why I can't spend the rest of my life bound to your son."

He raised a brow and waved the servant away with a whisk of his hand.

Taking this as a cue for me to continue, I grappled for my next words. "All I ask for is mercy. Please, Your Majesty. Please annul the bargain. I agreed to it unknowingly, and only because I wished to reclaim the property that was stolen from me."

"Miss Payne, you have found yourself in a unique position. A position for which many women, and men, for that matter, would kill not only an acquaintance, but probably a favored kin. You are in the position to inherit the queen's throne one day. Do you understand the power my wife has?"

"I understand that, Your Majesty." Though I didn't, really. I didn't get the impression that Queen Evangeline had much sway in how the kingdom was run, but nevertheless... "I do not desire the throne."

"Is that so?" The king cocked his head, studying me, and then in a sultry voice, not unlike the one his son so often used, he asked, "And what do you desire?"

I swallowed. I hadn't noticed until just now how commanding the king's presence was. How brilliantly handsome he was. It wasn't attractive so much as it was devastating. Still, I straightened. The king might have been handsome enough to knock my carefully practiced speech right out of my head, but his question was simple, one I might as well have been practicing my whole life to answer.

I knew what I wanted.

I always had.

"To transform my father's business into something not only practical, but beautiful. Unprecedented…and—"

"Could you not be more successful with the allowance you'll receive as a princess?"

Allowance. I shook off the interruption. "I know it sounds foolish, but I don't believe it would be the same, Your Majesty. The joy I receive, the thrill… It's inseparable from the work, the process, the steady progress. If I were simply given the money… Well, I don't know that I would find as much pleasure in it."

"I see. And is that all?"

"Not quite. I—" This part felt silly, and it didn't escape me how ridiculous it was that I was having this discussion with the King of Dwellen. "I wish to marry for love. It's a value instilled by my parents, and their parents before them. I can't marry for money, so I will make it myself. And I can't take the money from your son, either, for then I'd be robbed of the chance of marrying for love."

The king stood from the table and advanced. He placed a firm hand on my shoulder, and for a moment, I wondered if it had been wise to desire a private audience with the most powerful male in the kingdom. If perhaps Evander had misjudged his father's devotion to the queen. I fought the urge to recoil, and he craned his neck ever so slightly. "Hm. You're an honorable young woman, Miss Payne. I have to say, I admire your values."

Hope rose in my chest, even if the king's touch had me reeling. It had worked. The prince—that idiot—he had actually come up with a plan that worked. Maybe he wasn't as stupid as everyone thought, after all. This mess was going to be resolved, and all it had taken was—

"However, I cannot fulfill your request."

"I…What?" I asked, losing all pretense of propriety as I followed him across the hall to the door. "What do you mean, you can't? Wasn't that the whole point of having you cosign the prince's bargain?"

The king withdrew his hand and sighed. "Forgive me. I misspoke.

What I meant is not that I *can't* do as you ask. It's simply that I *won't* do as you ask."

My jaw dropped. Came unhinged. Decayed and rotted and crashed to the ground, creating a pile of dust for the servants to certainly grumble about. "Why not?"

"Because, *Lady* Payne, the reason I cosigned the bargain was because I thought it was almost certain that my son would make a poor choice in a future queen. Which he would have, had his bargain not been so poorly and rashly worded. At the beginning of this dinner, I had every intention of undoing the arrangement, after what I was sure would be a long evening of a power- and money-thirsty maiden buttering up my queen and myself with praises of our generosity and compliments regarding aspects of ourselves the maiden was sure to know nothing at all about. Oh, but what a pleasant surprise it was to meet you, instead."

"I don't understand…"

"Ah. Let me make it clear for you. I don't believe my son could ever pick a female as fit for ruling as you."

I shook my head, as if doing so would dislodge me from this ridiculous nightmare I'd found myself trapped in. "But I don't care anything about power."

"Exactly. That, and the fact that you're clever and possess inge- nuity about you, makes you the perfect candidate for a future queen. In the case that I meet an unpleasant end, of course."

My heart sank. "But what about my father's business? I…I told you about my desire to marry for love. Why did you ask me what I wanted if you had no intention of holding it in any regard? Surely you're not going to punish me for your son's folly."

The king sighed and, not for the first time, I noticed the weariness, the fog that blurred the edges of those gray eyes. "That, my dear, is the trouble with it all. As much as I hate to punish you—and believe me, I do—my son is as you say. A fool. He has paraded about his entire life as if his actions have no consequence on anyone around him. As he is now, he is not fit to rule. A king must understand this quality, to his very core. That his actions are not his own, but the rudder that shapes the course of every soul entrusted to him. My son must learn that his rash nature is harmful to others. If I fix his mistake on your behalf, how will he ever learn?"

I blinked at the burning tears that were now obscuring the king's beautiful, horrible face as I tried my best not to break down in front of the only being who had the power to free me. The power to ruin my life.

For all the certainty I'd possessed just a few moments ago, all I could manage was a whisper. "Please don't do this. Please."

"My dear," he said as he turned away, "I have utmost confidence that a woman as industrious as yourself will learn to make the most of it."

IT HADN'T WORKED.

I stood gaping at the open door through which the king had just exited, my legs and fists wobbling.

I hardly noticed when Blaise and Imogen came to retrieve me.

Convincing the king to revoke Evander's bargain had been our one shot at getting out of this marriage, and we'd failed.

I'd failed.

The life I'd planned for myself unraveled with every turn of a marble staircase, every curve in the stone corridors of this wretched castle.

I could hardly keep it together as Imogen and Blaise led me back to my quarters.

Relief swept over me when we finally arrived at my door, but it was short-lived.

Someone had carved my name, *Lady Elynore Payne, Crown Betrothed*, into the door.

They might as well have carved the knife into my gut.

Blaise unlocked the door and propped it open for me. I swept inside, grateful that I was only moments away from having time to myself, a moment to weep without having to deal with Imogen's uncomfortable stares.

After both maids helped me out of my gown, Imogen curtsied and left me be, wishing me goodnight in a mumble I almost couldn't detect.

Blaise stayed, lingering by the door, fiddling with her keyring.

"It didn't work, did it?" she asked, her tone absent of that carefree aura she so expertly adorned.

I swallowed, turning toward the bed so she wouldn't have to watch my tears ruin the paint she'd taken so much care to perfect. Imogen had tried to wash it off, but it had taken all my willpower not to burst into tears as she and Blaise undressed me, so I'd told them I'd rinse it away myself.

I wasn't sure how she'd known what Evander and I were planning, but since they appeared to have a relationship that exceeded that of a servant and prince, I figured Evander had kept her informed.

"No," I said, clutching the edges of my nightgown. "It didn't work."

Blaise went silent for a long while, and for a moment I wondered if she had slipped into the corridor, but then she spoke, her voice soft. "I'm sorry. I know this isn't what you wanted for yourself."

"You don't have to apologize. It's not as if it's your fault."

Footsteps padded against the rug, and soon the warmth of a hand landed gently on my shoulder. I turned to Blaise, and she chewed her lip, concern etched across her brow. "I know you'll probably hate me for saying this, but you could do worse than Evander." When I opened my mouth to protest, she shook her head. "I imagine you could do better, too. He's definitely got his flaws. But he's not like his father. He'll see to it you're taken care of."

Silver lined Blaise's lower eyelids, and I wondered then if she was speaking from experience. Blaise hadn't struck me as the most sentimental person, but there was no mistaking the gratefulness that welled in her eyes.

Or the sadness. Or perhaps it was pity. I couldn't tell if it was for me or Evander, or the both of us, but there was something raw about it.

"You know what it means to have the future you expected stripped

95

away from you." I'd meant for it to be a question, but it didn't come out that way.

She offered me a tight-lipped smile and nodded. The momentary sadness disappeared, and she donned that carefree mask once more.

Then she slapped me on the back like we were old fishing buddies, and grinned. "It seems to me that we're both the type to make the most of it."

CHAPTER 12

EVANDER

She'd failed.

I'd stood outside the dining hall, eavesdropping on the conversation between Ellie and my father.

Ellie had failed to convince my father to sever the bond, and now I was going to be stuck with a woman who thought little more of me than a common whore for the rest of my life.

Well, her life.

Which, in a faltering moment of my character, I was thanking the Fates was going to be a relatively short one.

Truth be told, I have no desire to flirt with someone with a list of bedmates behind him that could probably span the length of this table.

I couldn't decide which was worse, the words or the crimson that had flushed my mother's cheeks at the statement.

I'd told Ellie to sell it—her hatred for me. Not to humiliate my mother.

As if that weren't enough, she'd failed to convince my father of much of anything except that she'd make a better ruler than me.

Well, that part was probably true. I wasn't fit for the crown. I knew that. My father knew that. The entire kingdom knew that.

My feet found their way down the cold stone hallways without my help. Through the castle's South Gate, where the night watch received a monthly bonus from my personal allowance, and had for at least a century. The gate I could pass through without question, without word making it back to my father.

By the time I reached the grungy pub on the south side of town, my anger had multiplied, swelling within my chest, threatening to explode.

I'd never been the type to take out my anger on inanimate objects. After all, they never did anything to cause my frustration. That was the point of being inanimate. As a child, I'd mostly noticed the practice in the more dull-witted of my father's soldiers, and I'd had no desire to turn out like them.

I punched a city wall on my way to the pub.

It made my knuckles throb in a somewhat satisfying way, so I punched it again.

Perhaps the soldiers had been onto something.

When I finally reached my destination, a seedy pub run by an even seedier faerie, I pulled my hood over my face and slipped into the musty tavern.

The seat in the shadowed corner of the bar was empty. A tankard full of ale sloshed on the table before I even had the chance to sit down.

I may or may not have been a regular customer.

The bartender may or may not have figured out who I was a few decades back, and I may or may not have been paying his lease in exchange for his discretion.

Whatever. This place had been good to me.

Oh yes. It's been real gracious, supplying you with cheap ale that has you in bed all day with women you can hardly get to leave it, was what Blaise would say if she could hear my thoughts.

Not half a drink in, and I was thinking of Cinderella. Six in, she could have been sitting right across from me, as far I as knew. Fates, she'd been pretty. I ran my fingers through my hair, as if she were there to see me do it. To be charmed by it.

I wondered where she'd disappeared to. Was there someone at

home who hadn't realized where she'd gone that night? Overprotective parents who held a grudge against the fae and wouldn't allow their daughter near one, even if it meant saving themselves from squalor? A master, perhaps, less than thrilled about the idea of having to free his slave? A jealous lover? A husband?

My mind throbbed at the thought, and the ale churned in my uneasy stomach.

Surely not.

While my reputation among women was fairly accurate, my subjects seemed to be under the impression I'd sleep with anything with a set of breasts.

While I could see how they came to that conclusion, I did have rules.

I didn't mess with married women. Not knowingly, at least.

The bartender sloshed another drink onto the table.

I chugged it and asked for another before he made it back behind the bar.

How many drinks before I could flush that souring thought from my mind—that Cinderella had a husband back home?

It would make some sense. Explain why she'd left so quickly, why she hadn't made herself known.

My father's voice rang in my head. *Perhaps she had the good sense not to tie herself to a brother-killer. Perhaps she saw right through you.*

I shook my head. The bartender must have been serving me the cheap stuff. Usually the drink drowned out my father's voice.

Well, that wasn't entirely true. At least, not since Jerad.

Before my brother's accident, alcohol had been a balm. Something that whisked away my worries, warmed my hands and feet and made my face buzz.

Now it just sort of numbed everything. It wasn't a great feeling, but it was better than the pain.

Usually.

Despite myself, my mind wandered to Ellie.

Arrogant, better-than-me, life-ruined-because-of-me Ellie.

If I had to be chained to a self-righteous bore for the next five

T.A. LAWRENCE

decades while the only woman I'd ever loved grew old and died, at least she was pleasant to look at.

Once she wiped that sneer off her face.

Okay, she was still gorgeous when she was sneering, but that was difficult to appreciate in the moment.

"You're looking lonely over here," a sultry voice purred.

I raised my eyes to find a busty woman peering down at me like a lioness ready to strike. She looked familiar, and I wished I could blame my inability to recall her name on the alcohol.

I held up my tankard, and it splashed all over my sleeves. "Got plenty of company right here."

Apparently she wasn't convinced, because she slid into the booth next to me, her curvy thigh practically resting on top of mine.

I flashed a feral grin at her, aware that it was all she could see of my face with my hood shading my eyes. "I said I'm not interested."

Her seductive grin soured into a sneer. "Well, that's a first," she hissed as she popped up from the counter and strode away.

Did she mean that was a first coming from me, or the first time she'd been turned down by a drunk male in this tavern? It made my head pound to ponder it, so I didn't.

I left way too much coin on the counter for the barman, considering what I paid him under the table, but the ale was making my head spin, and I didn't have the mental energy to count what I owed.

When I stumbled into the streets, the castle loomed over me.

I made it a good three steps before I vomited. At least I made it into the gutter.

Ale has no place in the mind of a king, Jerad's voice reminded me. That's what he'd always say when I tried to convince him to come out with me.

"Well, I'm not king yet," I spoke to no one in particular. "And if our father has his way, I'll never be."

If something ever happens to me, the responsibility will be passed to you. Are you ready to give up your childish behavior?

"Too late, something already happened," I choked. "Shouldn't have come with me that night."

100

A slurred voice cut through the alcohol clouding my mind. "You're the one who shouldn't have come out tonight."

Firm hands gripped my shoulder, then someone kneed me in the gut.

The pain buckled me, my drunken limbs swaying in shock.

The man holding me spit in my face. "You must not be from around here. Otherwise you'd have known to leave your jewelry behind."

A fist caught me in the jaw. I swung, but the man before me caught my hand midair. He wrenched a golden ring off my finger—Jerad's ruby ring, before shoving me to the ground.

"Give that back," I hissed, but the words came out slow, slurred. Unintimidating.

"Yeah, okay," the man chuckled.

I spit on his boots.

Something collided with my skull, then everything went black.

"WHAT IN ALONDRIA is wrong with you?"

The voice was familiar enough that it stirred me from sleep, but I found myself annoyed at being ripped away from the darkness so hastily. It had been peaceful in the darkness.

Now the street lanterns blinded my eyes, amplifying the pounding in my head.

A shadowy figure stood over me, concern etched across her brow.

Blaise.

The grin on my face came out of nowhere. Everything hurt, and I'd almost been murdered and left for dead by a bunch of lowlifes. I wasn't sure what I was happy about, but the giggles burst from me all the same.

Until Blaise slapped me in the face, that is.

"Ow."

"Get up."

I nestled into my almost-grave, burying my face into the ground to shield it from her open palm. "You know, I think I'll just stay here."

Scrawny arms looped underneath my underarms and tugged.

I hardly moved. Another giggle escaped my lips. "You're so tiny. Did you know how tiny you are? You used to be even tinier. I remember one time—"

"Shut up and help me," Blaise snapped.

I frowned. Blaise was mad, but I couldn't figure out what for. But I loved Blaise, and I didn't like it when she was upset. "Okay, okay." I let her help me to my feet, leaning against her slight frame for support.

We hobbled up the street like that, Blaise yelling at me every few minutes when I tried to convince her the better path home was through the moat.

"I think Cinderella is married," I found myself saying.

"Yes, well, you're quite drunk, so see if you still think that in the morning."

"No, think about it. Why else would she have left me? Why would she not come back?"

Agitation spiked in Blaise's voice. "I don't know, Andy. Did you ever consider—" But then she took a breath, her face softening. "I don't know, but surely that wasn't the reason."

"It's probably for the best, anyway."

"Yeah, why is that?"

"Because she wouldn't have loved me if she had known."

Blaise stilled, her shoulders going rigid under my weight. "Known what?"

"Oh, you know, Blaise. About Jerad. About how—"

"I don't want to talk about this."

"But I need to tell you. I found him, you know. And he was—"

Blaise's voice was shaking now. "You're drunk."

"What's that got to do with how Jerad—"

Her tone shifted, spiked in the frigid air. "I don't want to talk about this."

"Oh." My chest sagged, and so did my eyelids.

Somehow, Blaise managed to get me all the way back to my chambers before I collapsed onto my bed face first. She tugged at my limp body until I lay on my back.

"Are you mad at me?" I asked.

Blaise sighed. She sure looked mad. "No."

"Are you sure?"

"No."

For some reason, that made me smile, and when I smiled, her face softened, her brow sagging. "I'm going to help you, Andy. I'm going to help you find a way out of your bond with Ellie."

I didn't know who that person was, but I thought better than to tell that to Blaise.

CHAPTER 13

EVANDER

I woke to a splash of cool water bursting through my nostrils and stinging my brain.

A string of curses escaped my mouth as I choked and sputtered. With the whoosh of a nearby curtain, light swarmed my bedroom, illuminating the cedar furniture Blaise had picked out for me while simultaneously scalding my unprotected eyeballs.

"Get up."

Blaise.

Just who I wanted yelling at me at this hour of the morning.

"It's past seven. You're about to miss breakfast." Fates, it was as if the girl could hear my thoughts.

"Didn't really need it while I was sleeping," I moaned, covering my eyes with my wondrously cozy blankets.

Blaise ripped them away from me.

Normally, she wouldn't have been able to do that, but even a fae's reaction time could be easily limited by a good old-fashioned hangover.

When I rolled back over and shoved my face into my pillow, something slammed me over the head.

Another pillow, sure, but even a pillow can feel like an anvil when you already feel like your skull is about to crack open.

"Get. The. Crap. Up," she seethed between blows. "I'm. Done. With. This. Behavior."

"Okay, Mother."

That earned a sharp twist of my ear.

All other options exhausted, I rolled over and faced my unwelcome wake-up call.

Of course, as soon as I got a good look at my friend, her eyes puffy and swollen, try as she might've to cover the discoloration with paint, my heart softened.

And as it softened, that gave room for a pricking sensation.

"I'm sorry." I mumbled the apology, though I meant it.

She gave me a few more whacks over the head with my pillow, then sighed and collapsed into my nearby chaise.

"I know. You always are."

That stung a bit, too.

"Do you even remember last night?" Her cheeks were pale, her tone flat.

I reached backward in my mind, trying to grasp onto any clues to what I'd been up to last night other than drinking myself into oblivion, but I came up short.

I remembered nothing.

And as much as that had been the point, there was something unsettling about it, too. Losing that much time.

It was one thing to lose time as I slept. At least then, I could be fairly confident I wasn't up and about making a mess of my life or the lives of others.

"Didn't think so," Blaise said.

For a moment, I thought Blaise would hop up from the chaise lounge and leave, that she'd finally decided she was done with me. She scooted forward like she meant to, and even braced her hands on the armrests of the chaise, her pale knuckles bulging.

But in the end, she just slumped back into the soft material and rubbed her temples.

"Did I rope you into the drinking too?" I teased, hoping to lighten her mood.

"No."

Obviously, my efforts were ineffective.

"I'm sorry, Blaise."

"Sorry for what? You don't know what you did."

I sighed, pushing myself up against the backboard of my bed. When I did, I sucked in a gasp, pain rippling through the muscles of my back. Blaise opened her eyes and took a passing glance at my abdomen, where the remnants of welts were starting to heal.

I shuffled uncomfortably, more careful with how I moved my back this time.

They must have beaten me fairly badly if the wounds hadn't completely healed overnight.

Fae wounds were like that. If I cut my hand, it would likely heal within the hour. If I cut my hand twice, it might take a handful of hours to heal. Cut my hand a thousand times...

Well, there was only so much the fae healing magic could do at once.

"They look better now than they did last night," Blaise said, her gaze averting to a portrait of Jerad that hung on my wall.

I squirmed a bit, immediately regretting doing so as a storm of sharp pricks ricocheted through my muscles. My wounds had been cleaned—the ones where the skin had clearly been broken the night before. I pulled up my blankets slightly to peer underneath, and to my relief, I wore the same pants as I'd donned last night.

Blaise must have caught the subtle movement, because she let out a cruel laugh. "Oh, so you can't be bothered with how you ended up left for dead last night, but you'd be embarrassed if it was me who changed your trousers so I could clean your wounds."

I opened my mouth, but she wasn't done.

"You know, maybe if you don't want me dragging you back to the castle, all of your weight supported on my shoulders, which are much tinier that yours by the way, then maybe don't drink yourself into a stupor and get yourself mugged and beaten and left for dead all over some random girl you danced with at a ball for a handful of minutes."

I went silent, and so did she, crossing her arms.

"I'm sorry," I said, though I'd lost count of how many times I'd said it at this point.

"For what?"

"You're going to make me list all the reasons?"

"Yes, I am."

"I'm sorry I went off and got drunk and got myself in a bad spot with whoever did this to me." I gestured at the welts on my body. "And I'm sorry you probably have a crick in your neck from supporting my massive weight. And I'm sorry you had to find me like that." That last one, a tad more genuine.

Blaise glanced back and forth from the floor to me.

"Okay. I accept your apology."

"Thank you."

"But you're not doing this anymore. I forbid it."

"You forbid it?"

"Yes, I do."

I sighed, leaning my head back against the backboard. It was worse having this argument, because she was right. Blaise was undeniably right. It wouldn't have been a good decision for a peasant to make, to get themselves plastered and mugged and left for dead. But I was the prince, sole heir to my father's throne.

Things could have been much worse for me.

I shuddered to think what might have happened had those men recognized who I was. They could have very well killed me, simply for not being the brother they so loved and adored. Some would have tortured me for what they believed I'd done to Jerad. Others would have taken me and chained me and held me for ransom.

Others might have sold me to the highest bidder.

There were quite a few perks that went along with being a fae prince.

There were dangers attached to it, too.

The consequences for harming a fae prince were severe across all the kingdoms of Alondria, but there were plenty of beings in this realm whose purses sang louder than their sense of self-preservation.

Like the Avelean collectors who would have killed to stuff me and turn me into their dining room rug. Or maybe they'd just keep me alive and talk to me like they would a pet parrot.

Either way, if Blaise hadn't shown up…

"Thank you," I said through a dry mouth.

"Just don't do it again." Though her voice was still tight, I could feel some of that temper dissipate.

"Also, I'm going to be needing another thank you soon." She crossed her arms, certainly pleased with herself now that she felt she'd gotten a sincere apology out of me. Then she pulled a book from her sack and rested it on her knees, opening it facing toward me so I could see.

"You planning to bore me back to sleep my reading this to me?" I asked, though Blaise's sacrifice in the gesture wasn't lost on me. Blaise was literate, but reading had never come easily to her, and it almost always resulted in a pounding headache.

She shook her head. "No. I'd like to beat you over the head with it, though."

"Fair."

"It's the third volume of ancient fae law code. I'm reading through the section on fae bargains, specifically how they can be broken. I think that if we can find an ancient law that serves us, maybe we can get you out of your bargain with Ellie. Then," she said, pulling out what looked to be a directory of the entire world given its size, "we can use this to find Cinderella."

Instinctually, I reached for the directory, my heart listening even as my head pounded at the thought of finding her.

Blaise jumped backward, wagging the directory just out of reach. Normally, I would have snatched it from her, but she had carried me home last night, so I supposed I owed it to her not to.

Plus, I was so achy it hurt to move.

Blaise clicked her tongue. "Nope. You're not getting your hands on this until we find a way to sever your bond with Ellie. I won't have you going after another woman while you're engaged, or worse, if we fail, married. I love you, but I'd rather not be disgusted by you."

That comment stung more than I thought she meant it to, but then again, maybe that was exactly how she meant it. She was clearly still angry with me about last night, and for good reason.

I sighed. "I hope you know I would be faithful to Ellie if we can't figure a way out of this bond."

Blaise shifted in her chaise, reading the ancient law book and pretending to ignore me. Probably so she didn't have to answer.

After last night, no, she did not know what I would or wouldn't do.

Out of habit, my fingers reached for Jerad's ring but met only flesh.

My stomach twisted as I felt its absence.

His absence.

"Did you happen to remove Jerad's ring while I slept?" I asked, my throat dry.

Blaise only answered with a look. The knot in my stomach morphed into a hole.

When she tossed volume IV of the law book in my direction, she aimed for my groin.

She didn't miss.

CHAPTER 14

ELLIE

I'd been under the impression my future was ruined.

I'd been wrong.

Apparently, my future was to be cut short.

Breakfast the next morning was tense, to say the least. I'd expected as much, which was exactly why I had begged Imogen to inform the family I was ill and could not join them.

It hadn't worked, of course. Blaise hadn't shown up for her morning duties, and Imogen had tiptoed around my request. I was fairly certain she really did want to please me, but we both knew who employed her. At the end of the day, she certainly didn't want to get on the king's bad side.

I couldn't exactly blame her.

Though, had I possessed the foresight to thrust myself onto the king's bad side, I might not be in this situation.

"I can't lie for you. I'm their servant," she had reminded me.

"It's not a lie. *Ill* can mean a lot of things. Besides, I feel ill. I look ill." As evidence, I pointed to my puffy eyes, which had almost sealed shut from all the crying I had done the previous night after Blaise had left me alone to grieve the loss of the life I'd dreamed for myself.

Even if Blaise believed my life here wouldn't be so awful, that didn't mean she'd convinced me.

I wasn't so self-centered that I couldn't concede that I certainly wasn't in the worst of situations. My mother and I had always laughed at the heroines in faerietales. They somehow always managed to act like being swept out of their squalor and forced to live out the rest of their days as a princess—waited on by a host of servants, never having to eat the same meal twice in one week or run out of steaming water for their bath—was what any reasonable person would consider torture.

Not to mention the way they always turned their nose up at their new selection of dazzling imported gowns.

I wouldn't turn into the person I'd scoffed at my entire life. I'd relish the hot baths and the exotic, hand-carved soaps and the gem-encrusted gowns and the tiaras.

And who didn't love a good tiara?

I'd make the most of what the Fates had placed into my lap, sure. But I had been happy in my parents' cottage, sweating away as my blow pipe warped glass into art, dreaming of my little shop in the art district.

The royal family might have showered me with riches, but they'd exacted something precious in exchange. The feel of the soft parchment against my skin as I read the daily news, the low grumbling of my father as he pretended not to enjoy discussing current events, the crisp scent of brewing coffee mingling with that of my mother's pastries wafting into our breakfast room from the kitchen.

Would I become a sniveling princess constantly complaining about the weight of the gold and precious jewels resting upon my shoulders?

No, I would not.

Would I pretend to be excited about what was typically my favorite part of the day being spent with a king who reveled in being needlessly cruel, a queen who despised me (understandably so, I supposed), and the reckless prince who had gotten me into this mess to begin with?

Also, no.

. . .

THERE AT THE breakfasting table I sat, next to the king as I had just last evening.

Except this time, I wasn't quite so pleasant.

Well, I would have liked to claim I was downright spiteful, a force to be reckoned with, a woman no one dared to spite for fear of her wrath, but if I was being honest with myself, I likely came across as more sulky than anything as I slurped down my meal in silence.

I spent most of the meal ignoring the royal family, most especially the king, as I counted every single speck in my oats. The oats weren't even that good. Once, as I reached for the bowl of brown sugar, my hand grazed against Prince Evander's, a consequence of my refusal to look up from my bowl. Our fingers brushed, sending my hand jerking backward and the hairs on the back of my arm standing up. We made the briefest of eye contact, at which point he gestured to his own eyes and frowned.

Did he really have the gall to ask me what I'd been crying about?

Come to think of it, the prince didn't look so good himself, what with the dark bags underneath his eyes.

I shot him a glare and tried to find the speck in my oats where I'd left off counting.

"Are you enjoying your breakfast? I wasn't sure what to ask the cook to make for you." The queen's voice was cool, impassive.

Reluctantly, I lifted my head to look at her. Did I want to talk to the person who adored the vile creature sitting across from me? No. But I still felt somewhat guilty for embarrassing her last night, especially when it turned out I'd done it for nothing. So I figured I should at least be polite.

"We eat oats every morning at home," I said, and the way the not-lie rolled off my tongue sounded so fae, I might have gagged had I not been fairly certain that was considered poor table manners.

"But I'm sure you prefer the way your mother cooks them." The queen smiled politely, though I could tell the edges of her mouth were resistant to the expression. She didn't like me. That much I was sure of, but I couldn't exactly blame her for that, either. It almost made me feel worse that she was still trying to be kind to me, even though it clearly took extreme effort and self-control on her part. I wondered how often in her centuries of life she'd been forced to practice being the bigger person.

"I guess I'm inclined to be partial to hers," I said, trying my best to fake a smile. I figured my strain probably mirrored the queen's, and that we both looked as if the corners of our lips were being held afloat by metal hooks.

I gulped down a few more bites and went to excuse myself from the table, figuring that probably wasn't the proper move. Perhaps even hoping this was the case. I didn't really care at this point if I disappointed my father-in-law-to-be.

When I stood, the king placed his hand on my arm. "One moment, Miss Payne." I froze at his firm touch and found my eyes locked on the prince's in alarm. He tensed and gave me the subtlest of nods, an earnest suggestion that I sit back down.

I did, and had to hold back a sigh of relief when the king relaxed his grip.

He eyed my unfinished breakfast with a look of mingled distaste and satisfaction, a combination one could only master after centuries of practice, I figured. "Now that you've finished your breakfast..." His gray eyes flickered to me, amusement curving his lips. "I wish to debrief you regarding your Trials."

The queen sputtered, shooting coffee splattering across the crystal table.

Evander choked on his breakfast roll.

It took him a moment to regain the ability to speak, which had me wondering if even the immortal fae could perish from something as inconsequential as a pastry. Hm.

"Trials?" he practically croaked. "You can't be serious, Father."

"Why should I not be serious?" the king asked, looking anything but. In fact, he looked like a child whose parents had brought home a new puppy. "The Trials are not only sacred tradition, but law. And for good reason, I believe."

"What are the Trials?" I aimed my question for the prince, since I'd made a vow to myself that I wouldn't give the king the honor of my full attention any more than was necessary to keep myself alive. Or from being thrown in the dungeon.

Assuming this castle had a dungeon.

Who was I kidding? All castles had dungeons.

Evander's voice ripped me from the machinations of my all-too-active imagination, which was in the process of reminding me how much I'd taken having a private bathroom for granted.

"It doesn't matter, because they're not happening."

I stole a glance at the queen, who was staring at me, her painted cheeks white with horror. Her back had gone rigid, and she hardly seemed to notice the servant hastily wiping the spewed coffee off the table. When I caught her stare, she quickly averted her eyes back to the king.

My stomach knotted.

"Marken, dear, don't you think the Trials seem irrelevant in this unprecedented situation?" the queen asked, her voice sweet but strained.

The king took his wife's hand and pressed his lips against her palm. "What about them do you find irrelevant, my love? You had no objection when you endured them so many years ago. I seem to remember that you actually got a thrill—"

The queen blushed and, quick to interrupt, said, "Yes, dear. But I am fae, after all. The Trials were crafted by the fae with fae in mind. They did not account for marriages with humans."

Though his eyes never left his wife's sickly face, the king played with his fork, smashing at his pile of breakfast peas until they reminded me of the churning contents of my stomach. "But that doesn't detract from the reasoning behind the Trials, dear."

"What in the name of Alondria..." Evander muttered under his breath as he pushed his palm into his face, creating creases in his forehead where his fingers bulged as he closed his eyes.

"Would someone mind explaining to me what a Trial is?" I asked, irritated now at the conversation that was happening around me, especially since I didn't have enough knowledge about the situation to offer input.

Evander leaned forward, knocking an empty bowl to the side. "I'll tell you what it is. It's a horrible, outdated custom that hasn't occurred in centuries. And for good reason."

"That reason being that there hasn't been a royal wedding since your mother's and mine," the king corrected.

"No, the reason being that it's archaic," Evander hissed.

"I don't know why you're acting so surprised, son. We've discussed this possibility many times—"

"Yes, when the assumption was that I would marry fae!" The prince jolted up, towering over us, my chair skidding underneath me as I started. Any semblance of that boyish charm was gone, wiped clean by the wrath on the prince's face.

I'd been so wrapped up in being irritated at his rash behavior, I'd almost forgotten *what* he was.

The king bared his teeth in a false grin. "Which you had ample opportunity to do. Instead, you broke not only dozens of hearts, but dozens of potential alliances, as well."

"What are the Trials? Please, Lady Queen," I pleaded, realizing that I was balling my napkin in my fists. What in Alondria could be so horrid that it got Evander of all people riled up like that?

The queen sighed. "The Trials were set up as a failsafe for forming marriages within the royal family, to ensure the unions were in the best interest of the people of Dwellen, as well as the royal family."

I frowned. "Wouldn't the fact that a marriage has to be cosigned already take care of that?"

She nodded, placing her spoon upon her plate with such graceful-ness, the collision of silver and crystal made no sound. "One would think so. However, the people of Dwellen didn't find the cosigning adequate. They worried that their king might be biased toward his sons and daughters. That a father might put his children's wishes above the people's." She paused, and the silence around the table was thick enough to taste. "So the Trials were created. They are as they sound. Tests, designed to prove that the royal couple is marrying for the right reasons."

Evander snorted. "And does being tricked into marriage count as a *right* reason?"

The queen frowned at her son, though there was little rebuke in the expression, and turned back to me. "To pass the Trials, the betrothed couple must prove their ability to unite under pressure, as this is crucial for a ruling family." She slid her hand across the table to her husband, who took it, caressing it with uncharacteristic gentleness. He flashed a dazzling smile in her direction, and her cheeks tinted as she continued. "A vital part of the process is the non-royal member proving that he or she is not marrying the royal for power or money. And the royal must prove that the marriage alliance is not…" She stumbled over the words, glancing at her husband with a girlish grin. "Well, a result of lust and the desire to sidestep proper rules of society."

The king snorted.

Evander's sea-green eyes glistened as he sat down and leaned back in his chair, cradling his head in his interlaced fingers. "Father, I hope you're not implying that I would attempt to sidestep the proper rules of society. You should know better than anyone that I've only ever sought to plow through them."

"And how are we supposed to prove those things?" I asked, before the answers to my questions could be derailed by an argument breaking out between the two males at the table.

The legs of Evander's chair clacked against the marble floor, and as he rested his elbows on the table, clasping his hands together, his green eyes flashed. "Oh, just a series of puzzles and tests that will kill us if we don't solve them."

"Surely not." My heart seized up, and I looked between the king and queen, waiting for them to dismantle the prince's claim.

I found no such reassurance in their faces—only grim trepidation from the queen, and a satisfied smirk from her husband.

Evander, looking pleased with himself as always, reclaimed his previous position in his chair, this time propping his feet on the table.

When my exasperated stare gained only a shrug from my *betrothed*, I straightened my shoulders and said, "I refuse to take part in these trials that are most likely going to kill me, especially since there's no way I can prove that my love for you is true. Because it isn't."

The king chuckled, but the queen's countenance drooped.

Evander didn't seem all that put out, because he said, "Well, technically, it's not a qualification that you love me. You just can't want me for my money. And I can't want you for my bed. So it seems we're straight there."

"Evander!" His mother gasped, whether at the barbs in his words or the uncouth innuendo, I wasn't sure. But I didn't have time to care about his petty insults. I wouldn't be reduced to being someone's source of entertainment before I died.

"I refuse," I said, turning my glare upon the king.

"Well, then," he said. "To refuse the Trials is to refuse to marry my son."

I made to bite back, but his words hit my chest like an arrow.

My throat closed.

I willed my lungs to move, but they wouldn't obey. Panic set in as the king stared me down, his gray gaze a challenge, daring me to blink first.

My heart pounded in a flurry of panic. I couldn't breathe.

What in Alondria...

What was happening?

The king flashed a set of feral teeth. Was he...was he doing this?

My mind whirred through a series of headlines, but my memory wasn't functioning properly, and none of the headlines stuck. The royal fae were descended from the lines of the most powerful fae, those endowed with magic. But the royal family of Dwellen possessed power over plants, over flora...

So why couldn't I breathe?

I couldn't breathe, I couldn't breathe, I couldn't...

Dishes clattered and spikes of crystal shattered across the floor as the prince jumped from his seat, launching himself over the table. In a moment, his face was inches from mine, blocking my view of his horrible father. My lungs were burning now, my head spinning. The vision of the prince's sea-green eyes danced before my face. He grabbed my face between his palms, cradling my jaw in his warm hands.

I was going to die.

I was going to die, and Evander's shining eyes would be the last I ever saw.

"It's okay, Ellie. Take it back. Just take it back, and you'll be able to breathe again."

Take it back? Take what back? I tried to scream, to explain that I didn't understand, but the words caught in my throat, the air sealed in my lungs, the pressure building, threatening to burst.

"El. Take it back."

Evander's words were a command, but my lungs spasmed in a set of stifled whimpers. I gestured toward the king, praying to the Fates Evander would understand my meaning, that he could somehow convince his father to spare me.

Realization washed over Evander's hypnotizing features. "No, El. He's not doing this to you. It's the fae bargain. It's killing you." He shook my shoulders. "Do you understand that? It's going to kill you if you don't take it back."

The fae bargain.

I'd refused to enter the Trials, and by so doing, refused to marry Evander.

And the penalty for breaking a fae bargain was death.

"Fates, Ellie. Just take it back."

I gagged on the bulge forming in my throat. Hot tears stung my eyes and poured down my cheeks as I shook my head, my sobs silent, unheard. I couldn't do it. I couldn't speak, didn't have the breath to take it back. I'd broken the fae bargain, and the Fates required my life as recompense.

I chanced one last look into Evander's eyes. They were that same sea green, except now they were shining, a raging tempest, the kind that refused to relent.

At least if I was going to die, I'd gotten to witness someone looking at me like that.

Evander must have recognized the resignation in the way my brow sagged and my eyes fluttered, because he furrowed his eyebrows and pulled my face close to his. Then, as black dots began to cloud my view of him, I felt his hair graze my left cheek. His hot breath caressed my ear as he whispered, "Say you'll marry me."

What?

Everything was dark now, and Evander's voice, low and commanding, was the only thing still tethering me to reality.

I might have laughed, could I breathe.

What an absurd thing for Evander to ask, when we barely knew each other, hardly even tolerated each other.

Quite silly indeed.

This time, the hot breath against my ear made me dizzy. "Say it."

Fine.

Okay, I'll marry you.

"Okay, I'll marry you."

I gasped, air rushing into my desperate lungs. My eyes shot open, only to find that Evander had moved me to the floor, that he'd pulled me into his arms as I straddled the edge of consciousness, the edge of death. With one arm, he tugged me close, his hand clutching my waist. The other still cupped the edge of my jaw.

The light dancing in his green eyes winked. "See? I knew you wanted me."

And just like that, the spell broke. Came crashing down like a massive chandelier that someone had forgotten to reinforce.

I leapt out of Evander's lap like it was a den of snakes and not the source of the lightning scorching my senses.

He unleashed a cocky, lopsided grin at that.

I might have tried to wipe it clean off his face, if the king didn't get to it first when he said, "Interesting that you couldn't let her die, son. You could have freed yourself of the bargain."

CHAPTER 15

EVANDER

A more intelligent man—one with his brain capable of setting aside the excitement of the present for half a moment and remembering that the future, intangible as it might seem, did in fact exist—would have let Ellie die.

That would have been the simplest way out of my predicament.

She was just a mortal, after all. A human. Their lifespans were akin to those of bumblebees, buzzing around and keeping themselves busy just to die before they ever saw their work finished.

Well that was morbid.

I didn't actually think that, of course.

I mean, it was sort of true, but the brevity of the human lifespan didn't make them any less valuable. Perhaps I would have been under that impression if not for Blaise, but I didn't think so.

No, I'd been around a long time before Blaise's grandparents even met. And I'd never been convinced that humans' short lifespans made them any less valuable than the fae.

If I was going to sit here and fantasize about Ellie's lips turning blue and her last breath stealing away from her mouth and her eyes rolling back in her head, I couldn't very well use the classic, "Well, she's a human" excuse to make myself feel better, now could I?

So I guessed that meant no daydreaming about my betrothed's untimely demise.

I was halfway to the seedy pub before I realized where my feet were taking me. Before I remembered Blaise had forbidden me from taking another sip of alcohol.

It wasn't exactly her decision, but Blaise was one of the few people in Alondria who genuinely liked me. Her demands carried a bit more weight than most people's.

So instead of getting day drunk like a proper fellow, I wandered my way around the city, eventually finding myself in the art district. Now that I was here, I wondered why I didn't visit this part of the city more often. Even if the shops hadn't been decorated with colorful murals of dragons and sea monsters, the scent of lavender candles burning in the air, it would have been worth a visit just for the music.

This morning, a man had already set up a fiddle on a street corner and was strumming away at a lively tune. I stayed for a while, pretending to be interested in a local vendor's ceramics, just so I'd have an excuse to listen to him finish a song Jerad and I use to belt the lyrics to when one of us was trying to resolve a fight with the other.

When the man plucked the bridge, the tune pricked my heart. I listened anyway.

If I closed my eyes, I could swear I felt his presence standing next to me.

Towering over me. Outshining me, as always.

But at least he was here.

But the melody couldn't stretch on forever, and soon the fiddler took a break, eagerly captivating a passerby in a story about the time he played with "The Red," a red-headed flautist rumored to enchant entire towns with her songs, only to steal away their children in the middle of the night.

Musicians and their affinity for legends.

I found myself wandering away from the arts district and toward the main thoroughfare. My stomach was practically roaring. Even from several blocks away, I could scent freshly baked scones being pulled from the oven at Forcier's Sweets and Treats. As I walked the streets and the voice of the fiddler dulled, my mind wandered back to Ellie.

I shouldn't have saved her this morning. Then there would be nothing to daydream about. Her death would be a memory, not a sick fantasy, and I'd be free of this mess.

A mess you got yourself into, my brother's ever-present voice reminded me.

Well, yes, I suppose it would be unfair if Ellie had to die for my mistakes.

Still.

She certainly made it easier to fantasize about skipping away from her twitching body with a renewed spring in my step when she made comments about my sex life in front of my mother.

Fates, what had she been thinking?

I'd thought I'd gotten over that, but my entire body still cringed when I recalled what had probably been the most embarrassing moment of my two-hundred-year existence.

Still, I couldn't very well let her die, could I? It wasn't as if I'd exactly stolen the hearts of the Dwellen people since being shoved into the too-large shoes of the heir. I couldn't imagine it would soften public opinion if my betrothed died a mysterious death only a day after solidifying our engagement.

Though, I supposed we could have told the truth, that Ellie Payne had refused to marry me. That she was an insolent, self-righteous plague on my conscience who honestly probably deserved better than I could ever give her. Which made her extra hateable (because let's be honest, perfectish people are unbearable). And that she'd choked herself to death by disobeying the fae bargain.

That was certainly one option.

But knowing the people and their insistence on believing the worst about me, I was fairly certain they'd find a way to make Ellie a martyr and me her executioner.

Why was I talking myself through this like Ellie was dead and I had a decision to make, anyway?

Ellie was very much not dead. She was very much my betrothed, and she would stay that way until Blaise and I figured out a way to undo the bargain.

Or until Ellie died, possibly in the tournament.

I could let it happen, of course.

I could let her die.

In front of a crowd wasn't ideal, though it would be nice to have an audience to witness me wipe that smug look off her face.

Okay, even thinking like this was starting to make me cringe at myself.

I'd had no evidence that my father was the murdery type—I mean, obviously he was the king; he had a tendency to execute people without having to blink twice—but that was the kind of murder that most considered aboveboard.

I meant that I'd never known him to *murder*, murder. Behind closed doors. Dead bodies of his enemies popping up miles down the river, washed up on shore. That sort of thing.

Well, there was that female who laughed at my mother's new gown that one time.

They'd found her severed finger (they knew it was hers because of the gaudy sapphire ring) a few days later. A village boy had claimed it had fallen from the sky, dropped from the beak of a circling vulture overhead.

Well, there wasn't much finger pointing one could do when there wasn't actually a body...

Still, I was sure he had it in him—a good, vicious murder when the situation warranted one.

Now that I thought about it, my father, in a rare display of his magic, had unleashed an array of deadly vines upon the sister of the Queen of Naenden during the most recent Council meeting.

My father had refused to allow me to attend. Not that I'd wanted to, though apparently I missed quite the spectacle.

Luckily for Dwellen's relationship with the kingdom of Naenden, his attempt on the young girl's life had been thwarted by Queen Abra of Mystral. That, I wished I'd been there to see.

Perhaps my father was capable of true murder after all.

He hadn't passed that trait onto me.

I'd gotten his nose, and that was about it.

He would have said he hadn't passed along his intelligence or dignity to me either, that Jerad must have hoarded it all for himself.

Neither did he gift me his propensity for scheming.

Not that I didn't think about things before they happened. It wasn't as if I went into situations without knowing exactly what I planned to do.

It was just that rarely did I ever find a situation that turned out just as I had imagined it. There was always some unforeseeable variable (my father would have claimed there was no such thing), like Ellie Payne actually being an annoyingly admirable person, that required a change in the plan at the last minute.

So, yes. I had considered what I would do if Ellie refused to marry me. If she refused to take part in the Trials, and thus suffocated herself to death.

The plan had been to prop my feet up on the table as her own stubbornness squeezed the life out of her.

I just hadn't expected her stubbornness to be so stinking cute.

Because it wasn't stubbornness, not at all.

Mules were stubborn.

Ellie was tenacious.

I'd seen it sparking in her eyes, steeled in her expression, that unwillingness to yield.

It was so foreign to me, so unattainable. I couldn't let it die—that iron will. Couldn't let it burn and fizzle out, only to be seen again when the Fates decided they were done crafting new souls and decided it was time to recycle their Ellie pattern.

I didn't want to wait that long.

OKAY, none of that was actually true.

Ellie had stopped breathing. Those annoyingly adorable brown eyes of hers had gone wide with dread, and I'd been at her side in an instant.

There'd been no forethought. No current thought. Only ever afterthought, which was when I'd realized I'd made a horrible mistake by saving the life of the girl who would have been a whole lot more useful to me dead.

But what's a male to do when a woman like Ellie Payne is dying, except to jump a table and convince her to breathe again?

I imagined most reasonable families would have labeled my saving Ellie's life as "quick on my feet" or "thinking fast."

But no, in the eyes of my father, everything I'd ever done was "rash."

But rash and quick were just two sides of the same coin.

My father wasn't the type to acknowledge that coins have two sides, though. After all, his face was only printed on one of them.

Maybe I'd let her die. The first trial typically involved a feat of sorts, one that would likely not have been planned with a human contestant in mind. It would be simple to make it look like an accident.

But then again, she'd probably just turn those wide, beautiful eyes on me and I'd find myself cradling her in my arms and tracing my thumb over the curve of her jaw and...

Great. Now I was fantasizing about saving her.

Already I could tell that the Trials were going to be a raging success.

When I finally arrived at Forcier's, my mouth practically watering from the enticing scents of lemon and cinnamon wafting on the gentle breeze, I noticed that the cosmetics shop next door was barred up, a "For Lease" sign hanging in the window.

Strange. Madame LeFleur had leased the eye-catching purple storefront for decades, and from how Blaise scoffed at the hordes of women who frequented the shop (she especially loved to mock Imogen for it), I found it odd that she'd gone out of business.

But then someone opened the door to Forcier's. The scent of freshly baked apple fritters collided with my nostrils, and all thoughts of Madame LeFleur were gone.

CHAPTER 16

ELLIE

*I*t didn't end up mattering that the prince had prevented my suffocation, because nothing could have prepared me for this.

The pair of servant guards led me to a metal door that closed off the entrance of the cold tunnel where we waited. All I could hear was the sound of my own labored breathing. That, and the rumble of what I assumed to be the crowd outside.

The cacophony of voices shook the ground under my feet, only amplifying my nerves. As if the tremblings from which I'd suffered all night had suddenly bled out of me and now reverberated into the stone floor.

A familiar voice cut through the low rumble of the crowd, and though I couldn't distinguish any words, the voice itself was distinct enough. Especially since it needed only one word to send a wave of silence crashing over the crowd.

Out there, the King of Dwellen was addressing his people.

We listened to the few disconnected words that punctured the stone tunnel, and I found myself wishing that Evander and I could have been presented together. It wasn't that together was my preferred state of being when it came to the prince; I didn't exactly enjoy the prince's company, or even tolerate it.

He might have saved me from suffocation, but he'd gone back right to being insufferable immediately afterward. The prince had made a point of getting under my skin. Knocking on my door in the middle of the night belting sardonic poetry would have done the job just fine, but the imbecile went as far as stealing food off my plate, and that I could not forgive.

But if he were here, at least I wouldn't be able to hear shallow gasps that marked the panic in my breath. At least I'd have some rude comment to offend me, to take my mind off what lay ahead, rather than having to sit alone with my morbid thoughts.

I was going to die today; there seemed to be no question about that. At least not in the prince's mind, or his mother's. Whether the king expected me to live or not, I couldn't tell. I hadn't gotten the impression that he'd been lying that night, when he had sealed my Fate because he believed I might make a decent queen one day.

Unfortunately, becoming queen one day necessitated I outlive the king himself.

Which seemed improbable now that I had a moment of silence to really consider it.

Of course, he had never intended me to be queen. Why would that situation ever come up? If he hadn't been brutally murdered in the last millennia, or however long the king had lived, why would he expect it to happen during the next sixty or so years of my mortal lifespan?

So why was he doing this? Surely he had nothing against me personally. All of his anger seemed to be directed at Evander.

I didn't have time to answer those questions.

It occurred to me that I didn't have time left for much of anything at all.

The king concluded his speech, and the chains on the stone door scraped and reeled, allowing the sun to slip onto the tunnel floors through the widening crack at the bottom of the door.

Once the door had lifted high enough, the sun singed my eyes, but it turned out I didn't need them at the moment. The guards simply shoved at my back and pushed me into the arena.

How considerate of them.

The crowd went wild in a buzzing amalgamation of cheers and jeers. I couldn't quite tell the ratio of those in favor of my survival compared to those who would rather get their money's worth for the price of admittance by witnessing me torn to pieces by some rabid animal.

"Introducing the betrothed of the Prince of Dwellen," the king announced amid the crowd's screams.

"And now, my son, Evander Thornwall, the Prince of Dwellen himself."

The crowd lost it, though again, I couldn't tell whether the cheers outnumbered the booing. It wouldn't exactly have surprised me if the crowd was eager for the possibility of the prince's downfall. It wasn't as if he was popular amongst the fae or the humans.

But he was devastatingly handsome, so there was that.

I searched for him through the blinding light and found a shadow across the arena, appearing from a doorway. It took a moment for my eyes to focus, but I knew it was him before I had the chance to make out his features.

No one else swaggered quite like that.

The prince strode across the arena and presented himself before his father.

He didn't bother to bow.

His copper hair whipped into his face in the windy arena, his white tunic billowing, especially since the prince had not bothered to tuck it into his dark leather pants.

My heart skipped, and I told myself it was only because I had just laid eyes on the man by whose side I was surely about to die. The humor of the situation did not escape me. Me. The woman who'd never done anything with a male, was now going to die with one.

Great.

His green eyes found mine from across the arena, and he smirked.

And to think I had once entertained pity for him. Apparently, he couldn't even take our impending deaths seriously.

As I scanned the arena, I noticed what looked to be an obstacle course that ran through the middle of the colosseum. It had only taken a matter of days for the king's servants to assemble the monstrosity, though they must have worked on it all hours of the night. The first section looked to be a huge triangular prism made of wood. Something glinted at the top edge of the prism, but I couldn't make it out from such a distance.

Next to the long prism was a collection of vertical logs that looked like a forest of recently guillotined trees. Then, at the opposite end, was a huge metal box that looked like a receptacle, and though I couldn't see inside it, I was fairly certain the crowd could see into it from its open top.

I searched the crowd for my parents, though I had no idea why I thought I'd be able to find them in this colossal stadium.

And the stadium was packed.

From what I could tell, most in the audience were fae, though I could only differentiate the details of their faces within the first section of seats, and I wouldn't have been surprised if the humans had been placed in the topmost sections.

My chest ached for my parents. They'd written me every day since they received my first letter reporting that I wouldn't be back home anytime soon. Though I hadn't specified that the fae bargain I'd gotten myself into was the betrothal sort, the morning paper had spilled the news for me.

Father had been livid, of course. At least, that was the impression I'd gotten from the way he'd stopped referring to Evander as the prince, and had renamed him The Cad.

But I'd take my father's anger over my mother's sorrow any day. If it hadn't been clear by her letters that she missed me terribly, the tear stains that smeared her perfect script would have given it away.

I could only imagine how they'd felt when they'd read I was to participate in the Trials.

Part of me hoped my parents hadn't come. If I was doomed to die, as Evander had so kindly informed me at breakfast yesterday, I didn't want my parents to witness it. But it was a vain hope. There was no way my parents weren't somewhere in that stadium, hands clasped tightly together, praying to the Fates to spare my life.

If I had lost the will to live, the will to try, the knowledge that they were watching would have been enough to stoke a fire in me.

But I hadn't lost the will to live, and their presence would simply fan an already-roaring flame.

The king's voice boomed from his box that loomed over the section of the course with the lengthy prism. "Now, for the prince to escort his betrothed to their first trial."

Evander approached me and flashed me a dazzling grin as he offered me his elbow. I rolled my eyes at how calm he seemed. What were the chances that I, the human, died during this trial, while he, the fae, made it out alive?

I was no mathematician, but I was willing to bet they were favorable.

Good to know this ordeal would work out well for Evander. I would die, and he'd be free to chase after that poor woman who clearly didn't want him.

"Take it," he hissed through his grin, which I now realized wasn't for me at all, but for the crowd. Maybe he was concerned after all. "Please," he added, hastily.

"This is ridiculous. It's not as if you're escorting me to a ball." But I laced my hand through his arm anyway. I couldn't help but notice that the sleeves on his shirt were thin, hugging against his taut muscles where my hand rested.

Heat warmed my face, and I had a difficult time not noticing the firmness of his arms. Goodnight, did the male press tree trunks in his spare time, or were fae just born like this?

The prince strode toward the stairs at the bottom of the first obstacle, taking me with him. "Perhaps if you had attended the original ball, we wouldn't be in this mess to begin with."

"Oh, and why is that?"

"Because I might have met you and been so bored with your company that I never would have considered bedding a human."

"You're disgusting."

He cocked his head at me. "I said wedding a human. What did you think I said?"

I jerked my head to glare at him, at that plastered smile on his face. I opened my mouth to retort, but then the wrinkles around his eyes joined his smile.

He was teasing me.

I shouldn't have enjoyed it as much as I did.

CHAPTER 17

EVANDER

*W*hen I'd first offered my arm to Ellie Payne, her touch had been feather-light, as if she feared that the feel of her hand against my bicep (with a layer of fabric between them, mind you) would send my mind spiraling in a cascade of rakish fantasies.

I sometimes wondered who had first perpetuated the belief that sex was all we males were capable of thinking of.

That being said, Ellie Payne did look ravishing, but I found that fact more frustrating than enticing.

Someone had had the audacity to stick her in a dress after I had specifically asked the tailor to hem her a pair of trousers.

Normally, I tried not to be that guy. The rich cad who dressed his women like they were racehorses meant to be paraded. I'd had the tailors make a set of gowns for Cinderella, but I'd done it because I didn't know if she'd have anything to wear when she returned to the castle. Of course, it had been Ellie who'd ended up in that dress, the night she'd mortified me in front of my mother...

Anyway. This was a trial, and pants were in order.

My irritation rose when I noticed that not only had they put in her in a dress; they'd put her in a layered dress—the kind with enough fabric around the skirt to fuel Collins's oven.

We reached the steps that led to the first platform, and I almost groaned when Ellie lifted her skirts and I caught a glimpse of satin slippers on her feet.

My father had most definitely had a part in this.

Did he want Ellie alive or not?

Next to me, Ellie scoffed. "Really? We're about to face our almost certain deaths, and you're trying to steal a look under my dress?"

I let out a steadying breath. *Actually, I was calculating your chance of survival based on your footwear. You know, because I was concerned for your safety. My apologies for stepping outside my public image of mindless sex-monger for a breath of fresh air.*

I voiced none of that, of course. Instead I swallowed my annoyance, flashed her a well-practiced grin, and said, "What can I say? I'm an ankle guy."

The way Ellie's tongue groped for a response that never came was worth the ankle-fetish gossip that would certainly ensue.

As we ascended the platform, Ellie seemed to cast aside any scruples she might have previously held regarding clinging to me. By the time we reached the top, her delicate touch had morphed into a desperate grip, and I was pretty sure she'd grown claws somewhere between the ground and the top of the steps.

On the platform, we were now flush with the lower level of the crowd. Every time Ellie fidgeted, which was approximately every time I counted to two, the wooden platform groaned.

Forget the shoes and the dress.

Ellie Payne was going to tremble herself off the edge of this platform.

I couldn't help but frown. "You don't like heights?"

She swallowed, her throat bobbing. "It's not heights I mind. I'd just prefer to be on a more stable surface."

"So you'd be alright with the mountains?"

She almost looked like she wasn't going to answer, like it was a stupid question that shouldn't be graced with a response. But then... "Mountains are about as stable as things get."

"Good. It would have been a shame if I'd found out I was marrying a beach girl. I was hoping we could honeymoon in the Kobiis."

She snorted, but her lips broke into a smile, clearly disarmed by the ridiculous notion of the two of us honeymooning together. I grinned right back. "Better?"

Ellie nodded. "A little." And was that… Did I sense gratitude in her tone, or after two hundred years was my hearing beginning to fail me?

It gave me an idea.

I let my arm loosen, and when she frantically grasped to keep hold of me, I snaked my fingers down the bare skin of her forearm and interlocked my fingers with hers. "I am quite *experienced* in calming a woman's nerves."

The scoff she let out this time was a tad too breathy to be genuine. "And there you go again. You can't help yourself, can you?"

I turned to face her, then used her death grip on my hand to draw her closer. Her eyes widened, and when I leaned in, her breath hitched. "Not around you, I can't."

Had I not known better from all those dreadfully dull wielding classes my father pressured me to take as a child, I might have said my plan worked like magic.

Ellie's back stiffened, forcing her to stand taller. "You're trying to distract me."

A surprising lack of accusation in her voice. Only wariness. Noted.

"Is it working?" I asked, still in that intentionally seductive whisper.

"Yes, actually," she said, and I tried to ignore the way my heart leapt at her admission. Which ended up being for the best, because she immediately pulled away and said, "Disgust is a much more potent emotion than fear."

I couldn't stifle the annoyance that perhaps my idea had worked a bit too well.

Before I could come up with a snarky retort, my father's voice ripped my attention from our little game and back to the arena. "Prince Evander and his betrothed"—why couldn't he just say her name?—"are to face a series of three obstacles, each of which will

134

provide the couple an opportunity to prove their ability to work together. The Kingdom of Dwellen does not take marriage bonds of its future leaders lightly, and thus these Trials have been crafted to ensure that any future marriage alliance will benefit not only the couple, but also the citizens of Dwellen."

Applause and screams erupted from the crowd. How many of them had placed bets on whether Ellie would plummet to her death?

Ellie snapped her neck toward me. "Do you die if you fall from this height?"

I ventured a glance downward. "Likely not."

My father spoke again. "The rules to this trial are simple. The couple must make it through these three obstacles without falling or being otherwise impaled by iron..."

It took me a moment to realize it was back. The trembling. Rattling the platform and buzzing underneath my feet.

I turned to Ellie, whose brown eyes had gone wide, sending me right back to the floor of the breakfast room, holding her in my arms and hoping to the Fates she wasn't dead.

"Are you okay?"

I wasn't sure she could hear me over the sound of my father's voice.

She just stared.

My father droned on. "The first obstacle, the couple may attempt as they are. We will address further rules should they conquer the first. The couple must make it to the next platform without falling."

As if on cue, sunlight glinted across the razor edge of the lengthy prism that acted as a bridge to the next platform.

"Any tightroping experience around your belt, my impressive betrothed?" I asked.

She scowled. "You know good and well how to get past this."

"Oh, do I?"

"It's a fae competition. I've read about them," she said, her voice eerily impassive considering how I'd thought our conversation had been heading in a pleasant direction.

She was right. This obstacle was fairly simple. All we had to do was lock arms and walk on either side of the prism—the smooth portions. Our respective weights would serve as a counterbalance and keep us from plummeting down the sharp slope.

"Ah, well, since you already know how to play, this should be simple then," I said, offering both my hands. She crossed her arms rather than taking them.

"No."

My fingers twitched, begging to let me scrape them down my face. "If it's the height you're worried about, I assure you, you won't be tempted to look down. Not when my face will be directly in front of your vision the entire time."

Again, I reached for her hands, but she crossed her arms and pulled away.

Dread coiled in my gut. "We don't get to say no to this, Ellie."

Even as the words escaped my mouth, she gripped her throat. Not like yesterday, when the effects of rejecting the bargain had been sudden. Fae curses were tricky like that, as if they each had a dose of sentience about them, someone behind the veil making a judgment call.

Saying no to my help must not have been as grievous an error as refusing to do the Trials at all. For now, she was still breathing. Still, if Ellie didn't step off this platform soon...

"You'll drop me," she whispered.

There was no defiance in her face. No fury in her pretty brown eyes. Just fear.

Fear of me.

Something withered in my gut.

"Why would I do that?"

She nodded toward the ground, and this time when she spoke, I could hear the faintest edges of a wheeze. "If we fall, I'll die; you'll live, and you'll be free of me. I'm not stupid. This is just your and your father's way of bailing you out of your bargain with me without the shame of having to annul the agreement."

I glanced down at the ground, then back at the woman before me.

She was right. If she fell, my life would go back to normal. Blaise and I would find Cinderella, and this…this would just be a blip in my unending existence, a dog-eared page in an epic.

But then Ellie would be dead.

Why, *why* couldn't I just be okay with that?

I sighed and ran my hands through my hair. "I won't drop you."

"I don't believe you." Her voice was raspy now, breathless.

"By Alondria, Ellie, you don't have another choice." I reached out, my fingers grazing her throat, and I could feel the breath leaving her body, as it had yesterday.

"You say that a lot, you know. Perhaps you could come up with a more creative phrase to communicate your frustration."

I cocked my head in question.

"By Alondria," she explained, a warble in her voice even as she teased.

"You're stalling."

A hushed whimper rippled through the crowd. The attendees were wondering why we hadn't started the challenge yet.

She shook her head and winced. Fates, her throat was closing up.

"Ellie, please. I won't drop you."

"How do I know?"

"I can't lie, remember?" Which was exactly why it had been a stupid move to vow something like that. Now, if I did drop her, even on accident…

Well, she'd be dead, and I wouldn't be far behind her.

Then we'd be stuck together in the afterlife, too.

Either that was good enough for her, or her human instinct had decided it had had enough of Ellie's masochistic behavior, because she practically launched herself into me as she grasped for my hands.

Our fingers intertwined, and I ignored how much better I liked it this way.

"Good. Glad we're on the same page," I said, squeezing her hands and trying to offer a reassuring smile.

"Okay," she said, and she followed my lead as I stepped a foot onto the slope. Beads of sweat broke out across her forehead. Her right foot was shaking, still glued to the stable platform.

But those soft hands of hers were still in mine.

When she looked up at me from underneath those thick, dark eyelashes, my foot almost faltered. "Just don't let go, okay?"

As if any sane male would have wanted to.

CHAPTER 18

ELLIE

$\mathcal{W}$e stepped off together, and there was one terrible moment when I felt like my stomach was going to fall through my body. My weight lurched, and I knew I was falling. But then the tension between our crossed, interlocked arms went taut, and I found my body stable.

"See? Not falling," Evander said. "Now, don't you dare look down. Just look at me instead."

I did as he asked, grateful for somewhere to set my gaze other than the ground. I figured it probably wouldn't help our chances of making it through this obstacle alive if I lost the contents of my stomach on the already slick slope.

Fortunately, or perhaps unfortunately, there were worse places to look than Evander Thornwall's face. Where I'd only ever witnessed a pompous smirk, his expression had gone soft, confident, encouraging. "Now let's take another step. Together. Three, two, one." We stepped, and again, I felt as if I were falling for a fraction of a second, but it wasn't nearly as bad as when we'd initially stepped off the platform.

An annoyingly stunning grin broke across his face. "You're getting the hang of this."

"Don't patronize me."

He snorted. "Careful. I'm getting the urge to lift my hands up in my defense."

That didn't exactly serve to make me feel any better.

Still, he talked me through the next few steps, and I tried to focus on his eyes rather than how tired my hands were, how they were trembling and clammy enough to slip at any second.

His eyes. Just focus on his eyes, Ellie.

They were green, technically, but not green like the forest or the grass. It was a green that belonged to the ocean in the middle of a storm, the edge of the sea, where water met sand.

I could almost bet there had been women who had drowned in those eyes.

"See, one more step, and it's over," Evander said, and I felt my breath catch, which I told myself was due to the fear of losing my footing with only one step to go. My left foot landed on the second platform, and the steadiness of it washed me in relief, providing me with the confidence to move my right foot over.

"You don't have to keep staring, you know. The task is over," Evander said, a twinkle of amusement glinting in those gorgeous eyes. I ripped my gaze away from his in horror, to which he only smirked. "Though I don't mind if you wish to continue."

For the first time since the King of Dwellen turned down my request, I was actually thankful to hear the vile being's voice as it boomed through the stadium. "The prince and his betrothed have completed the first task. Now for the second. Guards."

Well, he had to go and ruin it, didn't he?

Two guards appeared, one behind Evander and one behind me. The former wrapped a piece of black linen over Evander's eyes. The latter leaned down and swatted at the hem of my skirt. I might have jolted or turned to kick him if my feet hadn't rooted themselves on the platform for my fear of heights. Thick rope scratched my ankles as the guard tied my feet together with a knot. The forced narrowing of my stance made me feel like I might topple over the edge at any moment now, and I reached out toward Evander to steady myself.

"That feels good." Evander purred at my touch, and even that stupid blindfold couldn't obscure the smugness that must have been flickering in his gaze. "And unexpected."

"Don't humor yourself," I hissed, and I could have sworn that Evander flexed his bicep under my grasp in response.

I didn't like this. Not one bit.

The king's voice boomed again. "Now that the prince and his betrothed have been sufficiently handicapped, the couple must traverse the logs before them, a task which symbolizes how, in a true match, one should be capable of offsetting the other's weakness with their own strengths."

I examined what lay ahead, where at least four dozen logs had been staked into the earth, forming a large rectangle. Their tops were bare, which I figured was a bad sign.

"Looks like you're my eyes now, El. What do we have ahead of us?"

I bristled at the nickname, and the edge of his smile quirked. It was unsettling how easily Evander could observe me, even with his sight taken away. I sighed. "Any chance you memorized the course before they blindfolded you?"

"Nope."

"Didn't think so."

"You'll have to lead me across."

I nearly choked. "Um. Only one problem with that. I can't step across the logs. Not with my ankles tied together."

He grinned, the edges of wrinkles poking out from under his blindfold. "Oh. Well, that is a problem, isn't it?"

"I don't know why you insist on acting like this is funny," I said.

He crossed his muscular arms. "And I don't see how acting like it's the end of the world is contributing to our success, given the situation."

"It's not like I can hop across the logs!" There was no way I could clear the distance with my ankles tied together, though the logs were spaced far enough apart that I likely wouldn't have been able to make the jump anyway.

"Don't fret, my dearly betrothed. I have an idea."

"Oh, really?"

141

"Oh, really. And the best part is that you're not going to like it."

I opened my mouth to retort, but I never got around to it, because Evander reached for my hand, then traced his fingers up my arm until he found my upper back.

My throat closed up, and not from the bargain this time. "Wha—"

Quick as an ember springing from a fire, he stepped closer, pulling me into him. For a moment, I thought the imbecile was going to kiss me right here in front of everyone, but then he leaned down, placing his other hand under my knees. The ground left me, and I found myself cradled against his chest as he picked me up.

My heart pounded.

Dizziness overwhelmed me.

I told myself it was the heights.

"No. Way. In. Alondria."

He smirked. "Do you have a better idea?"

Unfortunately, I did not.

"Just tell me where to step, my love. You've got my ears." The tips of his pointed ears perked, as if they too thought the situation was worthy of a joke.

I bit my lip. "Fine. Take a step forward. *A small ste—*" I yelped as he almost stepped off the platform. He grinned and drew his foot back to the edge. My chest was practically rattling, and I shot him a scowl. "You did that on purpose."

"I'm blindfolded, remember?"

"That sounds like a way to get around a lie."

He craned his neck so that his nose practically scraped mine. "You know me so well. No wonder we're getting married."

I coughed in his face, which he answered with a grimace. I turned away, trying to focus on the bald edges of the logs rather than the ground far below us. "Alright. Now shuffle to the right a bit." He did as I asked. "And you're going to have to take a step out, probably about half of your leg span."

"How long have you been noting my proportions, Ellie?"

I groaned. He was going to get us both killed. With a jolt, he did as I asked, and I had to fight back a squeal. If I was going to die today, in front of all of Othian and my parents, I was not going to go down squealing. Even if every inch of my body claimed otherwise.

His foot landed on target, and I sighed. One launch later, and both his feet were on the narrow log.

"Well, look at that. Those were pretty good directions, after all. You really must have been paying attention to my physique."

"Just shut up while I try to think," I said, my head spinning at the height.

"I thought you'd enjoy me distracting you."

"Well, you thought wrong."

"Noted. Heights are not a turn-on. I'll remember that for when we're wed."

I blocked him out and searched for the nearest log. Unfortunately, the nearest log was thin, and would probably only support one of the prince's feet. In fact, as I looked around, all the nearest footholds seemed to be too small to bear the entire weight of both of us.

Great.

There was one pole, an extra row down, that looked like it was large enough for two feet. But we'd have to traverse the small logs to get to it.

"Okay, listen—"

"What else am I going to do? I'm blindfolded, remember?"

"All the poles surrounding us are too small for both your feet. You're going to have to step on one of them with one foot and use it to launch off to the next log."

That wiped the smug look off his face.

"Are you sure?"

"No, Prince Evander. I'm just trying to trick you into misplacing your foot so that we can both fall, and so I can die a romantic death in your arms."

"For the record, if you're going to use my name to be snarky with me, it sounds better if you just call me Evander."

I grunted and decided to ignore him. "The first log is pretty close, probably about three cubits away."

"The fae don't use that method of measurement. It's not precise enough for our tastes. After all, isn't there variation in the length of a human forearm?"

"Agh!"

"My apologies, Lady Ellie. I'm just kidding. I know how long a cubit is."

"Anyway, it's to your right, on a forty-five-degree diagonal. You'll have to launch off of it with your right foot to get to the log to your left diagonal, which you'll probably have to jump for."

"How far?"

"Far."

"You do know that far for a human is not the same as far for a fae."

I gritted my teeth. "Like I said, *far*."

"Oh."

"Oh, indeed."

"Very well then."

I closed my eyes. Evander jumped, and my mind desperately grasped for signals that we wouldn't be falling to our deaths. Our momentary weightlessness. The sensation of my belly compressing. The pressure of his foot landing on the first log. The burst of speed when he jumped again.

I couldn't bear to open my eyes to see if he had judged correctly. Our collective weight collided with the log, and I opened my eyes and sighed. My relief was short-lived, however, as his other foot mis-stepped and met the air rather than a solid foothold.

We toppled, and try as I might to grab onto his neck, I slipped.

My hands traced his forearm.

When I fell, my scream curdled in my throat.

CHAPTER 19

ELLIE

*I*t seemed as though whatever magic had bound the lying curse upon the fae had taken a liberal interpretation of what it meant to drop me, because Evander could still breathe well enough to yell.

"El!"

Evander's knees buckled, sending his chest colliding with the top of the log as he reached for me.

For half a moment, staring up into his blindfolded face, his mouth screwed up in panic, I was certain this would be the moment I died.

Elynore Payne, may she rest in pieces.

May her spirit remain whole, though her bones did not.

It's funny—the way one's brain has the time to come up with these things when you're plummeting to your death.

But then Evander's fingers locked into mine, the force of which sent my entire body weight flying into the pole.

Fear gripped me as I dangled over the ground. The only thing keeping me from plummeting to my death was the prince's clasp on my wrist.

My head swam. Evander's face was flushed red, his teeth gritted as he tried to keep a hold on my wrist while maintaining his balance as he lay sprawled over the top of the pole.

There was no way we were getting out of this. On purpose or not, he was going to drop me. Tears stung at my eyes as I pictured my parents watching, huddled together, white-knuckled as they squeezed each other's hands, unable to peel their eyes off of me.

"Ellie, listen to me. Tell me where the next platform is."

I didn't have time to argue. "Directly to your left."

"Is it large enough for both of us to stand on?"

I nodded, then realized he couldn't see me. "Yes."

"I'm going to swing you over."

"What? No!" But my protests were too late, the breath I'd spent crafting them useless, because now I was sailing through the air. My feet hit the wide platform, and since I couldn't hold my balance with my ankles tied together, the force of my landing launched my face onto the wooden surface.

For a moment, I savored my safety, but then I remembered Evander straddling the pole with his chest, and how it must have thrown off his balance to toss me over. I whipped around and found him grunting as he pulled himself up to the top of the log where he had just slipped. The muscles of his upper back rippled through his thin shirt, and I thought the fabric might rip apart with the force he was exerting. But then his chest hit the top of the log, and once he had his balance, he pushed himself off with his arms, swinging his feet until they landed in place.

The dynamics of the motion made no sense to me. It was like watching a double-jointed acrobat who could clasp their hands behind their back and pull them over their head.

Never in my life...

"Evander," I called out to him. His pointed ears perked and moved in my direction, and he launched himself off the log, landing safely on the platform. "You didn't wait for my directions."

He crawled over toward where I was lying. I ran my fingers through his hair, tucking them under his blindfold as I pulled it off, revealing those stunning sea-green eyes.

Which immediately dipped to my mouth.

"I didn't have to. I just followed your voice."

His gaze lingered on my mouth for a moment, and I swallowed. In an unforeseen turn of events, he averted his gaze, almost awkwardly, then rushed to my ankles. As he undid my restraints, he didn't look at me, for which I was thankful.

It occurred to me that, had Evander fallen to his death just now, I would have been free from my bargain.

I hadn't thought of that in the moment. All knew was that I had desperately hoped he wouldn't fall.

Huh.

Evander must have sensed the delicate flower of goodwill blooming between us, because he immediately overwatered it by saying, "You know you were trembling the entire time I held you. Was that for my touch?"

The king's voice saved me from having to respond. "For our third and final trial of the day, the prince and his betrothed are to enter the pit. Guards, gag the woman."

Instantly, someone stuffed a piece of stretchy fabric into my mouth and tied it tightly from behind. I winced as it dug into my skin, and Evander frowned.

"You don't have to tie it so tight," he said through gritted teeth, but the guard didn't bother loosening it. Instead, he grabbed me by the arm and led me to a platform that hung over the metal pit. I looked down and instantly regretted doing so.

I didn't fancy myself squeamish, but then again, I didn't usually find myself being forced into a den of giant ants, either.

Myrmecoleon. The lions of ants. I'd heard about them in stories my father used to tell me before bed. The kind of stories that had always gotten him a scolding from my mother.

Their teeth were as sharp as razors and could rip even fae flesh to pieces.

And they were swarming the bottom of the pit.

Great.

Bile stung at the back of my throat, soaking the gag stuffed in my mouth.

The other guard led Evander away to an opposite platform across from me, but he kept craning his neck to keep his eyes on me. Concern etched his brow.

The king drawled, "It is well known among those bound by the covenant of marriage that the males must learn to read the unspoken signs of their females. A respectable husband must be able to interpret her needs without requiring an explanation in order for the marriage to be effective."

Evander laughed dryly across from me, even as the words crept under my skin and boiled my blood. At least Evander, too, found this notion ridiculous. I'd never understood people who didn't just tell the other person what they wanted, nor did I think it was anyone's responsibility to learn to interpret—excuse me, assume—someone's desires based on their body language.

"Through this trial, my son will demonstrate that he is able to decipher his betrothed's mind, without the use of words between them."

"Oh, this should be great." Evander laughed, though he kept looking nervously at the bed of myrmecoleon crawling down beneath us.

"The betrothed will be provided a rendering of an item. She must communicate to the prince without her words what item is on the paper before the platforms descend and deliver them to their deaths."

"You've got to be kidding me," Evander said, his words echoing my thoughts.

So our lives depended on my ability to play charades.

This was it. We were going to die.

I found myself wishing we had simply fallen from the prism. At least that death would have been quick. Not to mention less humiliating.

Would you rather smash your skull against the unforgiving earth or be eaten alive by a swarm of giant ants?

After being forced to play charades in front of a bloodthirsty stadium.

Hm. What a tough choice.

A guard handed me a rolled up piece of paper. My hands shook, and the platform jolted beneath me, descending much more quickly than I would have preferred.

Eventually, I managed to untie the knot on the scroll, but by the time I got to it, we'd already dropped a few inches.

"Ellie?" Evander asked impatiently. "I'd rather not have my flesh ripped apart today, you know."

I unraveled the scroll and opened it before me. It was a map of Alondria. So familiar, I'd seen it a thousand times. It laid out all the kingdoms—Laei, Naenden, Charshon, Avelea, Dwellen, and Mystral— the major rivers and mountain ranges that separated us. I had half a mind to toss the scroll to Evander, as technically that wouldn't be breaking the rules, but a guard reached down and ripped it from my hands as soon as I'd gotten a good look at it.

"Well?" Evander called from across the pit.

I groaned and pointed a finger into the air, tracing the outline of Alondria as best as I could.

"A jagged blob?"

I shook my head, though I was almost certain he hadn't been serious, anyway.

I turned around so he could watch me trace it from behind, thinking he might understand it better if it wasn't a mirror image he was looking at.

"Seriously, Ellie. What is that supposed to be?" His words lacked unkindness, but I could hear his pitch tighten as we descended further.

I squinted my eyes tight and tried to think. I turned back to him and broadened my hands, as if to encompass the world in them.

He squinted. As if his perfect fae vision wasn't seeing my motions correctly. "Big?"

I nodded, excited now. Maybe I could get him to the answer step-by-step.

I lifted my arms to the side and spun around, intending to convey that it was all around us.

"A strange human dance I'm unfamiliar with?"

I shook my head, aggravated now, and flung my hands out wide.

"A big human dance I'm unfamiliar with."

"AGH." My grunt came out garbled from underneath the cloth jammed into my mouth. My head spun as I tried to think of a way to communicate this to him. How was I supposed to mime an entire continent? For something so large and concrete, suddenly it seemed like an abstract idea.

"Ellie?" Evander crossed his arms and tapped his foot on his descending platform. We had sunk halfway down the pit by now, and I had run out of my two ideas.

Panic set in, and if my brain had intended to help me today, it certainly had given up hope now.

I frowned and shook my head at him.

I don't know how to do this.

My meaning must have been clear enough, because his arrogant smirk twitched and faded into something else. Panic. Fear.

"Come on, Ellie. You have to think of something."

By Alondria, it was like I was being trapped in some horrible version of charades where everyone was about to watch the skin get ripped off my face as penalty for a brain block.

By Alondria.

That was it.

I spun around and found the ropes that were lowering my platform into the pit. The ropes slithered downward, propelled by gears at the edge of my platform.

This was stupid.

This was so stupid.

But it was going to work.

I was going to make it work.

I grabbed one of the ropes and pulled. It was taut, and it resisted me, but I finagled it to the side, pinning it between two gears. That platform shuddered to a halt, and the crowd gasped.

The guards murmured above me, something about cheating and whether to drive an arrow through my heart.

"No," the king said. "The gears are sharp. They will simply rip through the ropes."

It was true. The strings at the edge of the rope were already starting to fray, splintering one by one. It wouldn't take long for the gear to sever the rope, sending me plummeting to my death.

"You have to undo it. It won't work. You'll just fall early," Evander warned from the other side as he descended lower and lower into the pit.

I ignored him and placed my fingers around the other rope.

"Ellie, seriously. I really don't want a giant ant chomping into your flesh to be the last thing I see in this world." There was humor in his words, but only in his words. His voice had risen to sheer panic, reflecting what I was experiencing on the inside.

This was going to work. This had to work.

I yanked at the other rope, jamming it inside the second gear.

The rope on the right popped loudly as it snapped. The left rope was the only thing holding me up at this point.

Evander lost it.

"By Alondria, what do you think you're doing?"

I whipped around and waved my arms frantically toward the king, toward the guards, toward anyone. When they looked at me like I was a lunatic, I jabbed a finger toward Evander.

The king cocked his head at me, then a pleased smile washed over his cruel face.

"Stop the platforms," he said.

"But sire, they haven't solved—"

"Stop the platforms," he yelled this time. The guard did as he was told, and both of our platforms screeched to a halt.

"Sire, they didn't solve the trial," the guard said, confused.

The king fixed his calculating stare on me. "But they did. The rules stated that the prince must state the item on the scroll without hearing the betrothed's words. The word was Alondria, was it not?"

The guard paused, his mouth agape. "Yes, but—"

"Did my son not just utter the word Alondria?"

It almost looked as if the guard was chewing on air for a moment as he tried to process what had just happened. Tears burned at my eyes, but I blinked them back. By the time the king and I were face to face, I wanted him to see nothing but determined victory in my stare.

Evander let out a sound that sounded like a kitten being strangled. When I glanced back at him, his mouth was hanging in an open-mouthed grin, his eyes sparkling.

"You're...you're..." He laughed, something like hysteria mingled with disbelief choking his words.

The guards had to find a rope ladder to hoist me back up, since I had broken their contraption. Evander had beaten me to the top and was already there to greet me. He offered me his hand, and I let him help me off the ladder.

Before I could register what he was doing, he had slipped his fingers into the curls at the nape of my neck. My heart faltered, sure he was going to kiss me, but then my gag fell loose, and I realized he'd only been untying it.

His bright eyes scanned me, not in that disgusting, assessing way I'd seen when we'd first met, but as if he was taking me in as a whole. As if he'd lived his life in the desert and had glimpsed his first snowflake.

I shrugged and swallowed, uncomfortable with his extended gaze, but if he noticed my cue to look the crap away from me, he didn't take it. I had to clear my throat and cut my vision over to the king just to break the stare.

"Prince Evander, the prince's betrothed, congratulations on passing your first trial." The king's eyes flared. "May you succeed in those to come."

My heart stopped. "There are *more*?"

Evander peered down at me and squeezed my hand.

It took me all afternoon to convince myself that the flutter that hiccupped in my heart had been a result of passing the Trials.

CHAPTER 20

ELLIE

*W*hen Imogen brought me back to my quarters, I crashed on the bed and slept for the majority of the afternoon. It was strange. I would have thought that coming so close to death twice, if not three times, today would have invigorated me, prodded me to get off my butt and make something of my easily extinguishable life.

But no, I pretty much just wanted to sleep.

In fact, I slept so hard that I didn't realize Imogen had entered the room until she was already next to my bed.

I jolted, the realization of a presence standing above me striking a whirl of fear in me I hadn't expected.

"My apologies, my lady. I didn't intend to scare you," Imogen said, still blinking down at me with her pinprick eyes.

"That's fine," I said, clutching my chest and regaining my breath. "I didn't hear you come in."

"I knocked. You didn't respond, so I let myself in," she said.

I sat up in the bed and rubbed my eye sockets. My head was pounding. "How long did I sleep?"

"Most of the day, but I'm to dress you for dinner."

I groaned and plopped my head back on my soft pillow. "I'm not going to dinner." It felt good to say. To be able to refuse something for once without my throat closing up and choking me. They could make me participate in the Trials, and they could make me marry the prince, but where I chose to take my food had nothing to do with this stupid bargain.

To my surprise, Imogen nodded. "Very well, I will inform the prince."

That caught my attention. "You're not going to fight me on it? Aren't you worried about the king relieving you of your position?"

"The invitation was not extended by the king, but by His Highness, Prince Evander. He requested that the two of you dine alone tonight."

I frowned, suspicious. "And you're not afraid of the prince relieving you?"

"The prince is kind, my lady. Besides," she said, straightening somewhat awkwardly and poking her chin out, "it seems to me you've been through enough today, and that if you desire to keep to yourself this evening, then your wishes should be respected."

I smiled, my heart warming to the girl. "Thank you."

She returned my smile, a look of relief softening her face, and left. I laid my head back on the pillow and had almost fallen back to sleep again when I heard a knock on my door. Imogen's voice sounded muffled, nervous. "My lady?"

"Come in," I groaned.

The door burst open. "I cannot believe you refused my invitation to dinner."

I jumped up to find Evander striding into my room as if it were his own, the nervous Imogen eyeing him from behind as her fingers jittered together.

"I'm tired," I said, as blandly as I could manage.

"That's because you've been sleeping while the sun is out. Last I checked, humans aren't supposed to be nocturnal."

"Yeah, well, humans aren't supposed to be lowered into a pit of myrmecoleon either, so I'll take my chances with the napping, thank you."

At that, Evander's faux outrage broke with a betraying smile that gaped between his top and bottom teeth. He ran his hand over his mouth, as if to cover it up, and I couldn't help myself. I found my mouth curving too.

"Ellie. Will you please have dinner with me?" His eyes sparkled, and the voice that came from his mouth sounded so unfamiliarly earnest, I almost had the inclination to search the room for where it had come from.

"You're not demanding?"

He shrugged, tucking his hands into his pockets. "No, you seem to dislike that, so I'm trying another tactic. Asking. Desperately, really."

That broke me. I laughed. The hesitant type, but it was a laugh nonetheless.

My laughter must have been fodder to this strange being, because he pointed to Imogen and said, "Seriously, Ellie. I sent Imogen up here to ask you because I was too nervous to come up here myself. Imagine my disappointment when she told me you'd chosen sleep over my company."

"I can't imagine that was how she worded it." I glanced over at Imogen, whose wan face had gone scarlet. "It's alright, Imogen. You did the best you could. It's not your fault he's incessant."

This only intensified the blush on her face, and her eyes flitted nervously to the prince.

The prince didn't seem to notice, though. He was too busy grinning. He clapped his hands together. "Now that that's settled, I'll meet you down at my dining quarters in an hour. I'd say we meet sooner, but I imagine you'd rather not trek through the castle in your nightie. Though I can't say I'd complain."

"How thoughtful of you," I said, waving him away. He strode out of the room and passed Imogen, who seemed to let out a long-held breath once he was gone.

Imogen was quiet as she fixed my makeup and hair. She wasn't as naturally talented as Blaise, but she was fairly proficient at making me look like someone who could potentially be a princess, and I was impressed. But she was still eerily silent—more jittery than normal— and it bothered me.

"Are you okay? You're quiet tonight," I said, looking up at her through her reflection in the mirror as she braided a vine of blue wisteria into my curls.

"Yes, my lady," Imogen shot back in a tone a little too high to be genuine. Rather, it sounded as if she was trying to force the melancholy from her voice.

"Are you sure? You seem upset. Are you ill?"

"Perhaps I am coming down with something," she said, clearing her throat.

I frowned, the looks of which Imogen seemed to be avoiding as she focused keenly on my hair.

"Was the prince unkind to you when I sent my refusal?" I asked.

Imogen's eyes flickered up to meet mine, and she bit her lip. "I'd rather not discuss it."

This set my stomach roiling. "You can tell me anything, you know. I know I'm not technically royalty. But I'll do what I can to protect you. Even if it is just sharing a secret. If something happened..."

"Nothing happened," she snapped, her eyes going red as she blinked voraciously.

"Very well," I said, biting my tongue.

We didn't speak again until she led me to the prince's quarters.

CHAPTER 21

ELLIE

I expected Evander's style in decor to be lavish with a dash of excess.

I couldn't have been more wrong.

Actually, Evander's quarters were far from extravagant, which surprised me. Given his reputation with women, I had expected his dining room to be dripping with wealth. After all, wasn't dinner where seduction usually began? Although now that I considered it, I wasn't sure that Evander had to use dates in his arsenal of tactics. The thought irritated me, and between that unpleasant realization and my concern over what had transpired when Imogen had gone to tell Evander of my refusal, I found myself in quite the ill mood by the time Imogen escorted me to the dining room.

The walls were a subdued sage green. The dining table was carved not of ivory, but ivory-painted wood. Its carving was intricate and fine, of course. But it was what I would have expected to see in a nobleman's dining room, not a prince's.

Simple but elegant clay plates lined the table, a pleasing aesthetic that was actually quite tasteful. Some might even say modern.

Huh.

Imogen escorted me to my seat, and I stood behind the chair waiting for the prince.

He arrived not a moment later, waving a hand at me. "Oh, you don't have to bother with those formalities. They're all cumbersome in their own way, and a waste of time."

"Like having to say Prince Evander?" I asked, calling back to his comment just before our Trials.

"So many syllables," he agreed.

I sat and he joined me, though Imogen stood just behind me, hovering like a twitching shadow cast by a dying flame. My stomach twisted, reminding me of how uncomfortable she might be if Evander had been unkind, or worse, to her earlier.

"You don't have to stay, Imogen," I said, smiling gently. "You deserve the evening off, anyway."

Imogen blinked and shot a nervous glance in the prince's direction. Then she leaned over and whispered in my ear. "But it's improper."

"I'll be fine," I said, trying to be reassuring. Though I wasn't convinced Evander hadn't done something to deserve Imogen's nervous behavior, I also figured her timid nature and position of employment gave him greater power over her than it did me.

"But—"

"You have the evening off. Go spend it in town, or on something fun," Evander offered.

Imogen gulped, but she nodded and scampered off.

When I turned back to the prince, he was eyeing me mischievously. "You wanted to be alone with me, didn't you?"

"Not particularly. I simply didn't want Imogen to have to suffer in your presence."

He raised an eyebrow. "What? Imogen? Suffer? I think she rather enjoys my company."

Something twisted in my gut, and as I unraveled my napkin, my silverware crashed against the table. "Not every woman desires your advances, you know. To assume such... It doesn't give you the right to..." I stumbled over my words, too angry to form coherent sentences.

He narrowed his brow, a look of genuine concern spreading across his face. "To do what?"

I could only manage a whisper. "To take advantage of your servants. You're in a position of authority, you know. Even if she makes it appear as though she welcomes your advances, that doesn't mean she does. There's a pressure that she feels—"

"Ellie," Evander said, blanching as he touched my hand. "By Alondria, please don't finish that sentence. Nothing happened between me and Imogen. Unless you count me making myself look like a fool for being too nervous to ask you to dinner myself lest you chuck a glass slipper at me or something."

I jerked my hand away, the phantom brush of his touch still warm on my skin. "I—nothing happened with Imogen?"

"No. Why did you think something did?"

Out of habit, I searched his face for signs of a lie. Until I remembered that he was fae. He couldn't lie. "Because she..." I fumbled over my words, realizing only now how many leaps I had taken to come to my conclusion. My conclusion that had been false. "Well, she seemed off after talking with you. And when I asked her about it, she said she didn't want to talk about it. And then your comment about her enjoying your company made me think..."

"Go on," Evander said, clearly suppressing a grin as he pressed his lips together.

I scowled at him. "I won't have you make me say it and embarrass myself."

He dabbed his mouth with his napkin, despite the fact we hadn't begun eating yet. "It appears it's too late for that now, doesn't it?"

I thought to bite back at him, the mortification of my poorly placed accusations stinging at my cheeks and threatening to prod me into lashing out. But then I remembered how allowing my tongue to loosen at dinner with the king and queen had ended—with the queen despising me, and for good cause. I sighed. "You're right. She was probably upset about something else entirely."

Evander shrugged and traced the patterns on the wooden table with his fingers, avoiding my eyes.

My jaw dropped. "You *do* think she was upset over you, don't you?"

Evander threw his hands up. "I open my mouth, and you accuse me of being an arrogant pig. I keep it shut, and you come to the same conclusion."

I rubbed my forehead. Of course. If Imogen had a crush on Evander, it would upset her that he was inviting me to a private dinner. And that I had accepted it. And that she had been forced to deliver the invitation herself.

Evander sighed. "I didn't pick up on it until I saw how red her face was when I was flirting with you earlier. Had I known, I wouldn't have asked her to deliver the message. And I certainly wouldn't have made a scene about inviting you to dinner in front of her."

"It seems a bit unnecessary for a prince to change his actions just to spare the feelings of a servant."

Evander scoffed, placing his elbow upon the table and tucking his chin into his palm. "You don't believe that. You just don't want to admit that I can be a nice person."

I smiled softly. Apologetically. It was true. I was surprised that Evander considered anyone's feelings other than his own. Especially those whom I would have assumed he thought beneath him. He hadn't even offered an explanation as to why Imogen had been upset. Why? To save her from embarrassment? That was a kindness I didn't expect from civilized company, much less the careless prince.

But hadn't he already shown me that he cared? After all, during the first trial he'd gone to great lengths to assuage my fears. He'd also kept me from plummeting to my death, I supposed.

Mercifully, the cook entered not long after with a serving cart, from which he produced two large, steaming plates and set them before us.

Lobster.

I *loved* lobster.

I inhaled the main course, though I could have cursed the crustacean for making it so difficult to get to the delicious soft meat underneath its exoskeleton.

When I was done with the meat and had ventured on to the garlicky noodles, Evander spoke. "So, you made those shoes?"

"Are you still trying to convince yourself that your mystery lover isn't a thief?"

"No, I've resigned myself to being in love with a petty criminal. But at least she's pretty."

I laughed, despite the fact that my mouth was full of pasta.

"How long did it take you to perfect the design?"

"I've been working on them for over two years."

He frowned. "You must have been devastated when they went missing."

I nodded.

Half of a smirk stretched the corner of his mouth. "But not devastated enough not to shatter the only pair you had left?"

"Well, being tricked into an unsavory engagement will do that to you. And it wasn't a pair. The other one is still out there somewhere."

He raised his glass to that and took a sip. "Are shoes your passion, then?"

I cocked my head at him, surprised by the question. No one had ever asked me that before. Not even my parents. What was my passion? Certainly not *shoes*, of all things. That seemed too simple, too inconsequential to label as a passion.

"The shoes are the most beautiful thing I've ever made. So yes, in that way, I guess they're my passion. But it's about more than just the shoes. I want to reframe the way the world looks at glass. I want to bring beauty to the common people. The rich have their crystal and diamond and gold and precious stones. But to take sand and fire and craft something that makes people's eyes sparkle—that's what I enjoy. It could be stained glass, or glass slippers, or even just glass-blown globes. It doesn't really matter. I'd just like a workshop named after my father, where people come from miles and miles just to see a Payne."

Evander's eyes flickered. "So you're an artist at heart, then?"

"That. And I like to think of myself as a businesswoman."

He laughed, but not in the dismissive way I might have expected from nobility hearing what must seem like such an insignificant dream to someone like him. Someone who had probably traveled all of Alondria by the time he was weaned. "I assume you have a lot to prove to your fellow humans."

I nodded, suddenly sad at the reminder of the dream that had been ripped away from me, so I changed the topic. "And what's your passion?"

Evander's smile didn't reach his eyes, so much so that it almost looked like a grimace. "That, I've given up searching for."

I shot him a knowing look. "That didn't directly answer my question."

"You're getting good at detecting my tactics. I'm not sure that I like it," he said, though his smirk might have suggested otherwise.

I shrugged. "Don't yank me out of a perfectly good nap to come to dinner next time, then."

"By the looks of that poor, devastated lobster, I'm sure I could find a way to bribe you out of bed. Or if I couldn't, my chef could."

I rolled my eyes and gestured, as if to stab him with the tiny lobster fork. "So what's your passion, then?"

He sighed and locked those deep, sea-green eyes on me. My stomach whirled. Probably from the lobster. "Her."

It took a tremendous amount of self-control not to gag. So I cleared my throat, the whirling in my stomach turning into something deep and heavy and not entirely comfortable. "And by her, I'm assuming you mean the mystery girl who swiped my shoes?"

"That would be the one," he said, resting his chin upon his hand, lost in some dreamlike state.

Everything in me wanted to say that any respect I had gained for him had been lost in that one word. *Her.* Blech.

In fact, I found it irritating that he had gone to the effort of arranging this private dinner, even going as far as flirting with me about being too nervous to ask me himself, yet he still found it appropriate to bring up another woman.

Not that I cared.

Still, he wasn't exactly placing great care into the kind of signals he was putting off. And even though I *wasn't* under the impression the prince felt any romantic interest regarding me, that didn't mean I *couldn't* have gotten that impression from his actions this evening.

Then again, he had been kind to me about my glassblowing dream when he could have just as easily mocked it. Perhaps I should return the favor.

"Tell me about her, then," I said, almost having to force the slimy words out of my throat.

Apparently, the effort was obvious, because he shot me a suspicious look. "You don't really want to know."

I sighed. "Alright. You got me. I don't. But..." I said, lingering on that word, "that lobster might have been the highlight of a terrible week, so if you would like to talk about her, then I will, you know, listen. And then promptly scrub my ears out."

"A true friend," he mused.

"Oh, is that what we are?"

"I could keep calling you my dearly betrothed, if that's what you want."

"Friend is fine, thanks."

"I thought so. Anyway, back to my story."

"Gladly."

"When my father announced we'd be hosting the ball, I planned to dance the night away with the help and refuse to pick a bride by the end. But when I arrived, there she was, standing under a chandelier, sparkling in that blue dress of hers..."

I thought back to the dress I had worn my first night at the castle, the one the prince had requested the tailor make for his mystery woman.

"And I knew I had to talk to her. There was something..." He grinned sheepishly. "You're going to tease me if I tell you."

"I'll probably tease you either way, honestly."

"It was as if I'd known her my whole life. And when she looked at me—her eyes, I'm telling you, Ellie, I must have seen those eyes in my dreams, they were so familiar."

"Are you saying this girl is your fated mate or something?" I asked. It was a superstition my father had told me was held by many fae—one that, in my opinion, did more harm than good; it tended to excuse a male's possessive behavior in the name of some ancient, unbreakable bond.

I expected an "of course not." Instead, he shrugged, and I watched his jaw work. "I don't know. Maybe. I never believed in that sort of thing until..." He swallowed. "But I asked her for that first dance. And then the second."

"And then all the rest, yeah, I heard," I said.

"And that was it. She stole my heart."

"Just like my shoes."

He frowned. "I'm sure she had her reasons. Perhaps she's poor and wasn't able to buy clothing for the ball."

I quirked a brow, slicing a stalk of asparagus in half with my fork. "And that excuses the fact that she stole from me?"

"No. Of course not. It's just—"

"It's just that you can excuse it, because you never would have danced with her in the first place if you had known she was poor?"

He groaned and pressed his thumb against his forehead. "I shouldn't have said anything."

My heart faltered with guilt. Evander wasn't exactly the model of what I wanted in my future husband. But he had been kind to me today about my fear of heights. He'd even helped me, when he could have easily let the fae bargain do its work, making his problems disappear as quickly as it would have taken me to suffocate. "I'm sorry. I'm just a little bitter about it. That's all. She's the one who got me into this situation to begin with."

"Yes, and what a torturous situation it is," he said, scraping his empty plate with his tiny lobster fork.

"Yes. Actually. Having to dangle over a pit of myrmecoleon kind of does count as torture."

"That's not what you meant, though. You meant having to marry me." His bright eyes blazed, reminding me of a puppy that had just gotten into a freshly baked wedding cake and was now relying on adorableness to win its owner back over.

I coughed, not entirely unaffected by the annoying puppy eyes. "That's not fair. You don't want to marry me either."

"That's different," he said. "I don't want to marry you because I'm in love with someone else. You don't want to marry me because you think I'm an idiot."

I opened my mouth, trying to come up with a way for that not to be the truth.

I came up empty.

We sat in silence for a moment until I couldn't bear it any longer. "There had to be something else, though. I mean, I'm sure you've danced with plenty of beautiful women. There had to be something else that was special about her that made you want to bargain your life away."

"And there I was, beginning to believe you thought me shallow."

"I do," I said, carefully considering my next words. "But probably not when it comes to making serious decisions. Like who you want to spend the rest of your life with. Or, you know, the rest of her life, in the case with a human."

He sighed, wincing at the reminder of the girl's mortality. "She just... Well, she understood. All my life, I've been treated as an afterthought. As a backup plan to my brother. That's what's always been expected of me, and I was content with that role. But then... Then he..." Evander shook his head, as if to dislodge a memory. "And now, instead of ignoring me and pretending I don't exist like he always has, my father can't seem to stop criticizing me for how I turned out. For how he always expected me to turn out. I understand why he hates me. It was my fault, my fault that..." He paused, his mouth hanging open, as if the words had simply run out. As if there were none that existed that could explain what had happened. What it had done to him.

I remembered reading the article. How Prince Jerad, the heir to the throne, had died in an accident. An accident involving a stunt that his younger brother had roped him into.

He shook his head, as if to expel the memory. "She just understood, that's all. We talked, and she understood. All my life, the people who should have seen me, should have noticed the pain. What it was like to grow up unloved, unwanted by my father. The pain I must have gone through when my brother died… No one close to me saw it. Not even my mother. And now the entire kingdom acts as if it's my fault that I'm the lesser choice for an heir. Believe me, I know that. But no one stops and asks why I was never put in the same classes as Jerad. Why my father never invited me to his study to explain the ins and outs of ruling a kingdom. Why I was left to my own devices. She understood. She saw me. She didn't tell me what an honor it was to become the heir of Dwellen, she didn't ask me why I didn't…. or what my plans were, she asked me…"

"How you were coping with your brother's death," I said.

He nodded, covering his eyes with his fists, causing his forehead to bunch. "I wept every night and every morning for months after it happened. That night, not once did she treat me like the heir to the throne. She just treated me like I was someone who had caused the accidental death of his best friend."

Something knotted in my chest. The way the papers had covered the death of Prince Jerad, one would have thought he and Evander had been childhood rivals.

That was clearly not the case.

Somehow, my hands found his shoulder blade, my fingers pressing into the curve of a knot that had formed in the muscle. He tensed at my touch, but I might have imagined it because he immediately lifted his face from his hands and grinned.

"Look at you, always finding an excuse to touch me."

CHAPTER 22

EVANDER

*S*ince waltzing into my life, Ellie Payne had laid waste to quite a few of my plans.

The first and most obvious was my betrothal to Cinderella, of course.

But Ellie Payne was starting to interfere with other aspects of my life.

Francesca Aberdeen, for example.

Francesca Aberdeen had always excelled at one skill in particular— being the perfect distraction.

She had the body of an hourglass, the face of a demure lamb, and the cunning of a serpent.

And whenever I called, she answered.

I'd always liked that about her, or at least I'd always told myself I liked that about her.

Really, I thought I despised it, for as much as I enjoyed her company in bed, I really just reveled in the fact that there was at least one other fae in this world more vain and shallow than I was.

By far.

When I invited Ellie for dinner, it had been with the intention of making an ally of my future wife. Though neither of us wished to enter into this marriage, there was no reason we shouldn't at least try to enjoy one another's company, especially since it seemed we were going to end up stuck together for the next few decades.

What I hadn't expected was to still be thinking about my dinner with Ellie well into the evening.

It wouldn't have been so much of a problem if I hadn't invited Francesca Aberdeen to my bed.

At first, I hadn't felt an ounce of guilt for extending such an invitation. I had strict boundaries regarding marriage and infidelity, but being engaged still felt like a gray area, especially when my betrothed would have rather not been my betrothed.

This was my first time calling on Francesca since the night of the ball. I hadn't wanted to after I met Cinderella, after that question of hers had consumed my every waking thought.

It hadn't even been as much of a question as it had been an acknowledgment.

It must hurt to have lost him.

But Ellie was right; my father was right.

I'd proposed to Cinderella, and she'd fled.

I was the Heir of Dwellen, and I'd found the one woman in the country who didn't want to marry me.

Well, the second, I supposed.

Ellie didn't exactly want to marry me, either.

I'd been an arrogant fool to expect otherwise, first with Cinderella. I mean, what kind of scoundrel must I be if a woman quite literally fled from my presence and I interpreted that as her wanting to be chased?

It reminded me of something one of my father's creepy advisors would do. Receive obvious rejection from a young female and assume it meant she desired an increase in his efforts.

Blech.

And then I'd come onto Ellie, assuming she wanted me, too.

I knew she found me attractive. I could hear the way her heart pounded when our bodies were close, could sense the hairs on her arms standing up, the quickening of her breath.

But Ellie Payne was not one to let carnal desires cloud her judgment.

And clearly, being with me was poor judgment.

I hadn't really wanted to seduce her the first day she arrived in the palace. By Alondria, she was stunning, sure, but I'd still been convinced of Cinderella's affections for me and had desired no one but her.

I'd just wanted to prove that Ellie was secretly excited about a chance to be a princess, that she was inwardly greedy, grasping for the power of the throne.

I supposed I'd wanted to absolve myself of the guilt of ruining her life by proving she secretly wanted this.

I'd been wrong, of course.

That was a pattern, apparently.

Still, she'd been a genius in the Trials, and I couldn't help but admire the way her sharp mind had cut a loophole in the rules. How quick she'd been in a pinch.

And then there was the way her heart pounded in delight when I lifted her into my arms, the way her body betrayed her in that moment. She'd been stunning, in more ways than one.

Ellie Payne was a force of nature, resilient and determined and absolutely tenacious, and she deserved better than to be tied to me.

Though if I had to be forced into a marriage with a woman who thought I was an idiot, I'd probably gotten the better half of the deal.

But then Francesca had arrived, and every time I looked at her, something gnawed at my insides. Guilt, perhaps? Either that, or Francesca would say something, and I wouldn't hear her because I'd been too busy thinking about something Ellie had said at dinner.

In the end, I'd sent her home, spouting a flurry of awkward apologies about calling on her so late in the evening.

I didn't quite understand why I'd done it.

All I knew was that Francesca Aberdeen was not the female I'd wanted in my bed.

When I woke the next morning, I had an idea.

"So what? You just snap your fingers, and glassblowing workshops magically appear?" Ellie asked as we stepped into the abandoned barn on the West End of Othian Castle.

"Something like that." When she shot me a knowing glare, I couldn't help but grin. "Okay, maybe I don't snap my fingers. Maybe I ask very nicely and promise a handful of servants a generous Lunar Eclipse bonus, and then the workshop appears. Within three to five business days."

Ellie shrugged, hugging herself as she examined the workshop I'd gotten the idea for a few days ago. Unfortunately, my father was still denying Ellie a key to her room, but at least she could come here and work as long as she had an escort. I'd had the servants install multiple furnaces. Apparently the materials needed to be heated to different temperatures throughout the glassmaking process. The furnaces were already blazing, lighting up the abandoned barn and making me thankful I'd asked the servants to wipe the place of cobwebs. There were all sorts of other metal tools organized neatly, some on stands, others resting in iron bins.

"What do you think? Is this a conducive environment for Elynore Payne to work?" I asked.

Ellie bit her lip, and her shoulders dropped slightly. For a moment, I thought I must have placed the wrong artisan in charge of designing the workshop, that something was amiss and would cause it to be unusable, but then Ellie surprised me.

"It's...It's very nice. Well thought out, even down to where the furnaces are placed. It'll make moving from station to station easy." She paced toward what looked to be a long metal poker and picked it up, turning it over in her palms. "And the tools are good quality." She turned to face me, and in the flicker of the furnace light, I caught the way the edges of her lips twitched.

Like she was battling back a smile.

170

Elynore Payne might have been a formidable opponent to most, but she was going to lose that fight.

I'd make sure of it.

"Admit it," I said. "I did a good job."

"I thought you said your servants did all the work."

"Hm."

All right, so perhaps coaxing a smile out of her today was going to be more difficult than I'd anticipated. Challenge accepted.

"So where do we start?" I asked, striding up next to her and prying the metal prod from her hands. I took care to make sure my fingers lingered on hers as I did, and derived no small amount of satisfaction when her pulse skipped.

Ellie swallowed, tucking her dark ringlets behind her ear. Fates, she was pretty. The canary yellow day dress she wore was simple, yet it suited her. Her eyes were wide, a warm brown with tiny golden flecks around the edges.

Yes, Ellie Payne was very, very pretty.

"We?" she asked. "I wasn't aware you dabbled in glassblowing."

"Oh, I don't. Dabble, I mean. That's why you're going to teach me."

"REMIND me why you want to learn glassblowing again," Ellie said, not bothering to mask the suspicion in her tone as she peered over me, watching me spin a red-hot bulb of molten glass stuck to the end of a metal rod (which was called a blow pipe, according to Ellie) against a shaping mold. She was so close, I could feel the warmth of her breath.

Which would have been pleasant, had that breath not been directed down the back of my shirt collar as she reminded me what I was doing wrong.

This might have been my third attempt at forming a glass bulb. Ellie was of the opinion that I talked too much and let the glass cool too quickly before applying another layer of molten glass and returning to the furnace.

"I want to learn glassblowing because it's about the only skill I've yet to master," I said, unable to help but notice her pleasant scent—

fresh rainwater and lavender—even as it mingled with the cinders from the furnace.

She snorted, which I found adorable. Females of fae nobility never allowed themselves to snort. "I highly doubt this is the only one left."

"Try me."

"Sailing?"

"A solo trip across the Adreean on my sixteenth birthday."

"Taxidermy?"

"Unfortunately. One is not reared under the strict hand of my father without being forced to shoot and stuff one's own wall decorations."

I took my gaze off my glowing bulb for a moment to find Ellie grimacing.

She chewed her lip, staring me straight in the face as she pondered. "Playing the harp?"

"Unless you've invented a musical instrument I'm unaware of, you'll be hard pressed to find one I can't maneuver."

"What about magic? I thought the royal family had power over plants, but I haven't seen you use it," she asked.

"My sister Olwen's the magic-wielding prodigy in the family. I've never been much good at it."

"So you don't use it?"

"Do you enjoy tasks you're not skilled at, Ellie Payne?"

She cut her pretty brown eyes to the side, eyeing my misshapen orb. "You let it cool off again."

I tilted to the side, leaning into her. "What can I say? I find you distracting."

Ellie swallowed and directed me to start over.

By my fifth attempt, Ellie was tapping her foot against the ground, tugging at her skirt like she was trying to give her hands something to do other than rip the blow pipe directly out of my hands.

On any other occasion, I might have been annoyed by this, except that I'd let the fourth bulb cool on purpose.

"All right, you've got it this time. Just don't get distracted talking, and I'm sure this will be the one." Ellie scratched the stretch of skin under her jaw, as if watching me work was giving her hives.

"Perhaps it's not me that's the problem. Have you considered that it could be your teaching style?"

By the look on her face, Ellie clearly had not. "My teaching style? I'm telling you exactly what to do. You're just not listening."

I'd never had to fight that hard to suppress a grin. "I'm more of a hands-on learner myself."

Ellie's throat bobbed, and she took half a step away from me.

"But if giving verbal instructions is the only way you're comfortable teaching, then I underst—"

She flicked her wrist, banishing the rest of my sentence. My lungs were shaking now with the effort of holding back a laugh. Then, to both my eternal amusement and utmost disappointment, she shuffled around to the other side of me so she could place her hands on the rod while still being able to maintain space between us.

"See, you have to keep turning it consistently so the bulb with stay even."

"Got it," I said, turning the rod much faster than would be to her liking.

"Well, I suppose that's consistent, but—"

"I think we're in need of a demonstration," I said, passing the rod to Ellie. When the weight settled into her fingertips, her shoulders loosened, and the relief in her cheeks was palpable.

Then I wrapped my arms around her from behind, and every last fiber of Ellie Payne's body went rigid.

"I thought you said you needed a demonstration," she said, her tone warbling, but she made no move to push me away.

"No," I said, nuzzling in close so she could hear my low whisper. Her breath hitched as my lips brushed her ear. "I said *we're* in need of a demonstration. I'm demonstrating to you how to properly demonstrate."

When I pressed my chest to her back, the rod in her hands began to tremble. I let my fingers trail down her arms before letting them rest over her hands, my grip steadying the rod.

"Ellie Payne?" I asked, dragging my thumb across her fingers, noting every dip, every ridge.

"Yes?" she answered, her voice hardly audible.

"I think I'm ready to learn now."

CHAPTER 23

ELLIE

"Ou're going to give me hives with all that jittering of yours. I'm allergic to anxiety."

Blaise stared at my fingers, which were tapping against the library table where we were supposed to be studying decorum, with a look of revulsion.

"I'm not anxious," I corrected. "I'm just unable to ignore the fact that my father, who typically depends on my labor to fulfill his orders, is now short a pair of hands."

That wasn't entirely true. Evander and I had spent the better half of the day yesterday crafting windows, which he'd promised would be delivered to my father this week. Evander had said that in my free time, I was free to use the workshop, but given the reason Blaise and I were currently in the library, I didn't know how much free time I'd actually have.

Besides, the king still hadn't allowed me a key to my room, so I would have to have someone from the palace escort me anytime I wished to use the workshop.

I also had a feeling that my jittering wasn't isolated to my concern that my father's business might crumble. The phantom heat of Evander's chest permanently seared into my back, his fingers caressing mine as we maneuvered the blow pipe, likely also had something to do with it.

"There's a word for that, you know?" Blaise said, saving me from unwittingly replaying my and Evander's interaction in the sweltering workshop for the seventy-eighth time.

I raised an eyebrow. "I do?"

"It's called anxiety." Blaise rolled her eyes, then flopped her hands onto mine dramatically.

She'd been assigned to me for the afternoon with the task of preparing me for the queen's luncheon tomorrow. The queen herself was busy with preparations and, though she was the one requiring me to attend, she couldn't seem to be bothered with helping me navigate the tedious rules of high society.

So they'd made Blaise do it, who I was fairly sure wouldn't know decorum if it sniffed at her with an upturned nose while drinking bland tea, pinky-up.

Blaise slammed the book in front of her, the one we'd gotten about three pages into.

That was fine with me. I might not have been of royal blood, but my father's income kept us if not in high society, then at least adjacent to it. Our neighbors had never considered us truly wealthy. For some reason, it was more notable to have had money handed to you by your parents than to earn it yourself. But still. I knew a thing or two about which side of my plate the salad fork should go.

It was the left, by the way.

"We've got to find you something to do. I'm already going to hear your fingers tapping in my sleep. I'd rather it not persist to my grave."

My jaw hung open a little, and I considered spitting back a retort, but then again...

It really would be nice to have something to do other than want to claw my ears out as Blaise droned on reading the *Handbook for Proper Ladies* aloud.

"Fine," I said, wrestling the book from Blaise before she drooled on it, or worse. I rose and tucked the book safely back into its place on the library shelf and approached her. "What do you propose we do?"

Blaise brightened at that, her rusty brown eyes practically gleaming with mischief.

Blaise wasn't what I would consider a pretty girl—at least, not when I'd first met her. But when she smiled at you like that, like there was nothing in the world she'd rather be doing than doing nothing by your side—I could see why the servant boys, and even some of the fae courtiers, fell all over her.

"Glad you finally asked."

I WOULD NOT HAVE THOUGHT that the King of Dwellen would allow such a thing as a servant girl *fencing*, especially while borrowing from the king's personal store of equipment, but according to Blaise she did it all the time.

I didn't believe her until she jabbed me in the crook of my shoulder before I even had time to flourish my weapon.

"Ow," I said as she pulled her helmet over her face, imitating me.

The courtyard had warmed in the midday sun. I might have flopped on the ground and soaked it up were I not so busy dodging Blaise's attacks. Still, there were bumblebees flitting between the tulips that decorated the grounds, and the breeze was ruffling the grass, and I couldn't have been more content.

We must have looked ridiculous. Well, Blaise certainly looked ridiculous. The fae were so large, there hadn't been a single adult fencing outfit for either of us to fit into back in the changing rooms. Blaise hadn't seemed worried about it, and she'd tossed me an outfit, telling me it was made for fae children, but that it would most likely fit.

Fit turned out to be a loose interpretation of the word. The white fabric was snug, but whatever fae material it was made of stretched. So there was that.

Blaise's hung off her slight frame instead of clinging to it, and the metallic mesh that shielded our faces while still allowing us to see one another left her looking like little more than a pale shadow.

A *fast* shadow. She moved in a blur of white and struck my belly this time.

I narrowed my eyes.

"Again?" she asked.

I nodded. This time when she struck, I was ready, and though I had few skills as far as sword play was concerned, I at least had the wherewithal to block her blow.

"Nice," she said. "Where'd you learn that?"

"Put my stick in front of your stick. It's not that difficult to intuit."

To my surprise, she laughed, her pale face lighting up.

"You're funny, Ellie Payne. I might not mind having you around after all."

After that, Blaise seemed more willing to actually explain to me the rules, the moves, and even a few strategies she claimed to have developed herself.

After about half an hour of haphazardly defending her strikes and parrying, I finally landed a blow on her shoulder. "Nice!" she said. "You're a quick learner."

I shrugged.

I didn't realize I'd be any good at hitting another person with a stick.

Then again, this was the first time I'd tried.

Hitting other people in a controlled environment turned out to be rather cathartic.

SWACK. I got Blaise one good time in the chest, and she coughed, a sputtering laugh spilling out of her. "Remind me not to put persimmon juice in your coffee," she giggled.

When she landed a blow to my side that had me clenching my waist, breathless, I said, "Remind me not to make you read boring etiquette manuals."

She laughed at that. "The only thing worse than etiquette manuals are the luncheons you're supposed to show off your skills at."

Apparently, she glimpsed my confusion through my mesh, because she explained, "My father was the king's ambassador to the humans for many years. He wasn't of noble blood, but the king treated him like he was." A sad smile shadowed her face. "He used to dread dragging me to dinners when all the families were invited. I always ended up with pudding on my gown or a slice in my finger or a bug in my hair—though come to think of it, I can't imagine how that was my fault."

I frowned, lowering my sword. "What happened to him?"

She shrugged. "He died."

"I'm sorry."

"And your mother?" I dared to ask.

"Also dead. But she died when I was too young to remember her."

My heart sagged. I wasn't exactly thrilled about my situation—betrothed to an imbecile who was in love with another woman. But at least I had my parents, my mother's warm dimples and my father's constantly consternated brow. Even the thought of them brought a smile to my lips.

I wondered if it still brought Blaise joy to think of her father—if it was bittersweet, or if the pain swallowed up all the good from her memories.

"Do you have anyone else?" I asked.

She shook her head. "No family. Well, not any worth mentioning. I hardly consider them family at all. At least I have Andy, though."

I frowned, confused.

Noticing my expression and realizing that it must have been strange for a servant to consider themselves so close to a prince, Blaise explained, "He and Jerad were always fond of me as a child. They'd entertain me as best they could during dinners so my father could focus on networking with the other diplomats. When my father died, Jerad went to the king and asked for me to be placed in the palace's care. I think Evander would have asked for it too, if he didn't think his presence would foil the chance of Jerad's request being granted. The king wouldn't think of adopting me, of course, but he's allowed me to stay on as a servant ever since."

A pretty horrible servant, at that, I didn't add. But things were starting to make more sense. Like how Blaise got away with doing

T.A. LAWRENCE

little to no work. If her employment was out of respect for her late father—"OW."

A blunt blade to my side wrenched me from my thoughts. Blaise cackled, and I unleashed all my maneuvers upon her—all three of them.

OUR STOMACHS WERE HOWLING by the time we'd changed out of our fencing gear and Blaise took me by the hand, skipping toward the kitchen.

I fought the urge to pull away from her grip. I'd never been one who enjoyed being touched.

Well, except for perhaps that time Evander carried me across the logs, pulling me into his firm chest, but there was no need to acknowledge that, even to myself.

When we reached the bottom of the winding staircase, Blaise released my hand and practically launched herself into the kitchen, pulling pastries and treats from every counter that a servant wasn't actively pulling a tray from.

They must have been preparing for lunch. I'd been having too much fun with Blaise to realize how much time had passed.

Something smacked me in the face, leaving a sticky substance on my cheek as a pastry fell to the floor.

"You were supposed to catch it," was about the only apology I supposed I was going to get from Blaise.

I couldn't say I minded.

"So, what are you going to do once you become queen?" Blaise asked, taking a bite of her fourth pastry and offering me one.

I couldn't stifle the laugh. "No thanks. I prefer lemon scones. And we both know that's never going to happen. The king will live another thousand years and Evander will be on his sixth wife by the time he gets the throne."

"Okay, fine. You'll most likely be cow food before the crown gets

A BOND OF BROKEN GLASS

passed on to Evander." She noted my bristling and smirked. "But hypothetically, if you were queen, what would you do with it?"

I bit my lip. I hadn't considered a question like that before. For some reason, that bothered me. Like the thought should have crossed my mind. Like I should have been channeling my energy into change, into something other than my glassblowing and my—

Blaise's voice cut through the thoughts. "You okay? You look like you're presiding over a rather intense internal trial."

I laughed. "Something like that."

Blaise speared a piece of a nearby cake with her fork and pointed it toward me. "We'll have none of that. The question is supposed to be fun. But since you can't seem to take anything not-seriously"—she swallowed the piece of cake—"we'll have to try another method."

That couldn't be good.

Blaise swung her body up on the counter and let her legs dangle off. "Would you rather—"

I couldn't help it. I was already laughing.

"—use Dwellen's massive treasury to commission a fleet of ships made entirely of glass or purchase a bale of talking turtles from Laei?"

"The glass fleet, obviously."

Her jaw dropped. "Really? You wouldn't even consider the turtles?"

"They freak me out. I don't like thinking about what they look like under their shells."

She waved her hand dismissively. "Right, well, I guess I gave you an easy one to start off with. I was afraid you'd deliberate too much if I gave you something with stakes."

"I'm going to choose not to take offense at that."

"You shouldn't. It just shows that we've been friends for a day now and I already know basically everything about you. We're practically best friends."

The way she said it was so nonchalant, so everyday, like it was common. But it wasn't common to me. I'd had girlfriends growing up, liked the women whose social circles I ran in, even. But the other women always had a way about them, how they could be strangers one moment and the best of friends the next.

That, I'd never understood.

So I'd grown up on the periphery. Well-liked and well thought of, except for my nasty habit of making money for myself, but that wasn't polite dinner conversation anyway.

To be fair, I hadn't exactly been regimented about pursuing those close relationships either. Not when I had my sights set toward the future.

I knew she was teasing, just being informal, irreverent Blaise who probably said something one moment and forgot it the next, but... but still. She'd noted my anxious tapping in the library, my limbs practically dying for something to do, so she'd snuck me into the fencing quarters. I'd thought it was simply a pastime she enjoyed, but was it possible that she'd noticed that I needed something to do with my hands, with my body, or I was going to go crazy?

"Okay," I said, crossing my arms and meeting her challenge. "Since you think I'm not capable of being any fun, what about this? If you were queen, would you rather..." I pondered for a bit, tapping my finger against my chin. "Use up the entire treasury to fund a standing army and have no money left over to fund the roads, or have roads but no standing army?"

Blaise's cheeks sagged, and she ran her hand down her face. "You really don't get the point of this game, do you?"

"Yes, I do. The point is to give a choice between two options that are impossible to choose between, is it not?"

"Yes," Blaise said, sitting up straight. "But the options are supposed to be fun. Not political." She stuck her tongue out as if politics were the opposite of fun.

Before I could respond, she jolted to her feet. "Oh! I've got one. Would you rather fall in love with Evander and get out of your marriage bargain—but you can never be with him? Or would you rather never love him and be stuck married to him for the rest of your life?"

My heart jolted as my mind was swept back to the workshop, to Evander's lips grazing my ear. My grin threatened to falter, but I wouldn't let it slip. Blaise was just trying to have some fun, and she'd provided me not only with an escape from my boring tasks for the day, but also with companionship.

It wasn't her fault that the way my betrothed behaved was…confusing.

She must have sensed my discomfort in the air, because she frowned. "I'm sorry. That wasn't funny. I just—"

"Miss Blaise, why in Alondria are you stuffing your face down here when the foyer is yet to be scrubbed?"

Blaise blanched, and I turned to face the head maid, who nodded at me gently and said, "Milady," before turning her bulging eyes on Blaise.

IN THE END, I helped Blaise scrub the foyers, much to the head maid's horror. I didn't care about her bustling and grumbling, though. Not when Blaise was trying so desperately not to let me see the tears of gratitude constantly trying to slip down her pale face.

CHAPTER 24

ELLIE

I'd anticipated an afternoon of cheap conversation, vain gossip, and prattle regarding the latest fashions.

I couldn't have shown up more ill-prepared.

Imogen was the one who escorted me to the veranda where the luncheon was to be held. Apparently Blaise was still suffering under the stern hand of the head maid, tasked with shining the insides of the metal suits of armor as a punishment for shirking her responsibilities yesterday.

My escort was skittish, and as always, I couldn't decide whether to be annoyed with her nervous energy or pity the poor girl.

I figured pity was a tad kinder, if not also a tad condescending.

"Your hair looks nice," I tried, noticing that she'd styled it differently today, the brownish-blondish knot at the nape of her neck shinier than usual.

"Thank you, milady," she said, bowing slightly, her eyes buzzing about like a pair of bumblebees.

When my attempted conversation died, I pressed, "Are you using a new product?"

"I am."

I took a breath and attempted to steel my patience. Ever since Evander had invited me to his quarters for dinner, Imogen had been short with me—almost unpleasantly so. "Did you buy it at Madame LeFleur's? I know her products are quite popular amongst the women in town."

Also quite useless, but I didn't think Imogen was likely to engage me in such a topic.

She shook her head, almost violently. As if I'd asked her if she drank puppy blood to stay youthful. "No. I wouldn't go there. My stepmother says that woman's a witch."

"Right."

I officially gave up on engaging Imogen in conversation today.

She led me out onto the veranda. The floor was lined with cedar planks, the table wooden as well, though intricate designs of mountain peaks had been carved into its face, likely to represent the Kobii mountains that served as the border between Dwellen and Avelea to the south.

Imogen had delivered me early, as she'd promised. I'd wanted to arrive before the queen's other luncheon guests. Sure, it was uncomfortable sitting around and waiting, but at least if I arrived early, I could greet each lady one by one, learn their names, and tuck the information away.

Perhaps I even had a chance of gaining their approval this way.

Women were like that, I'd decided. It was easier to sidle up to their good graces individually than trying to force oneself into an already familiar group.

Attempting to do so could so easily be interpreted as a wedge.

Plus, arriving early would keep me from the awkward situation of walking in late and having a host of fae females staring at my every asymmetry.

The queen was there when we arrived, her delicate frame like a dewdrop on a leaf, with the veranda overlooking a garden of evergreens that must have been planted to resemble a forest.

She stood at the wooden table, peering over a collection of papers, one hand perched on the wood to support her weight, the other running a finger over the lines as if searching for something.

"Ah!" A self-satisfied grin that reminded me of a hand patting a back broke across her beautiful face.

Only then did she look up to find me standing across the room from her.

Her back stiffened, and though the pleasant smile remained plastered to her face, it dimmed at the edges.

"Ah, you've arrived early. Good. Thank you, Imogen." She nodded to the servant girl, dismissing her.

I fought the urge to clear my throat. Though Blaise and I hadn't gotten very far in the etiquette handbooks yesterday, I was fairly sure it was against decorum for a lady to clear her throat. Unless it was the queen reprimanding someone, of course.

Things had been a bit tense between the queen and me since the night I insulted Evander's reputation in front of her.

That was yet another reason I'd had a bad feeling about this luncheon. Blaise had informed me I'd been personally invited by the queen, and for some reason getting thrown into a pack of hungry fae noblewomen didn't seem like the most benign of invitations coming from someone who already didn't like me.

Perhaps I could prove her wrong.

Her sharp blue eyes took one rushed sweep over my attire, and her throat tightened.

I'd asked Blaise yesterday to find something appropriate to wear for the luncheon. She'd obtained a modern contraption masquerading as an outfit—one she insisted was all the rage in fae social groups.

I hadn't thought to ask her *which* fae social groups.

By the fleeting look over the queen had given me, I was inclined to think it wasn't the royal ones.

The suit was one piece, the top made of two strips of cream-colored linen that were attached to the waistband. Imogen and I had struggled with dressing me this morning, Imogen cursing Blaise under her breath for picking an outfit so unreasonable, then not bothering to be around to help me get into it.

I was inclined to agree.

Finally, we'd decided the material was designed to cross over my chest, intersecting in the front, draping over my shoulders, then crossing again in the back. I was fairly certain that was how it was meant to be worn, with my belly and sides exposed and the rest of the fabric cascading down my back in a sash tied into a bow.

I made Imogen help me wrap my torso in it instead.

By the end, we'd constructed a well-formed bodice I'd thought was rather elegant, in an earthy kind of way.

Perhaps the lower half of the garment was the offensive part. While the taupe fabric flowed loose like a dress, these were most definitely pants. I wasn't accustomed to wearing pants, not even while working in my father's workshop, though now that I'd tried them out I thought I might have to make them a regular piece in my wardrobe.

Just not to be worn at another luncheon, clearly. If I ever got invited to one again.

On second thought, perhaps I should wear pants to every royal gathering I deemed an unpleasant waste of time.

The queen's eyes landed on me, and a somewhat forced smile crossed her cheeks. Not the saccharine smirk of a conniving female attempting to ensnare a young girl with flattery so she could backstab her with little resistance. No, this was the pained smile of a woman who looked as if she were trying to truly force herself to be happy.

Like the queen figured that if she pretended to like me, it would eventually come to pass.

"Our dear Blaise must have picked that out for you, then?" she asked, her shoulders tense, but her voice steady and sweet. "She's always possessed a keen eye for which fashions are about to peak the horizon. I've always been a bit too timid to let her dress me, much to the poor girl's chagrin. You would think by the way she looks at my dresses that I were threatening to bore the girl to death." She flourished at her own gown, and now that she pointed it out, it really was quite simple to be adorning a queen. A rose-blush dress, structured at the bodice with a flowing skirt that revealed little of what I imagined must be a beautiful form. Even her hair was simple, tied in a simple plait that had been tucked underneath itself just behind her left ear. Her fae features might have kept her looking barely older than me, but her dress, her hair, even the way she carried herself, suggested a female from a different time.

"Careful, dear. My other guests have more sense for fashion than I do. They might threaten to rip that right off you." The smile that overtook her face was real this time, a gentle, teasing fondness for a group of females apparently more cutthroat than herself.

While I might have interpreted the words themselves as a threat, coming from the queen's mouth, they sounded more like an invitation.

Guilt twanged in my chest at that thought. I'd given her every reason to despise me, yet she was still trying to get along with me.

"To be quite honest, I would have much preferred your gown to this..." I gestured to my garment. "Whatever this is called. You wouldn't believe the tribulations Imogen and I faced trying to get it on."

At that, a genuine laugh threatened the wrinkles next to the queen's sparkling eyes. "I can only imagine."

The room went quiet, and I felt pressure to keep engaging this female in conversation, lest the opportunity slip away from me. If I were to be her daughter-in-law, stuck in this palace for the rest of my life, I figured it would make life easier if we got along.

She'd never make up for my mother, of course, whom I missed desperately. There was even a pang of guilt in my chest for even attempting to befriend the queen, like I was betraying my mother.

But no, Mother would want me to make the best of an unpleasant situation, so I would.

I could sense the moment fleeing, slipping from my fingertips, so I grasped at the only bit of conversation starter I could find in the vicinity.

I nodded at the pieces of paper on the table. "What were you studying when I interrupted you? You seemed pleased with yourself."

The queen gestured for me to join her side, and I did. The scent of cloves and cinnamon wafted over me as I approached.

Were the fae obsessed with perfume, or did they just come out of the womb bearing their own unique and lovely scents?

Good gracious, just standing next to her gave me the urge to flee back to my rooms and bathe in scented oils, though I'd done so just this morning.

"This," she said, pointing to the paper, "is my cheat sheet."

"I thought the fae had near-perfect memory."

She waved a dismissive hand. "Oh, is that another thing humans have made up about us? They act like we're mystical beings."

"Well, you did enter Alondria from another realm," I said, then as her expression soured, added more meekly, "didn't you?"

"I suppose we did, waltzing into another world like we owned the place." She rolled her eyes, which shocked me a bit. Was that disapproval I sensed in her voice?

"I suppose you do own the place now," I said.

She met my gaze. "Yes, I suppose we do." Her attention returned to the sheet of paper. "Regardless of what the humans make up about us, no, we do not have perfect memory. Which becomes quite the struggle when one lives for centuries. Especially as a queen, when I'm expected to remember the names of a lord and lady I met one time three dozen decades ago."

Even the idea made me want to scratch at my throat, like it was giving me hives.

"So was born the cheat sheet," she said, flourishing at the neatly scribed parchment. Then, with a mischievous glance I'd only ever seen on the face of her son, she said, "After I accidentally mistook a minor lord's wife for his mistress and called her by the mistress's name."

My hand found my mouth as I tried to stifle the bout of laughter.

"No need to hide your amusement on my account, my dear. I was not the one who went home to an empty bed that night." Again, that pleased look crossed her face. Was...was the quiet, austere queen making a joke about... "Still, while I wasn't sorely disappointed in myself for exposing the lord's indiscretions, I decided I'd rather not do so on accident in the future. The wife was quite upset. It would have been better for her to discover it in private..." The queen frowned at the memory, then quickly straightened. She pointed to the column on the left of the page before reciting the intention of each. "Here's the list of each person's name. This is a record of their physical description...much easier with fae than humans. Oh, I can hardly recognize the human ambassadors after a decade of not seeing them. It's mortifying and I've yet to come up with an adequate system for it. And here is where I keep my less than pleasant tidbits of information: affairs, scandals, that sort of thing... I know you're probably thinking I'm horrible, keeping people's darkest secrets here, but I try not to use them unless it's absolutely necessary. They mostly keep me from treading on topics that are uncomfortable and might inhibit trade relations if brought up. You must think me horrible," she repeated.

"No," I muttered, half flabbergasted, half in awe. "No, I don't think that at all. I think it's..." Diabolical? Wonderful? Beautifully organized and intentional and plotted and... "Strategic. I think it's strategic. That has to be a vital part of being a queen, is it not?"

A pleased smile crossed her pursed lips. "Indeed."

I wondered then how many beings she'd shown these records to. Likely very few.

I wasn't sure whether to be honored or debilitatingly horrified, or a little bit of both.

"Oh, and lest you think me a gossip-mongerer, I do keep the pleasant things too. People—human and fae alike—respond well when you take the effort to remember something specific about them. It doesn't even have to be anything profound or amazing. Even a simple recollection that they prefer a specific sauce with their vegetables can go a long way."

"A long way toward what?" I asked.

Again, that naughty grin that strikingly resembled her son shone on her face. "Anything you need it to, my dear."

· · ·

IT SHOWED a great deal of self-restraint on my part that I didn't break out a notepad a quarter of the way through the luncheon and start scribbling notes furiously.

What I had expected from this luncheon was a droning lull of idle chatter, vain gossip, and the endless discussion of whose offspring had recently procreated.

What I got—well, it was still all those things, but underneath the innocuous talk of familial relations and upcoming styles was a battle-field of wits and wagers, and the queen was at the head of the fray.

"Oh, Your Majesty, you remembered my sensitivity to wheat," said the Duchess of Cornwraith as she peered with delight down at a plate that to me, looked very sad indeed without the rolls I'd had to force myself not to devour in one bite.

I also had to fight suspicion from creeping onto my brow, as it seemed quite unlikely to me that beings as healthy as the fae would have food sensitivities.

If the queen was also suspicious, she did not let it show on her face. I'd come to realize it was a mask, carefully crafted over the centuries to be whatever the queen needed in the moment.

I silently encouraged my eyebrows to take notes.

"How could I forget, after that lovely dinner you and the duke hosted at your manor?" the queen said. "I came home and straight away asked my cook if he could recreate that salad simply from my description. Though arrowroot is difficult to get in the city. I inquired, and it seems your province is the only one in all of Alondria where the conditions are right to grow it. I suppose that's why you can charge so much," she said with a wink in her eye.

The duchess nodded smugly.

"Though I have heard Charshon produces it as well, though I can't imagine it's of better quality. We at the castle can afford yours, of course. But I hate that the people of Dwellen can never seem to get their hands on it, and I suppose even a lesser quality crop from Charshon is better than nothing."

The duchess's smile faltered a bit, then quickly regained its bril-liance. "Oh, far be it from us. There's no reason for your merchants to exert themselves and waste a trip to Charshon for their lesser quality crops. I can assure you, my husband would sooner keel over than have Charshon of all places beat us out in trade. And you've been so kind to us, I'm sure we can manage a special price."

The queen clapped her hands together, a charming grin lighting up her face. "Oh, that would be delightful. I cannot wait to see the rush of business it will create for the taverns in town. Everyone will be rushing to get a bite of arrowroot salad, though I imagine none could cook it as well as your staff."

"Indeed, I would think not," said the duchess.

Duchess of Cornwraith—wheat sensitivity; she and her husband were conned by a lord of Charshon in a trade for corn. Their cook makes the best arrowroot salad.

I had to keep my jaw from dropping.

It had been right there, scrawled in the queen's carefully organized notes.

I watched in awe as the queen did it again and again. Kind words here, bringing up an old feud there, until half the females at the table had sworn a better price on crops, a lower fare for using their roads, a lower tariff on imported goods. I wondered how many of these females actually had control over such things, with their husbands holding the true power.

The sparkle in the queen's eyes each time she won one of them over told me they possessed more power than I'd once thought.

Perhaps influence and power were one and the same, after all. Two sides of the same coin.

Only once during the luncheon did the queen seem at a loss for words. She'd been discussing the price of fish with the wife of a coastal lord, and the female, clearly shrewd herself, had reminded the queen that, as theirs was the only fish-heavy coast on this side of the continent, there simply was not enough fish around to lower the prices.

After a game of flattery, the queen had gotten nowhere, and had about given up, when I got the excellent idea in my head that I would go head to head in a verbal sparring with a high fae lady of Alondria.

"What if there was another resource Dwellen could purchase from your shores? One less troublesome to collect, which could be sold at a fine profit?" I asked. "Surely that would help to offset the price of the fish."

The lady eyed me with curiosity, as if noticing me for the first time, which I knew was not the case at all. Everyone had been sneaking glances at Prince Evander's human betrothed all throughout the luncheon, though most had attempted to be discreet about it.

It was sort of impossible to be discreet when *everyone* was staring.

The queen eyed me with a careful suspicion, and though the look made my mouth go dry, I ignored the scratching sensation in my throat and continued. "The eastern shores of Avelea are dense with fossil beaches, are they not?" I asked.

The lady's back was rigid, but she answered all the same. "To our ever-loving detriment, yes. Worthless stretches of land. We can't build there, and the beaches themselves aren't even enjoyable. You can't walk across the sand without slicing your feet."

"Yes, but inconvenient as it may be, the sand from fossil beaches can be used to make glass."

"Glass?" the lady questioned.

I might have been waiting my entire life for that one-word question. "It's similar to crystal, but it's made, not mined. It's frequently used to make windows in Dwellen, and I imagine the trend will spread to the rest of Alondria before long. Right now glassmakers have to import their sand from Charshon."

The lady shot a look at the queen, requesting confirmation.

"It's true. Glassblowing is a thriving business in Dwellen."

"Hm," the lady said. "What a thought. That there's a use for those dreadful beaches of ours all along. My husband will be glad to hear of it, I'm sure."

I tensed with excitement, awaiting her next words with bated breath. Even the queen seemed to be tilted forward in her seat. "I suppose the girl has a point. If it's true...and only if it's true, that sand is as lucrative of a resource as you suggest, the gain our community might receive from trading it could offset the loss from discounting Dwellen's fish."

Well, she referred to me in third person as "the girl," but I would take what I could get.

The look the queen sent my way was a subtle one, one hardly any of the other females at the table would notice.

The queen was like that, I realized. But no amount of subtlety could hide the pride beaming in her eyes.

CHAPTER 25

ELLIE

*A*pparently it was important to the citizens of old that the heir and his betrothed knew one another on a deep emotional level. I actually found this news to be quite progressive of them. Most brides of the pre-faeistic era were such only due to the fact that they had either been kidnapped from a neighboring land or practically sold like property by their fathers.

That didn't mean I didn't think the way they went about it wasn't stupid, though.

I stood not in a stadium this time, but in the king's council room.

Apparently, this was where the Council, the union between all the kingdoms in Alondria, gathered whenever their meetings were to be hosted in Dwellen. The room was vast, with a circular table in the middle large enough to accommodate at least fifty royals. Dark wooden stands fanned the edges of the chamber so citizens could witness the Council's public meetings. Though I couldn't imagine why anyone would want to attend. It seemed to me that any conversation the Council chose to make public was likely scripted and of little consequence.

Now, to sit in on an actual Council meeting? One involving treaties and uprising and trade? That, I might actually enjoy.

Careful, or you might get used to the idea of being queen, a little voice inside my head whispered.

I wondered whether queens were allowed on the Council. Surely some of them were, for the Kingdom of Mystral was ruled by Queen Abra alone. At least, it had been since her husband died a mysterious death that everyone in Alondria knew to be at her hands, though there wasn't any physical proof. Surely she attended the meetings. But with a husband tying me to my status, would I be allowed admittance?

Many things that might not happen at all would have to occur for that to be the case. First, I couldn't die in these Trials. Second, the king would have to die one day in order for Evander to take the throne. Perhaps by then I could convince Evander to bring me along. Though I had little training in politics, I figured I would have ample time to learn, as I couldn't imagine that the entertainment duties of a princess could be all that taxing, especially when the queen already did most of it herself.

What a strange thought.

I was beginning to think of myself as a future princess. And not hating every bit of it.

Well, if my mother had taught me anything, it was that the resilient could always make the best of an unpleasant situation.

Surely that was all it was.

Surely.

I shook the thoughts from my head and returned my attention to the event unfolding before me.

Evander sat on the other end of the table, the crowd encircling us buzzing with excitement. He combed through a pile of letters, though *combed* was probably too strong a word. Instead, he flicked his eyes over the first few lines before tossing the letters to the side. Sometimes it appeared as though he wasn't even reading the letters, just noting their length before disqualifying them.

Clever male.

I couldn't help but smile in anticipation, surveying the edges of his smirk, the corners of his bright eyes, for the flicker of amusement that would surely overcome his face when he found my letter.

The task was simple, and much less dangerous than the previous, thankfully. A scribe had appeared at my door last evening and had informed me I was to dictate a love letter to the prince. The scribe had visited a plethora of other eligible women in the kingdom during the past week and had collected countless love letters.

The idea was that if Evander and I truly knew each other, we would be able to figure out which love letters were written by the other. If we each guessed correctly, we passed the trial. The dictation part was to keep us from recognizing each other's handwriting.

Though even the assumption that we'd written to one another before was laughable.

Evander's eyes lit up and darted across the table to me. He turned his chin to the side and flashed me that dazzling smile, the one where he opened his mouth just barely so his teeth didn't touch. I returned the amused grin, pleased with myself.

Evander held up the single piece of parchment, signaling the scribe to waltz over and select it from his hands.

The scribe took one look at the paper, his eyes flitting with exasperation, before saying, "The first portion of the second trial is complete. The prince has identified his betrothed's letter."

The crowd erupted into a roar, and I wondered not for the first time whose side they were on. Though the Kingdom of Dwellen unanimously hated their prince, they had seemed excited by our success so far. Maybe it had nothing to do with Evander at all. Nothing to do with how fit they found him to inherit the throne, nor how fit they found me. Perhaps they would have cheered just as loudly during the first trial if the two of us had been gobbled up by the myrmecoleon. Perhaps all they wanted was a show, an afternoon of entertainment to distract them from their menial lives.

I tried not to let my bitterness show as the attention of the crowd shifted to me.

My turn.

The pile stood as high as the length of my forearm. I wondered if it would be as easy to spot Evander's letter through the pile as it was for him to find mine. I snuck a peek at him. He pressed his lips together, as if he were trying desperately to hold back a laugh. Warmth and amusement filled my belly at this confirmation that we had both taken the same approach to this task without plotting together.

The crowd went hushed as I opened the first letter, which I found to be ridiculous, since it wasn't as though I was going to be reading the letters aloud. There was no need for the audience to remain silent.

As I unfolded the parchment, I immediately had the urge to toss this paper to the side. The letter was five pages long, written in the scribe's tiny, parchment-saving scrawl. There was no way that Evander had spent this much time on crafting a letter for me. Still, my desire for perfection, my inherent need to be so thorough that I never questioned my own decisions, overcame me, and I felt compelled to read at least a bit of it, just in case the five pages were full of insults.

MY DEAREST BETROTHED,

When I consider all the women of Alondria, the vast number of events that must have occurred—the stolen glances of our great-great grandparents, the decisions of where to live, who to associate with, the millions of seemingly inconsequential moments that had to occur to bring the two of us into this world, to set our paths so that they would cross at the perfect time, so that our souls could collide, so that we could fall so desperately in love...

OKAY, so that one was going in the "not it" pile, for sure. I tossed it aside, trying to suppress a snort, and started on the next few letters.

MY DEAREST BETROTHED,

You are as beautiful as...

I SCANNED the letter to make sure there was nothing in there about me being as captivating as a rhinoceros. When all I found were mentions of sunsets and daisies—my least favorite flowers—I tossed this one aside, too.

The next several minutes were spent in a similar manner. I would open an envelope, find a generic letter that could have been written to anyone and no one in particular, then toss it. One of the letters was actually a poem, an ode to my beauty, and it actually compared my skin to goat's milk, which I couldn't help but think would be offensive even to pale-skinned women. In fact, I was quickly struck by how many of the letters focused on my beauty alone. Even in the letters from men who seemed to have a clue about who I was and what I looked like, I found them all to be empty, devoid of anything substantial, and I wondered how many women in Dwellen received love letters so bland. And if any of them actually enjoyed them.

Not that I minded the occasional appreciation of my appearance. I wasn't that prudish. But still.

The next letter I opened was the shortest one yet.

ELLIE,

Thanks for talking to me the other night. If I'm to be forced into a celibate marriage, I'm glad it's with you.

Not in love,

Your reluctant betrothed

I BURST INTO GIGGLES. I couldn't help it. When I snuck a glance at Evander, I expected to find that mischievous grin. Instead, his lips tugged into the softest, most genuine smile I'd ever seen from him. Something in my chest turned over.

"This is the one," I said, my throat going dry as Evander stared at me.

"You don't wish to look through the others?" the scribe's voice drawled with annoyance. I ripped my eyes away from Evander's smile, at great pains, to answer.

"What, you don't want to have to read this in front of a crowd?" I asked, teasingly. I did feel a little bad for the poor scribe. He'd been sent to fulfill a simple task, but part of the trial included him reading off the selected letters in front of the crowd.

He did not seem the type to find our responses amusing.

"It was painful enough having to listen to the words spout from the two of your mouths the first time," he said before snatching the letter away. I brought my fist to my mouth and pressed my knuckles to my lips to squelch the laughter. If anyone was looking closely, they would have seen the way my shoulders and chest were bobbing in silent cackles.

Though, *someone* was looking.

I knew, because I was looking back.

Evander was silently giggling, too.

The scribe took my letter and moved to face the crowd.

"The heir and his betrothed have succeeded in identifying one another's voices in the letters." While cheers erupted from the audience, I couldn't help but notice that some of the beautiful women in the front row were sighing. I supposed they had been counting on their letters breaking up our engagement so they could have a chance to steal the prince.

A thought battered the inside of my skull.

I could have picked the incorrect letter on purpose.

I could have ended our engagement by failing the trial.

The crowd buzzed. My head, more so. Why hadn't I even considered that? Had I really gotten so tickled and amused by the little joke I'd had the scribe jot down, that I'd completely forgotten that I didn't want to marry the prince?

Was that even true anymore?

My own thoughts tasted like betrayal.

I didn't want to marry Evander. I didn't. I wanted to marry for love, and I didn't love him. And even if I did love him, he was irresponsible and a rake, and would take mistresses. Was probably already taking mistresses, and that wasn't the life I wanted.

Even if he did remain faithful, that didn't negate the fact that he was in love with someone else.

I wanted someone committed to me. Not because they accidentally got stuck with me and were making the best of it. Someone who
would have committed their life to me on purpose. Someone who had
the choice to walk away, but every single day would choose not to.

Someone who loved me like my father loved my mother.

The scribe continued on, but I couldn't hear his words. *You have to
be rational about this*, I told myself. Just because I couldn't see any
immediate danger in this particular task, didn't mean there wasn't
any. If the king had been willing to allow a trial where both his son
and I would have died if we had failed, then why should I assume that
I wouldn't have been killed if I had purposefully sabotaged this trial?

What I had done had simply been subconscious self-preservation.
That was all it was.

That was all it was.

The scribe read off the letter that Evander had written me, and the
crowd gasped, which hurried me back to reality. I chanced a glance at
the king, whose lips were pursed and eyes narrowed in displeasure. I
wondered if Evander would receive a tongue lashing later. Would the
king consider it to be an embarrassment upon the crown?

The grimace currently smearing the king's face answered my
question.

The queen blushed, and when she clasped her hand over her
mouth, I couldn't decide if she was preventing a gasp or a chuckle
from escaping her lips.

Even from the crowd, I could hear a few giggles, a few subdued
bursts of laughter.

At least someone thought it was funny.

Then it was the scribe's turn to read my letter.

My face went hot, my hands clammy. I hadn't considered the fact
that this would be read aloud when I'd dictated it to the scribe. I'd
been secluded in my room for the past few days, except for mealtimes.
Apparently, the lack of socialization had gotten to my head.

I scanned the crowd for my parents, hoping to the Fates they
weren't here to watch me embarrass myself, but no... Only nobility
had been invited to this trial.

The scribe opened his mouth.

My dearest, darlingest, prince,
For what it's worth, you're hotter than your dad.

Evander burst into a proud grin, but he was about the only one. A few stifled chokes of laughter broke the air, but otherwise, the crowd went silent. I told myself I wouldn't look at the king, I wouldn't meet the gaze of the king, but my primal need for self-preservation got the better of me.

I chanced a look and instantly regretted it.

The mild displeasure that had been brewing on the king's face since Evander's letter was read was nothing compared to the shadow that cloaked his face now.

Pure rage. Teeth gritted, eyes blazing.

When I'd first arrived at the palace, I'd found myself on the king's good side.

The cruel smile that curved on his ancient lips might as well have sealed my Fate.

I'd lost the favor of the King of Dwellen, and I would suffer for it.

CHAPTER 26

EVANDER

This was one of those situations where, if Jerad had still been with us, I would have sidled up next to him in the corridor, dangled his favorite pastry underneath his nose, and asked him for a favor.

He would have known immediately what I wanted. It was always the same—there was something I needed from Father that would only be granted if requested by his favorite son.

I couldn't think of a single time when Jerad hadn't come through for me. It didn't matter how petty the request was, or even if it were something so frivolous it was likely to get him stuck mucking stalls for a week. *Our boys need to learn the consequences of a mislaid request,* our father would often say when my mother attempted to intercede for us.

Father preferred Jerad to me, but their relationship wasn't perfect.

Sometimes I'd sit outside the throne room, my ear pressed against the door as they launched into a screaming match over something Jerad couldn't care less about.

But Jerad always convinced him.

Always.

Even if it meant enduring hours of intensive training or a night spent in the dungeon as punishment for asking.

Well, this was one of those big things, and Jerad wasn't around to present my case.

Or, more accurately, to present Ellie's case.

I just had to pray to the Fates I could make him listen.

I'd seen his face at the end of the second trial when the scribe had read aloud that delightfully inappropriate note in front of the crowd.

My father had favored Ellie.

It had taken Ellie ten words to obliterate that favor.

I had to get it back.

I inhaled a ragged, shaky breath and let myself into my father's office.

It was as neat and pristine as he was, marble bookshelves lining the walls, all the books special editions my father had rebound in silver ghost leopard leather to match. The desk in the center of the room was white granite, which would have been a foolish choice for someone less intentional with a quill and ink than my father.

If his verbal words were carefully selected, then his written words were selected like one might appoint officers as personal guards.

The office was beautiful in a sterile kind of way. Also like him.

He didn't look up from his parchment as I entered.

I cleared my throat and received no response.

"Father," I finally said, agitation already setting in. He hadn't even spoken to me yet, and my anger was already simmering. Off to a great start.

He still didn't look up.

"You're angry with Ellie. I can tell."

My father let out a measured sigh before placing his quill back in the ink bottle, folding his perfect, suspiciously not-ink-stained hands together and meeting my stare with a boredom to match my resentment.

There was resentment there too, though, hidden under than unruffled facade. My father wasn't one to flush from embarrassment. Such outward expressions of emotion were deemed beneath him.

So he masked it in the rage reddening his cheeks.

Because, as everyone knows, anger isn't an actual emotion.

That would be feminine.

"Have you come here to defend her? Surely Miss Payne is more fit to such a task."

Like I said, great start.

I breathed through his insult, refusing to allow it to find root. "What do you plan to do with her?"

My question hung there in the silence for a moment, my father letting it, probably reveling in my discomfort. He'd always complained that I was an impatient child, but it wasn't as if he ever tried to accommodate for that.

"Why should you care, my son, my heir?" There was something about that word, *heir*, that he always enunciated like it was an explicative. "You do not wish to marry her, correct?"

I swallowed. "Of course I don't. But that doesn't mean I wish any ill to befall her."

A smile snaked across my father's marble-cut face. "Now, why would you think I intend any such thing?"

I gritted my teeth, fisting my hands to keep them from trembling in rage. "Because I know you, and I know she embarrassed you today."

"Embarrassment does not befit a king. Jerad would have known that."

I couldn't fight back the wince that jolted through my jaw at the sound of his name on my father's lips. "Be that as it may, there's flesh and blood underneath that iron exterior of yours, Father, and there's nothing that makes it past your armor like a few well-placed words."

I thought I sensed my father bristle. Actually bristle. But his face hardened, and I decided it must have been a trick of the light, a game of shadows that his flickering lamp now played.

"Embarrassment does not befit a king, and ill humor does not befit a princess," he said, his smile eerily pleasant, but his jaw bulging as he gritted his teeth all the same.

I let out a scoff. "What do you mean, ill humor does not befit a princess?" My memory flitted back to the first dinner Ellie ever ate with my parents. *I have no desire to flirt with a male with a list of bedmates behind him that could probably span the length of this table.* "I seem to remember you enjoying her ill humor when it was directed toward me."

Again, that eerie smile overtook his face. "You're correct. I find Lady Payne amusing. But the time always comes to put away amusing things."

Put away. I didn't like the sound of that.

"What will you do to her?" I tried to keep my voice steady as I asked, but the edges of a plea dripped through. That wouldn't do. I wouldn't add a single day to Ellie's life by sounding like a beggar.

"Me?" he asked. "I will do nothing."

Yep. I was definitely right to feel that dread pooling in my stomach. As much as my father liked to pretend that he was misunderstood by his younger son, I'd dealt with him long enough to recognize vengeance when it worked underneath the stony cut of his jaw.

I didn't even know what to say. I could ask more questions, but he clearly planned on answering only in vaguely ominous non-answers.

I let out a scoff, one I injected with as much disappointment as I could. It wasn't difficult. I'd hoarded up plenty of it over the past two centuries.

His eyebrow quirked. "You're fond of the girl."

That was it. I exploded.

"Me? *I'm* fond of Ellie? Unbelievable." My fingers ran through my hair of their own accord. "*You're* fond of her, Father. In your sick, twisted kind of way. Or have you forgotten why you denied her request to rid herself of the marriage bond? You spent an hour with Ellie, and you saw in her what you never saw in me."

His face hardened. His pointed ears twitched as he drawled, "And what, exactly, do you think I saw?"

I huffed. "A leader, that's what you saw. You saw vision, and the ability to execute it. You saw a queen. And who could blame you? Anybody would. And yes, she might have offended you today. She might have embarrassed you, though why you allow such an emotion into your heart when you're literally the most powerful being in the kingdom is beyond me. But that fire, that ember of rebellion you witnessed in Ellie today, it's the same spark that feeds her drive, the same spark you admired in her. So no, I won't sit around and let you forget the vision you saw for this kingdom when you laid eyes on her. Because you don't get to have it both ways. You can't admire her strength and cleverness, then punish her for being bold and shrewd. So, no. I'm not in here *defending* Ellie. I'm simply calling to your memory who she's been all along."

My father hardly moved, but his ears twitched.

I held my breath.

"Well, son. It seems you've finally sprouted a backbone after all," he said, his eyes blazing. "I'll spare the girl from punishment."

I let out an exhale just a moment too early, because as soon as I made it to the door, he added, "She and Jerad would have made a good match."

CHAPTER 27

ELLIE

I knew the knock was coming before I even felt footsteps approaching. I knew because I'd been imagining it all afternoon. Though I'd distracted myself with a pile of books I'd requested Imogen fetch me from the library, I hadn't been able to focus on any of them. I'd catch my eyes slipping over the words, realizing after a dozen paragraphs I hadn't retained a word.

I'd been thinking of Evander.

Mostly his smile, those glances we'd stolen during the most recent trial. I'd asked the scribe afterward if I could keep the letter Evander had written me. Judging by how quickly he shoved the letter into my hands, the poor male was glad to be rid of it, as if even holding the letter had soiled his perfectly trimmed fingernails.

I'd pulled out the letter multiple times and read it repeatedly, in between searching for a book that would actually grab my attention. The nuance of the letter brought a renewed thrill to my chest every time, and my cheeks were starting to hurt from smiling. I traced every line with my gaze, well aware the perfect script belonged to the scribe, not to Evander.

It was ridiculous; I knew that. I mean, what woman in her right mind fawned over a letter about a celibate marriage?

Fates, it was practically half-insult.

There was always the interpretation that Evander was glad that our marriage would be celibate, the subtle jab that he abhorred me physically. But that was half the fun of it, for I knew now that he'd never say something so unkind if it were actually true. Not now that we'd become friends.

And I liked being his friend.

That was what I told myself, at least.

After all, friendship was all the note promised. The insinuation being that, should we be forced into marriage, we would likely become the best of friends, one another's confidants. The ones that made the other laugh, that knew the other's most precious secrets.

I had known of more amorous marriages that had gone poorly for a lack of companionship.

Making the best of our situation. That was what we were doing. That was all we were doing.

I meandered over to my desk.

Several times today, I'd pulled out my quill with the intention to write my parents, but I'd only succeeded in ruining half a dozen sheets of parchment.

There was so much to tell them, but each time I started, I found my pen had a tendency to make all the sentences start with "Evander." And that would not do.

They hadn't been allowed to attend the second trial, as it had been an exclusive event for fae nobility. As much as I would have loved to see them, I couldn't help but be a little relieved that they weren't there to hear the contents of my and Evander's letters.

They'd read about them in the papers tomorrow, of course. But I wouldn't have to witness that, would I?

I was just about to begin a letter focused entirely on explaining my developing friendship with Blaise when the knock sounded on my door.

I jolted from the desk and stuffed both Evander's letter and the letters I'd drafted to my parents under my pillow.

"Yes?" I called.

"My dearly betrothed, would you please let me in?"

"Oh, gladly, my beloved," I called, giggling with the ridiculousness of it all. Again ignoring the rush that shimmied down my spine when he had called me his betrothed.

Evander strode in, dressed in an outfit similar to the one in which he'd competed during our first trial. Imogen stood behind him in the shadow of the doorway, peering in nervously. She watched as Evander plopped himself onto my bed, sprawling his legs out like a cat that might fall asleep in the sun.

"You know, if you want a mattress like mine, I'm sure no one will deny you," I teased. "There's no need for you to continue to bother me and pretend you enjoy my company."

He rolled over on his side and propped his head on his hands. "Actually, I have every reason to visit. In fact, I believe it's the other way around. I pretend to enjoy your mattress as an excuse to come see you."

My teasing grin faltered as something quite unwelcome whooshed in my stomach. My face went hot, and I struggled to hide my reaction underneath the ruse of flirting. "Not every young woman is interested in such persistence, you know. It might do you good to learn to take a hint. Maybe if you had, you wouldn't be trapped with me to begin with."

I measured my words, the look on his face—fearful that I had gone too far, teased him about too sensitive a topic. But he searched my expression, my nose, my mouth, with those blazing sea-green eyes of his for a moment before a knowing look spread across his face.

"If, by that, you mean to accuse me of not being able to take a hint when my mystery woman fled from me at the ball, I choose to interpret that as a sign of your jealousy regarding my affections for another woman, and consider it the utmost flattery."

I rolled my eyes and chanced a playful shove at his shoulder, noting where my fingers met solid rock as I did. "You're insufferable."

"And yet, you choose to suffer me. I wonder why that could be."

That gave me the footing I needed. "Oh, I don't know. Perhaps it has something to do with the fact that my body will strangle me to death if I don't."

Evander shrugged. "Say what you will, but I know the truth."

I opened my mouth to respond. *And what might that be?* But I thought better of it.

"So, why did you come here?"

"I wanted to ask you to go on a walk. And to prove I'm not entirely lacking in the gentleman department."

"It's a little too late for that."

"But I can try, can I not? Go on a walk with me?"

That last question sounded a bit too earnest, and the eagerness in his boyish expression twisted at my chest.

I did wish to stretch my legs, to let out some of the nervous energy that had bounded my chest all afternoon since the trials.

"I suppose your company is a smidge more entertaining than counting the notches on my bedpost."

Regret swarmed my stomach as soon as the words had fallen from my stupid, traitorous lips. *Why? Why did you have to select that particular string of words, Ellie?*

Delight twinkled in Evander's eyes, and I shoved my hand over his mouth. "Don't you dare comment on that."

True to his nature, Evander bit me.

I EXPECTED Evander to take me to the gardens to walk, so I was surprised when we turned toward the woods at the back of the castle walls instead.

"Do you intend to lure me out here to murder me?"

He shrugged. "If I'm still in the mood for it when we get there."

I laughed, overly aware of the timid presence that followed us from behind.

Evander turned to face my maid—well, one of my maids. She'd informed me earlier that Blaise was sleeping in. Apparently it was indeed possible for a person to sleep past lunch. "You may leave,

Imogen," he said, then he turned to me with a polite nod, "If the lady allows it, of course."

I weighed the possibilities in my mind as Imogen widened her eyes. If dining alone with Evander was improper, traipsing through the woods with him alone was downright inappropriate. Scandalous, even. If Evander's suspicions about Imogen were true, which would torture her more? Chaperoning us all afternoon? Or sending her away, forcing her to spend hours letting her imagination run away with what we might be doing together alone in the woods?

Her fears weren't rooted in reality, of course. Evander and I had become friends, sure, but nothing more. Though I had grown fond of him and even allowed myself to admit there was a bit of attraction there, that didn't change our situation. I wouldn't be handing my heart on a platter to a being who had bedded more suitors than I had friends. Mostly since he'd given me no indication he intended to cease the habit once we wed. We could be friends within a forced marriage, sure. But I would protect my heart at all costs.

I gazed at Imogen, noted the horrified look on her face, the tenseness that seemed to exude from her, and decided that I didn't need that kind of energy following me around like the shadow of a storm cloud on such a beautiful afternoon. If she allowed herself to dream up that something more was occurring than was, that was not my responsibility. I had no control over her thoughts. "You're dismissed for the afternoon, Imogen."

She glanced back and forth between me and Evander, eyes wide, then curtsied and shuffled off.

My heart sank. I hoped she wasn't going off to hide and cry somewhere.

"I know you're fond of her," Evander said, "but if you allow yourself to feel guilty for crushing the heart of every woman who fancies themselves in love with me, you're going to have to bear the responsibility of quite a lot of tears that aren't yours."

I couldn't help but snort. "How humble you are."

Evander grunted. "I don't mean that I'm deserving of every woman's love and affection. Only that there are plenty out there who believe themselves to be deserving of mine. Never mind the fact that none of them actually know me. Not really."

"Oh," I said, embarrassed that I had, again, assumed the worst.

He shrugged. "It's fine," he said, though I hadn't actually apologized.

We strolled in silence for a moment until we reached the edge of the woods. The trees cast shade over the ground, and as we continued on, the gentle breeze invigorated my blood, which had felt like it had gone stagnant from being trapped inside the castle for the last few weeks. My mind dwelled on what he had said. Something about his tone had made me wonder...

"Are they true? The rumors?" My words echoed off the forest canopy, and Evander didn't look at me for a moment. My face went hot, and I was grateful for the songbirds who filled the space left agape from my inappropriate question.

"Which rumors?" he finally asked, that smug grin plastered across his face. But nothing about his green eyes glinted. How many years had he spent perfecting that mask, only to miss the most telling part?

Eyes did not lie, and there was no tricking them into it.

"The ones about your reputation."

He stepped in front me of, stopping me in place as he leaned in close, much too close, tilting his head so that his lips lingered just above my forehead, a blade's width away from brushing my skin. "Why do you ask?"

My blood went hot as my heart pounded. His breath was warm and soft on my face as he inched closer.

I cleared my throat and stepped back. "Stop trying to deflect."

The seductive look drained clean from his face. Only annoyance was left over. He stepped back and placed his hands in his pockets. He started walking backward, and I followed him, refusing to let him avoid answering me that easily.

"If you mean the rumors that I take a different female to bed every evening, then no."

Heat flushed my face as my throat tightened in discomfort.

"Embarrassed?" An almost mean-spirited smile spread across his face. I swallowed. I didn't like that look on him. The way his perfect features formed into a sneer looked too terrifying. Too real.

I straightened my back. "Yes, actually. But I thought I'd risk the embarrassment to give you a chance to talk about it."

Confusion softened his stare. "Why would you think I wanted to talk about it?"

"I don't know. Maybe because I just figured I wouldn't like it much if my sexual history was being gossiped about by people who didn't even know me."

"Do you even have a sexual history?" he asked, his lips forming into a sneer yet again. But instant regret twitched at the edge of his smirk, and he frowned. "I apologize. That was unkind."

But I was prepared for it this time.

"No, but I'd rather people not talk about that, either. And I'd especially not like them making up rumors."

He shrugged and turned, walking further into the woods. I followed him as we cut through the brush. The forest was beautiful. Pine needles brushed my cheeks as we walked, and there was an impressive lack of thorns in the bushes. Ivy clothed the thick tree trunks, and when I imitated Evander, who grazed the trees with his outstretched fingertips, I found the surface to be as soft and inviting as a homespun quilt.

After a long silence, he spoke. "There's probably more truth to it than simply gossip, though people do like to exaggerate." He turned to look at me, and his shoulders sloped as he sighed. "There's something about realizing that you're immortal. As a child, you think it's a blessing. But when your mind finally works out its own thoughts, you start to realize there's a weight to eternity. That, even though the possibilities seem endless, there's not really a potential for limitless pleasure. Eventually, I'm going to run out of the things that bring me enjoyment. That's the thing about thrills—they have a tendency to grow dull so very quickly. But pain, El? There's an infinite amount of pain to be suffered."

My heart sank, and I wondered if he was thinking of his brother.

As if reading my thoughts, he said, "I don't know if it was as bad for my brother. He had a purpose, at least. Something to work for, people entrusted to him. I always thought it was an illusion—that his life had meaning—but I was jealous of it all the same. So, for a long while, I drowned the pointlessness and the emptiness with the parties and the so-called friends and the countless females."

"For a while?" I asked. Were the rumors no longer true? They had sure seemed true, the way Evander talked to me that night he first came to visit my room. In fact, he had actively worked to perpetuate that persona.

"After Jerad died, I threw myself into that life more than I ever had. There's something about it that's numbing. And it was nice to be numb for a while. But then." He looked at me, clenched his teeth, and swallowed. "But then, one day, it wasn't so nice anymore."

I nodded, mostly because I didn't know what to say. The silence surrounding us went thick, which was probably why I asked, "And Blaise?"

Evander frowned. "What about her?"

I chewed my lip. "The two of you seem close."

Evander practically gagged. "I've known Blaise since she was a toddler. She's like my sister. An even better one than my actual sister."

The way his tone soured when he spoke of Olwen, his sister who was rumored to now reside in a tower crafted of vines after refusing to go forth with the marriage arrangements King Marken had prepared for her, I didn't think it best to pursue the subject. The papers made it seem like Evander and Olwen had never gotten along, and the way his jaw clenched at the thought of her, I was inclined to think the articles weren't simply hearsay.

"I figured," I said, returning the conversation back to Blaise, "but you never know."

Evander crinkled his nose as if I'd presented him a rotten spud. He cleared his throat. "Do you have someone back home? Someone you love?"

The question startled me, especially since I hadn't expected the conversation to turn so quickly to me. Not after what the prince had just confessed.

"Um, no."

"Are you telling me the truth?"

"Yes, why wouldn't I?"

"So you've never had anybody? Loved anybody?" he asked. "No rugged window-installation man you had your eyes on? Anyone like that?"

"No," I said, laughing. "My father installs all the windows. Besides, I've been too busy with my glassmaking. I love it. And, well…" I paused, not sure that I was ready to reveal the next bit.

He cocked his head to the side. "What?"

"Well, I guess I've been waiting until my business takes off, until I have some real money to my name, to worry about it."

He raised an eyebrow. "Don't your peers typically solve the problem the other way around?"

"Well, yes. But I didn't want to have to marry for money. I wanted to marry for love. And I figured if I had the money to support myself, I wouldn't have to worry about money being a barrier."

"Huh," he said.

"What?" I asked, suddenly embarrassed.

"Marriage for love…" He grinned. "What an interesting notion."

I rolled my eyes. "Oh, don't act as if you couldn't have married for love if you had wanted to."

"I tried, didn't I?"

"Well, yes. Let me rephrase that. Don't act as if you couldn't have married for love if you had wanted to and been smart about it."

"Ouch."

"Well."

"Why do you think I was free to marry for love?" he asked.

The question surprised me. Why couldn't he see it? "Because you're one of the richest people in the kingdom. Money isn't an object for you."

He laughed. "Is that really what you think?"

"Isn't it the truth?"

"Ellie, you have to understand, the rich hardly get away with marrying for love, even if they think that's what they're doing."

"Why not?"

He threw his hands into the air. "Because everyone wants us for our money!"

I shrugged. "Then just find someone who already has plenty of money, and it won't be an issue."

He plucked a leaf from a tree branch above us and brushed my nose with it. "That's not how this works."

I jerked away from the leaf tickling my skin and stopped. "Then pray tell me how it works, exactly."

"It's not like really rich people get to a certain amount of money and then decide they're satisfied with it. It doesn't matter how rich a rich person is, they need for that wealth to grow and grow, otherwise they feel like it's slipping away from them. So no, I couldn't have just picked a wealthy woman. Then it would have certainly been for the money."

"That doesn't make any sense. Why would you need more wealth when you already have more than you could ever hope to spend?"

"Security, Ellie. It's all about security."

"Security?" I laughed. "Is having castles and servants and enough gold to fill the Gulf not enough?"

He shook his head and smiled. "Nope. Never."

"But to be as rich as you, these women could lose, what, ninety percent of their wealth and still be clothed and fed with a roof over their heads?"

"How would you feel if I asked you if I could cut off your pinky toes?"

"I'd rather you not."

"Why not?"

"Because it would hurt."

He shook his head. "No, women choose to go through childbirth all the time. So it's not the pain. It's because you're used to having it. Used to living with it. Used to how it keeps you balanced and from toppling over. Sure, you could live without it. But you're not *used* to living without it. It's a part of you."

I crossed my arms. "That's not a perfect analogy for so many reasons. I wouldn't even know where to start."

He shrugged. "Still. It's like that for the upper class. Our money defines us. That's why we can't marry one another for love. There's always some business transaction going on underneath the surface, even if it's subconscious. That's why I was so thrilled to find someone of no material or social consequence at the ball."

"You mean the same person who stole my property so she could fake being rich?" I asked. "Yes, I'm sure your money never crossed her mind."

"Yeah, well, maybe she thinks similarly of you."

I huffed in exasperation. "And why would she have any right to think that?"

A wicked grin spread over his face as he shrugged. "Oh, I don't know. You did steal her man, after all."

WE ALMOST MADE it out of the forest without me asking a question I'd regret.

Almost.

Speckles of light snuck through the jagged spaces between the overhead leaves, raining sunlight upon us. Through the brush I caught a glimpse of the open gardens. Tall sunflowers, so easy to spot from a distance, waved in the breeze.

I wasn't sure why I asked it. Probably because Evander and I were alone, away from prying ears, and though I was to be his wife, I wasn't confident of how many more moments like this we would get.

"How did he die?"

Evander went still. The fae kind of still, like a leopard waiting to strike.

I got the instant urge to apologize, but I bit my lip, allowing the silence to linger between us. It wasn't simple curiosity that had me asking.

It was the way he'd talked earlier, of needing to numb himself to the pain of his brother's loss. It was the way there was a mystery surrounding his brother's death, one the papers could only speculate about.

Secrets were venom. And Evander had a secret.

Finally, he sighed, tucking his hands behind his head without looking at me.

Then, with less emotion than I thought possible, he told me.

"Jerad never celebrated himself. It didn't matter how far he advanced in the military, how many medals he received. He never let himself have any fun. His birthday rolled around, and we hadn't celebrated it in years, so I hounded him until he went camping with me. He never drank. Always said it made him feel vulnerable. But I convinced him, kept pushing the ale on him until neither of us could put a foot in front of the other. Or so I thought." He ran a hand through his hair, still looking straight ahead. "When I woke up the next morning, he was gone. I thought he'd gone to relieve himself or something, but when I called his name..." He swallowed, his voice eerily even.

My pulse raced, my stomach aching, and I opened my mouth to tell him he didn't have to finish the story if he didn't want to, but he simply said, "I found him at the bottom of a ravine."

Horror gripped me, and I couldn't help but clamp my hand over my mouth.

"He was dead," he added, as if that needed to be said. "I guess he wandered off in the middle of the night and was too drunk to realize he'd come to a ledge."

I didn't know what to say, couldn't formulate words. But I couldn't just do nothing. At least, my body didn't seem to think so, because before I knew what I was doing, I had wrapped my fingers into his.

He blinked, clearly surprised, and stared down at our interlocked hands.

Embarrassed, I made to take my hand back, but he only gripped it tighter. Not tight enough to hurt. More like a plea than a command.

"Don't bother telling me it's not my fault. The people who know what actually happened—my father's advisors—they're always saying that. That it wasn't my fault. Funny thing is, I never said that it was."

"Don't worry. I won't."

His sea-green eyes finally flickered over to me, and a pained smile broke the edges of his lips. "Well, at least you're honest with me."

I frowned. "That's not what I meant. I only meant that it wouldn't do you any good. You're going to blame yourself whether it's rational to or not."

He exhaled a long breath. "How optimistic of you to say." But then he smiled, more genuinely this time. "It is refreshing, though. That you get that."

"What do you think your brother would think about the situation, if he were here to talk to you about it?"

"I don't think he'd exactly be happy about being dead."

"I know. But what would he say about your part in it?"

Evander leaned up against a nearby tree, taking my hand swinging in his as he did.

He didn't let go.

Then he closed his eyes, straining a smile. "He'd probably say, 'This is what I get for breaking the rules.' Claim that he should have known better or something. He was always complaining about that. About all the crap I pulled without getting caught, where if he snuck an extra roll from the dinner table, Mother would sniff it out."

We didn't talk much after that, and only when the sun began to set and a chill began to sweep through the forest did he slip his hand from mine.

EVANDER RETURNED me to my rooms, and my heart sank a bit as I watched him unlock the door with the heavy brass key. As was his custom, he'd borrowed it from Blaise before he invited me on the walk, and as was her custom, she'd threatened him within an inch of his life if he didn't bring it back.

Apparently Blaise didn't have much confidence that Imogen would let her use her copy of the key should she need it.

Of course, Imogen had arrived at my door soon after Evander came to get me, so it hadn't ended up mattering.

The lock clicked, and the door swung open.

I entered my room, noting the bright swaths of sunlight that brightened the blue wallpaper and shimmered against my silver bedspread.

Evander lingered, propping himself against the doorpost. He crossed his arms, the deep cut of the muscles of his forearms visible where he'd rolled up his sleeves.

"What is it?" I asked, suddenly suspicious of the careful way he was eyeing me.

"Promise you'll stay?" was all he asked, his sea-green eyes gleaming as his voice deepened an octave.

My mouth went dry, my lips fumbling for words. "I don't really have a choice, do I?"

He shrugged, and it was as if I'd imagined the intensity in his stare. He dangled the key before me, its metallic sheen gleaming in the light coming in from the window. "I mean if I leave this here, you won't run off, will you?"

I went to snatch the key, but he caught my wrist with his free hand. As fast as he'd grabbed me, his touch was just as gentle as he pressed the key into my palm.

I found it was difficult to breathe.

A lazy grin spread across his face, and before he could say something that would inevitably hurt my feelings, I cut him off. "Wouldn't the fae bargain suffocate me if I tried to run away?"

Evander returned to crossing his arms, and I felt the absence of his touch more than I should have. "Maybe. Maybe it would think you were trying to refuse the bargain. Or perhaps it would think you'd gone out to town to purchase me a lavish wedding gift."

I turned the key over in my palm, the cool metal like a gentle breeze against my fingertips. "Is that your plan, then? Gift me a key so I'll run away, accidentally kill myself by refusing the bargain, and rid you of me once and for all?"

I waited for Evander to confirm it, to parry with some teasing insult, but it never came. When I met his gaze, there was something uncharacteristically earnest in the way the edges of his eyes creased, the way his jaw clenched ever so slightly.

"You won't try to run," he said. "You're too smart for that, anyway. I'm just tired of you being caged up. That's all."

A lump in my throat swelled, and I opened my mouth to thank him as I clutched the key to my chest, but he was already gone.

CHAPTER 28

A cool shudder snaked the plain girl's spine as the moonlight delivered control of her body, authority over her mind, to the parasite.

The parasite sighed, stretching out her limbs as she always did, cranky and weary and tired of being stuffed away into the suffocating mental prison that encroached on the back of the plain girl's mind.

She didn't bother looking into the mirror that perched atop the vanity across the small bedroom before she shifted.

Bones cracked. Skin stretched. Muscles bulged in an instant.

Ah, here we are, the parasite thought, unable able to help herself now as she glanced into the mirror.

The woman who stared back at her was the definition of modern beauty. Large, bright eyes. Thick eyelashes. Full lips. Smooth, blemishless skin matched with curves for days.

The parasite couldn't help but admire her handiwork.

Things had not gone entirely according to plan, but during the past mooncycle, while the parasite had been tucked away, locked up, she had not wasted the passing of time by sulking.

She'd done as she always had.

She watched. She listened. She lurked.

The ball had gone smoothly enough. It had taken little more effort than crossing the prince's line of vision to catch his attention. Far less effort to hold it.

A dazzling, wanton grin had crossed his handsome face at the sight of her. In less than the time it took for the parasite to breathe, he had been before her, taking her hand in his and kissing her palm.

He'd asked her to dance, and she'd offered a delicate smile in response.

Then he'd whisked her onto the dance floor, and that had been that.

Except that *hadn't* been that.

The parasite had attended the ball with a singular focus: seduce the prince into offering her his hand in marriage. She'd had to make the brief encounter count, for she knew she only had hours until she transformed back into the plain girl's body. That she'd need to secure the prince's devotion, infiltrate his wildest fantasies, if she expected him to still be pining for her after the passing of a mooncycle.

And she needed the prince to pine. At least, until she could secure the marriage alliance that would make her queen. After she ridded Dwellen of its current monarch, of course.

Then, when she had the entirety of Dwellen's resources at her disposal, she would use them to find a way to inhabit this body permanently.

Of course, she would have to make sure the marriage bargain between herself and the prince would be specific enough to keep him from taking legal actions against her while she was trapped inside the plain girl during the rest of the month.

But that could be arranged.

The prince already fancied himself obsessed with her, thanks to the talents of Madame LeFleur.

The slipper left on the palace steps had also been intentional—a token of the mystery girl, a promise of yet another dance, something for the prince to remember her by until she returned.

The slipper had been about the only intentional thing that had happened that night.

For example, she'd meant to charm him, and she had, she supposed, but not in the manner she'd planned. When he'd pulled her onto the dance floor and laid his hand upon her waist, grinning down at her in awe, something had tugged—actually tugged—inside of her chest.

She was used to the sexual nature of humans. It was a perk she frequently indulged in during her limited moonsoaked moments.

But this had been different.

It had to have been the girl, she'd realized. This occurred occasionally, if she happened to be in the presence of someone her host had developed intense feelings for—jealousy, love, obsession. She tried to stay far away from such people. They served as a distraction. Besides, the parasite didn't exactly enjoy getting tangled up in sporadic human emotions. She had to deal with them enough as it was throughout the mooncycle.

But then she was dancing with the prince, and he was dazzling her with his smile, making her poor mortal heart forget to beat.

Human hearts were stupid like that. It was a wonder any of them survived puberty with the way they ceased beating at such little provocation as a crush's stolen glance.

The plain girl must have known him personally, at least in some stretch of the word, the parasite realized.

She had been right. When the plain girl woke in the streets to a ray of moonlight glowing against her closed lids, her ordinary clothes returned to her body (unbeknownst to her, a dazzling blue gown soiling in the dirt underneath a nearby rosebush), she'd frowned and, thinking Madame LeFleur had scammed her into buying a sleeping draft rather than a beauty elixir, had drummed back to the castle defeated.

She'd stayed up all night tossing and turning, imagining a thousand different scenarios, a thousand different beautiful women vying for the prince's hand. A thousand different proposals, none of which were made to her.

The parasite had possessed little patience for the girl's tears, but it wasn't like she could just leave the room, now could she?

225

Relief was a moderate term to describe what the girl had felt when she learned the next morning that the prince had squandered all his dances on a mystery woman who'd fled at the stroke of midnight.

Jealousy had existed too, souring the girl's belly and tasting of lemons to the parasite, but at least the mystery woman was gone.

The day had been a whirl of emotion for the pitiful girl, and when she'd learned of the prince's accidental betrothal to Ellie Payne, the parasite shared her shock and outrage.

The parasite knew from the beginning that Ellie Payne would try to get out of the marriage, but it didn't take long for this jealous little girl to figure it out as well.

She'd even grown to like Ellie, in whatever way a human could like the woman betrothed to marry the love of her life.

It helped that Ellie wanted out of the marriage, too.

Naïve little girl.

The magic that bound Ellie's future to the prince's was ancient (though not quite as ancient as the parasite), and not to be underestimated. There was no getting out of this marriage without the king's consent, and the parasite had been in proximity to enough fae rulers to know when a male's mind was beyond being changed.

No, there was only one way out of this predicament.

If the parasite were human, she might have regretted that Ellie Payne had to die.

CHAPTER 29

ELLIE

That night, I dreamed of Evander.

Well, I wished I had dreamed of Evander.

Because at least then I could have blamed it on my subconscious.

The truth was that I lay awake for hours, playing over every conversation we'd had. Every tease, every smirk I could remember. I searched my memory for moments that we'd touched, though I spent most of my time reliving how long Evander had held my hand in the forest.

Other than that and the time in the workshop, most of the times we'd touched had been constrained to when my life depended on it.

Though I supposed Evander hadn't needed to risk his life the day of the first trial.

He could have simply let go of my wrists as we traversed the prism.

No one had forced him to promise that he wouldn't drop me.

In fact, he could have let me suffocate in my own refusal.

As far as I knew, just because one person refused to go through with a bargain didn't mean that the other suffered for it. Not magically, at least.

But he had risked his life anyway. He'd made a vow to me, just so I would feel safe enough to step off that platform. Just so I wouldn't kill myself from fear.

So, in a way, maybe it had meant something, the flirtatious remarks and the winks and the grins that seemed to overtake his entire face...

I kept the key to my room underneath my pillow, and my fingers kept finding it, twiddling with it. Like it were some sort of lavish gift —an emerald necklace or an opal ring, and not just a stupid key.

But I would have taken the key over a fine piece of jewelry any day, so maybe it wasn't so stupid after all. It allowed me to roam freely through the castle, and I wasn't sure what Evander had said to his father to convince him to let me have it. But I was grateful all the same.

Not long after Evander left, the click of the key in the lock signaled Imogen's arrival. I still kept my door locked when I was inside my quarters, though. I didn't exactly trust the king to employ the palace guard based on how trustworthy they were around females. Imogen's timing had me wondering whether she'd been lurking around the corner, watching my door to make sure Evander returned me to my quarters at a decent hour.

Still, I was glad to see her. I was dying to explore the castle, but I'd only ever been escorted from room to room, and Blaise liked to take different paths every time—something about keeping things interesting.

Imogen hadn't exactly looked pleased about the idea of me wandering the castle without an escort, but she'd drawn a map for me just the same.

Granted, her script had been almost impossible to decipher, given the way she left so little space between her characters that they practically ran together.

But I'd made it all the way to the library and back to my rooms without getting lost, so I supposed the map was functional.

Now, as I took another glance at the map, I couldn't help but notice that Imogen had failed to label Evander's quarters.

Not that I was searching for them.

Without my permission, my mind wandered back to our walk. How he'd stepped right in front of me, so close that I could have kissed him if I'd wanted to.

I told myself I hadn't wanted to.

But then I had to shake my head and remind myself that it hadn't been real. Prince Evander, heir to the Throne of Dwellen, had told me himself that he was well practiced in wooing women. That his frequent dalliances had meant little to him. Recently women had been a means to numb his pain. And before that, even worse, his boredom, since he couldn't think of anything better to do with his immortality and riches.

I rolled my eyes, agitated now. Evander might have shown me his softer side; he might have opened up to me about his brother, but that didn't make him any less of a spoiled brat.

And that was the worst part. I didn't want him to be a spoiled brat.

There was a time when I had. I had wanted very much for him to be every vile, annoying, self-absorbed inch of his reputation. It had been easier to hate him then. Easier to hate this life for being so different than how I'd imagined my future.

But hating him wasn't quite so simple anymore. Now all I could feel was irritation when I remembered how foolish he'd been... how wasteful. How he'd squandered years of his immortal life and riches on parties and women when he could have been helping, well, some-one. Anyone. Funding orphanages or building homes for the widows who roamed the streets of Othian.

And now I was angry at him for not being that person. For not being benevolent or wise or...

Well, for not being his brother.

My heart twinged at the thought. I didn't want to be like his father, requiring Evander to be someone he wasn't. But it wasn't as though I expected him to become a different person entirely, to change his personality and dreams and demeanor just to fit someone more adequate to take the throne. No. That wasn't it at all. Because there was something about the mischief in the corners of his glances, the eagerness with which he teased... Something about how, even in his

229

grief, he found a way to make others laugh… That was what he'd done with me, wasn't it? Seen my distress on the platform of the first trial and gotten under my skin until the anxiety was…not gone. But bearable.

That part of him, I didn't want to change.

But a person didn't have to change themselves entirely to become kinder, more generous. To consider the needs of others.

Or perhaps they did.

My heart sank. Who was I to expect Evander to change at all? Sure, I was his betrothed, and if I survived the next trial, I would become his wife.

Just not the wife he wanted.

I figured he had resigned himself to our fate well enough, just as I had. He found me pleasant to talk to, an interesting enough person to have around.

A friend.

The mingled delight and torture that word provoked within my stomach threatened to make me ill.

And then there was the mystery woman, this Cinderella. The girl from the ball he'd been so quick to try to snag into marriage. I knew I shouldn't waste my thoughts on her, that it was unproductive to do so. But that was easier said than done. At least during the day, I typically had something to distract me. A duel with Blaise or a luncheon with the queen or a trial to prepare for.

But now there was only the moonlight slipping through my window, spilling light like glowing white ink onto the floor. And it wasn't much of a distraction, was it? During the last full moon, Evander had been whisking a beautiful stranger onto the dance floor, laughing and talking and falling in love.

Was Evander still in love with that woman? Even after he'd had time for the facts to settle in, the undeniable truth that she was nothing but a petty thief? And if so, what was so special about her, other than her apparent ravishing beauty—obviously—that gave her such a hold over him?

The night Evander had invited me to dinner, he'd told me she was the only person who'd ever treated his brother's death as a matter deserving of grief rather than a political discussion. She'd spoken to him as a person, not a prince.

But, I realized, hadn't I done the same, if not better?

The thought settled uncomfortably in my stomach. It was the kind of arrogance that my mother would have had me cleaning the window sills for as a child. Hadn't the prince mentioned earlier how, all his life, women had assumed they had a right to his affections? What I had begun to expect was little better. I was playing into that same age-old assumption.

That because I loved him, I deserved his affections in return.

I stumbled into sleep over a bed of cold, sharp thoughts.

CHAPTER 30

She stalked in a cool blanket of shadows, a predator as much as a parasite. The plain girl's bedroom allowed quick access to the kitchen, so it had been no trouble to snatch a carving knife.

It really couldn't have worked out better than this, the parasite mused— *a royal servant wandering into the Madame's shop.* She knew every winding staircase. Every long passageway. Each shortcut to Ellie Payne's room.

They'd locked her in for the night. It had taken little effort to secure the key.

When she crept into Ellie Payne's room, the woman didn't stir. Moonlight danced across her face, highlighting her deep brown cheeks as she slept. Even unconscious, the woman was breathtakingly beautiful, her cheekbones high, her lips full, her eyelashes thick and curling.

Before, the parasite had considered it a shame that Ellie Payne must die, her talents with her.

But now, as she stared at the woman's beautiful face, something unpleasant stirred within her, puncturing her insides and making them ooze bile.

Perhaps I've made a mistake, the parasite thought, examining the woman's flawless details. *Perhaps I chose the wrong sort of beautiful.* Suddenly the perfect body she'd just admired in the mirror only minutes ago seemed cliche. Predictable. Unremarkable, in Ellie's Payne's presence.

The venom in her gut heated as she thought of the way the prince sometimes looked at Ellie Payne.

It made it that much easier to plunge the knife into Ellie Payne's stomach.

CHAPTER 31

ELLIE

Something was wrong.

I woke to a gasp escaping my lips, to a hazy awareness that I hadn't woken from a nightmare or bodily needs or even anxieties, but from something else.

Someone else.

I opened my eyes and promptly screamed.

The shadow over my bed was a woman's and, in a moment of unclarity, I thought she must be the messenger of death. Her pale white skin and hair were so fair they almost blended into the moonlight coming from my window. And in her hands was a knife, glinting in that same light. Dripping from the knife was a dark, scarlet substance. Blood.

My blood.

The sound that clawed through my throat was not my voice, but something more primal. An ancient survival instinct. Another being, who had resided in the back of my mind all this time, who had never alerted me that I was sharing my body with someone else.

That was the being who screamed.

I knew, because in that moment I couldn't move.

"You weren't supposed to wake up," the woman hissed in a voice dripping with such hatred I no longer wondered if I would die. It was only a matter of who would find my body first.

But then the woman fled, and the scrape of a key turning in a lock sounded behind her as she slammed my door.

She had locked me in.

That was when I remembered the blood.

The shock that had kept my limbs immobile dissipated, and I grasped at my belly. Something hot and sticky and wet soaked my fingertips. My breath tightened.

My blood.

That knife had been dripping with my blood.

I screamed again, this time intentionally. "Help me! Please, someone help me!"

I searched my body for pain, for any other indication besides the blood for how severely I'd been injured, but my mind must have erased the pain.

It knew I just needed to survive.

Footsteps sounded in the hallway outside. "Lady Payne?" I didn't recognize the voice and assumed it must have been a guard. "Lady Payne?"

"Yes! Please, I've been stabbed!" I gasped.

Voices murmured in the hallway outside as the doorknob creaked and rattled. They were locked out. The woman had locked me in here, and the guards didn't have a key.

I scrambled for the one tucked under my pillow, but my fingers were slick with blood, and in my haste, I knocked it off the side of the bed.

Another voice, this one familiar, yelled, "Get Blaise! No. Get Imogen. Imogen, the lady's maid. She'll have a key."

The clock struck midnight.

Footsteps again. The guard must have run off, because footsteps pounded in the hallway before they went faint.

"Evan..." I struggled to coordinate my breath with words. I could hardly speak, much less lower myself to the floor and grab the key.

"Ellie? *El!*" The door splintered, and in sauntered Evander, stomping over shards of wood as if they were blades of grass. In seconds, he was at my side, stroking my forehead with one hand, examining my wound with the other.

"It's going to be alright, Ellie. It's going to be alright. Forrest! Call the healer. Then call the one from town."

"Your Highness..." said the guard.

"Now!" Evander barked. Then he grabbed my bedsheets, ripping a strand from them with his bare hands. "I'm going to put pressure on this, okay?" He wadded up the sheets and pressed them against my torso.

I yelped. Now that Evander seemed to be balancing the entirety of his weight upon my wound, the pain began to pulse, thrumming against my stomach. Or perhaps the shock was just wearing off.

"El, it's okay. They're getting the healer. The healer is on his way. I just need to keep applying pressure."

"I know how it works," I croaked, trying to nod my head.

A distressed smile broke out across his face, and for the first time I noticed he was sweating.

"Who did this to you?" Evander gritted his teeth, set his jaw. "I swear, when I find out who did this to you, I'll—"

"No, stop," I gasped. "I don't want you to get yourself into another bargain you don't...wish to...keep."

He frowned and cocked his head, his brow furrowing. "Who, El?"

"I... I don't know." It was the truth, at least in the most exact sense. I didn't *know* the name of the woman who had just tried to kill me in my sleep, who had glared at me with such hatred, such vengeance, that it was clear she felt I had cheated her out of her happiness. Out of a life that was rightfully hers.

So, yes, I didn't *know* who the woman was.

But I had a pretty good idea.

And from the way Evander's face blanched as white and frothy as the winter's first snow, I figured he did too.

Evander said something, but it was as if the words had to swim through sludge before they could reach my ears. My vision went spotted around the edges, and before I could unscramble Evander's statement, the darkness took me.

CHAPTER 32

EVANDER

*T*he day immediately following the attack, the corridor outside Ellie's room had been buzzing with members of my father's staff. Mostly guards assigned to investigate exactly how an intruder had snuck into and out of the castle grounds unnoticed.

So far, they'd come up with nothing. The theory so far was that somewhere among the entrances, there was a stationed guard given to strong drink, one who had allowed the perpetrator to slip by without raising an alarm.

It wasn't exactly the most helpful theory. What guard was going to turn himself in for getting drunk on duty when the penalty for such an infraction was death?

After a few days, the traffic subsided, and a silence settled over the entire corridor off of which Ellie's bedroom resided.

If there had been one more second of chatter in the hallway, if the shuffling of feet had continued to mask her shallow breathing, the steady drum of her heartbeat, I might have lost it.

But there she lay, flat on her back with her beautiful face resting to the side, very much alive.

Rays of sunlight crept through the window and caressed her cheeks. I could never decide whether to crack the window or leave it shut, but there was something about the state of Ellie's health that had me feeling like the exact temperature of her room was of dire importance.

She'd made the window. I found my fingers tracing the carved initials every time I tried to determine whether the fresh air would do my betrothed good or harm.

Ellie had hardly breached consciousness in the few days since the attack. Peck, a faerie healer who'd been in the service of the royal family since before my grandfather had taken the throne, spent hours at a time by her bedside, tending to her wounds and whispering enchantments over her injuries.

I watched wide-eyed with horror while he dressed the wound. At first I'd averted my eyes to maintain her privacy. Sure, we were to be wed, but I wouldn't force Ellie into anything that marriage would typically require, and I had zero expectations of laying eyes on my wife's form. Other than the curves that couldn't quite hide under the delicate fae fabric of her gowns.

But I couldn't help glancing at the wound.

It had become a bit of an obsession, actually.

When Peck ripped her gown apart at the waist to examine the wound that first night, it had seemed to gape, open-mawed, ready and welcoming to any infection that might come Ellie's way. Maybe it was the blood that pooled around her, dripping off her smooth brown skin and splattering against the sheets that gave that impression.

Once he'd cleaned it, I'd felt a bit relieved at its size and averted my eyes once more.

The second day it had swelled.

The third I thought I glimpsed signs of infection, but Peck assured me the puss was simply a byproduct of the wound purging itself. Using Peck's magic as a catalyst to do so more quickly and fervently than human skin would typically be capable of.

I stayed through all of it.

And when Peck left her side to get some rest of his own and replenish his magic, I stayed then, too.

This was my fault, after all.

I couldn't quite bring myself to admit *why* it was my fault, at least not without skirting around the edges.

So I told myself it was because I'd been a fool and placed that fae bargain on that stupid shoe, not considering the consequences if the shoe might fit someone other than...

I shoved her name from my mind. I'd deal with my concerns about her later.

Right now, all that mattered was Ellie making it through this.

I held her hand most always, rubbing my thumb across her feverish arms, sometimes using both palms when she began to tremble and I worried she'd gotten too cold.

As soon as Peck returned, he usually commanded I stop. That he was hydrating Ellie as best as he could with magic. If I kept rubbing the same portion of her skin like that, I'd give her a blister. That sort of thing.

Sometimes Ellie would shiver uncontrollably, and Peck would tell me he'd done all he could, that his magic was fighting off infection, giving her the best shot at survival.

Once, the shivering got so bad I considered slipping into the bed with her. I'd already pulled back the sheets when Blaise arrived and offered to do it for me.

She'd snuggled up next to Ellie and fallen asleep, weary with dread herself, and I'd watched as the new heat source assuaged Ellie's shivers.

I'd had an awful thought that night.

I'd been annoyed with Blaise, wishing it could have been me who soothed Ellie, whose body warmed hers.

That thought got tucked away with haste.

Besides, Blaise had taken to Ellie.

The night of Ellie's attack, Blaise had burst through the doors an hour or two after Ellie had slipped from consciousness, out of her mind frantic. She'd muttered something about hearing a commotion in the hall, how a servant had informed her what had happened.

She hadn't even taken the time to put her slippers on before sprinting up to Ellie's rooms barefoot. I'd had to catch her before she launched herself onto Ellie, weeping.

She'd fought me for a moment, tears streaming down her pale face and soaking my arms. I'd just held her like that, pulled her against my chest as she kicked and punched at me until, all at once, the fight and frenzy in her seemed to be snuffed out, and she sank against me in a puddle of tears.

I'd let her sit next to Ellie after that, and she'd gotten into nearly as much trouble as I had with Peck. Except with Blaise, he claimed she was rubbing Ellie's forehead too much.

Blaise had hardly left Ellie's side, except for the day after the attack when she'd run to town for a few hours and returned with a basket full of sticky buns and lemon tarts from Forcier's.

My mother had supplied the bedside table with a fresh vase of lilies every morning.

Even Imogen came and visited, her sallow cheeks waning still. She would show up for only minutes at a time, hovering by the door quietly, as if she hoped not to be noticed. Her fingers would jitter, and she'd chew her lip before slipping into the hall, only to return a few hours later.

From the look of the shadows that rimmed her eyes, she wasn't sleeping.

"Do you think we should read to her?" Blaise's voice broke me from my dazed thoughts, and from an almost-nap. I'd spent the nights in the armchair beside Ellie's bed, Blaise and I taking turns staying awake to monitor Ellie through the night, but the little sleep I managed to snag was fitful, and I often found myself drifting off during the day.

"I'm going to be honest with you, Blaise," I said, stretching my feet out, like that would somehow make up for the deprivation I'd put my body through the last few days. "I don't know that my eyes can focus enough to read right now."

She waved me off, already bounding down the hall. She came back a few minutes later, an armful of books retrieved from the library.

"Listen, if those are romance books, I can't sit here and listen while you read the—is that a glassblowing manual?" I squinted my eyes, which were surely deceiving me.

Sure enough, my fae eyesight didn't disappoint. Blaise held a stack of nonfiction in her arms.

Before the books could tumble to the floor from how thoroughly she'd piled them, I grabbed one from the top of her stack. *"How to Start Your Own Shop and Turn a Profit within Three Mooncycles, The Origin of Glass..."* I said, reciting the names of three other business books. "Are you trying to bore her into healing faster?"

Blaise glared at me, and for the first time in several days, a smile tugged at my lips. I was fairly certain listening to a manual was the last thing Ellie would enjoy, even if it was discussing her passion. Ellie was a hands-on kind of woman, and somehow I knew having her artwork broken down into dry, precise steps would be about as interesting to her as watching Peck measure Ellie's drafts.

But still. It was sweet. And Blaise rarely allowed anyone to glimpse that side of her. Probably because she was pretty awful at it—hence the manuals and business books.

So Blaise recited the arduous process of making glass. Every time she stumbled over a phrase or mispronounced a word, a twinge of gratefulness to my friend tugged at my heart.

CHAPTER 33

ELLIE

I awoke to Prince Evander of Dwellen in my bed.

In fact, I was fairly certain his snores were what rattled me awake.

That and his warm breath against my cheek, his arm stretched across my abdomen, tucking me into his chest as he interlocked my fingers with his.

Of all the ways I could have returned to consciousness after having a lunatic disembowel me, I supposed this wasn't the most unpleasant.

It was, however, the most problematic.

Any moment now, someone was bound to waltz through my bedroom door and find the Prince of Dwellen spooning me.

"Evander," I whispered, my voice dry and crackling from disuse.

He groaned and readjusted, but instead of waking up and scooting away from me like I'd hoped, he roped his arm around my ribcage, pulling me into his warm chest. Maybe it was his fae instinct, but his fingers skirted my injury. Like he knew the boundaries of my wound so well, he could avoid it in his sleep.

The male went so far as to nuzzle his face into my neck.

Heat soothed my sore stomach.

Well, at least he'd stopped snoring.

It was...nice, I supposed. Being held like this. His firm chest pressed against my back, and the weight of his arm left me feeling secure. Safe.

It was so pleasant, in fact, my heavy eyes fluttered. Evander's breathing slowed again, his inhalations a steady pulse against my spine.

I allowed my eyes to rest. Perhaps I could go back to sleep like this. Then, maybe he'd wake before I did, slip from the bed, and both of us could pretend this never happened.

His thumb brushed my ribcage, and I shuddered. Electricity shot through my body at the subtle caress, and I found I wouldn't be going back to sleep. Not anytime soon.

Okay, never mind.

Staying like this was a bad, bad, bad idea.

Sure, Evander and I were engaged to be married, but he'd said it himself, hadn't he?

Unless I'd misinterpreted the context clues of the word *celibate* growing up, I was fairly sure he had no intention of bedding me once we were married.

Clearly, he'd only been trying to warm me. I'd flitted in and out of consciousness the past few days, and Blaise had been doing the same. I'd never quite been alert enough to communicate with her, but I'd appreciated her sharing her warmth as I'd shivered through my fever.

Blaise had needed a break, and Evander had done what any friend would do.

He fidgeted again, this time adjusting his neck so that his warm lips pressed against the bone behind my ear.

Nope, nope, nope.

"Evander," I hissed, louder this time.

"Mmm?"

"What do you think you're doing?"

He lazily traced his finger over my shoulder.

Then he jolted. "You're awake."

Was that *embarrassment* I sensed in his voice?

I wasn't quick enough to find out.

"You're in my bed," I said. I made to roll over to face him and had to fight back a groan as my stomach twisted, but he placed a firm hand on my shoulder.

"Easy. Peck's already had to stitch you up twice. Turns out you're an active sleeper."

I couldn't miss the glimmer of amusement in his tone. Still, I took it slow. Once I was facing him, I tucked my sheets up to my neck and shot him the nastiest glare I could muster.

He'd propped himself on his elbow, his bronze hair disheveled and falling across his brow. "Right. You're wondering why I'm in your bed. Well, I figured since we only have a few weeks before we're married, we should take it slow. Wouldn't want to blow your mind on the wedding night or anything. So I figured we could start with spooning. Then maybe next week I can hold your hand. Oh, wait, we already did that. Excellent. I'm hoping by the wedding, I'll have you adequately warmed up for a kiss, but—" His words faltered as his gaze dipped to my mouth. I tensed, readying myself for whatever mortifyingly inappropriate innuendo was about to come out of his mouth, but his voice only softened. "It's really good to see you awake."

I stiffened, and he smiled, shrugging as he supported his weight on his elbow. He looked more sheepish now, his tanned cheeks slightly tinted. "You had a really nasty fever. Peck was having a hard time breaking it with his drafts. Blaise has been keeping you warm most of the time, but to be honest, she was getting to where she stunk, so she went to bathe and get you some more books." He rolled his eyes, and I shot him a questioning look. "Oh, don't tell me I suffered through the *Encyclopedia of Glass*, and you didn't hear a word of it."

I chuckled, which was a mistake, because it hurt like crap to laugh. Evander frowned, having caught my wince. He opened his mouth slightly for a moment, but then he shut it and swallowed. In an instant, the vulnerable expression was gone, replaced by a familiar cocky smirk.

T.A. LAWRENCE

"Well, it seems your fever finally broke." He pulled down the blankets, gesturing to his shirt. Which happened to be soaked through. Mortification blistered underneath my cheeks. Evander just winked. "It's okay. You're cute when you're sweaty."

I threw a pillow at him.

The pain that rippled through my stomach and had me choking back a sob was worth it.

EVANDER VISITED me what felt like once an hour for the next few days. At first, the castle healer, Peck, a birdlike fae with the looks of a human except for the feathers that covered his skin, put up a good fight against Evander's visits, claiming that I needed the rest. But eventually Evander won out, as, I assumed, he was fairly used to doing by this point in his life.

I always pretended to be asleep during his visits, which I think was the only thing that kept Peck at bay. It wasn't that I didn't want him there by my side. In fact, I relished his company, just knowing that he was sitting next to me in the rocking chair he'd carried up to my bedroom. Sometimes he'd stroke my hand, and I'd try not to let myself tense up as the motion sent a crackling sensation up my arm. I was pretty sure I wasn't fooling him. Surely, with his fae senses and nothing else in the room to distract him, he could tell that I was faking sleep. But if that was the case, he didn't push it. Instead, he allowed me to pretend.

Maybe because he knew what I was really avoiding.

Maybe because he wanted to avoid it, too.

If I were in his shoes, I wouldn't want to talk about how the love of my life had just attempted to murder my betrothed.

The more I considered it, and, truly, I had nothing else to consider as I lay in bed all day pretending to be asleep, the more I convinced myself it was her, the more I remembered that flash of envy in her blue eyes and knew, deep down, that she'd tried to murder me because I had taken her prince.

Well, she had taken my shoes, so...

"Ellie." Evander's voice summoned me from my irritable thoughts.

I tried not to stir. I wasn't ready for this conversation yet.

Besides, my stomach still ached, and stirring, rather, moving at all, would have only irritated it further.

"What? Are you just going to pretend you've fallen into an eternal slumber?"

"Mm. Peck says I need rest."

"Peck says you need to eat something. Don't you, Peck?" Evander asked pleasantly.

"As much as it pains me to do so, I agree, your Highness," Peck said without looking up from the salve he was mixing on my desk.

"Great, because I ordered that lunch be delivered at noon."

"Thank you, but I'm really not hungry," I said.

"Just try it." He smiled. "And we can talk while you do."

"I'm too tired to—"

"Okay, no. We're going to talk about who did this to you," Evander said.

"Why are you pushing me about it when you already know the answer?" I asked through gritted teeth. I wasn't sure why I was so angry all of a sudden, but I was. And for some reason, my heart seemed to think that Evander was to blame for it.

"Ellie," he said, taking my hand. My heart lurched at the feel of his soft caress as his thumb stroked the back of my hand. "Please. Just tell me who it was."

I sighed. "She looked to be about my age, maybe a little older. She had really pale skin and hair to match."

Evander swallowed. "How pale?"

"She could have disappeared into the moonlight easier than trying to hide in the shadows."

I watched his face, searching for any hint of recognition. Of admission.

"Did she say anything to you?"

I shuddered. "Just that I wasn't supposed to wake up. Then she disappeared."

Evander let out a slow, controlled breath. I waited. I wasn't going to be the one to say it out loud. Not when it would make me sound like a jealous lunatic.

And I wasn't a lunatic.

"Anything else about her?"

"Her eyes were blue."

"Are you sure you're getting all the details right? I know you must have been so terrified, and it was dark in your room…"

"Evander."

"Yes?" His eyes glistened. Pleading.

"Have you ever described your mystery girl to me?"

"A few times—"

"No, I mean what she looked like."

He shook his head.

"And does what I'm describing sound like her?" There, I said it.

He clenched his teeth, and his jaw bulged before he nodded.

"Don't you think it would be a bit too much of a coincidence if it wasn't her?"

"You could have heard descriptions from the servants. Some of them were there the night of the—"

"You think I'd make this up? That I'd lie to you about it?" My voice went high, hoarse from when I'd screamed so loudly. "Why would I do that? What, do you think you're just *that* irresistible, that women would go to any lengths to have you? You probably think I stabbed myself just to get your attention, don't you?"

He clamped his mouth shut, but not in the way he did when he was angry with his father, when he ground his teeth and looked as though his jaw might rip through his skin. No, his mouth just seemed as if it had simply run out of words and decided to close up shop accordingly.

The rage in me wilted at that expression. "I'm sorry. I know you weren't accusing me of that."

He shook his head and rested his chin on his hand. "I was hoping it was a subconscious thing. That you'd heard her described and forgotten about it, and you only thought you saw her that night. Like your mind was playing tricks on you in your stress."

"I've never been told what she looked like, Evander." Well, other than her skin being pale.

Peck tensed in the corner.

"That seems clear enough now." Evander sighed as he stroked my hand before setting it back on the bed beside me. My heart hung in the air a bit as he let go and folded his hands in his lap. "What I don't understand is why."

I forced myself up in the bed by my elbows.

"Here, let me help you." Evander placed his powerful hands on my shoulders and helped scoot me up. When he pulled away, I could still feel the buzzing imprint of his fingers on my shoulders.

"Isn't it clear why?" I settled into my new position on my favorite pillow. "She's jealous that you're marrying me. She wants me out of the way so she can marry you instead."

He frowned, a crease forming above the bridge of his nose. "That doesn't make any sense."

It was my turn to frown. Despite the railings I'd heard from women at social gatherings, I had never been under the impression that males were actually as oblivious as women made them out to be. I always figured it all was some master scheme to keep women from expecting too much of them. "It makes perfect sense. She's jealous, and she wants me dead."

"But, no, it doesn't. I understand that she'd rather us not wed, but I thought…"

"What?"

"Well, I guess I thought she knew better than that. That I love her, not you."

Two projectiles penetrated my heart in that moment. The first came from the words themselves—the admission that he didn't love me. The second came when, once again, I remembered Evander's fae heritage meant he couldn't lie.

If he said he didn't love me, I couldn't blame it on his inability to verbalize the truth.

If he said he didn't love me, then he didn't.

"I didn't mean it like that," Evander said, taking my hand. I cleared my throat and pulled it back. "Of course I've got a soft spot for you. You're... Well, you're the only real friend I've had in years, since Jerad, other than Blaise. I do love you, I do."

Love. What a strange word. You'd have thought we'd have come up with a better word to describe two completely different things.

"You're upset."

I snapped. "Of course I'm upset, Evander. You say that you love me. That I'm your friend. Yet you're sitting here admitting you're in love with the woman who tried to murder me."

"We don't know that she was trying to kill you. It could have been that she was just trying to scare you off."

I was pretty sure my face went void of all human emotion at that statement. "She stabbed me in the stomach. Either she was trying to kill me or she's an idiot."

"Well, that is what you think of me. So maybe one day you'll agree she and I are a good match?" His smile was genuine, apologetic, his tone playful. He knew good and well he was acting like a pitiful, lovesick puppy dog.

It wasn't cute.

"I'd like to rest now."

"I can stay long—"

"Get out."

He blinked and swallowed, as if to absorb my words and allow them to settle. "I probably deserve that." Then without looking at me, he turned and left.

Peck came to dress my wounds. How many royal conversations had he been privy to? The quiet being in the corner, holding everyone's secrets.

"I probably deserve that," he mimicked, almost to himself, in a high-pitched tone as his eyes widened and his face scrunched up in disgust.

The hinge on my jaw must have broken, because it seemed I was no longer in control of my facial expressions.

"You could do better, my lady," Peck said.

I groaned as the weight of being magically bound to a male who loved someone else settled in my stomach and soured. "Actually, no; I literally cannot."

CHAPTER 34

ELLIE

Once Peck cleared me to walk again, I...

Well, truth be told, my life didn't change a whole lot.

They'd changed the locks on my doors and replaced the key with an ornate iron one to match the ornate iron door handle. Which rendered the key Evander had given me useless.

Unfortunately, I was too irritated with him to ask for a new one.

Part of me thought I might return to the workshop Evander had set up on the castle grounds, but I didn't exactly want to relive the memories there, either.

The first day back in my service, Blaise had apologized what must have been fifty times for the whole incident, though it didn't seem to me like it was any one person's fault.

Imogen, however, seemed inclined to blame Blaise for the incident.

Apparently the key had been stolen from Imogen's keyring during the night.

Blaise had been a heavy sleeper all her life, so she hadn't noticed anyone sneaking into her and Imogen's shared room and swiping it.

In fact, Blaise couldn't figure out how Cinderella had gotten into her and Imogen's quarters.

Imogen, who kept my sheets fresh and my water jug replenished, had her own ideas of what happened. Apparently Blaise was notorious for forgetting to lock their bedroom suite.

At first it had seemed strange to me that Imogen hadn't been in her quarters when the key was stolen, but when I spoke to Blaise about it, she said Imogen had been mopey all day, her eyes bloodshot.

I couldn't help but wonder if she'd been crying over my walk in the forest with Evander, wishing to weep in private rather than in front of Blaise.

I couldn't exactly blame her.

Evander hadn't visited me since the day I'd blown up on him. Not that I wanted him to.

I hadn't been sure what to write my parents. Given the time I'd spent in a feverish, draft-induced coma, there had been a lapse in our daily correspondence. The papers hadn't printed news of my attack; King Marken had made sure of that. Probably by threatening the editors' relationship between their necks and their heads.

Part of me was glad for the discretion. There was no use in having my parents fret over my safety, not when there was nothing they could do to ensure it.

In the end, I settled on a letter apologizing profusely for my lack of correspondence, explaining that I had been terribly busy the past few days.

I figured that wasn't exactly a lie, as most rational people would agree that being stabbed was its own sort of busyness.

I'd just sealed the letter when someone knocked on the door.

I wondered if that was a fae thing. Could he make me think about him when he was near? Even the idea of it sizzled my bones.

I didn't bother to respond, so he let himself in.

"I'm sorry. I thought you must be sleeping."

I didn't answer.

"I take it you're still angry."

"Yes."

I expected some immature, spoiled response about how I shouldn't be upset with him, about how he couldn't help who he loved and I shouldn't expect him to.

But when he spoke, he caught me by surprise. "I'm sorry about the other day. I was insensitive."

"Oh?" I asked, cautiously. Was this going to be a real apology or was he about to offend me by calling me out for the real reason I'd been so upset?

The reason I'd refused to acknowledge to myself the past few days.

He walked over to where I sat in a chair facing my window. Then he sat down next to me on the floor, crisscrossing his legs. It made him look rather childish, in my opinion.

"It was selfish of me to talk about loving the woman who hurt you, and for trying to minimize what she did. Obviously, I didn't know her as well as I thought I did."

"Common mistake. Anyone could have made it. You know, we all agree to marry complete strangers from time to time. Usually, a few hours of dancing is a reliable measure. I hate that it didn't work out for you."

My insult was met with silence, and when it finally grated at my will enough that I looked down at Evander, he was staring at me and his bright eyes had gone watery. There was nothing but pure defeat on his face.

Something about the way he'd given up on picking a fight deflated my anger.

"That was unkind of me to say," I said.

He shrugged. "But not untrue."

"My mother always says you should always serve truth salted, if you must serve it at all."

He craned his neck at me. "Is the salt supposed to be kindness or cruelty?"

"Kindness. Don't you like salt?"

"Well, yes, but preferably not in my wounds."

"Hm." I'd never thought of it that way.

"I can't lie, so I can't tell you I don't still love her. But I intend to work on getting over it."

Something about the genuineness of that statement tugged at my heart. "Will you arrest her if you catch her?"

Silence.

"Hm." Okay, the anger wasn't completely gone.

"I want to get to where I can promise that to you. I'm just not there yet."

"The fact that she's a thief and a murderer isn't enough? How many crimes must she commit before you rid yourself of her affections?"

"Technically," he said, "she's not a murderer."

"Alright. So she's an incompetent murderer. I can see how that might be attractive."

A grin broke out over Evander's face, and I might have let it lift my spirits. Only a little.

He nudged my knee with his elbow. "I got something for you. As an apology present." Evander shifted on his feet before standing.

"You don't have it with you?"

"It's downstairs." He examined me, the way I sat upright in my chair, hardly moving, and a shadow came over his face. "Hm. I got so excited with the idea when it hit me, it didn't occur to me you might not feel like walking downstairs. I could...carry you?"

I shook my head ferociously. There was no way. Not only would that be humiliating, I was fairly certain sitting upright was the only pain-free position available to me at the moment. I would know, because I'd tried countless others, as the soreness from sitting in the same position had settled into knots in my back.

Peck cleared his throat. "If you'll forgive my interjection, Your Highness, I believe I might have a solution."

Evander nodded, and Peck scurried from the room. He returned a few moments later, pushing a chair that sat on two wheels.

"Did you make that yourself, Peck?" I asked in astonishment.

The feathers on Peck's neck bristled. A sign of embarrassment amongst his species? "I enjoy woodcraft in my spare time, my lady."

I grinned. No wonder I liked him.

The two males hoisted me into the rolling chair, a task I was certain either one of the fae could have accomplished by themselves, except that both insisted on helping. Perhaps male fae and human men had more in common than I had thought. I tried to bite back a groan as they moved me. Though Peck had used magic to heal my wound, there was still a lingering soreness.

"Ready?" Evander asked once they settled me in. He didn't wait for my response as he wheeled me out of the room and into the hallway.

The stairs might have been more of an issue if Evander's body hadn't been a monument to strength and agility. As we reached the stairs' edge, I opened my mouth to protest, but Evander spoke first.

"So I can bounce you down the stairs, or I can carry you. Your choice."

My immediate reaction was to make him turn right back around and deposit me in my room, but I was curious about his present. And I'd been cooped up in my room for so long by this point...

"Carrying me it is," I made sure to say glumly.

Evander looked as though I'd made his year.

Before I knew it, I was being cradled in Evander's arms and carried down the steps. It didn't exactly hurt my stomach as much as I expected it to. When we got to the bottom, I insisted he let me lean against the wall rather than him setting me on the ground.

Once he retrieved my chair, we wound through countless hallways, and for the first time I felt like I was getting the impression of exactly how large this castle really was. It seemed to me that this place was spacious enough that one who lived here might have never even entered some of the rooms.

"Have you explored all of it?" I asked, and my voice echoed off the stone wall of the particularly empty corridor we had just entered. It wasn't decorated with tapestries or busts like the rest of the hallways, which gave me the impression this part of the castle went unused.

"You forget I was a child here once," Evander said.

"*Was?*"

"Must you always be so condescending?"

"Yes. I must," I mused. "Have you brought me back to this light-forsaken part of the castle to murder me in the shadows where no one will hear my screams?"

"Well, the screaming was the part that ruined my plan when I sent my henchwoman to kill you the other night," he teased.

I stifled a laugh. Partially because I was still aggravated with him for not giving up his feelings for a murderer. Partially because laughing really, really hurt.

When we reached the end of the corridor, Evander opened the door to a narrow staircase. This time, I was ready when he hoisted me up and carried me down. To my surprise, the stairway led outside.

"Where are we going?" I asked.

"You'll see."

EVANDER PUSHED me down a pebbled path that led to the castle's south entrance, where a guard nodded and opened the iron gates for us. When he lead me through, I realized that this portion of the gate lead straight into the art district of town.

"I always saw the walls when I visited here, but it never occurred to me how close you lived to the city all this time," I said.

"It's an ancient city. The rulers of old benefitted from keeping it under such strict observation."

My chair bumped and vibrated as we wended our way through the streets, shooting needles of pain through my abdomen. But I tried to ignore it. If Evander noticed I was hurting, he might try to turn back, and I was thrilled to be back in town. In my favorite part of town, of all places.

The art district looked as it sounded. Most of the artists who lived here worked and set up shop out of their own cottages, which were all decorated according to each artist's particular style. Soria, the vendor who sold decorative plant arrangements, had a cottage that seemed almost overgrown with vines and flowers, though overgrown in the most flattering sense of the word. I often wondered if she had spent years teasing each vine into the perfect shape to decorate the face of her home.

Moran, who sold brass wind chimes, had a home that burst to life with music with every gentle breeze. Then there were the houses owned by the painters, each face boasting a mural, some of colorful Alondrian sunsets, others of epic battle scenes often including dragons—which were always said to be extinct by some and thriving in caves by others.

But Evander didn't take me to any of these. Instead, we stopped by a small cottage at the edge of the district that I had never noticed. Most likely because it appeared abandoned.

"You ready?"

"Ready? For what?" I asked, trying not to sound too disappointed that he hadn't taken me to any of my favorite shops.

He flashed me a grin that informed that me he was proud of himself and I should be concerned, then flung the door open.

He wheeled me in.

I gasped in horror, though judging by the grin spreading across Evander's face, he'd clearly interpreted it as indicating pleasure.

It was a storefront. One lined with tables and shelves. And on the tables and shelves sat the most beautiful pieces of glasswork that I had ever seen. Far finer than I had accomplished in my years of working in my shop. There were plates perched upon golden stands that sparkled in the light of the suspended candles from the ceiling. The intricacy of the designs I could pick out even from a distance. On one shelf was a beautiful array of glass figurines. Fire-breathing dragons that looked as though they were living and had simply been cursed to abide in glass form. A human woman, her forehead wrinkles caught in a laugh. A fae male whose ears appeared to twitch, though it could have been a trick of the light. Even the glass chandeliers above had been crafted with far more intricacy than my current skill level could have mastered.

In the back of the store was a large window, painted with a mural of the Adreean Sea. As the light danced through the glass, the waves rippled with delight, providing the illusion of tumbling waves.

And on the center counter was a pair of glass slippers, much like mine except that a floral design had been etched into the glass so that when the candlelight shone on them, a symbol of a daisy sparkled silver and gold on the adjacent wall.

"Do you like it?"

My heart sank. Recoiled. Shriveled. Whatever.

I swallowed, but the burning lump in my throat remained. My eyes stung, and I rubbed them, hoping Evander would think I was tired and not notice me crying.

This too, Evander misinterpreted. At the sign of my tears, he beamed.

"I knew you would like it," he said. "I had Father's master craftsman start working on it the morning after your... umm...accident."

Accident. The word flared within me. "They did all this in a week?"

He beamed. "Like I said, they're the best in the land. They were so thrilled to do it, too. Something about the artistic beauty of being able to create something extraordinary from such a plain substance. Apparently, working with crystal and fine gems wasn't doing it for them anymore." He rolled his eyes.

Something inside my chest had gone numb. "I would like to go back to my room now."

Evander's grin faltered as confusion swept over his expression. But then he cleared his throat and straightened. "Of course; it was a long walk from the castle. I'm sure you're exhausted from sitting upright for so long."

As he wheeled me out of the house and locked the door, he took the brass key and placed it in my palm, closing my fingers around it. "It's yours. I thought you could run it once you get better. Only if you want to, of course."

I opened my palm and stared at the key. "Thank you." The words came out flat, lifeless.

Evander opened his mouth, his enthusiasm fading with the daylight as the sun slipped behind a cloud. "You don't like it."

The lump in my throat grew, and I felt as though it might cut through my skin at any moment. "Thank you. I would like to go back to my room now."

He frowned but returned to pushing me. After we had cleared the art district and were halfway up the path to the castle walls, he spoke. "Clearly, I've offended you. But I can't seem to figure out why."

I couldn't bring myself to answer. He halted my chair halfway up the hill.

"I thought you would like it. I wanted you to know I was listening to you that night we had dinner, and you told me that it was your dream to own a shop that sold beautiful glassware."

My heart went numb at the explanation. The one that took my dream and diluted it and made it sound so, so bland. "You weren't listening at all."

He rounded my chair to face me, holding onto the wheels from the front to make sure I didn't roll right back down the hill as he kneeled in front of me.

That would be the perfect cap to my week, at the rate it was going.

His green eyes flashed with anger, though the rest of his face was subdued. As if he genuinely wanted to understand what he had done wrong, although his feelings were clearly hurt.

Rage unfurled in my chest at the thought. That he should dare to have his feelings hurt after he'd crushed my dreams.

"It wasn't about owning a shop, or selling pretty glass," I said. "It was about building something with my own two hands. About the hours I'd have to put in, the glass I'd have to toss, just for that moment of euphoria when I'd figured it out. And it was about other people admiring the beauty of what my hands had made, witnessing the innovation of what my father only ever saw as a material to make windows."

Evander's brow furrowed. "There's a workshop in the back of the cottage. You can still work there, or you're still free to use the one on the castle grounds."

"You're still not listening." My voice trembled, and I sank to a whisper in a failed attempt to conceal that fact. "Do you know how long it took me to make a pair of glass slippers I was proud of?"

"Two years."

I bristled. I hadn't expected him to remember, but it did nothing to diffuse my agitation. "I threw away almost forty different prototypes. I worked by lamplight so many nights just to get up at the crack of dawn the next morning to do it all again, just so I could catch a few hours before I had to work with my father. But you—you said a few words, and then your father's craftsman had it made in a matter of days. All you did today was prove that my dream, my years of hard work, could be done so much better by someone else. That feeling— the accomplishment, the one where I could finally hold something in my hands, something I'd carried in my imagination for so long, and the knowledge that I'd made it with those two hands—you stole that from me."

Evander's mouth opened as if to retort, but then his teeth clenched.

I flicked my wrist. "See? You can't even bring yourself to apologize. Because you don't get it."

"No, I don't get it," he said, his knuckles bulging as he held onto my armrests. "I tried to do something thoughtful for you, but you can't even see that. By Alondria, you can't even give me the benefit of the doubt, or admit that at least I tried. So no, I don't get it."

"No. The reason you don't get it is because you've never worked for anything more substantial than a lay a day in your life."

Evander's jaw tightened, and his eyes went wide with hurt. Then his cheeks softened and went sallow. "I'll take you back to your room. I'm sorry for getting you out just to make an already horrible week worse."

The bitterness of my harsh words landed in my stomach, souring and churning as I processed the weight of them. "Evander, I—"

"No, you're right. You don't have to apologize for simply speaking the truth." He forced a smile, but his eyes didn't partake. "Maybe your mother was referring to salt in wounds after all."

As he pushed me back to my room in silence, the wheels of my chair grinding against the uneven road, I couldn't help but notice that the gnawing in my stomach hurt way worse than the moment I'd seen my dreams realized by someone else.

CHAPTER 35

EVANDER

I had a pretty good idea what Ellie was doing.

We were seated around the dinner table, and she was ignoring me, while simultaneously flaunting how well she got along with my mother.

Man, she irritated me sometimes.

"Your Grace," she said, but my mother quickly raised a delicate hand.

"There's no need for formalities, Ellie. Not with family," my mother said, her soft smile resting gently on her soon-to-be daughter-in-law.

Ellie beamed.

Fates, she was gorgeous. She knew it too.

"Not quite family yet," I said, aiming to match Ellie's grin, though through gritted teeth.

My father coughed, and my mother blinked rapidly. "Why, Evander," she said, surely intending to scold me.

"Just wouldn't want to jinx it," I said, impressed that my smile had not faltered in the slightest.

Ellie simply ignored me.

"Evangeline." Ellie grinned, saying my mother's name like it was an honor. "Did I hear correctly that the trade deal between Dwellen and the villages of the Eastern Shores is to be finalized soon?"

My mother set her silverware on the table, and I braced myself for yet another evening of having to watch my mother, *my* mother, the female who was supposed to inherently prefer me, bond with a woman I was fairly certain hated me.

"How did you hear about that?" my mother asked, though it was clear she was delighted Ellie had even thought to bring up the subject.

"Blaise was in the library earlier and overheard—"

My father's fork scraped his plate. "Blaise? In the library?" Suspicion furrowed his stony brow. In her youth, Blaise had been known to throw the not-so-occasional temper tantrum during her reading lessons—the ones my father paid for. "That child would do anything to get out of a day's work, wouldn't she?"

Ellie's eyes went wide, and she swallowed. "I didn't mean to imply Blaise wasn't working. I only—"

"She was working. For me," I said. Ellie's slender shoulders sagged in relief, though she kept her gaze averted from mine.

My father traced circles upon the dinner table with his finger. "Pray tell, Evander, what task of yours is so important that you would encourage Blaise to shirk her duties?"

"Let's just say she's researching a certain engagement gift for Ellie." I kept my eyes pinned on Ellie, and I didn't miss the way she bristled, preparing herself for where this conversation was inevitably headed.

My mother huffed in exasperation at my disregard for manners. "Evander, you can't go about hoisting the responsibility of finding a gift upon someone else. It defies the whole point."

"On the contrary, Mother. I only thought Blaise's taste might be better suited to the task. Knowing me, I'd probably choose wrongly."

"Well. I'm sure Ellie would love anything you gifted her, just by nature of it being from you. Wouldn't you, Ellie?"

How I loved my mother.

Ellie practically choked on her asparagus, but she recovered quickly enough. "Of course. I'm of the opinion that gifts are the perfect way for a person to show how closely they've been listening to their loved one."

My mother's smile faltered, and she bounced her knowing eyes between the two of us.

My father appeared to be savoring his potatoes, a conniving smirk spreading across his mouth.

Fine, Ellie didn't like my gift. I was two hundred thirty years old; I wasn't going to let my feelings get hurt over something like that. She had every right not to like it if she didn't want to.

But to be angry with me?

When I'd *tried*. I might have failed, but I'd at least *tried*.

I didn't get it.

I didn't get it then. I didn't get it three days later, and I was still stewing.

My mother spent the rest of dinner initiating discussions that sputtered into nothing.

Ellie excused herself from the table early that night, my father on her heels. I supposed he'd gotten used to having her around to buffer my presence and could no longer bear sitting at the dining table with me any longer than absolutely necessary.

My mother stayed awhile longer as I picked at my chicken breast.

Everything was so bland today. Had Collins fallen ill?

"Evander."

My mother's voice was gentle, but there was a sternness to it I rarely heard, even in childhood. She'd always used that tone with Jerad, never me. I always figured she spared me many a reprimand, thinking I got more than my fair share from my father.

"Yes?"

"You're not being very responsive to Ellie lately," she said.

"I don't see why that's unexpected," I said. "Neither of us wants to marry the other, after all."

My mother frowned. "I understand that you say you don't have feelings for her—"

"Oh, I have feelings—"

"—but trust me when I say your life will be easier if you try to grow to love her."

My gut twisted at that. Was that what my mother had done, grown to love my father? I'd always wondered. She seemed much too kind to love someone so cruel. But perhaps that was a fault of kind people; they tended to see good where there was none. My parents had been married for centuries before I came along. From my perspective, my mother had always seemed smitten with my father, adoring him despite his manifold faults. But had she always loved him so, or had she simply done what she always did, and made the best of a less-than-ideal situation?

I couldn't decide if that made me proud or sad or a little of both.

"Yeah, well, that's the problem. I tried, but El's not so great at being on the receiving end."

My mother sat straight up in her chair. "What exactly did you do, Evander?"

"Like I said. I reached out. Ellie's always talking about setting up a glassblowing shop, except instead of windows and bland functional items, she wants to make art. Like crystal sculptures and plates and dishes, and all sorts of things out of glass, that way the working class can afford pretty things. So I spent all this time and effort recruiting artists who were up to the task and buying supplies, and I even got the deed to a shop that was perfect. And then we get there, and she acts like I've just murdered her favorite puppy. I just...I don't know how to win with her, Mother."

My mother's face remained pleasant and gentle, but there was something there brewing under the surface, a *knowing* look that always had me wondering what she was remembering from my child-hood that I didn't. "Why do you think Ellie was upset?"

I tapped my fingers against the table. "I don't know. Actually, you know what? I know exactly why. Because she's so stubborn, and she's convinced she has to do everything herself, and it's like if you try at all to help her, then you've soiled the whole thing."

"Hm," was all my mother said.

I craned my head to the side. "What?"

265

"Did you ever consider, Evander, that perhaps it wasn't the shop that was Ellie's dream, but the sense of accomplishment she'd get from building it on her own?"

I sighed. Ellie had said as much, but that was still beside the point. "It just aggravates me that she won't accept anyone's help."

"Help? Is that what you would call it?" my mother asked. "Because it sounds to me as if you didn't help her at all. In fact, you did all the work for her."

I huffed a laugh. "Most people would consider that better than help."

"Is Ellie Payne most people?"

I choked. "Obviously not. If Ellie was most people, she'd be basking in the riches and the fortune of her life. Fates, she happened into being accidentally betrothed to a prince. Instead, she spends all of her time thinking about how she can rid herself of me."

"But dear," my mother said, placing her hand upon mine. "Do you even like most people?"

CHAPTER 36

ELLIE

*B*laise must have either been feeling sorry for me, or gotten tired of my ill mood because she'd popped her head into my room an hour ago and announced that she had a surprise.

In waltzed my mother, and I couldn't have been more shocked. Or thrilled.

After a long moment spent hugging, Blaise had explained that she'd gone to the queen and gotten permission to bring my mother for a visit. Then Blaise had disappeared, leaving me with my mother… as well as her task of hanging my laundry.

"You could apologize, you know," my mother said, rearranging the dresses in my wardrobe that were not hung up to her standards.

I bristled. "Apologize?"

Evander and I still weren't getting along, and I'd been avoiding speaking to him unless it was absolutely necessary.

He hadn't exactly been keen to address me, either.

I supposed I was going to have to learn to be okay with that. Wasn't that what I'd expected when I first learned of the betrothal? That the two of us would live out our marriage on opposite ends of the castle, only coming together for evening meals and the occasional attempts to sire a royal heir?

It took me half a breath to shoo away that sort of thought. It wouldn't do me any good, letting my mind wander down that road.

Especially not in front of my mother.

I'd told her everything, of course.

Well, not *everything*, but I'd told her about my and Evander's burgeoning friendship. About how he'd effectively proven to me that everything I'd worked my entire life for could be accomplished by the fae on a week's notice.

Why did I have a feeling she was about to make me regret all that telling?

"How long did you say your lady's maid has been a lady's maid?" my mother asked.

"She was just promoted to that position since I got here. I have another lady's maid too." Though it had been a few days since I'd seen Imogen.

"Hm," my mother said disapprovingly as she looked into the wardrobe and straightened yet another dress.

"Also, you can't say something like that and then change the subject. Why do I have to be the one to apologize? He's the one that was being insensitive."

"No," she said, sauntering back over to my bed, "he was being oblivious. You're the one who was insensitive, as I recall."

I grumbled at that. I never should have told my mother the entire story. Had I any inkling she would side with the prince of all people, I wouldn't have bothered to bring it up.

"You understand why it upset me, though, don't you?"

"I understand exactly why you were upset. He rained on this dream you've had since you were a little girl. Don't think I've forgotten all the times you rambled on about it while following me around while we were feeding the chickens. Or how many times your father had to go get you from the workshop to come to the dinner table. It was your favorite play place since you could walk. So no, don't accuse me of not understanding."

I smiled at that, even though in my anger I didn't want to. "Thank you for bearing with me talking your ear off."

She hmphed. "You're welcome."

"But if you understand, why are you defending him?"

"Because, Elynore. That male tried to do something kind for you. Something truly kind."

I crossed my arms as I plopped on the bed. "All he did was show me that he doesn't understand me at all."

The skin at the bridge of my mother's nose crinkled. "And why does that matter to you?"

"Because...well, he's going to be my husband whether I like it or not..."

"Only legally, I would think. At least, I would assume that the two of you would occupy separate areas of the castle and keep to yourselves, except for public outings, correct? Assuming that your marriage is purely one of bargain and necessity."

"Am I supposed to be happy about that?" I asked.

"No, but that wasn't what you complained about. You're not complaining that he ignores you, that he pretends you don't exist, that he's unkind to you. And you're certainly not complaining that he doesn't at least attempt to make you happy. You're complaining that he doesn't understand you."

I huffed, hugging myself. "Isn't that part of making me happy? Isn't that why you and Papa are so happy together? Because you understand each other?"

My mother shook her head. "You forget sometimes that you were not always a part of our lives, Elynore Payne."

What an odd thought. Of course I knew it intellectually. But all my life I'd been the center of my parents' universe, second only to their relationship with one another. How odd to consider that there was a time in their lives when their world had nothing to do with me whatsoever.

She continued. "We were married ten years before we had you. Do you think we knew each other so well those first few years?"

"I know you were in love," I said.

She smiled. "Ahh, yes. Being in love, the thing that carries marriages through those first few years when you're only just starting to discover how much more selfish of a person you both are than you previously thought. By the time you came along, your father and I knew each other quite well. But that took ten years. And sometimes I still don't understand the man, nor does he understand me in all things. Why are you expecting so much of a male you've only known for a few months now, who has grown up in an environment completely different than yours?"

I didn't have much to say to that. I hung my head. Perhaps I had been too harsh with him. "It was unkind of me to say—the part about him never working for anything in his life."

My mother focused a knowing, scolding eye upon me. "If memory serves me correctly, that's not all you said."

My face went hot. I probably shouldn't have told my mother exactly what I'd accused Evander of working for. "I think I know in my heart I should apologize. But how am I supposed to do that if he won't talk to me, either?"

"And why is it necessary that he talk to you for you to apologize to him?" she asked. "Fae don't have some skill of turning their hearing off at will that I don't know about, do they? Have you tried starting with 'I apologize for' or 'I'm sorry'?"

"Well, no..."

"Hmph."

"Why do you always have to be right?" I grumbled.

My mother smirked. "It's a mother's reward for enduring all those late-night diaper changes."

I laughed at that.

Just then, someone knocked on the door.

"Yes?" I asked.

"Ellie?" Evander's voice sounded muffled through the door.

Mother raised one pointed eyebrow at me.

"You can come in," I called out.

He opened the door, and though I had an apology ready upon my lips, I couldn't help but burst into laughter instead. "What are you wearing?"

"Oh, this?" He peered down at the full suit of armor that covered his body. It might not have been so humorous, except the armor was old and metallic and reminiscent of the armor humans used to wear into battle before the fae took over Alondria and magic entered the world, which rendered such cumbersome items useless. It clanked as he walked toward me, and his face almost looked smushed underneath his helmet. He turned to look at my mother then turned the slightest shade of pink. "My lady." He bowed, and the armor groaned. "You must be Ellie's mother. It's a pleasure to meet you."

"Your Highness," she said, her voice icy with suspicion. I wondered if Evander could tell it was a show, that she really didn't hate him. What would he think if I told him that moments ago my mother had taken his side? Not that I could ever allow him to know that such conversations took place at all.

"I won't stay long. I just...if you're feeling well..." He gestured to the door and cleared his throat. Another guard walked in, carrying a full suit of empty armor in his arms. "I thought we could go for a walk."

"In that?"

"Peck told me you're all healed up now."

I stared at him, amazed that he thought my injury was the sole reason I found this request strange.

"Well, if you want her to try it on, I suggest you hurry on out of here and shut the door behind you," my mother said, shooting daggers with her eyes toward Evander.

"Of course," he said, signaling his guard to leave the armor on my bed, at which point the guard fumbled with it awkwardly as he tried not to damage any of the sheets or drag them off the bed.

They left and shut the door behind them, and it took a fist to my mouth to stifle a giggle.

LESS THAN HALF AN HOUR AND a few bouts of bickering later, my mother had the suit of armor securely fastened on me. It was much too large. Evander must have struggled to find one small enough and settled for one I at least wouldn't topple over in. I wondered what small adolescent boy this suit had been fashioned for originally, and I shuddered.

"Your prince is an odd one," my mother said, looking me over in the suit of armor.

"He's not my prince."

She shrugged. "Has anyone told him that?"

I toddled over to the door, the gaps between the suit plates that allowed for any bit of movement pinching my skin as I moved. When I reached it, I knocked, and Evander opened it.

He unleashed a mischievous grin I had gotten used to not seeing on his face, and my heart swelled a bit.

"You ready?"

"I—" But my mother had already pushed me out the door.

CHAPTER 37

ELLIE

*I*t took double the time to traverse to the art district in the cumbersome suits of armor than it had when Evander had been pushing me in the wheelchair. The suits allowed for only the most rigid of movements. Not exactly ideal equipment for trekking down a hill.

More than once, I stepped on a rock I hadn't been able to see because of the visor on my helmet obstructing my vision, and Evander had to lunge forward to catch me before I toppled over and rolled down the hill.

At one point, I considered doing it on purpose, thinking at least it would be quicker and I probably wouldn't get hurt considering the obscene amount of metal that surrounded me.

By the time we made it to level ground, I was huffing with exhaustion and cursing the design of these suits that made it so difficult to keel over and catch my breath.

"Listen," I said, heaving as we passed the guards at the walls and reached the edge of the art district. "I'm sorry for what I said the other day." I paused, wondering if that was too vague of an apology to be worthwhile. On the other hand, I doubted Evander wanted to hear me repeat it. "It was uncalled for and insensitive. I know you were just trying to do something nice for me, and it was wrong of me to lash out."

"So the scorned lady is capable of apologizing after all," Evander said, shooting me an arrogant grin. So we were back to that persona. Great.

But then he came to a halt and turned to face me, all evidence of his smugness dissipating. "I'm sorry too. I'm not entitled to you liking my gifts. Especially when those gifts involve crushing your dreams." He scrunched his brow in a wince. "Be my friend again?"

Friend. The word had my stomach squirming, and I couldn't decide whether it was with butterflies or bile. My tongue seemed to shrivel up, my response with it, so I just swallowed and nodded.

"Why are you bringing me out here in these suits to begin with?" I almost asked him if eternity really had made him that bored, but then I thought better of it. Perhaps I should keep my snide remarks to a minimum for now.

"Because I'm tired of us not talking," he said casually. How in Alondria he had gotten it into his mind that traipsing around in armored suits would get us talking again, I had no idea.

Now that I considered it, we had exchanged more words in the past half hour than we had since the last time we visited town.

"So we're just to walk about the art district looking like ancient knights?"

He shrugged, which made the metal plates of his shoulder pads clank. "I figure if anyone won't think it odd, it would be the artists."

As I glanced around in embarrassment, I realized he was probably right about that. Most of the artists paid us no attention, and I remembered that it was common for traveling performers to spend most of their time in the city in the artists' quarter. We probably just looked like a couple of traveling pre-faeistic reenactors.

When we rounded the corner and found ourselves back at the cottage that Evander had renovated into my glass shop, I froze.

"What are we doing here?"

"Oh, I don't know. I guess I just felt like picking a fight and reliving the moment when you helped me realize what a miscreant I am." He extended an armored hand and nodded his head toward the door. Which ended up looking more like a twitch, given the lack of mobility afforded by his helmet. "Just give me a chance, will you?"

I sighed and took his hand, our metal gauntlets scraping as I did.

I wasn't sure what I'd been expecting. Maybe that Evander had removed the host of glass objects that made me feel so inadequate. Like someone else had taken my dream and run with it, equipped with a thousand times more talent than I could have ever hoped to accomplish in my limited mortal lifespan.

But when we walked in, nothing had been touched. Nothing had been rearranged. Nothing had moved.

"Evander, I'm sorry how I spoke to you when I was upset, but it still doesn't change the fact that I *am* upset."

"Exactly." His green eyes flashed. He drew the sword at his left side and turned it so that the hilt faced me. "Take it."

Confused, I did as he said, though I had to curl both hands around the hilt to support the weight of the hefty blade.

He brandished his second sword, then gestured toward the table in front of us, which held a delicately arranged set of glass teacups. "Ladies first."

"What are you—" But then it hit me, why Evander had brought me here. "You want me to swing this sword at them?"

He grinned, and though the sword grew heavy in my already sore fingertips, something like elation filled my bones. "Won't the artists be upset that we destroyed all their work?"

Evander laughed. "If they want to wipe their tears with the gold-leafed linens these bought them, they're free to do so. I went back and paid them extra for the emotional damage of it, and none of them seemed to mind once they saw the sum of my tip."

My jaw dropped. But then my back went rigid. "This feels petty."

"Exactly," he said. "That's the fun of it."

"But it doesn't change the fact that—"

"Ellie." Evander stepped so close the metal of his chest plate scraped against mine. "Please, for the love of all things pleasurable, just shut up for half a second and let yourself have some fun."

It was enough to spur me into action. I gritted my teeth. I'd show him fun. In fact, I lifted the sword so swiftly, he had to launch himself backwards to get out of my way.

Time sped up, and my blade with it. The edge of the sword hit the first teacup with a crash before slicing through the rest, sending teacups and plates and saucers soaring through the air, splintering in the candlelight. It looked as though stardust was blazing through the air.

I huffed, clutching my sore torso as I glanced at my feet. Shards of glass littered the floor, and my heart was pounding.

"You see why I had us wear the armor?" Evander laughed. I turned back to him, and as he caught what must have been a look of savage delight on my face, he grinned. "My turn."

In a whirl, he spun to his right. He was upon the farthest shelf before my eyes could track him. He swung his sword upward, sending splinters of wood and glass skyward, shooting through the upper shelves and splitting them in two. The shelves crashed all at once, pouring heaps of glassware down their slopes and onto Evander's helmeted head.

When he looked back at me, he beamed, even as the glass formed heaps around him.

It went on like that, the both of us bursting through saucer after plate after cup after perfectly formed dragon. Glass mermaids ricocheted off marble counters. Miniature ships, so detailed a sprite could have taken up residence within them, sailed through the air before slamming into the ground and shattering across the floor.

My hands started shaking and trembling as they went numb from clutching the heavy sword. It clattered to the ground, and Evander looked at me from the middle of a pile of glass ash, a questioning look on his face, as if to ask if it was time to stop.

But it wasn't time. Not yet.

I lifted my hand and dropped my metal visor into place. Then I picked up a warped glass ball and chucked it right at him. A wicked grin spread across his face, but it was quickly hidden as he dropped his visor, too. He ducked, and the glass exploded on the wall behind him. A moment later, he hurled a replica of his father at my chest. The King of Dwellen broke his neck on my chest plate, though judging by the fact that it didn't hurt, I imagined my assailant had held back on the strength of his throw.

We erupted into a very irresponsible, much more fun version of a snowball fight, at the end of which we had both fallen to the ground laughing.

I tried to roll over in my suit to face him, but with all the giggles and gasping for air, I could barely move against its weight. Besides, my core hadn't regained its strength since the attack, and every muscle in my gut was on fire.

"Evander, Evan...I can't...I can't..." My laughter kept me gasping for breath and I couldn't get the words out. Crap, it hurt to laugh. His laughter rang on too, though it grew louder as he crawled toward me through the sea of shattered glass.

When he reached me on his hands and knees, he rolled over and plopped the back of his head on my armored belly.

"Ow," I complained, though I didn't try to push him away.

He made to move off of me. "I'm sorry, I forgot you're still hurt—"

I shoved his head right back down. "No, it's fine. Your head can act like a weight. Help me get my strength up."

"Pretty sure that's not how it works, but okay."

We stayed like that until the laughter died down into subdued giggles.

"Who are the poor souls who have to clean this up?" I asked him, not sure I wanted to know.

"Oh, I'm just going to pay to have the building demolished," Evander said carelessly.

"Oh."

He leaned his head over and unshielded his face. "Don't tell me you actually like this little shop?"

"I never said I didn't like the shop. I just didn't like that you'd already filled it."

He grinned, his eyes lighting up. "I'm only teasing. I've already told the castle's cleaning staff to be here in an hour or two."

I rolled my eyes in annoyance. "Has it ever occurred to you that you make their jobs harder on them?"

His sea-green eyes sparked with mischief. "Okay, Miss Judgmental. You shattered more glass than I did."

"I'll just have to clean it up, then. You can stay to help me if you wish."

He rolled his eyes and sat up, and I tried to ignore the emptiness I felt when the weight of his head no longer rested on my belly.

"I informed the cleaning staff beforehand and offered a hefty tip to anyone who voluntarily decided they wanted to help clean it up. Those who wanted the extra money agreed. The others stayed behind, specifically the older ones. Apparently, from what they tell me, they've had plenty of tips from me to fund their families' cottages in the city. And that I do too much for them as it is."

"Oh."

"Mhm." He stood to leave, and I struggled against my suit to follow him. A flicker of amusement crossed his lips. "I should just leave you here for your rude little comment."

I sighed and laid my heavy head back on the ground. "I can't say I'd blame you if you did. Sorry, I can't seem to stop the insults from flowing. I don't know why I do that."

Evander just laughed, and he scraped his gauntlet against his helmet, like he'd forgotten he couldn't scrape his fingers through his hair. "It's all right. I'd take your little snubs over your silence any day," he said before tossing his helmet across the room.

He extended a hand, and I took it. When he lifted me, my feet left the ground for a moment, and he drew me close to his chest. He pulled a bit harder than necessary, sending our armor clanking against one another's yet again. My breath caught as he drew his face close to mine. "Forgive me yet?"

I nodded, breathless, as he leaned in closer, his shining eyes piercing me through.

"Good," he said, drawing back quickly with an amused grin on his face that said only one thing: *I win.*

It took everything in me not to throw a rock at him as he made me trudge back up to the castle in that ridiculous outfit.

CHAPTER 38

ELLIE

I might have spent more time replaying my and Evander's escapades in the glass shop had I not happened across something else that snagged my attention.

By the time Evander returned me to my room, my mother was gone. She'd left a note on my vanity saying how wonderful it had been to see me and that she hoped I enjoyed whatever adventure Evander had planned for me.

It took me at least half an hour and a few scratches and yelps, but I somehow managed to free myself of the suit of armor.

I took one look at the pile of metal on the floor, buckles hanging loose like snakes from tree limbs, and decided I'd worry about it later.

Besides. I had an urgent need that demanded attention.

And Evander had left behind my brand new key.

Using the map Imogen had made for me before the attack that had left me unable to explore as much as I would have liked, I wound my way down staircases and through dark corridors until I reached the kitchens. Blaise had once mentioned that her and Imogen's room was close by... There.

A scullery maid pushed open a door, and behind her I caught a glimpse of a hallway full of doors. She took note of me, scanning me with skepticism, but she said nothing.

A moment later, and I was in.

Now to find Blaise and relieve the desperate need I suddenly had to discuss the blooming butterflies in my stomach with a girlfriend.

It was an odd sensation, a lovely one. Not just the whirl of emotion I got in Evander's presence, the song of his voice as it echoed in my ears. But the way it welled within me, filling me up until I was threatening to burst and just had to tell someone about it.

I had to tell *Blaise* about it.

Was this what all those girls growing up had been raving about— the instant bestfriendhood that had never quite been within my grasp?

It would probably disgust Blaise, the idea of her friend developing feelings for the male who was practically her brother, but perhaps she could put that aside for a moment.

I just needed someone to giggle with.

How odd.

When I knocked on Blaise and Imogen's door (thankfully there was a plaque with their names on it), no one answered. Though I could hear shuffling inside.

A moment later Imogen answered, though she cracked open the door only a smidge. "Milady," she said curtly, her murky eyes slit with suspicion.

I forced a smile to my lips. I tried to feel pity for Imogen; I really did. But honestly. I'd done nothing to encourage her mood swings or the venom that often seemed to leak from her presence. "I'm looking for Blaise."

"She's not here."

"Where is she?"

"I'm not sure. I think she went to town."

"Well, I can leave her a message so she'll know to find me when she gets back."

Imogen shuffled, not bothering to crack open the door. "What message would you like to leave her, milady?"

I fought back the urge to groan. "Just tell her to come find me when she gets back."

"Anything else, milady?"

"No, Imogen, that will be all."

Imogen promptly closed the door.

I made it halfway up to my rooms before I lost all semblance of self-control and found myself at Blaise and Imogen's suite once more. Just in case Blaise had returned within the past ten minutes.

When I knocked on the door, no one answered. Perhaps Imogen had left to perform her other duties.

Figuring I'd better just leave her a note myself, I nudged the door open. Thankfully, it was unlocked.

I stepped into the shared suite, making a guess at which side was Blaise's—the messiest—and scribbled a note on the pad of paper on her desk.

I turned to leave, but as I did, something caught my attention, just a flicker in the corner of my eye. When I turned, I found the edge of a piece of paper flitting from underneath Imogen's bed. The draft from the vents must have blown it out from under the bed. If it made it much farther, I imagined it would end up on Blaise's side of the room, and Imogen would be lucky ever to see it again, so I picked it up and placed it under a paperweight on Imogen's desk.

But then my eyes caught the title.

Shifters: A Believer's Guide to Transmogrify.

I couldn't help it. My curiosity got the better of me, usurping my manners, and I unfolded the paper.

It was a pamphlet—one you might get from a shady vendor pretending to sell youth potions, except in the dusty corners in the back of the shop.

The type of shop Madame LeFleur owned, where she pretended to make her living off the beauty product shams she sold to unsuspecting customers in the storefront, while she peddled away Fates-knew-what behind that always-drawn velvet curtain of hers.

The pamphlet read:

Do you long to tap into your beastly form? Do you crave the power to unleash the monster within? Follow the steps below to harbor your soul to the moonlight and forever leave behind your humdrum life.

I rolled my eyes. This probably had come from Madame LeFleur's shop. The peddler had likely written the instructions herself while drunk on faerie wine, then decided they weren't half bad and figured someone would be foolish enough to buy the faulty instructions.

Imogen, strange as she was, didn't seem like the type to wish to become a lychaen. Perhaps she'd bought one of Madame LeFleur's DIY-blemish eraser kits and the shopkeeper had mixed up the instructions.

But hadn't Imogen denied frequenting Madame LeFleur's shop, claiming her stepmother thought the Madame to be a witch?

Though I supposed if Imogen was in the habit of buying this sort of product from the Madame, she might wish for that fact to remain concealed.

I flipped the pamphlet over. On the back was a list of ridiculous directions, some of which Imogen had crossed out and annotated.

The handwriting was definitely Imogen's. Her script was fresh on my mind from trying to decipher the labels she'd written on my map —the way her letters ran together in a way that almost overlapped.

1. Collect five tail feathers from an albino raven fledgling on its first flight. Imogen had written *"How???"* at the end of this statement.

2. Steep the white tail feathers in a tea boiled to the temperature of the Oracle's Hot Spring. I had to read it twice to decipher it, but in the margins was written, *only three miles away, possible during a break on the third day of summer.*

3. Drink the tea as the lip of the full moon—full moon was circled twice—*crests the night's horizon.*

. . .

ON THE SECOND page was a list of symptoms, some of which Imogen had marked as well.

1. Lychaenism may cause increased irritability. There was a check mark next to that one.

2. Lychaens will often have no recollection of their nights feasting, and will often awaken disoriented in a strange place, not sure how they got there. Imogen had circled the first phrase for this point and placed a series of question marks at the end.

3. Unwanted hair growth while in humanoid form may occur. The last symptom was crossed out entirely, except for the word *humanoid*, which was circled twice.

AFTER EXAMINING THE ANNOTATIONS, how seriously Imogen was taking this, guilt roiled in my stomach and I returned the pamphlet to the place under the bed. That way Imogen wouldn't know I'd seen it. I knew Madame LeFleur and took little stock in anything she sold—at least, anything Imogen might have been able to get her hands on. While from a mental health perspective, it was a tad concerning that Imogen was weighing the pros and cons of becoming a lychaen, from a practical perspective—

Well, to be honest, I didn't believe in such things.

I mean, I believed in lychaen. I wasn't blind to reality. But it was common knowledge that, although lychaen had long been romanticized in horror novels, they were simply a subset of faeries, not all that dissimilar to the forest faeries of Avelea or the lightning sprites of Laei.

I didn't anticipate Imogen would be turning into a lychaen anytime soon. Besides, perhaps she'd met a lychaen she was interested in. While it was uncommon, it wasn't unheard of for humans to fall in love with faeries. I supposed it wasn't all that different from falling in love with the high fae. Perhaps she had the desire, misguided as it seemed to me, to follow the object of her affection into that sort of lifestyle.

I figured it was best not to mention it.

So I left, and didn't think a thing about it for a good while.

CHAPTER 39

EVANDER

I couldn't sleep, and it was all Elynore Payne's fault.

Her infectious laugh kept ringing in my ears, coupled with the echo of shattering glass as I lay awake grinning ear to ear replaying the events of the day.

In fact, I couldn't seem to wipe the grin from my face, which was unfortunate. I wasn't sure that it was even possible to fall asleep smiling.

It had worked. My plan had worked, and El had forgiven me.

I should've been able to sleep.

After at least an hour of restless tossing, I decided food was the only solution. It was almost midnight when I padded down to the kitchens. I supposed I could have called for a servant to deliver the late-night snack directly to my quarters, but I'd always hated waking them in the middle of the night. From what Blaise told me, the golden tassel that hung next to my bed sounded a bell in the servants' quarters that was loud enough to wake the entire floor, which seemed a tad excessive given all I was suffering from was a rumbling stomach and a scurrying mind.

I'd snuck a plateful of tomorrow's oatmeal cookies from the

kitchen and was on my way back to my quarters when I noticed the door to the library was ajar.

It wouldn't have been much of an anomaly, except that my father was particular about the door staying shut. Something about the draft from the hall damaging the books. Or maybe he was worried that bugs would get in and ruin his collection.

One would have thought all the paddlings I'd gotten as a boy from forgetting this rule would have seared my father's reasoning into my mind, but they clearly hadn't.

Figuring there was no need for a careless servant to face my father's wrath, I went to shut the door, but my gaze locked on a shadow draped across a wooden table by the library window.

As I entered the library and approached, the shadow began to take form.

Blaise had fallen asleep, sprawled across the table with her face crinkling the pages of an open book.

As I approached, Blaise stirred and readjusted her head, revealing the title of the book at the top of the open page.

A History of Nuptial Law Among the Fae.

My stomach gave a rather unpleasant twist. I'd completely forgotten about Blaise promising to find a way out of my betrothal bargain with Ellie.

It was sweet, of course. And definitely the kind of thing Blaise would do. She might have been the laziest servant to walk the halls of Othian Castle, but there was little she wouldn't do for a friend—even if it meant searching law code into the wee hours of the morning.

I should ask her not to, of course. It wasn't really Blaise's responsibility to claw me out of the mess I'd gotten myself into. It should be me spending my evenings researching a way out of this bargain, not Blaise.

I'd resolved to convince Blaise of such tomorrow morning, when an unwelcome thought breached my mind.

What if Blaise wasn't only researching for my sake?

What if she was doing it for Ellie?

My gut wrenched, but I ignored it. Of course Blaise would want to find a way out of the bargain for Ellie's sake. She and Ellie had become close friends over the past several weeks. Blaise had taken to her in a way I hadn't seen her with another female. It would make sense that Blaise wouldn't want her friend forced into a marriage she didn't desire. I wouldn't even be surprised if Ellie had asked for Blaise's help in finding a solution.

No. Definitely not surprising.

Expected, even.

And good. This was a good thing.

Because if Blaise could find a way out of the bargain, a loophole in the law, then Ellie and I could both have what we wanted.

And getting out of this bargain was definitely what we wanted.

Both of us.

Especially me.

I mean, I couldn't speak for Ellie. I wasn't Fates-blessed with the gift of mind-reading. I supposed it was possible that during our time together, her feelings could have grown into something more tender than friendship.

Like today. There'd been a moment when I'd leaned in, when I'd stared into her shimmering eyes... Her heart had skipped; my fae ears had sensed it. The way her breathing shallowed, the way her pulse had faltered.

I would be lying if I tried to convince myself I hadn't been glad for her human hearing, for what it might have sensed in me in that moment.

Okay, so Ellie Payne was attracted to me. And I to her. But why shouldn't we be? We were both conventionally attractive individuals. That didn't have to mean anything. Friends could be attracted to one another without truly wanting anything more, couldn't they?

Sure, I'd never seen the use in denying pleasure with someone I was attracted to in the past, given they also showed interest. But Ellie was different. She was intelligent and witty and tenacious. And she was my friend.

Because that was what we both wanted.

Out of this betrothal, and to remain friends.

"Andy?"

Blaise's slurred voice snagged me back to reality. Her dark eyelashes fluttered as she lifted her head from the pages of the law book. Pink ridges creased her cheek from where the edges of the pages had been digging into her skin.

"Seems like you're suffering from a reading hangover," I said, closing the book in front of her before she could drool all over its pages and incur my father's wrath. "Come on. We're getting you to bed."

I went to help her up, and she made an attempt to shove me away as she rubbed her eyes. "No, I have to put these books away." She gestured to the hefty stacks of books piled on and below the table.

"Fates, Blaise. You've read all of these?" I asked, running my hands through my hair as guilt twinged at my stomach. I'd noticed that Blaise seemed more tired than usual lately. I'd thought she'd been out with farmhands all hours of the night, not poring over law books on my behalf. Some of them weren't even law books, now that I looked more closely. Within the messy stacks were titles like *Breaking Bargains, The Human's Guide to Reversing Fae Magic,* and *Fae Divorce Law.*

There were even a few books on elemental magic, a type of magic uncontrolled by the fae and therefore highly illegal. Granted, it was a good idea. It was possible for elemental magic to supersede fae magic, another reason it had been outlawed. I supposed it made sense that a more powerful source of magic could erase a bargain made by fae magic, but still... If my father caught Blaise looking into this kind of thing on my behalf and punished her for it, I would never forgive myself.

"Not all of them..." she mumbled, her chin jerking as she fought to keep herself awake. Dark circles had begun to form underneath her eyes.

This time, she didn't fight me when I picked her up and carried her back to her room. As soon as I lifted her feet off the floor, sleep overtook her and she tucked her face into my chest, just like she used to do as a child, her black hair falling tangled and matted into her eyes. A smile tugged at my mouth. I couldn't remember the last time I'd carried her to her bed, but it would have been years ago.

I EXPECTED Imogen to be asleep in bed at this hour, but when I approached the door, the glow of candlelight was seeping from underneath the door. Given that she was clearly awake, it took Imogen longer than I would have thought to come to the door after I knocked. There was the scraping of a chair against the floor, like the sound had startled her, then a rustling of papers, the patter of feet, and the slamming of a drawer before Imogen cracked open the door. "Don't tell me you've lost your key a—Oh. It's you." Imogen's eyes went wide, and magically that sliver she'd initially allowed in the doorway widened. "Your Highness," she said, curtsying as her gaze flitted to Blaise, who was still limp in my arms.

For a moment, I thought I noticed Imogen's eyes narrow, but it could have been a shadow cast from the flickering lantern light in the hall. She moved out of my way, and I entered their quarters.

Instantly, I searched the room for evidence of what Imogen so clearly had been rushing to hide from Blaise. It wasn't that I was particularly suspicious of Imogen, but I couldn't help my curiosity. The ink on the desk was uncorked, like Imogen had been writing something, but there were no parchments in sight. Except for the corner of one that protruded from the closed drawer of Imogen's desk.

Oh, well. It wasn't really any of my business, was it? Perhaps Imogen had a suitor she didn't want Blaise to know about. I couldn't really blame her. Knowing Blaise, she'd probably tease Imogen about it endlessly.

I crossed to Blaise's side of the room, the boundary clearly marked by a line of haphazard clutter, and set her on top of the sheets. When her head hit the pillow, her eyes fluttered opened, and she smiled, drunk with sleepiness.

"I found it, Andy," she said, her words garbled by a yawn.

"Found what?"

She squinted, like she was trying to squeeze the drowsiness from her eyes. "At least, I think I found it. A way to break the bargain with Ellie."

I went very, very still.

Imogen shifted in the corner.

"You haven't said anything," I replied.

Blaise stretched her arms outward, fighting to keep her eyes open. "Yeah. I meant I just wanted to make sure…" She jerked her head toward me, blinking rapidly. "Are you mad?"

"I…" Imogen's eyes lit up as I glanced up at her. She wasn't exactly the witness I wanted to this revelation, not when she dared to look so pleased when I was…when I was…

I was happy. Of course. This was the news I'd been waiting for.

I swallowed. "I'm not mad. I just want to be sure… No need in getting Ellie's hopes up if it doesn't work." That was true enough. If anyone deserved a choice in this, it was Ellie. Granted, the idea of extending that choice to her gnawed a hole in my gut, one I would have rather ignored.

Even in her stupor, Blaise must have been able to sense the not-lie, the dodginess in my response, because she frowned and pushed herself upright, leaning against the headboard.

"You're upset."

"I'm not—" My throat hitched, that dreadful fae curse tugging on the latch of my windpipe. Imogen's eyes went wide. I turned my attention back to Blaise, whose brow had creased with concern. "Okay, I'm upset. I've grown fond of Ellie. Of her friendship. And I'll miss her when she's gone."

"Andy…do you love Ellie?"

Imogen coughed, then quickly excused herself from the room, muttering something under her breath about fetching Blaise a glass of water.

I couldn't help but notice that Imogen's footsteps didn't patter all the way down the hall.

"Does she eavesdrop often?" I whispered to Blaise, but my friend was having none of it.

"Fates, you do love her. Don't you?"

I blinked, forcing the little that I knew to be true from my lips. "I don't know." It was true. I didn't know what I felt for Ellie, but that wasn't even the worst part. I didn't even know what I felt for Cinderella. It should have been simple, after she outed herself as the murdering sort, but I couldn't deny there was still a part of myself I'd let her sink her claws into, the dark disgusting part of me I didn't like to admit existed. But Ellie...

Well, it hadn't been thoughts of Cinderella that had kept me from sleep tonight, had it?

Blaise's brown eyes shimmered, and she buried her face in her hands and...groaned?

"Blaise? What's wrong? Why are you—"

"Do you mean to tell me," she said, her shoulders slumping, "that I spent hours of my mortal existence scouring law code *for nothing?*"

I placed my hand on the nape of my neck and rubbed, unable to decide if I wanted to be amused or exasperated by Blaise's dramatics.

"Not for nothing," I said, running my fingers through my hair. "I'm sure Ellie will be glad of it, at least."

Blaise let her hands fall to her lap and frowned. "You think she'll choose to break the bargain?"

"I don't know what Ellie will do."

"But you're going to tell her anyway?"

"When I find the right moment, yeah."

Blaise reached out and held my hand, her already pale face white with sorrow on my behalf. "If she chooses to break the bond... She's my friend too, you know." Blaise chewed her lip, her eyes flitting back and forth. "I can always come up with excuses to get her to visit. You know, if you wanted to happen to be around at the same time."

Gratefulness for my friend welled in my chest, and I ruffled her hair, which she took about as well as expected, rolling her eyes at me.

. . .

THAT NIGHT, as sleep fled me, I tried to ignore the fact that when I'd told Blaise I would inform Ellie of the way to break the bond, I'd been careful not to mention a timeframe.

CHAPTER 40

ELLIE

*T*wo weeks had passed since Evander and I turned the glass figurine shop into a war zone, and the Prince of Dwellen was throwing yet another ball.

Because the last one had worked out so well for him.

Okay, it was really the king who insisted on the celebratory event, to be hosted the evening before our final trial. Apparently it was tradition, or something like that, and it had to do with the fact that, should everything go to plan, Evander and I would be wed within a week of the final trial.

All of Alondria had been invited to the ball.

Well, that's what the king had said. What he'd meant was the all the rulers and lords of Alondria had been invited, but Evander had kicked me under the table before I mentioned the discrepancy.

As much as I wasn't looking forward to being paraded around a roomful of bloodthirsty fae royals, I had to admit: the gown was a perk.

When Imogen and Blaise had presented me with a selection of fine ballroom gowns, all exclusive designs for the Prince's Betrothed, I'd almost—almost—let myself get excited.

They'd brought me five dresses, but I'd hardly noticed the other four.

I hadn't even needed to try it on to know.

Though I'd tried it on anyway. Obviously.

The gown was golden and sparkling and simple and everything I could have ever wanted from an article of clothing.

As Imogen secured the back of the dress, I grazed its soft material with my fingertips. A Fae-made fabric. Humans had never quite figured out how to make a fabric sparkle like starlight and retain its softness.

When I gazed in the mirror tonight, a familiar rush went through me, as it had the first time I'd tried on the dress. Except this time Blaise had completed the look—a slash of kohl across my eyelids, a braided updo that allowed a flurry of tight curls to frame my face, a golden circlet that lay across my brow with a single diamond adorning my forehead.

The dress itself reminded me of molten gold burning so hot it was almost white. It sparkled and shone in the light of the flickering lanterns. Perhaps that was what it reminded me of—the soft glow of candlelight.

The dress was of a simple cut. Its high neckline grazed my collarbones before settling into thin straps around my neck, covering everything except my shoulders. It had a snug but tasteful fit around my hips before flaring out slightly at the bottom, quite unlike the girlish ballgowns I'd seen other female humans don.

"You look nice, milady," Imogen said, to which I smiled. It hit me how dazzled I'd been with my reflection just now, something I hadn't bothered too much with in the years where I'd been hunting down any last second to spend in my father's glass-working shop.

Blaise scoffed, leaning against my bedpost. "Nice? That's almost an insult. You look breathtaking, El."

I shot her a grin, and she tossed it right back. I hadn't ended up telling Blaise about my burgeoning feelings for Evander. By the time I'd seen Blaise again, doubt regarding whether Evander returned my feelings had begun to creep in. It just seemed easier to tuck them away rather than admit them aloud.

"Wait!" Blaise said, going to the vanity and pulling a string of pearls from a velvet box. She strung the necklace around my neck and fastened it in the back. When she did, the scent of lilacs and rosebud wafted in the air.

"You smell…*good*," I said, a bit more suspiciously than I intended to. Blaise wasn't the type to wear perfume.

Blaise just wheeled me around and tossed her dark hair over her shoulder in a flourish. "Why, thank you. Thought I'd try something new."

I didn't miss the glare Imogen directed toward Blaise, who leaned forward and whispered, "I may or may not have borrowed it from her without asking."

I was about to remind Blaise that one couldn't exactly borrow perfume, as there was no way to return the amount that was used, when I heard a knock.

EVANDER OPENED THE DOOR, and his eyes swept over me. He let out a strangled noise, as if he had thought to whistle but had then thought better of it.

I laughed. Good choice.

"Trying to impress me?" he asked, his sea-green eyes glinting with mischief as he leaned against the doorpost. His ball attire had been specially tailored to complement mine. Not match. Complement.

If my gown was a newborn star, then Evander was the night.

He was dressed in sleek black from head to toe, the only color in his snug-fitting suit at his wrists, where two white-gold buttons boasted the Dwellen insignia, a mountain formed of geometric flowers. His bronze hair had been styled, lightly combed back so it was out of his forehead—an old-fashioned style that quite suited him.

"Oh, Your Highness, you know there's no trying involved," I said.

Evander grinned and offered me his arm, which I took, not for the first time. His muscles bulged under his dress coat, and I tried not to notice.

Well, kind of tried.

Blaise and Imogen followed behind us, and as soon as they moved, Evander went still, a look of confusion spreading across his face. "What's that smell?" he asked.

Blaise flitted her hand into the air haphazardly. "That would be me."

Imogen shuffled her feet, clenching her fists.

Evander swallowed, blinking rapidly. "It's quite strong, don't you think."

"Is it? I didn't notice," Blaise said, though the way she flung her hair across her shoulder, sending a whiff of perfume in Evander's direction that had him gagging, implied otherwise.

I couldn't help but laugh at the way Evander's nose turned up in disgust. I rarely thought about how much more sensitive the fae's sense of smell was. The perfume, which was pleasant to me, must have been an assault to his nostrils.

"It seems you're no longer in need of escorts," Imogen snapped, bouncing into a quick curtsy before dragging Blaise away.

Imogen must really have been agitated about Blaise taking her perfume to willingly leave me alone with Evander.

My date just shook his head, like he was trying to clear his senses of the overwhelming perfume. When he looked down at me, he was smiling again.

"So, what's the ruse for tonight?" I asked.

"Oh, since we played up how much we hated one another in the last trial, I figure we give the nobles something to cheer for tonight."

His words sent a pleasant shiver down my spine. "And how exactly do we do that?"

"Act the part."

"What part?"

"The part of two people, separated by class and mortality and magic and general upbringing, fighting against all odds for our passionate love."

"Oh, that."

"Shouldn't be too hard for you," he smirked.

I rolled my eyes. "And why is that?"

"Because you're obviously in love with me. You won't even have to act." The words were encased in a taunting, playful grin. He was just flirting, I knew that. But I couldn't help but think of the night he told me he didn't love me. How, because of his inability to lie, I had known it to be true. Suddenly, the words didn't feel like so much of a joke.

"Ahh, yes, I'm sure…." But I didn't know where to go from there.

He chuckled, but didn't respond for the rest of the walk to the ball.

When we arrived outside the ballroom doors—each crafted from three-inch-thick sheets of crystal, because why not?—laughter and music echoed from inside. A pair of guards bowed to the prince when we approached.

"I thought the ball was to begin at half past seven," I said, concerned. Evander had picked me up no later than seven, so we should have been early, not late.

"The ball began for them at half-past six. For us, it begins at half past seven," he said.

"Is that customary?" My blood simmered with the anxiety of arriving to the ball late with Evander. It was bad enough to be escorted by him, to have everyone's attention on us at all times. But the prince would turn heads if he made a late appearance.

"Of course it's customary. Royalty can't be found sitting around waiting for their guests to show up like any regular dinner party. It's assumed that we make an entrance."

"No, thank you," I said, gulping down the anxiety.

He raised a brow at me. "I don't remember you being this nervous about the crowd during our first trial."

"That was because I was tad distracted by my impending death," I hissed.

Smiling, he leaned in close and whispered in my ear, "Don't worry. Just hold on tight to me, and you'll be fine."

I cringed. Whether it was out of disgust at Evander's arrogance and blatant flirting, or the pleasant tingling on my cheek where his hair had just grazed, I vowed never to admit to myself.

He grinned. "Ready?"

"No."

The doors opened, and the noise of the partygoers swelled. The ballroom was enormous, and its ivory walls sloped into a dome over our heads. Fae nobility bedecked in an array of sparkling gowns and fine dress coats mingled in small clusters across the rooms, their chatter eager and lively. They all looked too lovely, too regal to be real —a duke and duchess whose matching tattoos snaked up their arms in a pattern of tangled thorns; a female dressed in garments the color of moonlight with hair and a diadem to match, a red jewel dangling from her wrist the only splash of color in her attire; a male who snatched a pastry from a nearby serving plate with a flick of his wrist and a gust of wind. Musicians played flutes and lyres—fae tunes that I had never heard. Songs that made my feet feel like dancing as soon as they hit my ears.

"Introducing Prince Evander and His Betrothed."

We stepped forward, and the crowd halted their conversations, erupting into applause.

Evander leaned into me again and grumbled. "I've got to tell them to start using your name, El."

El. It rang in my ears and warmed my heart, the sound of my name on his lips.

I shoved that thought, that feeling, deep down.

He doesn't love me, I told myself. *He told me himself that he doesn't love me.*

But then Evander dropped his hand down my forearm, firing a whir of warmth through my blood as he clasped his fingers around mine and sent me twirling before the crowd. The crowd gasped, and the applause swelled again.

By the time Evander caught me in his arms, I was already breathless. His lips twitched into a smile.

But then the herald spoke again. "And now, the moment you've been waiting for. His Majesty King Marken and Her Majesty Queen Evangeline."

A louder but somehow more reserved applause echoed off the marble ceiling as the king and queen entered behind us, and I couldn't help but wonder how genuine it was. Evander had told me that this crowd was full of noblemen and fae. If that were true, did the wealthy ruling class support the king's reign, unlike the poorer and middle-class humans? Or was there malice and envy lacing the applause?

Evander placed his hand on my back and turned me to face the king and queen, who both approached us with a flowing grace that I would never have bothered aspiring to.

Evander's father wore a silver dress coat with indigo lapels, while the queen sported a matching silver gown that flowed behind her in a train of silken starlight.

The king's steely eyes fluttered over me, and he smiled, a look that made my stomach sink into the pit of my stomach. "You look like a queen."

I pursed my lips and curtsied, lest I say something foolish. Just because the king tolerated me challenging him in private didn't mean things would go well for me if I tried the same in front of all his lords and noblemen.

It was already shocking enough that the king had yet to punish me for embarrassing him during the second trial.

"Doesn't she?" Evander asked, then turning to his mother, said, "I believe between the two of you, we've been graced with the two most beautiful females in Alondria."

I'm embarrassed to say, my beam probably outshone the queen's. Evander must have noticed, because he nudged me ever so slightly.

Evander wasn't the only one to notice.

The king's lips curled into the most unfriendly grin I'd ever had the misfortune to witness, but his gaze cut above my head, across the ballroom.

"My dear Lady Nightingale," he crooned, just as a stunning female with sleek black hair and tanned skin approached us.

I couldn't have missed the violence with which Evander flinched at her name if my limbs had been numbed by frostbite. I shot a questioning brow at him, but he avoided my gaze.

"My King," Lady Nightingale answered, extending her hand for the king to kiss. "It's been far too long."

"Indeed," he said. "Evander often complains of just that."

"Does he now?" Lady Nightingale's gaze flicked over to Evander, and with that one knowing look, I understood just why Evander had stiffened in her presence.

The former lover alarms that sounded in my brain could have rivaled the king's battle trumpets.

If someone told me that Blaise had painted the smile on Evander's face, I might have believed them. "My father is prone to exaggeration. It comes with the crown, so I'm told."

That the king didn't seem at all perturbed by his son's slight had me fighting to keep myself from rocking back and forth on my heels.

"Son, why don't you offer the first dance to Lady Nightingale? For old times' sake?"

The queen cleared her throat. "Dear, traditionally the first dance is given to—"

"I'm sure Lady Payne wouldn't mind." There was nothing but challenge in the king's cold gray eyes.

The muscles in my back knotted. My stomach clenched. If this female hadn't even bothered to acknowledge my presence, I doubted she'd bother acknowledging the betrothal that tied my life to Evander's, and with their obvious history...

"Of course I don't mind," I said, trying not to bare my teeth as I released Evander's arm. I'd rather not give the king the satisfaction.

"Lady Nightingale," Evander said, placing a warm hand on my back. "I'm afraid I intend to give the first dance to my future wife." My heart swelled at his touch, at the sound of those words on his lips. My future wife.

"Of course, Evander," she said, her voice saccharine, "I understand that you have *obligations* that must be upheld."

Something sparked in me. "You know what, Evander," I said, stroking his arm in a way I supposed I'd never done before given the way he rose his brow in surprise, "let Lady...what was it? Thrush?" Lady Nightingale's eyes narrowed. "Let her have the first dance. What's a first dance to me, when I'm the lucky woman who gets your last?" When I cut my eyes over at Lady Nightingale, I made sure to give her a smile that could have won awards.

She returned it, but I liked to think mine looked less forced.

Evander's mouth went ajar, and he swallowed. "If you say so." He took his ex-lover's arm and led her to the dance floor.

When he placed his hand on her tiny waist, my heart wilted, my smile with it.

"He kept her around the longest of all of them," the king crooned.

I no longer wondered how he planned to punish me for embarrassing him during the second trial.

CHAPTER 41

ELLIE

*L*ady Nightingale was a skilled dancer.

Watching her and Evander twirl around the dance floor with such grace and ease, one would have thought they'd done it a thousand times—oh, wait, probably because they had done it a thousand times, and it had me wondering just how long they'd been together.

"Two decades," the king said with that annoying little habit of his that had me questioning whether the Dwellen fae had also been blessed with the ability to read minds.

It was probably just my soured expression, though. Or the way I was crossing my arms so hard, my forearm muscles bulged.

Two decades? Evander had courted this female for longer than I'd graced this side of the sun.

Though I supposed the king could have made up a number just to get under my skin. The fae curse kept him from lying, but that didn't mean he couldn't spout out random numbers when he hadn't even been asked a question.

One dance, I told myself.

But when one had decades of history up their sleeve, did they really need anything more than a single dance to rekindle the flame?

As if in answer, Lady Nightingale leaned in close and whispered something to Evander. I averted my gaze to the floor and began counting marble tiles. I couldn't stand to witness his reaction.

My heart ached.

"Miss Payne, so they tell me?" A smooth, playful voice made me lose count.

I startled, suddenly keenly aware that whoever this stranger was, they had probably just witnessed me pining after Evander.

I turned to find a ridiculously handsome male peering at me, offering his hand as if he expected me to take it rather than continue gaping at him.

His wavy dark hair fell carefree onto his forehead, tousled in a manner that must have been meticulous and purposeful for the way it somehow managed to look both messy and put together. Pointed ears poked through his dark waves. A mischievous grin spread across his tanned face and a promise of adventure flashed in his pale molten eyes.

"I..." *Get ahold of yourself, Elynore Payne.* "I'm afraid you haven't bothered to tell me your name."

It came out with more of a bite than I intended it to. Amusement sparked in the male's stunning eyes.

"Just call me Fin."

Fin. The name sounded familiar, and it probably should have. Most everyone invited to this ball would have been mentioned in the papers at some point or another. But for some reason, I couldn't place it.

"It's a pleasure to meet you, Fin. I'm Ellie Payne."

A flash of white teeth. "So I've heard."

Right. He'd already said that.

He leaned in close, the smoked cedar scent of him lingering as he whispered, "If you don't take my hand, I'm afraid I'll never hear the end of it from my sister-in-law."

When I looked down, I found his hand still outstretched, suspended in the air expectantly. I took it, though as soon as I did, I found my eyes darting around the room for Evander.

I found him all right, dipping that Nightingale woman so low her silken black hair grazed the floor.

I hoped Blaise had slacked off on mopping that very floor.

When I glanced back at Fin, he was watching me intently.

"What?" I asked, as he locked his fingers into mine and placed a hand on my waist. My skin warmed and my heart fluttered at the touch.

"Half the dances at these royal balls never mean anything," he said knowingly.

I scoffed. "Evander can dance with whoever he wants."

Fin's lip twitched, and he pulled me onto the dance floor. His steps were quick and sure, leading me through the dance with such mastery I found myself not having to think about where my feet went. "You're right. I suppose you are being forced to marry him. I can understand the strategy in remaining emotionally detached."

Emotionally detached. Definitely. That was definitely what was happening. I rolled my eyes. "So romantic."

He quieted for a moment. The lyres and harps transitioned into a new song, this one slower than the last. I couldn't help but notice that Evander and his dance partner slowed too, the female so close to him she might have laid her head on his chest and fallen asleep.

Not just the first dance, but the second.

Strong hands pulled me close, and I found myself a breath away from Fin's chest. I resisted and pulled back, the nearness of the lanky fae male as unsettling as it was enticing.

I expected a flash of anger to cross his face. To be invited to this ball, he had to be of noble birth and likely would take offense to a mere human rejecting his advances. But Fin only grinned wider. "You're ruining my schemes, Ellie Payne. I'm only trying to help you out."

I bit my lip, irritation boiling. "Perhaps you might consider that I'm not interested in what you're offering."

He looked offended, but I was almost certain it was feigned. "And what exactly do you think I'm trying to offer you?"

My cheeks burned, and I considered waltzing away and leaving him stranded on the ballroom floor, but the king was already displeased enough without me snubbing one of his honored guests.

Still. I might have the sense not to spurn him so openly, but that didn't mean I couldn't speak my mind.

"Do you always assume that women want you to 'help them out'?" I could hardly contain my eye roll.

Suddenly Fin was very close.

Way too close.

He'd dipped me backward, pressing his forehead to mine until our noses brushed, his breath heating my lips. I gasped, stunned for a moment as he held me there, suspended with his palm supporting the small of my back.

I don't know what I was expecting to see in his eyes. Perhaps longing or hunger or a range of emotions that were not at all appropriate to feel for the betrothed of another. But then he winked, and his eyes darted to his right, signaling me to follow his gaze.

I took the chance and glanced to my left.

Evander was still dancing with his former lover, but his neck was craned at an angle that hardly looked comfortable, his jaw clenched tight. His tanned skin flushed crimson, his sea-green eyes glowing. Or rather, glowering.

"You're the noble type, aren't you?" Fin mused, still breathlessly close to my face. "I take it you don't play games, Ellie Payne."

I leveled a glare at him. "You don't have to use my full name every time you address me, you know."

He laughed.

I chanced one last look at my betrothed, the female in his arms now scowling with distaste, and I turned back to Fin. "I'm always up to learn something new."

He flashed me a wicked grin, and in a moment he had me twirling around the dance floor, the hem of my dress catching flight as I spun. The world whirled around me, and I couldn't help the girlish giggle that escaped my lips.

A tug at my arm, and he had me spiraling into his arms just as the tune slowed to an intimate lull, our faces so close that his lips almost grazed my forehead.

My back to Evander, I peered up into that face full of trouble and opened my mouth, but then bit back the question, fearful of looking too desperate.

"To answer your unspoken question, yes, the prince is still staring." His eyes flitted over the top of my head, then back down. "And yes, I will be up all night, knife clutched to my chest, lest he murder me in my sleep."

I let out a laugh, and he smiled. Not a seductive one this time. A genuine smile that, paired with his curls, gave him an almost boyish look. "I like you," I found myself saying. "I think perhaps we could be friends."

His eyes twinkled as he feigned a heartbroken frown. "Friends? Elynore Payne, you say that word like it isn't a bludgeon to the male ego."

A close-lipped smile tugged at the corners of my mouth, and I shook my head. "You're not interested in me. You saw me pining after Evander and thought you'd come to my rescue."

"Mmm," he said, dipping me once more, this time holding my stare instead of bothering to glance in Evander's direction. "And why couldn't I have done it for both reasons?"

I bit my lip as he yanked me upright. "Because you've been glancing past my shoulder this entire time." It was true. While I'd been focusing on Fin's handsome features to keep my traitorous eyes from checking that Evander and his former lover hadn't snuck out of the ballroom, he'd been fighting—and often failing—to keep his eyes off someone in the corner. "Tell me, Fin. Who are you using me to make jealous?" Where I expected smug denial, his smile faltered a bit, the mischief in his eyes dying out.

I frowned. "I didn't mean to call attention to a spot of soreness."

He shook his head, and as quickly as it had fled, the light in his grin returned. "You didn't."

This time, I took the lead, twisting us around so I could get a good look at who Fin had been staring at all night.

My stomach might have dropped a bit when I found the Queen of Naenden watching us intently with her one eye.

My breath caught, and I quickly positioned Fin in front of me to shield me from embarrassment.

Fin's eyes sparkled with amusement. "Don't worry. She's not nearly as terrifying as she looks. Except when she uses that Old Magic of hers…" He shivered, as if shaking off a memory.

I frowned, pieces of headlines fitting together in my mind. Fin…

I jolted my gaze up to him. "You're Prince Phineas of Naenden."

He groaned. "Okay, I'll agree to stop calling you by your full name if you agree to stop saying mine."

"And that," I said, barely inching my head toward his queen, "is your sister-in-law."

"Could there be any more judgment on your face right now?" he asked, eyebrow cocked.

I had half a mind to rip my hands from his and put them on my hips. Instead, I hid myself behind Fin's tall frame. "Next time, when you decide to use an unsuspecting woman to make a Gifted queen jealous, perhaps you should let her know in advance whose wrath she's incurring."

At that, Fin looked like he might choke. "You think I'm dancing with you to make *Asha* jealous?"

I stiffened, and it somewhat impeded our keeping with the beat of the music. Okay, well now I was offended on her behalf.

As if he could read my thoughts, Fin shook his head. "Don't get me wrong. I love Asha. But she's like a sister to me. Nothing more."

I frowned. "Then who were you staring a—Oh. *Oh.*"

I shot a wide-eyed, knowing expression in Fin's direction. "Well, I can see why you like her."

In fact, I couldn't believe I hadn't noticed her before. The girl standing behind the queen was one of the most beautiful women I'd ever laid eyes upon, her almond-shaped eyes sparking, her black hair flowing loose at her shoulders, an emerald diadem atop her head to match her silken dress.

Still, her posture wasn't that of a woman who spent much time considering her own beauty. She stood behind the queen, straight-backed and sure of herself, but seemingly all too willing to fade into the background.

"Who is she?"

"She is also my sister-in-law."

I shot him a disbelieving look. From everything I knew about Naenden, marriage was monogamous. Even if rulers had a tendency to keep mistresses besides their queens, they didn't actually marry more than one at a time.

I supposed the King of Naenden had meant to get around that by offering up a bride as a sacrifice every mooncycle so he could get himself a brand new one.

Now that I'd seen the Queen of Naenden in person, I no longer found it surprising that she'd found a way to survive.

"She's Asha's sister," he explained with an embarrassed flush to his cheeks.

"Oh. Well, that…" I swallowed my initial inclination to say that was really weird. I was trying out this sensitive thing after all. "That will make holidays convenient, I suppose."

He shot me a look that told me he saw right through my attempt at concealing my judgment.

"I'm not trying to make her jealous," he said with a resigned huff.

I glanced back at the girl, whose eyes kept flitting toward us, then quickly away. There was no anger or petty fury in them. Just discomfort and a twinge of sadness that I was sure cut deeper under the surface. "Then I'm afraid this isn't going to plan," I said, instinctively putting more distance between the two of us.

Evander was clearly jealous enough. No need to make the girl cry for no reason.

"She needs to move on," he sighed, his hand twitching, as if he were fighting back the urge to let go of me and run his hands through his hair.

I cocked a brow. "Why does she need to do that? I'm not exactly an expert on love, but I'm fairly certain people don't check on someone every three seconds if they harbor no feelings for them."

When he looked back at me, his eyes had lost some of that mischievous fervor. "Dinah's different. She's good."

"And you're not? Last I read the papers, you weren't exactly the evil twin."

He laughed, a dry hoarse sound. "No, I'm afraid that title still belongs to my brother."

My mind flashed back to a newspaper article from about a year ago.

Naenden King Executes Brother's Wife for Conspiracy Against the Prince.

I'd thought the entire situation was horrible, of course. And honestly, one could never be sure the writers of these sorts of articles were bothering to tell both sides of the story, especially when a fae as powerful and cruel as the King of Naenden was the subject. Did Fin not believe his brother? The article had claimed the king had killed the princess in his brother's interest.

Or maybe he did believe him, and something like that was just simply unforgivable, regardless of the intentions.

"I'm sorry for your loss," I said. The words felt weak coming out. Useless.

"Me too," he said, absentmindedly glancing back at Dinah.

I bit my lip, unsure of whether I was overstepping. But then again, I supposed he'd been overstepping when he'd whooshed in to rescue me from a night of pining after Evander. And he *had* made me feel better. "I'm sure it's difficult to move on after something like that. There must be a lot of guilt surrounding any feelings you might develop for someone else. Especially for someone who was fortunate enough to marry for love."

Fin scoffed. "Fortunate? Is that what you'd call it?"

I swallowed. Yes, I'd definitely overstepped. But still. "I apologize. I didn't mean to offend."

He glanced down at me, his eyes softening, then he broke into a sad smile. "You can go ahead and argue your point if you wish, but I assure you, you're not fooling me."

"Fooling you?"

"Into thinking I should listen to you because you have experience being betrothed to someone you don't love. Trust me, it took about three seconds of the prince waltzing with that female and half a glance at your face to know otherwise."

My stomach tightened, and my mouth went dry, irritation buzzing at my cheeks. "One might say it's even worse this way. To marry for love, when your betrothed is simply marrying for duty. What am I supposed to do?" My throat constricted, a painful bulb forming around my throat. The next few words I had to push out. "Sit around and pine after him as he takes his mistresses to bed? Throw myself at him, fully aware I'm simply one of many?" And then the true reason. "Love him, while the whole time, he's in love with someone else?"

My eyes stung, and Fin released my hand, bringing his to my cheek and brushing my skin with his thumb, catching a tear beneath his touch.

I couldn't help but glance over at Evander, who was now dancing with another woman...with...the Queen of Naenden.

"For what it's worth," Fin said, catching my attention once more, "my brother's a monster, and my sister-in-law won him over in the end. I'd say Evander's not nearly as far gone."

I sighed a smile at him. "This is pretty pitiful, you know. The both of us pouring our hearts out to complete strangers."

"Miss Payne," Fin said with faux offense, clutching his chest. "And I thought you said we were friends."

I let out a laugh-sob, and he leaned forward, pressing a kiss to my forehead.

"For what it's worth," I whispered, "I think Dinah would understand if you told her you needed time."

Fin flinched, and for a moment I thought I'd offended him, but then he pulled away, and I found it was a hand on his shoulder that had startled him.

Evander leveled a sickeningly forced grin at Fin, one that didn't even attempt to meet his eyes. "One more song and I might be tempted to take offense," he said, his voice lighthearted enough, though I could sense the tension behind it.

"And I'd never dare risking such a thing," Fin said, tapping Evander on the back.

Fin winked at me before he bowed and walked away.

CHAPTER 42

EVANDER

*I*t was as if all the thoughts that make a horrible person—
well, horrible—were all competing for first place in my
mind.

There was the obvious one, of course. The classic go-to.

The fae prince who'd stolen every single one of Ellie's dances that
night was irrefutably uglier than me.

Okay, maybe not. But he was shorter than me.

Maybe.

By at least an inch from the looks of it.

If he'd managed to keep his wife alive, then perhaps he wouldn't
feel the need to seek comfort in Ellie.

Okay, that was the truly despicable one—the thought I felt bad
about the instant it stroked my mind, threatening to fester there.

Honestly, though. What was he doing dancing so publicly with a
woman hardly a year after his wife's death? At the hands of his
brother, who currently sulked in the corner, no less.

Really, it was my responsibility as Ellie's friend to put a stop to it.
If memory served me correctly, Kiran, the King of Naenden, had
crushed the windpipe of Fin's late wife before reducing her to a pile
of ash.

The story that had made its way north to Dwellen was that Prince Fin's bride, Ophelia, had plotted against him, attempting to seduce Kiran into both her bed and her schemes to assassinate the prince.

That was why he'd killed her. Or so he said.

But who was I to assume he'd told the truth, when he very well could possess an innate jealousy over his brother's lovers?

I chose to forget my species' inherent inability to lie. It was more convenient that way.

Just by allowing this to continue, by allowing Prince Fin to spin Ellie around like she was a marionette, I was practically complicit in Ellie's untimely demise. Her fiery murder.

What kind of friend would I be if I stood aside and did nothing?

"Your betrothed looks like she's having all the fun, doesn't she?" an amused voice asked.

I turned, then practically jumped, gobbling up my shock too late.

My surprise quickly warped into mortification.

The Queen of Naenden stood before me, her frame tiny and delicate and not at all matching her face. The scars that cut across her cheeks. The patches of mismatched skin. And most shocking of all, the pinkish empty eye socket that should have mirrored a pretty hazel eye.

"Your Majesty," I said, clearing my throat. "I apologize. I didn't see you standing there."

"You don't allow others to sneak up on you often," she said, and I wondered whether that was a question.

I shook my head. "No. No, not usually. But it's been a long night, and I've been…distracted."

"By your betrothed dancing the night away with my brother-in-law."

My smile flattened, as hard as I tried to tug it upward on the edges. I had to remind myself that Queen Asha of Naenden didn't grow up in a royal court. If a member of the nobility used that sort of direct language, it was almost always with the intention of being disarming. Coming from a human raised in an impoverished neighborhood in Meranthi?

The queen was probably just blunt.

"Our marriage is arranged," I said. "There is little room for jealousy. That would require a sense of possession, and as I don't claim to own her heart, and I don't believe in owning her person, I have little claim to the emotion."

My jaw almost dropped, and I tried to remember the words just as they'd come out of my mouth, because it was probably the most eloquent thing I'd ever said.

"Mmmm..." she said, her crooked smile wry. "A pretty male with pretty words."

I wasn't sure that was a compliment.

I was also fairly certain this was the point at which it became rude if I didn't ask the Queen of Naenden out onto the dance floor. Which I would have been inclined to do, had her husband not been lurking in the corner.

Everyone in this room was well aware of his reaction to his first wife cheating on him.

It would make history books. It *had* made history books.

And so had the tiny human standing before me, waiting to be asked to dance.

One waltz was far from cheating, sure, but the King of Naenden seemed like the type to murder anyone who laid a hand on his wife—innocent or not.

I wondered if she was into that.

Even now the King of Naenden sulked in the corner, quieter and less gregarious than his twin by manifold. Well, sulking probably wasn't the right word. It was more like he was reserving himself, his shoulders tight, his spine rigid, his fire-wick eyes scanning the room as he brought his chalice to his mouth more times than I imagined he actually sipped it. That was something I'd noticed about people who kept to themselves. They were always sipping something, holding something in their hands.

It was almost as if the King of Naenden—

"Kiran doesn't enjoy crowds. I made him promise me the last dance, though he'd rather be in the gardens," said the Queen of Naenden, breaking me from my thoughts. When I turned my attention back to her, a girlish smile curved at her lips, as if she had referenced an inside joke I wasn't a part of.

The smile softened her harsh features, and a barb of guilt panged at my stomach for not noticing it before—the person behind the scars.

This woman, with all her rough edges, her mismatched features, had calmed the fiery torrent and saved a nation's worth of women with her words alone, and probably a little help from the Old Magic that was rumored to possess her.

I wasn't sure what I'd expected from the human Queen of Naenden. It wasn't this.

"If you don't ask me to dance soon, others will think you find me ugly."

I blinked.

She blinked back.

"You're not exactly the source of my hesitation," I said, shifting my gaze to the hulking monstrosity of a male in the corner. "I'd rather not end up burned to cinders."

She shrugged. "Yet you risk inciting his wrath should you insult my appearance. You truly are between a boulder and a vat of quicksand, aren't you?"

I eyed her with suspicion. "Are you sure my dearly betrothed didn't put you up to this?"

She scanned the room. "Is she the type? If so, perhaps I should leave you be and go dance with her. It seems as if she's the more fun of the two of you."

I let out a laugh that bordered on a wheeze. "Ellie Payne? More fun than me? Please don't torture me with such nonsense."

I offered my hand, and she took it.

THE QUEEN OF NAENDEN was not a skilled dancer, but she seemed aware of it, because she allowed me to lead.

Which honestly was a bit of relief, after dancing with Valia

Nightingale. She'd grown bored of me after the second dance. Or so she said.

She'd probably just gotten irritated with me staring at Ellie and the Naenden prince.

I couldn't help whose feet I stepped on when I was distracted.

"I misjudged you," said the queen, as innocently if that were an appropriate entry point into a new conversation.

It was my turn to quirk a brow. "Is that so?"

"Your reputation is rather colorful when it comes to women, yet you hold me as if your life depends on setting a chasm between us."

Indeed. A baby cow would have had leg room in the gap I'd measured between my body and the Queen of Naenden's.

"You kind of just say what you think, don't you?" I said, my gaze immediately flicking to Ellie. I immediately regretted doing so, as I caught a glimpse of the Naenden prince dipping her, her long beautiful neck exposed as she tossed back her head in a delighted laugh.

My dinner soured in my stomach.

She shrugged. "After my accident, my father lost hope that I would ever wed, so he raised me like a ruffian."

"You mean like a male," I said.

She laughed. "Yes, like a male. I don't think he had the energy to sand away the crude edges."

"He probably secretly liked you how you were and was glad for an excuse not to."

The Queen of Naenden beamed. "Yes, I imagine so. I'm fond of him myself."

For the second time tonight, her harsh features seemed to melt away, and I thought I caught a glimpse of the beauty her husband beheld in her. There had been whispers that the human queen had enchanted her husband, bewitched him with that "stolen" magic of hers. I supposed everyone thought it unlikely, if not impossible, for a fae as powerful as the King of Naenden to love a human so disfigured.

Those people were wrong.

Well, mostly.

I had a sneaking suspicion the queen had enchanted her husband, just not in the way everyone else assumed.

She went quiet for a while, and I noted, "My reputation with women might precede me, but I would never dream of coming on to a married woman."

"Hm," she said. "And what about coming on to a single woman once you're married?"

I almost choked.

She shrugged unapologetically. "You can blame my father for the question."

Again, I glanced at Ellie, her smile like a beacon drawing me to her, yet like the sun in how it stung to watch her dancing with the Naenden prince. "I won't be unfaithful to my wife. No matter what the papers may claim about me."

A slight smile curved at the queen's gnarled lips. "I'm glad to hear it."

I cocked my head, examining the woman before me. She was younger, far younger, than I'd first realized, the scars aging her face. But if I focused on her features, the ones original to her, I realized she mustn't have been more than two decades old.

She'd barely surpassed childhood, barely lived a life, yet she'd thrown it away to save her people.

Something stirred in me.

I wasn't sure if it was guilt or admiration. Was there a word for the mingling of the two?

I was used to women wanting to dance with me, throwing themselves to get in line, married women even.

But this queen had not approached me for a dance, I now realized. Should have realized immediately.

"Why are you here, Your Majesty?"

"My brother-in-law needed to get out. He starts to miss people after a while," she shot back.

I'd encountered Fin on enough occasions to know that wasn't true. He could retreat to spend time with himself as easily as he could charm women.

"Why are you really here?"

"We were invited, were we not?" she asked, feigning outrage. "If Kiran only pretended to have gotten an invitation because he wanted to come dancing..."

I settled my most unamused smile over my face. The queen's eye flickered.

"Naenden hardly ever makes an appearance at social gatherings of other nations."

She scoffed. "Well, that's because Kiran's father was a paranoid tyrant."

I almost choked. That he was. That he was.

"Kiran intends to rule differently than his father." The pride that emanated from the woman before me...it almost hurt. To have a wife who spoke about her husband with such confidence, such adoration...

I'd grown up in court, and though my mother hardly ever spoke an ill word of my father, I'd overheard plenty of my mother's courtiers bashing their husbands.

Granted, most of their husbands deserved little more respect than that which was granted to them.

But still.

I imagined that having a partner who spoke about you that way... Well, it would spur me to be a better male, that was for sure.

"I have no doubt about that." I omitted the part where I was fairly certain the king's change of heart had almost nothing to do with an innate sense of righteousness, and everything to do with the woman standing before me. "But just because your husband intends to rule differently doesn't mean he has to attend celebratory balls for which he clearly has no interest."

The Queen of Naenden sighed. "Fine," she said, "but if we're going to discuss this, I'd rather not have to shout about it from across the room."

I must have squirmed, because she rolled her eye. "I promise Kiran isn't going to turn you to ash just for dancing with me at a reasonably chaste distance."

"Yes, but you're a human. So is your promise really worth that much?"

She shrugged. "Fair."

Still, I couldn't help but be curious, so I pulled her closer, until the scent of smoked cedar and citrus wafting from her hair filled my nostrils.

No matter what she assured me, I still kept a platonic distance between the two of us, even as the music slowed and the crowd began to pull their partners closer, to sway in a rhythmic pulse.

"There was a human who owned a shop in town—her name was Madame LeFleur. I doubt you keep up with all the vendors in the city, but—"

"Madame LeFleur? I've heard the name." On the lips of many a woman I'd courted over the years, though I didn't disclose as much. I'd seen it on their bottles too, the ones they tried to leave in my bathing chambers as if they'd be back for another visit the next night. Plus, her shop was next-door to Forcier's. Hadn't I noticed something about it last time I stopped by? That it was up for lease, perhaps?

"Well, she's dead now."

So matter-of-fact, this queen.

"I'm...sorry to hear that? Was she of importance to you?"

Queen Asha groaned. "We believe she was involved in a matter that is important to our...kingdom's security."

That caught my attention. "I know Naenden and Dwellen are on somewhat friendly terms, but you know you can't just come here expecting to arrest a Dwellen citizen."

"I wouldn't call relations *friendly* after your father attempted to spear my sister with conjured vines during the Council meeting."

If my hands weren't otherwise occupied with the dance, I would have dragged them down my face. "I'd forgotten about that," I admitted.

"Yes, well, the Council has too given that he didn't succeed in harming her, but I have not." A wicked grin spread across her gnarled lips. "And neither has my husband."

This time I avoided glancing at the King of Naenden. It wasn't as if checking to make sure he hadn't moved would serve as a comfort.

"Okay, so maybe you deserve one under-the-table arrest," I said.

Her hand flitted in mine, as if she couldn't suppress the urge to wave my comment away. "We didn't intend to arrest her. Only talk to her."

I leveled a knowing stare at the queen.

"Fine. We would have brought her back to Naenden if we'd found her, though not as a punishment for any crime."

"Let me guess. She had something you needed."

"We didn't need it as much as we needed someone else not to have it."

"A weapon?"

The queen shrugged. "Of sorts. Not one that you or your father would be interested in, I assure you."

She must have realized I wasn't convinced, because she added, "Let's just say it's quite dangerous and only a fool would think he could wield it."

Her jaw clenched at that.

"Does this *he* have a name?"

"This *he* is hypothetical."

"No, he's not."

When she shot me a questioning look, I said, "Trust me, I've spurned enough women to recognize the expression. *He* is quite real."

She rolled her eye again, which I was beginning to find quite endearing.

"I take it she didn't have the weapon on her when you found her."

She shook her head. "We can't remain here and investigate what happened to Madame LeFleur. There are situations in Naenden that must be addressed, and our other avenue of extracting information is occupied at the moment. Kiran doesn't think your father is trustworthy, so we came to you."

"Why would I know anything about Madame LeFleur's death?"

Her mouth opened. "Because she was one of your prominent citizens. And she dropped dead out of nowhere, with no visible wounds, no murder weapon. Doesn't that make you the least bit curious?"

No. No, it really didn't. But I was raised in a palace court, and my tutors had drilled it into me that it did not behoove me to admit to such.

"No. No, it really doesn't." Okay, so the lessons they drilled into me didn't always stick.

The queen's jaw dropped, and she bristled.

"What? No offense, but humans die of relatively nothing all the time. You, for instance. You could suffer a paper cut tomorrow and fall ill to an infection that would kill you within the week."

Her mouth twitched. "I'm guessing this is not the particular brand of charm you use on the ladies who give you your glowing reputation."

I flashed her a grin. "No, no it is not."

"I agree that she could have died of natural causes, but when a weapon of that magnitude is involved, I can't help but think it could have been foul play."

"Do you do this often?" I asked.

"Do what?"

"Go sleuthing?"

She scoffed, but she didn't seem to have a response to that.

"You know what I think, Your Majesty?"

She gave me a look like she didn't want to know, but assumed I would tell her, anyway. She was correct.

"I think you get a thrill from a good mystery, and that is why you're interested in the death of Madame LeFleur."

Her hand jerked again, like she was waving me off. "Our palace in Naenden has plenty of mysteries to keep me entertained without having to drag myself north to suffer this obscene weather, thank you very much."

I twirled her, but she was still glaring by the time she got back around to facing me.

"Usually women like that," I teased.

"Well, it makes me dizzy," she said, and by her words alone, I would have thought she was sticking her tongue out at me.

That word, *dizzy*, had me thinking of Blaise, of that wretched perfume she'd been wearing tonight that had sent my stomach somersaulting. As soon as I'd sensed it, I'd been sure Cinderella had just strode into the room. Of course, I should have known Cinderella couldn't have been the only woman in Othian to purchase that particular scent. Humans weren't as bothered by having their scents match another's as the fae were. For the fae, scents were fundamentally attached to specific memories, certain people. Blaise might have been wearing the scent, but it was Cinderella my mind associated it with. Just one whiff had sent my mind spiraling into a frenzy, one I didn't at all want to experience. Not when I'd wanted the night to be about Ellie.

My head had swum until the scent of Blaise's perfume dissipated, and by the time Ellie and I reached the ballroom, I'd about decided to petition my father to outlaw whatever recipe that perfume was.

"I'm afraid I have nothing to offer you, Your Majesty," I said, returning my attention to Queen Asha. "My apologies that you came all this way for nothing. And didn't even enjoy the weather."

She was ruffled, and she gave me a look like she wasn't about to take no for an answer, but then the song ended, and she slipped her hands from mine. "Very well, then."

Asha said something else, but I didn't hear it.

My ears were ringing too loudly.

Because Prince Fin and Ellie had danced into my line of vision, and he had just pressed a kiss to her forehead.

I left the Queen of Naenden abandoned on the dance floor as I made my way over to my future wife.

CHAPTER 43

ELLIE

"*Y*ou look like you need some fresh air," Evander said, taking Fin's place in front of me and clutching the fabric around my waist.

My heart jolted to my throat at the tenderness of his touch.

The image of Lady Nightingale leaning into Evander popped into my mind, and I shot him a souring smirk. "Oh, I don't know. I was actually quite enjoying being breathless for a change."

I made to look like I was craning my head toward Fin, who had rejoined the Naenden entourage and was now looking as if he couldn't decide whether it would be more painful to speak to his brother or the queen's sister.

I didn't get the chance to see whom he chose, because Evander leaned into me, pressing his forehead against mine and blocking my view. The scents of pine and rainwater hit me, overwhelming my senses. Or perhaps that was simply my reaction to Evander's fingers, playing with the fabric of my gown.

"What about now?" he breathed.

"Wha—"

"Do you need fresh air now?"

Yes. Yes, thank you, I did.

I swallowed, as embarrassed as I was intoxicated by his touch. The ballroom was crowded, and as the ball was being thrown in our honor, I doubted very much that no one was paying us attention.

"Okay," I whispered.

"Okay." He bit his lip. Fates above, why did he have to grin like that?

A moment later, he'd led me to the balcony and shut the glass doors behind us. Instinctively, I made my way to the railing, but Evander didn't follow. "Wrong way," he said.

I wasn't sure how there could be any wrong way on a balcony, other than down, but I humored him anyway.

With about as much effort as driftwood employs to float, he jumped onto the roof overhang and extended his arm. "You coming?"

I bit my lip, then took a glance through the balcony windows, but no one was looking in our direction. I grabbed his hand, and he pulled me up with one arm.

"That's really not fair," I huffed as he steadied me on the roof by placing his warm palm between my shoulder blades. Rather gentlemanly for a male who'd courted so many females.

His sea-green eyes twinkled playfully in the moonlight. "What's not?"

"How you even have the core strength to do that," I said, rolling my eyes.

He sank to the tiled roof and sat with his legs dangling off the castle roof. "Are you complaining?"

He extended yet another hand, as if I needed help lowering myself a couple of feet. I brushed his hand away and kneeled by myself. Unfortunately, the white stiletto heels that had gone so perfectly with the dress didn't seem taken with the uneven roof. I stumbled right onto Evander, who reached up and grabbed my waist to steady me.

Before I had the chance to consider whether I'd rather plummet to my death or fall onto the balcony for every ruler in Alondria to witness, Evander pulled me into his lap, wrapping his arms around my waist as he tucked me into his chest.

"I'm glad you didn't take my hand," he whispered into my ear.

The feel of his breath on my ear had me squirming, which I ran with and disguised by wriggling out of his arms and plopping down next to him.

I topped it off with a roll of my eyes, but my agitation with embarrassing myself could only last so long as I looked out over the city.

Candles and torchlight flickered like lightning bugs across Othian, acting as reflections for the stars above them. It was as if we were gazing upon a massive lake. I truly wouldn't have known the difference. Above us the full moon watched over the city, looking especially large tonight without the clouds to obscure it.

"How many females have you brought up here?" I asked, trying my utmost to disguise the blatant jealousy wrapped within that question with a teasing lilt in my voice.

"Just the one." Just three words, and my heart skipped. When I turned to look at him to check his face for honesty, his eyes were skyward, and his constantly sneering mask had melted off. His sea-green eyes widened in the starlight, and the tension at his jaw softened.

He turned to find me examining him. "When are you going to learn that I can't lie to you?"

I shot my gaze away and went back to pretending to admire the city, but I could feel his stare boring into my face. My throat went dry. "Would you, if you could?"

"What, lie? About what? Why would I lie to the one person I never have to tiptoe around, waltz these stupid verbal dances with?"

"What do you mean?" I asked. "Everything you say is cloaked in flirtation or insult."

He smiled weakly, and it caught me off guard. When he smiled like that, with such sincerity, his charm took on a boyish quality, quite the contrast to his usual mask of seduction. "I know it seems that way to you, but you should see how I talk with everyone else. Besides, I never would have told anyone else what I told you about Jerad."

"You told her," I said, the contents of my stomach wilting as I imagined Evander and my almost-murderer dancing the night away, him entrusting her with his worst nightmares.

He smiled. "She asked."

"You mean to tell me you didn't bring her up here the night of the ball?"

He shook his head. "She left too early. If she'd stayed longer, I would have. Besides, all eyes were on us the entire night."

A thorn pricked at my heart, which irritated me. He'd said it before, that he loved her and not me, despite the horrible things he now knew about her. Despite the fact she wasn't as she'd seemed. But here I was, still waiting for the moment the veil over his love-struck eyes would be lifted. When he would finally realize she wasn't the type of person worth wasting his love on.

That I was?

I shuffled uncomfortably.

"Are you cold?" he asked. Before I could answer, he was unbuttoning his coat and draping it over me. His fingers lingered on the curve of my exposed shoulder just a tad longer than necessary.

I hadn't been cold; the weather tonight had been strangely mild for early spring, but the gesture made me glad I hadn't admitted to as much.

He pulled his hand away, waving it out into the starlight. "So, what do you think?"

"Think of what?" I asked.

He shrugged and avoided looking at me. "Of the kingdom you're about to be a princess over. Of this new life my stupidity forced you into. Of knowing that in less than a week's time, you'll be my wife."

My wife. Lightning bugs flickered in my belly at the sound of it. He turned his gaze to me on that word, his eyes wide. Vulnerable.

"That's only if we pass the trial tomorrow." I shuddered at the thought, which Evander must have misinterpreted as me being cold, because he wrapped his arm around me and pulled me in close to his side. I shivered at the heat emanating from him, at the closeness I'd never shared with a male.

"We'll pass. I'll make sure of it. Not that you need my help. You've proved that much." He craned his head downward so I could see his teasing smile.

327

So his face could be close to mine? My heart stuttered at the thought.

"I'm not sure which is more terrifying: dying, or being forced to live out my days bound to you." The words came out as I'd intended them, that perfect balance of teasing and meanness that my parents would have been considered a sign of affection.

But the life in Evander's smile dwindled, even if it remained plastered to his face. "Would it be so awful?" The teasing was there in his voice, too. Just not in the corners of his eyes.

"Oh, come on. You said yourself you don't love me. That's a bit of a nightmare, you know—for a woman whose dream was to marry for love. You'd get out of it, too, if you could."

Evander reached out and touched my cheek with his thumb, sliding his fingertips into my hair and cradling the base of my skull. "I intend to treat you as a queen. I hope you know that."

The muscles in my back tensed at his touch as lightning flashed through his fingertips and into my bones.

"Like how your father treats your mother?" I asked, if only to dissipate the tension I felt in this moment. The tension I knew was only one-sided.

He frowned, but he stroked my cheek all the same. "No. You'll be my partner, Ellie. My friend. And, if the time comes, you'll rule by my side, not through social parties. My mother was always too smart for the limits of her position. You're too smart for that. Truth be told, I was always terrified of inheriting the throne. But then you showed up and"—he slipped his thumb and grazed my earlobe, sending chills down my neck that I prayed he couldn't feel on my skin—"and I'm starting to think that maybe I could be enough. Enough for this kingdom. With you by my side, at least."

I swallowed, a desperate attempt to regain my breath, my composure.

I was on fire.

All of me was on fire, down to my toes. Surely he could sense that.

"I wasn't trained to do any of this," I managed to choke out. "I'm still not being trained to do any of this."

"You will after the Trials are done. And I'm with you. I wasn't trained for any of this either. But here we are."

He went silent for a moment and cocked his head, like he was taking me in. I tried not to get lost in those sea-green eyes of his, tried to remember all the reasons I couldn't fall in love with this male. Oh, and there were many. I knew that much to be true.

The trouble was, with his fingers stroking my neck and his mouth so close to mine, I couldn't remember what any of those reasons were.

He leaned in and brushed his cheek against mine. His warm breath caressed my ear as he whispered, "Would it really be so bad?"

I shook my head. No, no it wouldn't be.

And then his lips were on mine, warm and soft as he kissed me. The pads of his fingertips grazed the length of my neck and traced my shoulder before he ran them down my back and pulled me closer to him. I closed my eyes and allowed my limbs to go weak as the warmth of the kiss radiated through my toes, through my fingertips.

When he pulled away, I found myself leaning in closer, following him. Wanting more.

When I opened my eyes, he was smiling down at me. He ran his hand down my arm and locked his fingers in mine.

"We should probably get back to the ball," he said, to which my heart took a disappointed plunge. But then the grin spread over his face once more. "I wouldn't want you thinking your betrothed wasn't a gentleman."

CHAPTER 44

$\mathcal{T}$he plain girl was becoming suspicious.

It was getting to be a problem, which was why the parasite decided something had to be done about it. Tonight.

The night of the first ball, during which the parasite first danced with the prince, the girl had gone with the most reasonable explanation—the Madame had obviously scammed her out of her hard-earned coin and peddled her a sleeping draft instead of a beauty elixir.

But the girl had been so overcome with a flood of conflicting emotions—what with the prince's engagement and her reluctant concession that Ellie Payne was not as awful as she might have imagined—her indignation with Madame LeFleur had effectively slipped her mind.

That had all changed the night she'd woken soaked in Ellie Payne's blood.

The parasite hadn't had time to wash off, to burn the plain girl's clothes, to bury the evidence of what had happened like she'd intended. When Ellie Payne had screamed, she'd alerted every guard stationed within three floors. The parasite had done well to reach the servant girl's room before the moon peaked at its apex and the parasite surrendered the girl's body over to its host.

The plain girl had sobbed.

She'd at least had the presence of mind to wash the blood off herself, to throw the clothes that bore the blood of Ellie Payne into the burning hearth. Later that night, when the plain girl had gone to check on Ellie, she still stank of blood.

Thankfully, no one had noticed. Not with the scent of Ellie's wound overpowering her stench.

She couldn't remember what had happened before, but there was no questioning that she'd done this. Not once the girl remembered the night of the ball, the hours she'd lost, the waking up in the streets. Not remembering how she'd gotten there.

The girl was many things. Jealous and lovesick and desperate. But she was not stupid.

She'd had conflicting feelings when she heard the news: Ellie Payne would make a full recovery.

She lied to herself about it regularly, but she could not hide the truth from the parasite. Disappointment had dropped like a jagged mace through the pit of the girl's stomach. She'd shooed the feeling almost immediately, but not before the parasite tasted it.

The girl hated herself for that, even now. She considered it a lapse.

The parasite knew better.

The reaction had aligned with the girl's truest self, her utmost desire, though she tried to deny it to herself.

She was the most desperate thing the parasite had ever inhabited.

It was intoxicating.

The next day, the plain girl had snuck away to Madame LeFleur's, intent on demanding the shopkeeper confess what sort of draft she'd given the girl.

One "For Lease" sign and a handful of innocent questions to the neighboring shopkeepers later, and the girl learned of Madame LeFleur's mysterious demise.

The parasite had feared the whole excursion would be quite the waste of time.

But the girl had been convinced. She had murdered the Madame. She was sure of it.

So the plain girl had started researching. Pamphlets stolen from the back of Madame LeFleur's empty shop, books swiped from strange libraries on the outskirts of town.

With Madame LeFleur out of the way, the girl had no one to ask, no one to question.

Of course, with no professional direction, the girl had taken a wrong turn, chosen a faulty route.

She'd been wondering if she was a lychaen the past few weeks— not the faerie type, but the kind made from fanatical humans who dabbled in strange magic.

It had been dull at first, having to listen to the girl's inner monologue take her down an erroneous path.

But the parasite had paid attention anyway. Just in case.

The girl was bound to happen upon the right information at some point, the key to freeing the parasite from her moonlit shackles, the answer to taking this body as her own. Permanently.

Then she could marry the prince, murder the insufferable king, and become Queen of Dwellen.

It shouldn't have, but recently her thoughts had lingered more on the marrying the prince part than the becoming queen part.

Ellie Payne needed to get out of the way if that ever was to happen.

CHAPTER 45

ELLIE

J could still feel the warmth of his lips on mine, even when he escorted me to my room after the ball.

We'd danced to three more waltzes, until my feet were raw in my shoes. I would have danced with him more, would have ignored the pain for another fleeting moment as he twirled me around the room, that boyish grin on his face seeping into mine.

But he'd caught sense of my blisters and convinced me I'd danced enough.

And now as we stood at my door, I wanted nothing more than to feel his mouth on mine again.

"Goodnight, Ellie," he said, bringing my hand to his lips and pressing a warm kiss against it. My face rushed with heat.

"That's it?" I laughed.

He grinned. "What were you expecting?"

"You tried to seduce me back when you thought I hated you. Now you're just offering a goodnight and a kiss to my hand?"

"Oh, I won't be trying to seduce you again. Clearly that didn't work, so I'm trying out a different method."

"And what's that?"

He leaned over me, gently pushing my back up against the door as his face hovered just above mine. "Goodnight, Ellie."

The door creaked open behind me, and he flashed me a grin before sauntering away.

When I entered my room and shut the door behind me, I wondered how long it would take for the smile to fade from my cheeks.

Neither Imogen nor Blaise was here to help me undress, I realized —though the perfume Blaise had borrowed from Imogen still lingered in the room, and now that I stopped to pay attention, it really was a bit strong. But I was eager to get out of this gown and into some more comfortable sleepwear. I remembered I'd given them the night off without considering how I would get undressed, but I figured it wouldn't be too difficult. After all, I'd never had a lady's maid back home, and I'd gotten dressed and undressed just fine.

Of course, I hadn't had a dress as fancy as this one either.

Besides. If I could get out of that suit of armor, I could get out of anything.

It took me quite a bit of stretching, groping, and hopping, but I finally managed to pull my dress over my head. The problem was the cinched waist. It was too small for my ribcage. Much too small.

I hopped around in the dark, trying to wiggle myself out of my trap without ripping the undoubtedly expensive dress.

"Need some help?"

The quiet voice made me jump. "Imogen, you scared me," I said, trying to regain my breath. "Can you help me get out of this?"

"Imogen?" the sultry voice purred.

My heart turned to ice as I recognized the voice, as her last words to me rang through my head.

You weren't supposed to wake up.

Cinderella.

I opened my mouth to scream, but not before a hand clamped over my mouth, already stifled by my gown. "Scream, and this knife goes straight through your ribcage. And I won't miss this time. Do you understand?"

I nodded. I wanted to fight back, but there was no way I was making it out of here alive when I couldn't see and my arms were stuck, pinned upright by my gown.

"Now, you were saying you needed help out of that."

I bit back a gasp as pain sliced down my side. The ripping of fabric yelped in my ears. Fingernails dug into my ribcage, and the fabric split.

As it fell off me, the room became visible again.

"You're welcome," the woman smirked. Her almost-white hair had been braided into a crown atop her head. She wore a dazzling blue dress that reminded me of the one Evander had originally made for his mystery woman. The red paint on her lips and the kohl on her eyelids made her look older, but I still remembered what she'd looked like the night she stabbed me. Underneath all that paint, she couldn't have been more than a year older than me.

"What do you want?"

Cinderella traced my body, now clothed only in my undergarments, with a cool, calculating stare that made me feel extremely violated.

"I want you to put these on," she said, sauntering over to my dressing wall and pulling out a bag. She reached into it and tossed me a raggedy set of men's trousers and a tunic.

"I thought you were planning on killing me," I said.

She flashed me a bloodthirsty smile with those painted red lips of hers. "I am. But when the prince finds your dead body, I'd rather him not see you in your undergarments."

I might have laughed, had my life not been in the hands of this psycho lunatic. "Jealous, are we?" I rolled my eyes as I pulled on the smelly pants and trousers.

Her eyes bounced over my body again. Was I imagining it, or did her sharp gaze linger on every curve, every stretch mark I'd ever thought to be self-conscious about? She grinned. "There's no need."

I suppose the words were meant to cut, but I was having a hard time being too rattled by jabs at my appearance when she sported a knife glittering with my blood.

"I wouldn't stab me if I were you."

"Oh, no?" she purred, lightly tracing the edge of the blade with the tip of her finger, staining her fingertips crimson. "And why not?"

"Because I don't know that it's going to win Evander's heart over like you think it is."

Pain cut through my left bicep as she sliced at my arm. I stumbled back, but she turned the bloodied knife on me as I gripped the bed to stable myself. "Don't you dare call him by his given name. As if. As if…"

It was like she couldn't bear the thought of it, much less the words.

I couldn't help myself. "As if I know him better than you do?"

Cinderella lunged, but I was ready for it this time. I launched myself to the side, and she plummeted onto the bed.

"Help!" I screamed. "Help me! Guards! Anybody!"

I whirled just in time to dodge the knife again as the woman slashed at my chest.

This time when she threw herself at me, I didn't dodge quite fast enough. The blade sliced through the tunic and between the edges of my ribcage. I gasped in pain as the weight of her slamming into me sent me to the floor. When I looked up, her arms were raised above her head, the tip of the dagger pointed at my chest.

A knock rapped at my door. "Ellie?"

Evander's voice froze both of us. "Shh," the woman said, moonlight seeping through the window, casting shadows dark as bruises under her cheeks.

"Ellie, I have to say, as proud as I was for being a little tease tonight, I got back to my room and couldn't get over the fact I hadn't given you a goodnight kiss. I know what I said, but I'm afraid one kiss isn't going to be enough for me after all."

I stared up at the woman with pleading in my eyes. She cocked her head to the side, as if she was trying to figure out a way she'd misheard that word.

Kiss.

She placed a finger on my mouth before whispering, "Go to the door and tell him not to come in. That you're tired and don't want to see him tonight." She climbed off of me and I eased toward the door.

I fought the urge to remind Cinderella it didn't matter whether Evander walked in on her murdering me. He was still going to know it was her when my body turned up with stab wounds all in it. But clearly this girl was delusional anyway, so I figured there was no need to argue with a plan that might extend my life by only a few minutes.

I couldn't help but notice that she kept the knife dangling close to my back.

"Evander," I called through the door. "I don't think you should come in."

The girl hissed. "Are you always that meek sounding?" The point of the knife punctured my tunic, scraping my skin.

"Are you feeling alright?" Evander asked, his flirtation faltering, probably at my unconventionally not-snappy tone.

I took a glance at the woman, who nodded her head for me to respond.

"No, I'm feeling quite ill, actually." My head spun. Could he guess by my voice that something was wrong, or had that one kiss destroyed every bit of expectation he had about my willingness to show my vulnerabilities? Would he fall for the lies, thinking the sweetness in my voice was just a byproduct of a reformed personality, a byproduct of my feelings for him?

"Are you sure?" he asked, his voice muffled by the door. "Can I get you something?"

So quietly I doubted even Evander could hear her with those fae ears of his, Cinderella whispered, "Tell him your monthly bleeding has come upon you."

I couldn't decide whether she wanted to provide a reasonable explanation in case Evander scented the blood trickling down my side, or if she thought such an admission would run Evander off.

Probably a little bit of both.

"No, I'd rather you not see me like this. I'm afraid the way of woman is upon me." The words almost felt sour in my throat. He'd sat with me for days after I'd been stabbed. He'd held me through my fever sweats, for Fate's sake. Surely he wouldn't be mortified by the natural course of a woman.

"Uh. Goodnight then. I hope you recover quickly." His footsteps shuffled away, and my breath caught. He had bought it. He hadn't recognized the change in my tone, the difference in my personality that had meant to signal him that something was very, very wrong. My heart ached.

He didn't know me at all.

He didn't know me at all, and that was going to be the death of me.

The woman drew the knife down my back hard enough that it cut through my skin. "Now, where were we?"

BAM.

My door splintered. Pieces of wood went flying, lodging themselves in my cheeks and in the fabric of my skin. Cinderella recoiled and fell to the floor as Evander stormed into the room, his sword drawn.

"What's going on?" Evander asked, glancing from me to my assailant. His eyes widened as he beheld her face, as recognition softened the blaze of rage in his face. "You," he said softly.

"Evander," Cinderella breathed. She heaved, her breasts undulating (because, of course they were). Tears flooded her pale face and her eyes widened.

His face hardened, and though his sword shook, he pointed it at her throat. "What are you doing? How could you try to hurt her?"

My muscles froze as I watched them, as I beheld the shock on his face and realized for the first time that he really had convinced himself that it had been some other woman who had tried to kill me that night. Not his mystery woman, not the girl who had dazzled him at the ball by treating him like a real person.

Not his Cinderella.

The woman wept and her voice went soft, not at all like the sickly sweet but venomous voice she'd used on me.

This one might have fooled even me if she hadn't just had a knife to my back.

"Evander, I..." She took a dramatic look at the knife clutched in her hands, at her raw-white knuckles, and gasped. The knife clattered to the floor, and she scurried backward on her elbows, as if to get away from it. As if it had been the knife that had made her try to kill me multiple times. "Oh, no. Oh, no, no, no." She rocked back and forth like a child, and I realized she'd backed herself away from Evander's faltering blade.

"It's all a show," I said. "Don't fall for it. She had a knife to my spine just seconds ago."

Cinderella wailed. "Oh, I'm so sorry. I'm so, so sorry." She buried her face in her hands before peeking those wide, twin blue eyes at Evander. He blinked. Something curled in my chest. "Please forgive me. I don't know what came over me. Evander, please. I was so sick, so ill when I discovered that your bargain—the one you meant for us—had made a mistake. My love for you—it drove me out of my mind. The jealousy of thinking of another woman at your side, in your bed."

She clutched her chest as if she were running out of air. "This isn't me. Evander, I promise this isn't me."

The hard line in Evander's brow softened. The grit in his teeth went lax.

"Evander," I said, fear gripping me now. He couldn't believe her, could he? "She's lying. She tried to kill me. Don't you see? She's already tried twice. She's not going to stop until I'm dead."

He whipped his head toward me. "What are you asking me to do?"

I recoiled. "You're the Crown Prince of Dwellen. The executor of justice. I'm asking you to keep me safe."

His gaze whirled back and forth between me and the woman, the woman and me. This couldn't be happening.

"That's my blood on the knife!"

"Evander, please, no," Cinderella cried, tucking her knees into her chest. "I didn't mean to."

He gritted his teeth, and the resolve returned to his face. "Yes. Yes, you did."

Horror struck Cinderella's face, but as she examined his, as she detected the same determination that I did, she cocked her head to the side and a wicked smirk spread across her red lips.

She pouted. "You're not mad, are you?"

Even my blood cringed in disgust.

"How could you?" Evander asked, his breathing ragged, unsure. "You have my heart, Cinderella. Don't you understand that? You've gotten into the castle twice now. You could have come for me at any point. We could have been together. But you came for Ellie instead. Why? Did you think I wouldn't have accepted you?"

What? My head spun. He was lying. He was lying to disarm her, to get her away from me.

My heart plunged.

Evander couldn't lie.

And now I couldn't breathe.

Had this woman been on Evander's mind the entire time? Of course she had. He'd told me as much. I'd just thought that tonight... My face went hot. How could I have been so stupid?

Cinderella rose to her feet, her very aura commanding the room. "We have to get her out of the way, Evander. Don't you see that? You and I can't be together if she's around. Not in the way we deserve. That bargain you made—it was meant for me. For me. But this little thief stole it, and as if that wasn't enough, she's trying to steal your heart. She knew exactly what would happen if she put those shoes on, just like every little whore in the kingdom did. Didn't you hear about the girls who blistered their feet trying to force themselves into those shoes?" Evander's face faltered, and she let out a shrill laugh. "She convinced you that she didn't know any better, didn't she? And you believed her. She played you, Evander, with that little hard-to-get game of hers. But it was all just part of a scheme for the throne; can't you see that? She waited until she had you in her pocket, and then she allowed you to believe that you were chasing her, not the other way around."

Her gaze lingered on me in solemn judgment. "So don't you dare call me the thief."

Evander's gaze darted back and forth between us. "That's not true, and you know it," I said, but the pained look in his eyes assured me he wasn't convinced. Told me that, in just a few hours, that conniving little wench had learned him like the back of her hand, better than I had managed.

She'd taken stock of her target. And then she'd aimed for his greatest insecurity. That no one could ever love him just for him. That I had to have been in it for the money and power to begin with.

"It's not true. She's trying to manipulate you. Can't you see that?" I asked, my voice going high in panic.

"Can't you see that?" the woman mimicked. "See, Evander. She's caught, so she's trying to use my *tactics*, as she calls them. Now, does that say honest to you?"

"Why'd you run that night?" Evander asked her.

"You can't be serious," I groaned.

"No, I have to know. Why did you run? I would have wed you before the next mooncycle. If you want so badly to be with me, if you really love me, why did you run?"

Incredulity rolled through me. "Is that even a question worth asking? Is there any possible reason she could give you that would change who she is? She tried to murder me!"

Evander shot a silencing glare in my direction. Rage tied my tongue.

How dare he.

"Why?" he whispered.

Her voice went back to that tone, smooth and sultry and sweet as spiced milk. "Because I wanted you to chase me. And you did."

She beamed.

She was crazy.

I scoffed. "Yeah, he just got it all wrong. How romantic."

She ignored me, and as much as I hated her at the moment, I had to admit; I was impressed with her capability to control herself.

"I just wanted to be with you. That's all I ever wanted. We could still be together, you know." She addressed him, but rose and advanced toward me.

I stepped back.

341

Evander whipped his sword in front of me, as if to protect me, but I could tell that it was wobbling. And if I could see it, she certainly could. "You're not going to hurt her."

"Is there any other way? I don't share, Evander."

His mouth hung open. "We could find another way. There is... We think there's a way to break the betrothal bargain."

His words slapped me like the surface of a lake after a plunge off a nearby cliff.

What about how he wasn't afraid to be king now that I was by his side? What about all he'd said about how I'd changed him, made him braver, stronger? And then... "How long have you known about this?" I asked, my heart sinking.

He shook his head. "Only the past few weeks. It's not a firm lead. I didn't want to tell you until I knew for sure."

His words shattered my chest. The pain was so poignant, I couldn't decide what hurt more. That he had acted like he was looking forward to marrying me? That he'd kissed me under the pretense that he truly believed we could fall in love? Or that he had known there was a possibility of breaking the bargain and hadn't shared it with me?

He'd led me to believe that I had to marry him, and I'd decided to make the best of it. I'd opened my heart up to him...

"So it's not certain, then?" Cinderella asked, inching closer to me. "What if it doesn't work?"

"I have hope that it will," he said.

"I know something that would certainly work." She was so close now. Did she have another weapon on her? Would Evander hesitate if she attacked me?

"My love, I don't wish blood on your hands," he said with such desperation that my heart shattered to a thousand pieces. So stupid. I'd been so stupid to think he cared for me.

And I could tell she had heard the desperation, too. Saw how it convinced her, consoled her.

Cinderella glanced toward the window.

"Then I shall see you soon." She backed away with a seductive grin

342

toward my balcony, where I noticed for the first time a rope was tied to the banister.

Panic gripped me. "You can't let her go. She's just going to come back and finish me off herself."

Cinderella grinned, her blue eyes sparkling. "Only if it's necessary."

I turned to Evander, but if he noticed, he didn't show any such signs.

"Please. Please. She's lying. She's a liar. You can't just let her go free."

The woman smiled and gave one last lustful look at Evander before she grabbed the rope and slipped over the balcony.

I lunged for the dagger on the floor and ran after her. I'd saw the rope in half if I had to. She couldn't get away, not when she'd shown how easy it was for her to threaten my life.

But strong arms surrounded me, stopping me in my tracks.

Hands clutched at my fingertips, the same hands I'd allowed to caress my cheek, my back, my arm just a few hours ago.

Evander pried the knife from my hand.

"She won't hurt you," he pleaded. And as I lost grip on the handle, my weight collapsed to the floor. "Ellie, I'm so sorry, but she won't hurt you this way."

I pushed him away, crumbling to my shaking knees and burying my face in my hands. "Go away."

"I couldn't let her hurt you. I had to say those things."

I had to say those things. The words only implied that he hadn't meant them, though the literal interpretation guaranteed no such thing.

And he hadn't been lying when he told my almost-murderer that his heart belonged to her.

I spun on him and launched to my feet. "You could have stabbed that sword straight through her heart. That's what you could have done."

His jaw dropped, and he grasped for words, but I wasn't done.

"You could have overpowered her. She's a human girl, for Fate's sake, Evander. She could be in the jail cells right now awaiting sentencing for attempting to murder the heir's betrothed. But no. You let her go."

"I—"

"You let her go."

"I don't want you to get hurt, El. I care about you. And you know that's true, because I can't lie."

"Yeah, well, then I also know that what you told her was true, too. That you've been looking for a way to end this betrothal. That you've found a way to do it, and you didn't tell me. What were you planning to do? Was getting me to fall in love with you just a back-up plan to make marriage to me more convenient for you if you had to go through with it? Or were you ever going to tell me there was a way to break the bargain?"

"I—"

"No. Stop. I'm not finished. Was that the plan all along? Did you decide to leave out that important information because you and your father think more alike than you've led me to believe? When did you decide that I'd make a convenient queen? That I'd run things behind the scenes so that your lazy butt wouldn't have to?"

His eyes watered, but I didn't care.

"When, Your Highness? When did you remember that your marriage bargain with me wouldn't prohibit you from taking a mistress? Sure, obviously she wants me dead, because she wants it all —the power, the glory, the throne, to be seen with you in public. But you were holding onto that idea, weren't you? That I could be your queen and free you up from your responsibilities so you could have more time to spend with the woman you actually care about."

"El, I—" He shook his head. "I care about you."

My voice went quiet. "Stop."

"El—"

"Stop calling me that."

Evander's mouth opened, but nothing came out.

"You know what the worst part is?" I asked. "You can say that because you actually believe it to be true."

"It is true," he breathed.

"Get out."

"El. Ellie—"

"Get. Out."

He did. And when I stayed up for hours, weeping into my pillow, he didn't return.

I told myself I hadn't wanted him to.

CHAPTER 46

EVANDER

$\mathcal{M}$y feet traced the familiar path back toward the South Gate, past the guard whose summer homes I paid for, yet I hardly noticed him when he waved at me.

I made it all the way to the seedy tavern just to stand in front of the wretched building, unable to make myself go inside.

There was drink in there. Strong drink that would make the past few hours dissipate into nothingness if I let it.

But that would only last me a few hours.

Then the truth would assault me again, except this time I'd have a pounding headache.

The morning would come, my body would purge itself of the alcohol, and I'd still be left with the memory of what I'd done.

I'd chosen Cinderella over Ellie.

That hadn't been the plan.

The moment I'd sensed the dread in Ellie's voice, that quavering timbre humans had such a difficult time masking, I'd determined to put an end to the woman I'd once thought I loved.

But then I burst through the door, and I'd seen the adoration in her blue eyes, scented that familiar smell of lilac and rosebuds, heard the longing in her voice…

That Fates-cursed mating bond had sunk its hooks into my beating flesh, and my heart had faltered.

My love for Ellie had faltered.

And I wasn't sure if I could live with myself knowing that.

So I left the seedy bar and wandered into the woods.

IT WAS first light by the time I arrived, the glowing sun making its appearance, the silvery moon finally slipping past the horizon.

My father hadn't wanted to bury him here, not initially. No, my father had wanted pomp and circumstance in the gravestone that would honor my brother, honor his heir.

I'd convinced him otherwise.

It was the first request he'd ever granted me.

I'd been shocked when he agreed, thinking the grief of my brother's loss must have altered something ancient in him.

It hadn't in the end, unless you counted being more irritable, but that didn't matter so much.

I'd asked him to bury Jerad back here, and he'd let me.

In the center of the castle grounds, there was a casket in a tomb large enough to pass for the resting place of a Fate, but the casket was empty.

My brother lay here, far away from tourists and prying eyes and citizens who liked to gossip and speculate about just how exactly my brother had died.

My father had granted me few gifts in my life.

If I had to pick just one, this would have been it.

His gravestone was simple, only his familial nickname carved into its face, lest someone stumble upon in and realize who was buried there.

JED
A SON, A BROTHER, A FRIEND

347

I SETTLED into the earth and dug my fingers into the soil. Something about the feel of earth between my fingers made me feel connected to him, like he'd returned to being part of the earth and was sitting here with me, just with another form, another purpose.

I could work with that.

"I keep messing up, Jerad."

Is that anything new? I could imagine his voice, the low timbre that never let anything provoke it. Could hear it like he was speaking to me now.

It was why I liked this place.

I laughed. "No, but at least when you were around, you could fix it for me."

Perhaps it's for the best that I left, then. You always need a bit of prodding to grow up.

"Well, I wouldn't exactly call your death a prodding. More like a staking, but okay."

Let's hear it then. What have you done this time?

"I fell in love with the wrong woman."

Also not a first. Surely we could sift through some of our old talks and get a head start on figuring this out.

I shook my head. "It's different this time."

If you're saying one's the wrong woman, I'm going to take a gander and guess there's a right woman?

I chuckled, but it sounded more like a cough.

And what, exactly, makes her the right woman?

"Well, she's my betrothed, for starters. I'm to marry her in just a few days."

Ah, yes. It would have been convenient for you to fall in love with the woman you were actually planning to marry, wouldn't it?

"Not just convenient," I said. "It would be... it would be perfect. I've never met a woman like her, Jed. She's got this drive that would level a continent if she thought that was what needed to happen to reach her goals. And she's so stinking clever. Not just with her craft. I mean, the art she can make with her hands—that's amazing. But she's just so funny. I never know what's about to come out of her mouth, but it has me flabbergasted and exasperated and delighted all at once. You would have liked her. Probably would have stolen her from me, honestly. Though I would have let you have her. She deserves to be loved. Deserves better than what I can give her. Besides, I think she would like you better than she likes me. The two of you could be boring and responsible together.

I thought you said she was hilarious. She doesn't sound boring to me.

"You're probably right," I said, breaking apart pieces of a leaf and tossing it to the side.

Probably.

I sat in silence for a while. Knowing someone for two hundred years is like that. You can sit there and have a conversation with them like they never left you, like they never died, and you even know where exactly and for how long they would insert dramatic pauses for effect.

So about the other woman? The wrong woman?

"What about her?" The pile of dead, torn up leaves was growing before me, getting to be bulbous at the top.

Well, that's just it. You've said nothing about her at all. Other than that you're in love with her.

I tossed the rest of the leaf at his grave. "What more is there to tell?"

You had plenty to say about the other woman. The woman you're not in love with. There was knowing in his voice, the kind that made him sound like Mother and made me want to strangle him.

"Jed, do you believe in Fated mates?"

My brother would have squinted at a question like that. *Do you?*

"I didn't. Not before. But you don't understand. It's like when I'm around her… It's like there's something *feral* inside me, and that *thing* wakes up, and it's…and I'm obsessed with her."

Hm. I can't say I've ever seen much evidence for a Fated mating bond.

349

Perhaps there's something about her that you love so intensely that it feels as though it's Fated? Can you think of what that might be?

"You know, after you...you know, left..." I swallowed. In my mind, his brow would have quirked at that—at my refusal to acknowledge aloud that he was dead. But he would have let me continue, so I did. "I didn't meet a single woman who wouldn't bring up you and my new responsibilities as heir in the same breath. 'Oh, Your Highness, what a weight you must bear now that you're the heir in the wake of your brother's passing. Oh, my condolences about that, by the way. Now back to the part about how you'll be the richest and most powerful male in all of Dwellen should you be fortunate enough to suffer the death of your father as well.'"

I'm sure they didn't say it quite like that.

It was my turn to quirk a brow. "You'd be surprised. Anyway, I just got so tired of it. So tired of women so blinded by my position that they forgot how much..." I swallowed again. "How much..."

I couldn't do it, couldn't say it, not even to the forest brush and my brother who couldn't hear me, not really.

"She was the first woman, other than Blaise, of course—"

Does our dear Blaise count as a woman?

"Hardly. She tells me she's eighteen now, but I think she must be lying. She can't be more than seven."

Jerad smiled fondly, and I couldn't help but allow it to spread to my face.

"Cinderella was the only one in a year who looked at me and saw my situation for what it was. Who looked at me and remembered that I wasn't thinking about being the heir or what I had gained. All I could ever think about is what I lost that day, Jerad. And so I know you think me foolish for giving my heart to a woman I hardly know... Fates, you don't even know the half of how foolish it is..."

I'm just a memory, a figment of your imagination, Evander. I know as much as you do.

I swallowed, wincing, somewhat delirious at this point. "Then you know I'm in love with a lunatic. She's insane. Out of her mind, crazy psycho jealous. Remember Nightingale? A thousand times worse. She's already tried to kill Ellie. Twice. And I had the chance to stop her, the chance to imprison her, to keep Ellie safe, and I..."

My brother waited.

"It would be nice if you'd say something about now."

I'd rather let you finish.

"Ellie's a good person. Sure, she gets under my skin, and half the time I think she thinks she's better than me. Which, she's a smart woman, so what else would she think, I suppose? But she's good in her heart, and she's my friend. Well, she *was* my friend. I think I might have ruined any chance of her staying that way. And she's going to be my wife..." My breath caught. Had I said that aloud before? Surely I had.

"Ellie Payne is going to be my wife." It shouldn't have felt the way it did on my lips. It should have felt like dread, and it did in some ways. Ellie hated me. She wouldn't forget that I'd chosen Cinderella's freedom over her safety, not for a long while. Perhaps never.

But Ellie Payne was going to be my wife. For some reason, the way my chest clenched at that thought seemed a whole lot less like the anxiety of a male forced into an undesirable marriage, and a whole lot more like nervous jitters.

The nice kind.

"You know, you really haven't given me much advice. You've mostly just asked me questions and given me non-responses. I should have known you wouldn't be that helpful," I said to the trees or my brother or the squirrels or whoever might be patient enough to listen to my ramblings.

Do you need advice, Evander?

"Why do you think I'm sitting out here in the cold?"

My brother's eyes wrinkled, tugging at something in my chest. *Very well. But I have little to say, and I fear my advice also comes in the form of a question.*

"Typical," I said, tossing a pine cone at his grave this time.

This Cinderella woman—you say she was the first to see your pain.

"That doesn't sound like much of a question, or advice, for that matter."

That's because I'm not finished.

I gestured for him to go on.

She might have been the first to see your pain, but who do you anticipate will be the last?

CHAPTER 47

ELLIE

By the time a pair of soldiers led me into the arena the next morning, everything was numb.

My legs felt as though they were only being propelled by some primal part of my brain, something that had kicked on automatically, much like my breathing or my heartbeat. Steady, sure. Not at all commanded by me.

Evander and I walked together, my hand limp in his arm as the king presented us to the crowd. I couldn't feel my fingertips against his coat, against his arm. The applause from the onlookers sounded like a buzzing hive to my ears, and the king's announcements were dull. Quiet.

Nothing could drown out the deafening emptiness in my chest.

I hadn't asked if there had been any developments during the night. Whether the bargain could be broken. It didn't matter, really, because Cinderella was loose. I had kissed her prince, and it didn't matter if he chose her over me, if the bargain was broken and they lived out their happily-ever-after together. She would always remember that he had kissed me after he had loved her.

One day, probably sooner rather than later, she'd drive that dagger through my heart.

My days were numbered. I could only hope that by then I'd grown wiser than to lay bare my heart, to leave it unprotected.

Hearts were too easy to stab.

I'd hardly slept at all. Guards had been in and out of my room trying to figure out how Cinderella had managed to sneak into the castle yet again, even after the king had ordered double the number of guards to be stationed at entryways for the ball.

They still didn't know how she'd made it into the castle, but they figured she slipped into my room during the ball and waited there for me to return.

All the keys to my room were accounted for, and when the guards berated Imogen and Blaise about whether they locked my quarters before the ball, neither of them could remember.

I'd wanted to come to their defense, but I'd been too distracted by Evander's reaction to the perfume that I hadn't paid attention.

For all we knew, Cinderella simply tested the doorknob and found it opened without resistance.

The crowd applauded again, tugging me back into the present, and I noticed two large black boxes in the center of the arena. Evander and I would complete our parts of the trial alone, separately. That much I remembered from my discussions with the queen this morning, when she'd snuck up to my rooms and given me as much vague information that she could afford.

I searched for her and found her seated next to her husband, her face twisted into a mingled grimace of concern and serenity.

She'd be rooting for me, this much I knew. Probably rooting for her son, too. I wondered how she would feel, how her intentions might shift, if she knew what had gone on just a few hours ago. If she knew her son had allowed my attempted murderer to go free. If she realized he still loved Cinderella.

Would she still root for me? Would she take my side, acknowledge my pain and fear? Or would the fact that Evander was her flesh and blood override the fair female's sense of justice?

I'd probably never find out.

From what I remembered, this trial was supposed to measure whether my and Evander's love for one another was pure.

But love was a funny thing. In its molten state, it ran hot and pure and unstoppable. But when it cooled, when it hardened... Well, then it resembled love about as much as stone resembled lava.

And whatever was in my heart for Evander had gone cold. Static.

It didn't matter whether Evander eventually found a way out of our bargain. Because I was going to die during this trial. I was sure of it.

Evander lead the way, and my feet followed until we reached the looming boxes. The king's voice rang, and someone—a guard—took my arm and led me toward the left box. My hand slipped from Evander's arm and fell limp against my side.

The door to the box opened, and the guard nodded for me to enter without him.

The door slammed behind me. Utter darkness surrounded me.

For a moment, all was silent. The box blocked out any noise from the crowd, any outside light. Perhaps this would be one of those tests where they saw how long one could stand being deprived of one's senses before the hallucinations set in.

A few minutes passed in silence. At first, I welcomed the reprieve. But after a few more, my mind began to race with all the thoughts and anxieties that had seemed stunted since last night.

In the darkness, there was nothing to distract me from the warmth of Evander's lips on mine, from retracing the path of his fingertips as they'd slid from my cheek to my ear, my ear to my back, my back to my shoulder, before caressing my arm and settling into my interlocked fingers.

Over and over I played it back, relished in that fraction of a moment when my world had been okay again. When I hadn't been scared at all. When my senses had flared up within me, coating my blood with heat and setting my senses on edge.

But then Evander's words would play over in my mind.

You have my heart, Cinderella. Don't you understand that?

We could have been together.

Did you think I wouldn't have accepted you?

I'd crush the thoughts out with silence before finding myself trapped in the same loop.

"My lady," a small voice piped up from the box. I jumped and let out a short scream, though it occurred to me that no one from the stadium could hear me.

"I apologize for frightening you," the voice said.

I shuffled, dysregulated. "Isn't that the whole point of a lightless, noiseless box?"

"I only enforce the trial. I did not devise it," he said, somewhat disapprovingly. "Though I am grateful for the anonymity it provides."

"Who are you?"

"The enforcer of your intentions."

Ominous, much? "What in Alondria is that supposed to mean?"

He paused. "I suppose that depends entirely upon you."

I waited for him to speak again. For him to tell me what sort of trial this was or to provide me with a riddle, but nothing came.

"Well?" I asked. "You're here for a reason, aren't you?"

The voice sighed. "Ah, yes. I suppose I am. Though I count myself unlucky to have been chosen."

The hairs stood up on my arms, not from any malice in the creature's voice, but from the regret tinting the edges of his words. What kind of trial was this?

"As you know, this trial is meant to certify that your love for the prince is pure, and that his love for you is likewise. I am tasked with giving you a choice to prove such."

He paused again, his intentions impossible to interpret in the dark.

"What choice?" I finally asked, disturbed by my inability to read the male's expression.

"It has been judged by the committee that you, as one of little power and few riches, might be motivated by such to marry the prince. This would be considered an impure motivation."

I laughed. Well, this would be easy. "I care nothing about that."

"I see…" He hesitated. "This is your choice: You may choose to take the prince's inheritance for yourself, as well as your freedom. I must explain that, if you were to marry the prince, though you would live in luxury, your inheritance would not be your own, and you would only inherit an inconsequential sum should the prince meet an unfortunate end. With the prince's inheritance, you could build your own castle and inherent a significant portion of Dwellen while the King of Dwellen still lives."

My skin prickled, not at the inheritance, but at the chance to get my life back. Still, it seemed too good to be true. Why would the king offer me Prince Evander's inheritance without price? "What's the catch?"

He continued on as if I hadn't spoken. "If you so choose to sever the bargain and claim the prince's inheritance, the prince will die."

I stifled a shocked chortle. "What? No. Who falls for this? There's no way you're going to kill the prince. If I were to choose that option, it would just mean I'd failed the test and you would execute me for treason."

"On the contrary, my lady. The committee who originally constructed this trial held the highest standards for an heir to the throne. It was their opinion that an heir to the throne who was stupid and lovesick enough to pick a bride who would betray him for money and power did not deserve the throne. They believed such a fool deserved to die for his lack of discernment, when the people of Dwellen were at the hands of his decisions."

"What about an heir who is stupid enough to enter into a marriage bargain with the wrong woman?" I scoffed, but it sounded more like a labored exhale than an expression of derision. He couldn't be serious. Regardless of the backwards notions the committee of old had held regarding the value of their potential heirs' lives, Evander was still the only heir. The king and queen had no other children. There was no one else for the crown to pass on to. They wouldn't have put their only living son through this trial, if…

Wait. That wasn't right.

Evander had a sister.

Princess Olwen.

My heart stopped. Surely not. As much disdain as King Marken held for Evander, the king despised his daughter. The ancient fae would rip his own heart out before giving the title of heir to his daughter who had shamed him publicly by refusing her father's plans to form a political alliance through her marriage.

But, then again, how much control did the king have over the results of the Trials? When he'd first told me of the Trials, I'd thought he meant to punish me. Except what motivation had he really had? For all I knew, the king took an oath when he was coronated that he would uphold the outdated tradition.

Did he have the power to save his son from death, even if he wanted to?

My stomach twisted.

"I have yet to finish."

I crossed my arms. "By all means, go on." The darkness in the room seemed to thicken.

"If you were to choose the money and power, the prince would die. But the prince has also been given a choice. A choice between what the committee decided would be the greatest temptation to the prince, and your life. If he severs the bargain while you choose to maintain it, then you will die."

My heart faltered, started back up, and raced in my chest. Surely he wouldn't. Surely not.

"If you choose to kill the prince, and he chooses to kill you, then both your lives will be spared, and you shall both have that which your heart most desires. If the prince chooses to kill you, and you choose to spare him, then—"

"Then I die," I breathed. "I know how this works."

"Correct. If you choose to kill the prince, and the prince chooses to spare you, then he dies. If you both choose to spare one another, then you each forfeit that which is most precious to you. Your bargain will remain, and you shall be married in a week's time."

"And what exactly do you think is most precious to me?" I asked, hardly daring to breathe.

"I'm afraid I cannot tell you that."

"Of course you can't." My mind whirred.

"I did not make the regulations."

I shuffled through the possibilities. What was most precious to me? My stomach seemed to shrink when I thought of my parents. I couldn't breathe. I didn't want Evander to die, not even if I hated him... But my parents... I couldn't...

As if reading my mind, the voice said, "In addition, the rules of the Trials state that no one will be put to death due to the decisions made by the prince and his betrothed."

Relief washed over me, but it was short-lived. My parents wouldn't die if I made the decision to spare Evander, but would I even live to see them again?

Evander thought I hated him. I did hate him. Would he assume I'd want him dead? Given my anger at him last night, he might assume I'd murder him anyway, regardless of the reward. Then he'd surely choose to kill me, thinking he could spare himself.

If that was the case, I could agree to kill him and we'd both be spared.

But, then again, what if he chose to spare me?

I hated him. I hated him for loving a thief and murderer above me. I hated him for choosing a single night of euphoria over the friendship I'd thought we'd built. I hated him for letting her go free, even if that meant risking my life. And I hated him for using me, for playing my affections, so that I could rule not with him, but for him, in the future.

I hated him, sure.

But enough to kill him?

My heart lurched.

"If I choose to kill the prince, that guarantees that my life will be spared, correct?"

"Indeed."

I numbered the alternative situations in my mind, as if somehow that would make the choice lest daunting. Less permanent. *1) I sever the bargain, but Evander spares me. That would leave me free and Evander dead. 2) I spare Evander, but he severs the bargain. Then Evander would be free, and I'd be dead. 3) We both spare each other, choosing to lose what is most dear to us and go through with the marriage. 4) We both sever the bargain, and we both get to live, while keeping what is most dear to us.*

My heart raced. I didn't want to die. Perhaps I'd felt numb this morning, but mostly because I knew I'd have to live in fear of waking up with that horrid pale face grinning at me above my bed, a dagger in hand. Perhaps already lodged in my chest. I didn't want to die, not yet. Could I bring myself to kill him if it guaranteed sparing myself? He'd already proven that my life wasn't the most important thing to him. If he'd really cared about my wellbeing, he never would have let her go. Never would have risked it.

He was going to choose to kill me, I realized.

Because there was something out there more important to him than my life and safety. Something the committee had surely caught onto.

Her.

He could kill me and have her.

My pulsed raced, the walls of the box crowding in on me.

Be reasonable, Ellie. Evander could have killed me at any point since our betrothal, I reminded myself.

But this was different. His life was on the line this time. And he knew I hated him. Why would he risk his own life, when surely he was convinced I would choose to kill him?

"Have you made your decision?" the voice asked.

"I...um..."

"Take your time."

But I didn't want to take my time. Because the longer I spent in the darkness, alone, hidden from the outside world, protected from the judgment of my parents' knowing eyes... I knew where the darkness would take me. It was all part of the trial.

The longer I spent in the darkness, the brighter the obvious path shone. It was Evander's fault I was in this position to begin with. He and his family had forced me into a betrothal I hadn't wanted. He'd ruined my life, soiled my dreams. Then he'd had the audacity to steal my heart, all while his belonged to another.

If he died, it would be his own doing. Not mine.

And even if I spared him, if we both spared each other, what would I be giving up?

That which you hold most precious.

It hit me then. What I'd be giving up.

No. He couldn't have it. Evander could take my heart and rip it to shreds, but he couldn't have *that*.

Objectively speaking, the correct choice, the rational choice, would be to sever the bargain with Evander. Because if we both chose to forfeit the bargain, then we'd both be spared. We could both have what we wanted.

Surely Evander would realize that. He was rash, sure. But he wasn't stupid. He would expect me to make the rational choice, and he would act in turn.

"I've made my decision," I whispered.

And then I chose.

The voice hesitated. "Is that your final answer?"

THE BOX OPENED, and light poured in, blinding my eyes. I searched the compartment for the owner of the voice, but my eyes weren't adjusting quickly enough. Everything had gone a bright orange, and before I could squint to make out the creature's face, a guard grabbed my arm and pulled me from the box. The door slammed behind us, though something was off.

I realized the crowd wasn't cheering. I turned to my left, only to see a shadow standing outside the other box. Evander. I couldn't make out his face. What would I find there? Had he condemned me to death?

Why wasn't the crowd cheering?

My limbs began to shake.

What had I done?

The king's voice sounded, and I clung to every word. "The Heir and his Betrothed have each made their decisions." He must have explained the rules to the crowd while we were in the boxes. My eyes started to make out more details, and there was a grim look on the king's face. My heart sank. That could mean only one thing.

But then his grimace softened at the edges. "Each has decided to put away their utmost desires for the other. Both the Heir and his Betrothed chose to spare one another's lives."

My heart lifted from my chest.

The crowd roared.

He spared me.

Evander spared me.

He couldn't let me die, couldn't risk severing the bargain.

Just like for the life of me, I couldn't stand to forfeit his.

I'd changed my mind as soon as the dreadful words had come out of my mouth. Never in my life had I been so thankful for a second chance.

I'd have kissed the owner of the voice if he hadn't been disembodied, just for giving me the opportunity to take it back.

I turned to look at Evander, to share the relief, but his body was rigid, his tanned face gone pale. He was looking straight ahead, and his mouth was twisted, as though he might vomit.

"Evander?" But the thundering crowd swallowed my voice. He was trembling. Why was he trembling?

What had he given up?

When the guards escorted us from the arena, they took us separately.

It was only once we reached the quiet tunnel that I realized the tips of my fingers had gone numb.

CHAPTER 48

ELLIE

I wasn't sure what I was expecting when I received word that Evander had called me down to his father's office to meet him. I wasn't even sure if I wanted to see him. Sure, I was thankful he had spared my life. But the way he had refused to look at me after the trial, the way he'd stared across the arena with an unsettling emptiness in his eyes…

When the guard escorted me to the king's office and announced my arrival, Evander hardly acknowledged me. Instead, he rifled the papers on his father's desk.

The king wasn't there.

"What's going on?" I asked.

The scribe standing next to Evander—the same one who had assisted us during the second trial—was the one who spoke up. "Lady Payne, the prince's associates have been on the hunt for a while, ever since the erm, unfortunate misunderstanding, for a means to free you both from the bargain." Oh, this again. My shoulders went rigid. "And we believe we have come to the conclusion that there is a definitive way to nullify the bargain."

I was free. I was free—so why did my soul feel as though it had been turned to lead?

"You were right then," I said, addressing Evander with the most obvious statement in the world, if only to pull him into this conversation that I shouldn't have had to have with a stranger.

"Yes," he said, still shuffling through the papers.

"Are you going to explain it to me or leave me to wonder?"

He glanced up at me, his usually bright green eyes pale, murky. Dark circles had formed under his eyes.

Before he could respond, the scribe interjected. I didn't take my eyes off Evander though. "It took a great deal of searching through the ancient laws. Most of the ones that would have been useful to us have been repealed, but there happens to be a clause from the second century that we believe is solid grounds for breaking the bargain."

"Fae curse magic cares about fae law?" I asked, rolling my eyes. "If that were the case, couldn't the fae have just made it the law that it was legal to lie, and then they could get away with it?"

"Not quite." The scribe coughed. "But few bargains are made in this era without a clause to allow one out of it."

"Right, that's why there's a cosigner on the marriage bargains between royalty," I said, annoyed that information I already knew was getting in between me and some answers.

"Exactly, my lady. Fortunately, your bargain with the prince specified that it was made by the authority of common fae law, and therefore can be annulled under any clause properly ratified by common fae law."

I chewed my lip. "Is a law from the second century considered common?"

The scribe let out a weak, unsure smile. "It is, so long as it has never been annulled. This law might have been forgotten over the years, but, as far as we can tell, it was never formally repealed."

"And what's this law?"

Evander was the one who answered. "Your parents have the legal right to annul any marriage bargain you enter into, as long as they make their intentions clear before the couple is formally wed."

I chewed my lip. Happy, Ellie. This was happy news. So why didn't it feel like it? "So I can't go back on a bargain I didn't mean to agree to, but my parents can?" No wonder the ancient law had been forgotten in the modern era.

Evander's fingers went rigid over the papers on his desk. "Yes."

I scoffed. "I assume you've already sent a carriage for them, then."

Evander and the scribe exchanged a knowing glance.

The scribe answered first. "His Highness wished to wait for your permission before calling your parents."

"My permission?" I eyed Evander skeptically. There had been a moment after the third trial when my heart had again warmed at the sight of him, at the knowledge that he'd chosen to spare my life. But that warmth had not been returned.

His face was cold, impassive, bordering on—my gut twisted —resentful.

He nodded. "I'm done assuming what you want. The carriage and the messenger are prepared, should you wish to summon them. But the choice is up to you." Those last words came out pained.

My mouth went dry. "And what, exactly, do you want?"

"For you to be happy." The words were immediate, not in the rehearsed kind of way, but in the manner in which people said things that they believed to their core.

The truth of that struck me.

"I won't force you into a marriage you do not want."

I swallowed the discomfort of finally being given the choice for which I'd hoped for months now. I could have laughed at myself, at my folly, if I didn't think laughing would cause my already sore chest to ache.

How foolish I'd been to fall for him. How foolish I still was. For even as he stood across from me, even though I knew in my heart that he'd chosen her over me by allowing her to escape, by sealing my fate, I was still allowing the feel of his warm lips on mine to slip in. Still hurting for the fact that I would never feel that again, that in the moment, I hadn't made the mental effort to hold onto that sensation. That I hadn't memorized his kiss. Because I'd assumed there would be a thousand more.

I couldn't allow myself to continue in this folly, couldn't allow myself to pine over a male who viewed me as his second choice.

I wouldn't be anyone's second choice.

First choice, or nothing at all.

"She'll still come after me. You know that," I said. Evander winced.

"You'll continue to have full access to your guards."

"That never helped me much here. Why should it help me at home? Why should I believe it will keep my family safe?"

Evander shook his head and sighed. "You'll receive the finest this time. Double the guards."

My heart ached. He had already thought of any objection I might have. Had already come up with the solutions should I try to stay within the bargain.

He wanted out.

"Very well," I said, my mouth going dry. "Call them. Let's end this."

A LONG HOUR filled with silence later, my parents arrived in the prince's office. My father, whom I hadn't seen in months, rushed over to the chair where I sat and kissed my forehead, lifting me off my chair and wrapping me in his strong embrace. I fought back the tears, but only because I was tired of shedding tears in front of Evander. Tired of shedding tears at all.

"The king won't punish her for this?" my mother asked as she held an inked quill warily over the signature line. Ink dripped off the tip, staining the parchment.

"No," Evander said. "My father is not above Fae law. He took an oath to uphold it."

My mother nodded her head, though she didn't quite look convinced. Then she pressed the quill to the parchment and signed her name. My father released me and followed suit.

"That's it?" he asked. "She's free now?"

"It can be tested," the scribe said.

Evander nodded. "I refuse to wed Elynore Payne."

I watched his chest. It ebbed like a river after a spring rainstorm.

"I refuse to wed Prince Evander."

Nothing happened.

The torrent of relief and loss swept over me, drowning one another in their own brands of intensity.

My mother took my hand as I savored my breath.

Evander and I stole one last glance.

I realized then that we were both complicit in killing each other. Not the versions of ourselves that would walk out of this white-washed office and go on with our lives.

The carefree prince, confident for the first time in his ability to lead. The dreamer girl, willing for the first time in her life to be content.

Together, we'd killed them, those versions of ourselves.

"Let's go home, Ellie," my mother said.

I turned for one last glance, one last word of well-wishing, but Evander had already disappeared.

He hadn't bothered to say goodbye.

CHAPTER 49

ELLIE

"So you're really leaving then?" Blaise asked, as if we both weren't packing my bags.

I'd amassed few belongings of my own while living in the castle, and though the queen had insisted I take the gowns and outfits, I couldn't quite bring myself to.

I didn't exactly want to be reminded of this place, pleasant as some of my experiences had been.

"I have to leave. You know that," I said to my friend.

My friend, who, true to character, was watching me pack my bags rather than helping.

But she was here, and that was enough.

Blaise shuffled on her feet, guilt spreading across her face.

I cut my eyes at her as I set a half-folded blouse on the bed. "What's wrong?"

Blaise's gaze skirted mine, scanning the ceiling. "I shouldn't have kept it from you—what Evander and I were up to."

I bristled at that. It had bothered me initially when I'd found out that Blaise, too, had known for quite some time that there was a way out of the bargain and had hidden that information from me. Perhaps my heart wouldn't be in this twisted mess if I'd discovered the truth earlier, before Evander swept my heart off its hinges and...

I swallowed any bit of anger I harbored against Blaise. She wasn't the source of my hurt, anyway. "It's not your fault. It was Evander's responsibility to tell me. You were only giving him the chance to be honorable and do it himself. Besides, Evander and you were friends long before I came along. I understand why you wouldn't want to jeopardize his trust."

A shadow darkened Blaise's face. "Still. I'm afraid I've jeopardized yours."

I turned toward her, propping myself backward on the bed, and smiled. "You don't have to pick between us, you know. You're welcome to visit me anytime, so long as you're okay with pretending a certain irritable and irresponsible prince doesn't exist for a few hours."

Blaise smiled at that, though it was the weakest smile I'd ever seen cross her lips. A single tear streamed down her face as she threw her arms around me and wrapped me in her embrace. "I'm really going to miss you, you know. It's been nice having another girl around."

"You have Imogen," I mused as her stringy hair scratched at my face.

Blaise humphed. "I'm pretty sure Imogen would slice my hair off in the middle of the night if she thought my retaliation wouldn't be a thousand times worse."

I happened to agree, but thought better than to admit as much. No need to put ideas into Blaise's head.

She finally pulled away, still sniffling as I packed the last of my things. "I'll call for a coachman, then," she said, wiping her nose on her sleeve before she scurried from my chambers.

Alone now, the beautiful room with all its fancy embossed wallpaper and ridiculously ornate mirrors and excessive bottles of perfume seemed to encroach on me, threatening to suffocate me in memories.

Evander, that first day. Backing me up against the bed. Threatening to murder me and frame my death on a household servant. I bit back a laugh. I'd been terrified of him then, his hulking form, his lightning-quick speed.

Now that I knew him, I was fairly sure he was the type of person who would stop a carriage to pick up a turtle from the road and move it to safety. Not exactly the murdery sort.

My cheeks heated at the memory of him so close, and my mind flitted to the night of the ball, the way my heart had skipped when he'd cut into my and Fin's dance, a rage of possessive longing steaming underneath his cocky gaze. Yet on the roof, he'd been quite the gentleman. Gentle and kind and unwilling to push any boundaries I might have.

Though perhaps that was simply because his mind was elsewhere, wishing for someone else's kiss, lingering on someone else's body.

My cheeks heated again, and this time the feeling sharpened, traveling to my chest and localizing there, pinching my lungs and making it hard to breathe.

I had to get out of this place. I'd miss parts of it—Blaise and the queen. My heart dampened as I thought of Evander's mother, the friendship we'd kindled. My friendship with Blaise might have been independent of my betrothal to Evander, but such was not the case with the queen. She was my friend, but before that she was a mother, and her loyalty to her son would supersede any fond feelings she might harbor for me.

The queen and I would part as friends, but we would part all the same.

It hurt more than it should have.

And then Evander...

If only I'd protected my heart, kept that vow to myself I'd made so long ago, then perhaps it wouldn't ache so much—leaving him. We could have been friends, he and I, had I not diverged from our shared mission of severing our bond. I'd still be leaving, but it would be with a promise of seeing one another again.

But that was silly, too, wasn't it? Once I was out of the way, Evander's psychopath love would step into my shoes—figuratively, this time—and there was no way in Alondria she would let me anywhere near him, even if it hadn't been for that cursed kiss...

Well, it wasn't so cursed, now was it?

A knock on my door, and my heart jolted, but it was only Blaise poking her head back in.

I tried to ignore the way my heart deflated at the sight of her, like I was expecting someone else to stride through that door.

You're being irrational, I reminded myself. *What are you expecting? Some faerietale gesture of true love?*

It was a silly hope. A child's hope. Besides, what could Evander possibly say that would convince me he loved me more than he loved her?

No, even if he could convince me of that, it wouldn't be enough.

I didn't want to be loved more than another woman.

I wanted to be the only woman.

I deserved as much.

So it was silly and foolish to imagine Evander striding into this room with some grand declaration of his love for me, because he'd already proved his lingering feelings for her the moment he'd allowed her to escape.

Nothing short of her head on a stake as a peace offering would convince me otherwise, and I considered myself a reasonable enough person not to expect something so dramatic.

"They're ready for you," Blaise said, even her voice drooping.

I nodded and grabbed my bags, straightening my shoulders. A footman hustled in and tried to take my luggage from me. "There'll be no need for that," I said. "It's not as if I'll have anyone carrying my luggage where I'm going. No use in getting used to it."

He hesitated, but must have been too timid to put up a fight, because he nodded and backed away.

When we left, Blaise pulled the door shut behind her. The thud of it closing sounded more like closing the door to my future.

No, not my future. One of many possible futures.

I'd simply find myself a better one.

"Ellie?" she asked once the footman rounded the corner.

"Yes?"

"Do you love him?"

My breath caught; my words hitched in my throat for a moment. But I recovered quickly enough. A child of my mother's would. "I suppose I did... I suppose I do. But I won't for long. I won't give my heart to someone who doesn't want it. At least, I won't let him keep it. Not for much longer, anyway."

Blaise swallowed, and for a moment I thought she might cry again. I'd never seen that before, not from anyone other than my parents—someone hurt like that on behalf of someone else. I wondered then how often Blaise absorbed pain that shouldn't have been her own, how much she hid underneath that free-spirited, lazy facade of hers.

"For what it's worth, he should have picked you," Blaise said.

A pained smile tugged at the corners of my lips. "That's certainly worth something."

"I think maybe," she said, looking up at me, "I think maybe you're the right choice for him. But perhaps he's not the right choice for you. If he was, then he would have seen that."

I nodded, too overcome with conflicting emotions to respond properly.

Blaise must have understood, because she took my hand in hers and walked beside me as I left this version of my future behind.

CHAPTER 50

EVANDER

*I*t'd been an entire mooncycle since I'd seen Ellie Payne's smirk, sensed her laugh upon my ears, thought I'd heard her laughter echoing down the corridors.

Yet still, Ellie Payne, that relentless, insufferable, unforgettable woman, refused to give me a moment's peace.

The footsteps in the hallway were always hers. Until they weren't, and Blaise or Imogen or any number of servants peeked their heads into my room to ask if I was hungry or thirsty or in need of anything.

I never was, though sometimes I would tell Blaise that if she could find me a glassblower with an affinity for lobster, I'd be much obliged. She'd hide her wince at my desperation behind a joke about how I should ask Imogen to do it.

And then Ellie Payne was in the forest, infecting my nostrils with the scent of rainwater and lavender as I attempted to get some fresh air to clear my head.

She was completely ruining my desire for exercise.

I'd come to dread lobster night.

I used to love lobster night.

Yep. Ellie Payne was in my life for a grand total of two months, and she'd managed to ruin my immortal existence.

Two months. That was 1/1200 of my life.

I'd calculated it; that's how bored I was without her.

The castle had become too stuffy, too quiet, so I'd found myself wandering into town, a hood pulled over my face so no one would recognize me.

I'd even walked all the way to her family's cottage one day.

Okay, two days.

Maybe three.

But I'd stopped doing that. One time was one thing. Three times was bordering on stalker behavior.

It wasn't that I was trying to stalk Ellie, though. Every time I found myself straying down the path toward her family's cottage, it had been with the intention of banging on her door, demanding to be let in.

I'd prepared at least sixty-three speeches. Unfortunately, there weren't many variations of *I love you* that made up for the fact that, in a moment of rash decisions, I'd picked the freedom of a psycho murderer over Ellie's safety.

Rash. It'd been the part of me my father had always despised, the thorn lodged within my soul he'd expected to be my ruin.

My father hadn't been wrong.

In my rash moments, I'd chosen Cinderella.

But in the quiet moments, in the longs walks past the sunflower fields with the dust caking my shoes and the snowcapped mountains in the distance, in the eerie moments of silence before I fell asleep, when nothing in the castle seemed awake, not even the crickets that dwelled within the cracks in the mortar... In those moments, I chose Ellie every time.

Perhaps that was what kept me from knocking on Ellie's door, despite the speeches I'd prepared—Fates, I had a robust collection of wilting flowers piled up in the corner of my room collecting dust, from all the times I'd stopped by the florist and purchased two bouquets— one for Ellie, one for her mother in case Ellie decided she wanted me thrown out of the house before I got the chance to speak my mind.

Ellie probably didn't like flowers, anyway. She'd probably interpret

my getting them for her as yet another example of how I didn't understand her—not really.

The women had come calling again, ladies of varying noble rank
flocking to the castle in hordes as the news of my and Ellie's failed
engagement spread through the kingdom like wildfire.

I might have found it amusing, if I weren't so miserable.

They primped and preened and had a tendency to find themselves
"lost"—conveniently in my quarters and scantily clad.

Poor Blaise had the misfortune of being the one to escort them out
of the castle. She'd complained of having half her robes soiled with
snot from rejected women who assumed Blaise would be eager to
offer them comfort.

I was probably ruder to them than I had to be, but that was for the
best.

Let them spread the rumors that Prince Evander of Dwellen was
intolerable. If it kept them away, I'd wear the reputation proudly.

It was in their best interest, anyway.

There had been whisperings about what had occurred in my and
Ellie's final trial, within the confines of those boxes. The theories
regarding what we'd faced had been endless:

*I heard they looked into a mirror that showed them the other's truest,
ugliest self.*

Well, I heard they both gave up their hearts to save one another.

No, no. It was their firstborn they had to give up.

No one had guessed what I'd actually given up to save Ellie's life.
No one had come close.

If they had, there wouldn't be a line of females queued up outside
the castle right now.

When I'd made the decision to spare her, I expected it to hurt
more, for me to feel the loss. I'd known then that Ellie would never
forgive me. I'd known then that I was going to tell her about the
exception Blaise had found. That I had to let her go.

It had hurt, what I'd given up, and I'd been shaking when I stepped
out of that box.

375

But the more days I spent away from Ellie, the less I cared about what I'd forfeited.

I didn't want it if it wasn't with her.

My door creaked open, and I closed my eyes, sprawling out on my bed to pretend I was asleep. Blaise had been incessant about checking on me lately. The crease between her brow furrowed itself with such frequency, I warned her it was bound to get stuck that way permanently.

Let her think I was still asleep. I didn't need her looks of pity to remind me of what I'd lost.

The moonlight shined so brightly tonight, it seeped through my closed eyelids, lighting them up with a muted white glow.

Tonight was a full moon. Which marked a month since I'd made the stupidest decision of my life.

The door creaked again, and footsteps pattered against the floor.

I let out a snore.

That should have deterred her, but I supposed Blaise knew me well enough not to be fooled when I was faking sleep. Still, I'd pretend as long as I needed to before she gave up. I wanted nothing more than to be alone tonight.

She was close now, and I could hear her breaths, sense her heartbeat, wild and erratic.

That was strange. Why would Blaise—

A weight settled on top of me, and the warmth of soft skin brushed against either side of my torso.

My stomach tightened with alarm as I snapped my eyes open. "Bla—"

It wasn't Blaise.

A CURVY FIGURE, clad in nothing more than a flimsy blue nightgown, hovered over me, straddling my torso with her legs.

Her white-blond hair shone in the stray rays of moonlight sneaking through the window.

She traced my stomach with her finger, leaning over me, wanton desire caking her face.

Lilac and rosebuds filled my nostrils, swarmed my mind, making me dizzy.

I wanted her. I wanted her just as badly as I'd wanted her the first night I'd laid eyes on her.

I wanted her, and I hated myself for it.

She must have seen it in my face, because a triumphant smile spread across her lips.

Unfortunately for her, I'd recently come to the conclusion that getting what I wanted wasn't worth it half the time.

Besides, there was something I wanted more.

Another blink, and I'd pinned Cinderella to the stone floor by her throat.

"You tried to kill Ellie," I hissed, knowing as soon as the jealousy flashed in Cinderella's eyes that I'd made a mistake. It was no matter, though. She wouldn't leave this castle ever again. I'd lock her up in the dungeons and leave her there until she was a distant memory. An unpleasant dream. The type you shake off when you wake up, then move on with your day.

On second thought, I didn't want her prison anywhere near me. I'd send her to Naenden and have them lock her up and leave her to rot.

"Of course I did," she said. "It was the only way to be together."

Tears welled up in her stunning blue eyes. That sultry look was replaced by one of horror as my fingers dug into her flesh, trapping the air above her lungs.

My hands shook, and I thought to end her right then, crush her windpipe and be done with the woman who'd ruined my life, but then I thought of Jerad, of his desire for justice, and I allowed my fingers to loosen, only barely.

She gulped in a gust of air like she might never taste it again.

She might not.

"I promise not to hurt her again. You have to understand, Evander.

I've been out of my mind thinking of you marrying her. I thought it was the only way. But now that the bond is broken and she's out of your life, we can finally be together."

I made no attempt to restrain the scoff that crossed my lips. "You're delusional if you think I'd ever want to be with you."

Her blue eyes twitched, almost like she'd caught herself in the middle of a wince. But she regained that haughty smirk soon enough. "Oh, Evander," she said, the feigned innocence gone now. "I like you when you show your fangs."

"I'm finding the darkest, dingiest hovel in all of Alondria, and I'm sticking you in it to rot," I seethed.

Playfulness flashed in her eyes. Was she enjoying this? My threatening of her? "I'm sure you will," she said. "But I believe that can wait until morning, don't you think?"

She snaked her finger down my torso and—

"Stop that." I grasped her hand, yanking it above her head and pinning it there.

She seemed to like that more than I intended her to.

"Just one night, Evander," she whispered, biting her lip. "Aren't you the least bit tempted? I know you are."

I sighed, and she must have thought I was reconsidering her offer, because feral delight broke across her face.

"I can't do this," I said, my breathing going ragged.

"But you *can*. You're the Heir of Dwellen. You can do anything you want."

I kept her hands pinned above her head, but I loosened my grip on her throat, allowing my fingers to graze the soft skin of her neck. I traced them up her jaw and ran them through her hair, and she shuddered at my touch.

When I leaned closer to her, her whole body stilled in silent expectation. Wanton desire devoured her blue eyes.

When my lips touched her ear, this time, it was her breath that went ragged.

And when I whispered what exactly I'd given up in the third trial for Ellie, I decided Cinderella's wail of rage was the best sound I'd heard in a month.

"You fool!" she screamed, any trace of wanting on her face now extinguished by her anger.

"Careful, friend," I laughed, launching myself to my feet and jerking her to hers as I twisted her arms behind her back. "Defeat isn't flattering on you. I'm afraid you don't have the face for it."

Her scowl had me in a better mood than I'd been in for weeks.

"*Do you have any idea what you've done?* What this means for an heir of Dwellen? You've ruined your chance at—"

"Oh, just shut up already. You act like it's your loss, not mine. But it was never yours, Cinderella. Just like those shoes weren't yours. You're just a sad, pathetic girl who has to take from others to distract everyone around you from how insane you actually are."

It felt good. Talking to her like that. That probably wasn't for the best, but right now—

Cinderella let out a cry of anger. Pain exploded in my head, and everything went black.

When I woke, my head spinning in pain, there was a note crumpled in my fist.

I opened it, the script scribbled in almost illegible letters, probably in haste.

When I held it under the moonlight, my heart stopped.

My dearest Evander,

So you'd choose Ellie Payne over me after all. Well, then. Let's see who you choose now.

Meet me at the Payne workshop before the moon reaches its apex. Otherwise, I suppose you'll have to read in the papers how Ellie and Blaise met their ends.

CHAPTER 51

*I*t had been unlike the parasite to leave the note.
Sloppy even.

The parasite wasn't used to being sloppy.

Efficient? Precise? Ruthless? Yes.

Sloppy, never.

She'd made a mistake picking this girl as a host. The parasite had always found it easy to construct walls between her consciousness and the minds of those she inhabited. There had been the hosts: living out their day-to-day lives as normal, perhaps a bit concerned about how they occasionally awoke in strange places once a month, but too superstitious to admit such to their relatives lest they be burned as a witch.

And then there had been the parasite, lurking in the shadows of their minds, prepared to take over when the glint of that horrible, glorious moonlight crossed the horizon.

But this girl was different. The parasite had known as much the day the girl had first shuffled into the shop, plain and wide-eyed and so deliciously desperate.

The girl was already so used to morphing herself into whatever she thought others wanted. Never bothering anyone with her pain while she inwardly drowned. Once the parasite had slipped into her body, shifting had been like slipping on a pair of shoes someone had already broken in.

But there was something in the girl that the parasite had failed to recognize. She might have scented it, had it not been so utterly masked underneath the girl's noxious desperation to be wanted.

There was a strength to the girl the parasite had missed, one she never would have tolerated in a host before.

The parasite had always avoided strong-minded hosts because they were difficult to wield. Unyielding and a pain to stuff into the backs of their minds, kicking and screaming and scratching the entire way.

That's what the parasite had told herself at least.

The truth was that she found that kind of strength intoxicating. More treacherous than the stubbornness, the refusal to be completely locked away, was how that sort of defiance tasted. Sharp and bitter and utterly all-consuming. As biting and decadent as dark chocolate.

The parasite had a difficult time shielding herself from it.

Had a difficult time not letting a little of her host slip through.

Not enough for the girl to gain control of her body, of course. Never enough for that.

No, the parasite kept the girl in iron chains of magic. The girl couldn't even remember the parasite's actions when she awoke.

But still. The parasite allowed bits of the girl to influence her, to shape her.

It had served her well at first, allowing the girl's undying love for Evander, her knowledge of his inner struggles to guide the parasite's words as she stole his heart the night of the ball.

The girl hadn't even known what she was doing, hadn't been aware of it, really. But the prince's face had been too deeply engrained in the girl's subconscious. He'd passed right through the bars of the cage the parasite had constructed for her host. The parasite had let him.

So the parasite had told the prince exactly what he wanted to hear. That she was sorry for the loss of his brother.

She'd known to avoid bringing up the fact the prince was the heir. Something in the recesses of her host's mind knew he hated that.

The parasite had assumed the girl's closeness to the prince would be a strength.

She could not have been more wrong.

At first, the parasite had assumed that her attraction to the prince was rooted in lust. After all, the parasite had known carnal pleasures during her centuries of moonlit escapades—and there was no denying that the prince was a perfect specimen.

She'd told herself she would enjoy him immensely once she found a way to free herself of the moonlight's curse and join herself to the girl's body permanently, using her shifting abilities to remain Cinderella forever and erase the girl's plain face from existence.

When she discovered that Ellie Payne had tried on the shoes and accidentally bonded herself to the prince, acid had settled over the parasite's consciousness. But she'd attributed it to annoyance that Ellie Payne would take the parasite's place as a princess, ruining her chances of ridding the castle of its monarch and becoming queen herself.

And when she stood over Ellie Payne with that knife, she'd told herself she was taking pleasure in it because she would have finally cleared the path to the power she'd always coveted.

The parasite had told herself many things.

Most of them had turned out to be lies.

She'd gone too far. Allowed too much room in the cracks of her subconscious. And though the girl had no physical control over her body, she'd soaked into the parasite, staining her and soiling her with her love for the prince.

Love was a dangerous thing in the heart of a parasite.

All a parasite was good for was taking what they wanted.

And she wanted Evander.

Not his title. Not his throne. Not his power.

She wanted *him*.

She wanted the prince to drown himself in his obsession with her, to double-cross his every moral code to defend her. She wanted his body and his obsession and his heirs swaddled in her arms.

Yet the parasite couldn't have that.

Ellie Payne had made sure of that.

And if the parasite couldn't have what she wanted, then she would do what she did best.

She would take him.

CHAPTER 52

ELLIE

*G*lass shattered against the wall of the workshop as the remains of my most recent project crumbled into a pile on the floor.

I couldn't get the slippers right. This had been my eighth attempt in the month since I'd left the castle. Yet I couldn't seem to replicate the shoes I'd once been so proud of.

That wasn't even the worst part.

I couldn't seem to get anything right. If I tried to cast a glass saucer, I'd heat it in the furnace too quickly, and hours of work would split in two. When I tried to etch flowers into a teacup, my fingers would falter, ruining the piece. Even the windows I helped my father make came out warped and uneven.

"Ellie, darling?" my father's voice called from the workshop door I'd thought I'd locked. It creaked as he entered. "You've only lit one lantern."

It was true. I preferred to work in the dark these days. Perhaps it comforted me to blame my regression of skills on not being able to see well enough to scrape an intricate design, to blow a perfect bulb in the glass.

Perhaps I was in denial, but I was content to abide there.

It was gone. My skill with glass was gone. I'd known it then—when I'd made the decision to spare Evander's life during the third trial.

That which is most precious to you.

The pitiful part was that I couldn't even bring myself to regret it. Because as much as I hated him for not wanting me like I wanted him, as often as I imagined his face as my target when I hurtled my failed projects at the wall, I couldn't take it back even if I had the chance.

Evander was alive. Alive and pining after another woman. But alive all the same.

I'd stopped reading the daily paper, so I wasn't sure whether he'd announced his engagement to Cinderella yet. I didn't really want to know if he had.

I'd broken my mother's favorite vase trying to get to the door when I'd heard someone knock last week.

It had been our milk delivery.

I couldn't even make her a new one.

My father sighed and sat next to me on my workbench. There wasn't enough room for both of us, and I had to scoot over and allow one leg to hang off the edge. His arm pressed against my shoulder, and it reminded me of how close I used to stand to him as I'd watched him work when I was a little girl, like I could absorb his talent and skill by just being near him.

He gestured toward the ever-growing pile of glass on the floor across the room. "Do you ever intend to clean that up?"

"No, I just plan to erect a monument to my failures." The words came out crueler, mopier than I had intended the joke to sound.

"I'm proud of you, you know."

I choked out a dry laugh. "Why's that?"

"You could have sulked in bed this whole time. I'm glad I taught my daughter that if you're going to mope, you can at least have something to show for it."

I huffed, picking at my fingernails. "You mean a pile of broken glass?"

"Something beautiful is going to spring out of that pile, I assure you," he said, and when he turned his wrinkled face on mine and smiled, I knew he believed it to be true.

I leaned my head against his shoulder, taking in the familiar scent of tobacco and firewood.

"Do you regret severing your bargain?"

The question took me aback. For all practical purposes, my father had always pretended that I was a little boy. He'd never once pressured me to marry or even acknowledged that I might someday like to do so.

"No. I will not be bound to someone who wishes to be bound to another."

"But you loved him, did you not?"

My shoulders tensed. "Are you saying I should have married him out of love, even though he loved someone else?"

"No, no, no. I'm not saying that."

"Then what are you saying?" I sat up straight, rubbing my sweaty palms against my forehead.

"I'm saying that perhaps you haven't allowed yourself the room to admit that you are hurting."

"I think I know better than anyone that I'm hurting, Papa."

"Hm."

I groaned. "You can't just say something like that, then say, 'hm.'"

"I think you're holding onto that anger in your heart."

My heart sank. "Are you saying I should forgive him? Aren't you supposed to take my side?"

He raised his eyebrows. "I will forever take your side. I hate to see you like this. But you're going to continue to hurt if you continue to harbor hate in your soul."

I pursed my lips, irritated that somehow, my father was implying I was in the wrong here. "He deserves to be hated."

"Maybe. But do you deserve to have to carry hate with you?"

I frowned and fidgeted on the bench. "Maybe. At least it makes it feel a little better."

"I think you'll grow to find that the little bit of relief you get is an illusion."

I sighed, having nothing left to say. My father rose to leave and kissed me on the forehead. But when he reached the door of the workshop, he turned back around and smiled, staring at the pile of glass on the floor. "You used to do that when you were little, you know. My little Ellie, the perfectionist. Everything always had to be just so, or you thought you'd failed."

My eyes stung, and I blinked hard as a painful lump formed in my throat.

"You were quite bad at glassblowing, you know. For a long while."

I let out a strangled laugh, hardly able to hold back a sob. "I think your comforting skills might be getting a little rusty, Pa."

As if he hadn't heard me, my father continued, "But you were convinced you were going to be the best glassblower in all of Dwellen. Surpassed me, even." I dared to look at my father. His brown eyes gleamed with pride in the lantern light. "I've always been so proud of you, Ellie. But I do miss it—you being little and needing my help. Teaching you about glass, watching your skills develop—those are some of my favorite memories."

My heart swelled with mingled pain and loss and nostalgia until I felt it might burst.

"I'd never wish this upon you—losing everything you've worked so hard for. But Ellie, watching you struggle, watching you fight…" A rim of silver pooled on the edges of his eyelids. "I wouldn't mind teaching you again."

Tears streamed from my eyes as something coiled up deep within me unraveled.

"Well, just think about it," he said.

I caught him in my embrace before he had a chance to leave.

I WAS STILL in the workshop when she came for me.

My father had already gone to bed. He'd encouraged me to do the same, but judging from the twinkle in his eyes, I figured we both knew it was a lost cause.

Tomorrow we'd begin our lessons, and Fates smite me if I wasn't prepared.

I was prepping the materials for a simple window, one of our standard, non-ornate versions, when I heard the sultry voice. It snaked the length of my back, sending shivers down my spine.

"Such a shame you seem to have misplaced your talent. I suppose I'll have to commission my wedding shoes elsewhere."

I grabbed for a nearby iron poker and spun around. My makeshift blade clanked against something hard as Cinderella lunged for me, sending her whirring backward.

She hit the wall with a thud...

And immediately began massaging her back against the wall post like she was trying to work a knot out of her muscles.

Fates, I hated her.

She must have caught the look of disgust that was probably smeared across my face, because she shrugged, the moonlight from the window highlighting her pasty skin.

Okay, she wasn't pasty. She was glowing.

Still, I preferred pasty.

I opened my mouth to scream.

"Uh-uh. Alert your dear parents, and I'll just have to kill them first."

The statement clamped my jaw shut as fear raced through me. Where were my guards? Evander had been true to his word; he'd sent members of his private guard to observe my house, to monitor me when I was out and about.

"How'd you get past the guards?" I asked.

She grinned, scraping the blade across her nails as if to trim them. For the first time, I noticed the blade was coated in blood. And I wasn't bleeding.

"I have lots of little tricks you don't know about. That no one knows about."

Fear coursed through my veins, and I inched my foot to the side, preparing to sprint if I had to. "Not even the love of your life?"

Hate flickered in her blue eyes for a moment before her expression chilled.

"Can't you give it a rest?" I asked. "You have what you want now. Evander's bargain with me has been severed. You have him all to yourself. You win."

"Ah, I wish it were that simple," she cooed, "but alas, when I'm lying in Evander's arms at night after he's—well, since you're an innocent I'll put it politely—after he's bedded me"—My blood coiled at the thought and vomit rose in my throat, but I swallowed it back down. My heart wouldn't hurt for him. Not in my last moments. I was too proud for that—"I can't help but stay wide awake. I can't seem to find that sweet sleep. You see, all I can think about is you."

"That sounds like your own problem," I said, clutching my poker firmer until my knuckles paled.

"Yes, well, I'll admit my body is horribly insecure. It tends to bring out my jealous nature," she said, even as my ears perked at the oddity of her word choice. *My body is insecure?* "I've tried to work on it these past few weeks, for my sweet Evander's sake. The male has a boyish heart and can't stand for harm to come to anyone. I'd like to be that for him, I would. But I can't do the sleepless nights anymore. He'll be upset at first, I'm sure. But he'll forgive me. He always does."

I swallowed. Maybe if I could keep her talking, I could find an opening. The idea of skewering her perfectly curvaceous body on my poker probably shouldn't have sent a thrill through me like it did. "I haven't seen any news of your engagement in the papers."

"Oh, you follow those? How pitiful."

"What? Is Evander embarrassed of you? Afraid it might get out what poor taste he has? Or is it the king who won't allow the news to go public?" I forced a wicked grin that mirrored hers. "But then again, I always was his favorite. You might have won Evander's heart, but the king will always be a bit disappointed in you, I imagine."

She gritted her teeth but didn't lunge as I had hoped. If I could get her to strike first, maybe I could be faster, dodge her attack and strike a blow from behind.

"We're waiting on the announcement. Wouldn't want the public to

389

think Evander has moved so quickly from woman to woman. The kingdom isn't aware, of course, that his heart has been mine the entire time."

"Oh, I think they're well aware of you, after you pulled that stunt where you fled at midnight." Hatred welled up within me, taking over my lips as I grinned and seethed. "I imagine their impression will be that the dog returned to his own vomit after being left at the altar."

That did the trick.

She pounced, but I was ready. I sidestepped and allowed her to pass me before taking a stab at her side. But she whirled quicker than I could strike, narrowly avoiding my poker. This time when she struck, I was unprepared, my arm extended into the air. The blunt side of her blade went slamming into my temple, sending dots of black across my vision. My elbows hit the floor, shooting another wave of pain up my arms and into my shoulders. She was on top of me then, scraping her knife into my face as if to carve letters.

Cinderella shoved her hand over my mouth before I could even let out a scream.

A muffled whimper escaped through the gaps between her spindly fingers.

"You shouldn't have kissed him," she whispered.

Fear propelled my arms and legs despite the pain, and I flailed at her, thinking to poke out her eyes or knee her ribcage. I landed a punch to her left ear, and the shock of the impact afforded me enough time to scramble to my feet.

It mattered little in the end, because she recovered quickly, and before I could react, she'd slipped behind me, tucking the edge of her blade to my exposed throat.

"Goodbye, Elynore Payne," she whispered, her voice curdling in my ear. "I do wish things could have been different between us."

I braced myself for death.

CHAPTER 53

ELLIE

*T*here was a moment when I could have sworn that hesitation dampened the craze in Cinderella's bloodthirsty eyes.

It only lasted half a breath, but it was enough to cost her.

"Get away from her."

In the throes of the struggle, neither Cinderella nor I had heard Evander slip into the workshop. How he'd known to come I had no idea, but that didn't matter.

His sea-green eyes glowed with rage, his perfect jaw set with determination.

It was then that I realized Evander was going to *kill* her.

The only problem was, she was going to kill me first.

Cinderella yanked me to my feet, placing me between her and Evander. My throat bobbed against the trembling knife pressed against my throat. Cinderella's hand was shaking, causing the knife to nick at my skin and draw blood.

Evander advanced on us, backing us into a corner as Cinderella drew me backward. "Draw one more *drop* of blood, put one more bruise on her neck, and I will *end* you."

Cinderella clicked her tongue, her erratic breath stinging my cheek. "You know I can't let her live."

This woman was insane. She was insane, and I was going to die.

"If she dies, you'll—"

"I'll what?" Cinderella snapped. "Regret it? Oh, I don't think I will. Because if she dies," she crooned, tracing the knife across my throat as Evander tensed, "then I'm free to have you."

I let out an exasperated cry. "You're insane. Can't you see I'm out of the picture? The two of you deserve each other. You can have him."

Pain flickered in Evander's eyes at my words, and I instantly wished I could take them back, swallow them, and bury them in the gaping pit gnawing at my stomach. His gaze flashed to mine, but only for an instant before he turned his attention back to Cinderella.

"Oh, do you not know?" Her voice was a serpent slithering through my ears, nestling into my gut, leaking trepidation into my veins with its sharp fangs.

I paid her no attention, my eyes set on Evander.

"Know what?"

He winced, his jaw working as if he was trying to formulate words, but his ability to process them was broken, rusted.

He ripped his gaze from mine, his voice going slack, desperate. "Please. Please, just let her go. I'll do anything you want, just don't hurt her."

"I can't have what I want, Evander. Not while she lives."

"*Evander*, what is she talking about?" My heart raced, frantic and wild and aimless as I tried to think of anything, anything at all that could make any of this make sense, but I came up short.

"Why don't you tell her, Prince? Why don't you tell Ellie what you gave up for her right before she walked out on you and practically spat in the face of your sacrifice," she hissed.

My heart stilled, my mind turned to stone. I couldn't think, couldn't speculate. All that was left was a quiet dread. A single question.

What did he give up?

I'd never bothered to ask him. I'd been too hurt, too heartbroken to give him the chance to admit the lengths he might have gone to in order to save my life that day of the third trial.

I hadn't wanted to know, not really. Because if he'd given up something great, if he'd done something reckless to save my life...

I would have rather gone on hating him in peace.

But now as I stared at the male in front of me, the male who'd occupied so many stations in my life: betrothed, enemy, friend...whatever else we'd been... I had to know. "Evander, what did you do?"

He swallowed, his throat bobbing. "I..." His face heated, and I could practically feel the warmth radiating off his cheeks. He swallowed again, more forcefully this time. "Our ancestors valued fidelity above all else. Apparently, all my ancestors, all the heirs of Dwellen, are required to give up the same thing. It's not all that bad, considering. If everything is as it should be, it shouldn't be a sacrifice at all..."

Cinderella hissed impatiently. "What the prince is beating around the bush to avoid saying is that, as long as you live, if he as much as kisses another woman, he'll die."

Shock hit me in the gut, swirled around for a bit, then climbed to my chest, rushing through me in a mix of horror and...and hope.

I could hardly breathe, but I forced out the question. "You gave up your chance to be with her, to be with anyone, to spare me?"

He cocked his head to the side, his eyes going glassy. "Probably not the wisest thing to blurt out while you have a knife to your throat, El."

I let out an exasperated huff, my mind spinning as the knife dug further into my neck, yet without drawing blood this time.

The final trial had occurred within hours of Evander letting Cinderella escape into the night, but come morning he'd chosen to keep me safe and, by so doing, sever any chance he had of being with her.

Prince Evander Thornwall, Heir to the Throne of Dwellen, had signed himself over to a life of celibacy in order to save my life.

And then he'd let me go, let me sever our bond and leave him in that sterile office, and hadn't uttered a word of complaint about it.

The blade slid across my throat again, hovering just above the point of breaking skin. "Luckily, there's a simple solution to our problem."

Evander ran his hands through his hair. He was fast, but was he fast enough to disarm Cinderella before she sliced at a major artery? Probably not. My hands sweated, my palms shaking. "There has to be something you want. Otherwise, you would have already killed her."

Though I couldn't see her face, pressed up next to mine, I felt the curve of her grin in the dropping temperature of the air. "I want you to bind yourself to me. A fae bargain, just like the one you made with Ellie, to wed me at the next full moon."

Evander took a breath, glanced at me, and with hardly a moment to consider the ramifications of this union, he nodded his head.

"No!" I cried out, but she only dug the blunt edge of the knife in harder.

Would that even work? Evander had been forced to ask his father for permission to enter a fae marriage bargain the first time around. But even the king had admitted this was simply a fae tradition, a safeguard against unsavory alliances.

A tradition Evander had feared enough to keep, but now, with my life hanging in the balance…

My heart sank.

He was going to do this.

He was going to bargain his life away for me. Again.

No.

Evander stepped toward us but raised his hands. "There will need to be conditions. You won't hurt Ellie. Not now, not ever. Even after we're wed. And you must promise me that Blaise is safe, and that you'll return her to me."

My ears perked at that. Blaise? Cinderella had Blaise too? Fear spiked within me. Cinderella was crazy; she might have already done away with Blaise, made up some fantasy in her head about how she didn't like how Blaise was closer to Evander than she would ever be.

But then Cinderella spoke, and the panic coiling in my belly loosened. "I agree to your terms. Blaise and Ellie will both remain unharmed."

I let out a strained breath. At least Blaise would be safe.

Evander would be linked to a lunatic for the rest of his life. Well, no, the rest of her life.

My heart ached at the thought, but though Evander and I would never be together, at least he'd be free of her after a few decades. There was a high probability I'd meet my end before then, but at least he wouldn't have to produce heirs with her. And he'd have a month of freedom before the next full moon.

My brain froze on that little detail.

Why had she specified that he'd marry her on the next full moon? If she was so desperate to be his bride, why not tomorrow morning? Or tonight, even? Why risk a month in which Evander might find a legal exemption out of the bargain?

As much as I would have liked to believe that Cinderella's obsession with Evander had been fueled by her desire to gain a position of power, the lust she felt for the prince practically rolled off her in waves. Surely she wouldn't be content being the prince's bride in title alone.

Fates, even *I* had wanted more than that.

And why had she taken Blaise?

Better than that, how did she know about Blaise? I searched my memories for a time when Cinderella might have run across my friend, but I could think of none. Sure, there was always the possibility that she'd been stalking us in the shadows for months now, but…

But then there was the full moon thing again. Hadn't the moon been full the first time she attacked me? Its rays had slipped through the window, causing her pale features to glow.

And come to think of it, I'd noted how pretty the full moon was the night Evander kissed me, the night of the second attack. We'd been up on the roof, and I'd thought the moon looked as though it was watching over the city.

My mind flashed back to Blaise and Imogen's quarters, when I'd found Imogen's pamphlet—the one about how to become a shifter.

Imogen.

A host of memories came rushing back to me.

Imogen with the strange pamphlet. Imogen upset when I asked her if she shopped at Madame LeFleur's. Imogen's jealous glances, her obsession with Evander. Imogen being the first to inform me that Evander's father could annul our betrothal bargain.

Adrenaline burst through me, rattling my brain and speeding up my thoughts. "Evander, don't. Don't make the bargain."

Unadulterated pain sliced the wrinkles at the edges of his eyes, and he shook his head. "I'm sorry, Ellie. I can't let you die. I *need* you alive. Even if I never get to see you again. It would be enough just to know you were safe."

My breath caught, but my brain stumbled for words, for anything to buy my mind more time to find the last piece of the puzzle, the part it couldn't quite grasp, no matter how ardently I fumbled in the dark.

What my brain latched onto wasn't much. I could only hope it would be enough as I blurted, "How long did it take you to summon up the courage to ask Madame LeFleur for something a little stronger than her usual brew?"

Cinderella stiffened next to me. When she spoke, her voice was an impatient command. "You'll need to enter this bargain now, Prince. Before I change my mind and decorate her father's workshop with his daughter's blood."

Evander eased toward us, his hand outstretched.

"No," Cinderella said, her words practically spat. "Do it verbally first. I won't have you yanking me away from her."

He shook his head. "You know that's not how this works."

"Then swear that you won't try to overpower me."

Evander clenched his teeth. Clearly, that's what he'd intended to do. "I swear it."

"Say the whole thing."

"I swear I won't try to overpower you when I take your hand."

Placated, Cinderella reached out, keeping her forearm braced to my neck so I couldn't move, the knife still in her other hand at my throat.

"If Madame LeFleur turned you into this, I'm sure she can turn you right back," I belted out, desperate now for anything that might rile her.

Cinderella cut her eyes toward me, a deadly sneer smeared across her full features. "That old hag is dead."

Dead?

The shock that must have crossed my face wasn't mirrored on Evander's. "Did you know?" I asked.

He grimaced. "Yes, but I didn't make the connection."

I turned back to Cinderella. "You murdered Madame LeFleur, didn't you? When she figured out that you'd used her potion to trick the prince into falling in love with you."

"And what if I did? Does it matter to you, Prince? Would you bind yourself to a murderer to preserve the lives of these little girls you hold with such fondness?"

Evander winced, but he didn't have to nod.

Everyone in this workshop knew the answer.

"Evander, please. You don't have to do this," I said, but the words died a breath away from my lips.

Of course he had to do this.

It wasn't just my life at stake. It was Blaise's. It was his life in exchange for ours, and he'd pay that price.

Perhaps if it had meant the fate of the kingdom, I could convince him otherwise. But as long as he lived, Cinderella would have no more power than Evander's mother.

Cinderella would never grasp even that, either. She could never hope to match the queen in wit, no matter how cunning Cinderella might be.

If Evander and his parents lived, that is.

I couldn't bear to think of what Cinderella might do to them if I was wrong about her feelings for Evander.

Perhaps even if I was right.

She was obsessed with him.

But how tested by time, how well-worn was the story of a scorned lover who murdered the object of their affection.

I had to do something.

Think, Ellie, think.

Cinderella slipped her delicate hand into Evander's.

They each shuddered.

I was going to be sick.

Evander's throat worked. "You first."

For a moment, I thought she'd refuse, but apparently she had little doubt that Evander would risk my life, because she rushed through the vow. "I vow that, in exchange for your hand in marriage come the next full moon, along with full legal immunity"—Evander groaned—"I shall spare the life and health of Ellie Payne and shall cause no physical harm to the servant Blaise."

The wording was strange—the way she separated her vows regarding Blaise and me, rather than lumping them together. Evander must have picked up on that, too, because he chanced a glance in my direction. Neither of us seemed to know what to make of it, though.

And why were her words so hurried, frantic, as if she was in a rush to seal this bargain? Of course, the sooner the bargain was made, the less chance of someone barging into the workshop and stopping it, the less time for Evander to change his mind. Still. Cinderella's gaze kept flitting toward the window. Did she expect someone to come after us?

Evander drew in a steadying breath.

"Just say it, you fool," Cinderella hissed. Was that my ears deceiving me, or was her voice actually trembling, not in a rush of excitement, but in trepidation?

Cinderella was working on a time crunch.

One that was about to run out.

Just like that, the missing piece clicked into my head.

Sure, Cinderella only appeared on the nights of the full moon, but...

At the stroke of midnight...

I'd thought the journalists had been sensationalizing Cinderella's premature departure from the ball, but even the night she'd tried to murder me, she'd slipped away before she had a chance to finish the job.

The clock in my room had struck twelve not moments later.

Cinderella had until midnight to seal this bargain.

One look out the window, at the moon cresting the peak of the sky, and I realized she only had moments.

I realized too late.

Evander let out a steadying breath.

What he said next shattered me.

"I, Evander Thornwall, vow to wed you, Cinderella—"

"—No! Evander, wait!"

—upon the next full moon, and offer you full legal immunity tied to this bargain."

My heart stopped. Cinderella's blade fell from my throat, but I hardly noticed its absence.

It was only me and Evander now, suspended in this moment I would relive for the rest of my life.

I'm sorry, he mouthed, and a part of me died.

My tongue worked, as if to tell him, but I swallowed instead.

What would it do to him? To tell him that if he'd merely waited a few more moments…

Evander's eyes widened in shock, and I didn't have to turn to know what was happening behind me.

Silverly moonlight slipped across the floor of the workshop, the moon having just hit its peak.

I turned to face Imogen and wondered if I'd hate her for what the magic possessing her had done.

I never got the answer to that question.

Because when I turned to face the woman who had ruined my and Evander's lives, it wasn't Imogen I found.

It was Blaise.

CHAPTER 54

ELLIE

*M*y mind sputtered, stopped, then restarted in a flurry of warped images, voices. Moments attempted to force themselves together like mismatched puzzle pieces to make sense of what I was seeing, but nothing seemed to fit.

Evander spoke first, his voice trembling. "Blaise?"

She was on the floor now, Cinderella's scandalous nightgown draped over Blaise's curveless body, lumping and protruding in all the wrong places. Blaise glanced down at herself, blanching at the sight of all the skin the sheer fabric left exposed.

As if out of some innate brotherly urge, Evander wordlessly tossed her a nearby empty sandbag. She wrapped it around her shaking body, her mouth moving and working, her lips parting and closing, as if she were trying to form words, but she'd lost the ability.

Evander tossed me a bewildered look, as if to say, *Please tell me you're just as confused as I am.*

My voice hardened. I had my guesses, but as I looked at Blaise, my friend, my confidant, something like hatred assaulted my chest. Though it was probably only betrayal—the realization that of course she hadn't actually been my friend—blistering between the sinews of my ribcage.

A BOND OF BROKEN GLASS

The silence, punctuated by Blaise's intermittent sobs, Evander's ragged breaths, and my feet tapping anxiously against the ground, swelled around us, wrapping us inside it, threatening to suffocate us.

But Blaise just swallowed, closed her eyes, then peered up at us, her gaze flitting between me and Evander, a strength there that hadn't been present only a moment ago.

Blaise had steeled herself, and now she was preparing to face her Fate. "You need to tell me what I did while I was..." She sucked in a breath, bracing herself. "While I was *her.*"

Evander let out a noise that straddled the definitions of a cry and a scoff.

I was the one who answered. "*We* need to tell *you?*"

Blaise shook her head. "I can't tell you exactly what her plan is if you don't tell me what she did."

It was my turn to shake my head. "You tried to murder me. Three times. You pretended to be my friend, and then—"

"No." Blaise stood, and in a moment, Evander had moved, his heaving body a shield between me and the girl he'd come to know as a sister.

At this point, I wasn't quite sure which one of us he was protecting.

"No. I was your friend. *Am* your friend, Ellie. None of that was fake, not a second of it."

I stepped out from behind Evander so I could see the lie written all over her face.

All I found was desperation.

My voice shook. "You killed Madame LeFleur."

Blaise winced, but she fisted her palms. "It was her. I swear."

"I'm just going to be honest with you, Blaise," Evander said, his jaw tight. "I'm not quite convinced there's a difference."

Blaise shifted her attention to Evander, a sadness wafting across her expression that ran deeper than her regret for me. "Please tell me what she did so I can fix it."

My heart constricted, squeezing and pinching and giving way to so much hurt. My friend had tried to kill me.

401

My friend had tried to kill me, and now she was going to marry the man I loved.

I couldn't breathe.

Apparently, Evander *could* breathe. At least, he didn't seem to have any trouble speaking. But when he addressed Blaise, it was not with the jesting tone a mischievous older brother might use in a younger sister's presence. No, when he spoke, his voice was a demand, uttered by the Heir to the Throne of Dwellen. "You're going to tell us what's going on. Now. Then we'll consider what you do and do not deserve to know."

Blaise didn't miss the condescension in his voice, the way he spoke to her as if she were a child. The hurt that flickered across her expression was more than offense. It was embarrassment and shame and something else just as sinister and intrusive.

She nodded all the same.

And then Blaise told us her story.

"I'd RATHER NOT START from the beginning," she said, her voice going dry. When Evander opened his mouth to protest, she shook her head. "No, I mean, I'll get to the beginning. It'll just take some...working up to."

Evander nodded, crossing his arms.

I just stood there staring, heart numb, as the girl I'd come to consider my friend told the story of how she'd come to be my attempted murderer.

"I didn't realize I'd been possessed the night of your first attack." She gestured to me, and I bounced away my gaze, unable to look at her for the bile that rose to the base of my tongue. She cleared her throat. "I woke in my bed, covered in blood. At first I thought my..." Her attention lingered on Evander for a moment before finding the floor. "I thought it was my cycle, come early." Evander didn't as much as flinch as he gazed upon her expectantly. "But the blood was all over me, most of it on the front of my shirt. And it was all over my sleeves, too. I knew then something was terribly wrong. But I was in such a panic. I'd passed out the night of the ball, too. Woken up in a ditch, and couldn't for the life of me remember how I got there. I brushed it off, came up with reasons that made sense, but when I woke up and smelled all that blood…" She gagged, her face paling. "I thought I must have started sleepwalking, or something. That I'd hurt someone in the night. I was in such a daze, I washed my clothes first, scrubbed myself down in the bath. What I should have done… I should have gone to look for you. I didn't know it was you I'd hurt, Ellie. Had no idea." She shook her head. "I should have gone to look anyway. I knew someone was out there bleeding, but I was so afraid I'd be called a murderer, that the king would lock me up… It wasn't right. I know that."

Evander's bulging jaw looked as if it were about to burst through his tanned skin.

Blaise sighed and rubbed her temples. "I hadn't had time to clean my sheets when Imogen found me. She rushed into my room just as I was getting changed into new clothes. Her eyes got all wide when she saw the blood on my bed. I didn't know what to do, so I laughed it off —said something crass and crude about my cycle to embarrass her, keep her from questioning me about it. I guess it worked, because she told me you'd been attacked in the night.

"I ran. I just…ran. There wasn't a thought in my head. Other than that you couldn't be dead, you shouldn't be…" Goosebumps trailed her arms at the memory. "When I got to your rooms, saw all the blood. I knew, I just knew I'd done it. The smell… It hit me as soon as I turned the corner…your blood. I'm so sorry, Ellie. I didn't know what to do."

Her eyes widened, like a puppy dog who'd gotten into dinner and ruined three hours' work of meal preparation.

Like she hadn't driven a knife into my gut and left me for dead.

Still, the longing in her gaze stirred something within me, and since I wasn't yet ready to accept that feeling as sympathy or some other generous emotion Blaise certainly did not deserve, I attributed it to betrayal.

Sympathy and betrayal. They didn't feel all that different when matched against one another. They both writhed in my belly, gnawing at my insides.

"You stayed with Ellie," Evander said. It wasn't said like a question, not in the typical sense, with his voice lilting at the end. But there was a question there all the same.

Blaise hiccupped. "Of course I did."

Evander shuffled. So did I.

"Were you going to kill me off, in case I woke up and realized it was you who'd tried to murder me?" I asked.

Blaise's eyes widened. "No. No, I'd never... Not while I was in my right mind. You don't understand, whatever's in me... it just takes over. I don't even remember what I've done when I wake up."

Evander held up his palm, silencing her. "She's not lying. I left her alone with you multiple times during those days when you were unconscious and recovering. If she'd intended to kill you, she could have done it then."

I crossed my arms. "If she'd figured out a way to get away with it. Perhaps she had the physical opportunity, but no way to hide the evidence."

Blaise shook her head, her eyes going weak. She rested her elbows upon her knees, and the burlap sandbag shifted around her. "I never wanted to hurt you. It wasn't me."

Evander threw up his hands in exasperation. "Then why didn't you tell us, Blaise? Why didn't you tell me? If you suspected you'd been possessed, why not get help? Why continue to put Ellie's life at risk?"

"Oh, don't give me that crap," she snapped at him. "If you'd just arrested her the night you burst into Ellie's room to save her, then whatever happened tonight—which neither of you will tell me— wouldn't have happened. Do you know how I felt, Evander, when I found out you had the chance to take me into custody, to discover what I was? It...it crushed me. It was like having the wind taken out of me. Because I couldn't tell you, couldn't bring myself to. I was just praying that you would figure it out, that you would..." Her shoulders sagged, and she slumped, running a hand through her long, limp hair. "Honestly, I'm just relieved this is over."

I couldn't help but think she didn't look it.

"Why didn't you tell me?" Evander whispered again, and this time, his inquiry was truly a request. One asked from one friend to another.

She didn't look at him; she just wrapped the burlap tighter around her shoulders. "I started researching as soon as Ellie made a recovery. I'd spend the night at the library trying to figure out what was wrong with me. Finding any books I could on magic possession and shape-shifting. I even researched the Queen of Naenden, but nothing useful turned up."

My brow furrowed at that, a memory forming in my mind. "Imogen must have been suspicious of the truth," I whispered as the other two stared at me. I tapped my finger against the air, as if to tap out the steps of the past. "I found a pamphlet of hers. She'd written all over it, taken notes about shifters. About lychaen. She must have noticed the attack happened on the full moon, and when she found you soaked in blood, she thought you were a shifter."

Blaise shifted uncomfortably, digging her fingers between the jagged floorboards. "It was my pamphlet you found. I broke into Madame LeFleur's shop and grabbed it when I was searching for anything that might explain what's happening to me. The pamphlet went missing weeks ago, and I figured it was Imogen who took it. She's been onto me for weeks, but she's too passive-aggressive to say anything. I guess she was waiting for sufficient proof to hand me over. But I was glad for the books she brought back, the ones she thought I wouldn't find under her mattress. I was desperate to find a way to expel the magic from me before she came out again. I hadn't figured out yet that she was tied to the moon. If I had, maybe...." She shook her head. "I don't know how, but maybe it would have helped..."

Evander ran his fingers through his bronze hair and muttered, "*A Human's Guide to Reversing Fae Magic*... I found it in your stack of books in the library. I thought you were researching how to undo my bargain with Ellie, but you were searching for how to reverse what-ever magic has its grip on you."

Blaise picked at a strand of her matted black hair. "I was researching both."

"What I don't understand is how she possessed you in the first place," Evander said. "What were you dabbling in, Blaise?"

Blaise's cheeks heated. With shame, perhaps?

"Blaise," I said, my voice remarkably even for the concentration of fury that rushed through my blood at the moment. "What happened to Madame LeFleur?"

Blaise lost the color in her cheeks, and for a moment, I thought she might misplace the contents of her stomach as well. "I didn't know she was dead. Not at first. The morning after you were attacked, I went back to her shop, but it was boarded up. I asked the baker next door—"

Evander's head snapped up. "You brought back scones from Forcier's that day."

Blaise blushed, chewing her lip. "I remembered Ellie liked them."

I worked my fingers through the pleats in my skirt, refusing to make eye contact with her.

"Anyway," Blaise continued, clearly dejected by my lack of acknowledgment of her sorry attempt to apologize for almost murdering me, "Mister Forcier said she'd been found dead the morning after the ball."

It was Evander's turn for his face to pale. "Blaise?" There was a question in it, one that, even now, he wasn't willing to ask. Moments ago, when she'd worn a different body, he'd threatened to end her for hurting me.

Would he do the same to Blaise? Would he follow through on his threat? If she'd killed Madame LeFleur, which appeared likely at the moment, would he bring her to justice as he would a stranger from the streets?

That was what she deserved, wasn't it? For knowingly putting the lives of others in danger to hide her own terrible secret?

Still, I couldn't bring myself to wish it upon her. Couldn't bring myself to hope the male she'd admired her entire life would bring a fist of judgment down upon her.

I didn't know what I wanted.

But it wasn't that.

I wasn't sure where that put me on the justice scale.

"I don't remember killing her," was all she said. She shrugged, as if in resignation. "It had to have been me, though. Or whatever's inside me. I was the only one there that night."

Something flickered in Evander's sea-green eyes. A curiosity of sorts, but a dreadful one, as if his mind had gotten snagged on a question he didn't want to ask. Didn't want to know the answer to.

I asked it for him. "Why were you at Madame LeFleur's the night of the ball, Blaise?"

Her head jerked up, like the sound of her name on my lips had been a beacon, guiding her back through the shadows to a friendship that no longer existed.

She must have seen the truth of that on my face, because the hope in the whites of her eyes wilted. "I went to her to ask for a potion."

Evander shifted, the fabric of his coat stretching against his muscular arms, his chiseled back. "What did you need a potion for?"

She wouldn't look at him, so instead she addressed me, as if I'd been the one to ask. "I asked her for a potion that would make me different...look different, I mean. I didn't intend for"—she gestured at herself, at the small body cloaked in seduction and shame—"this to happen. For her to change me entirely."

Evander took a step forward, and my heart clenched as he did. But then he was kneeling next to her, and two very opposing forces waged a battle within me.

There was the rage, the jealousy that Evander and Blaise had something so deeply rooted that he would reach out to her, forgive her for what she'd done to me.

Then there was the other force. This one meeker, hardly notable, except in the face of all that rage and jealousy and wrath, it stood firm. Small but resolved.

I think it was the part of me that would have liked to be loved like that. The part of me that watched Evander, his palm cupping the face of the little girl he'd taken in as his sister, and loved that part of him.

I loved it irrevocably, even if it ended up meaning that he'd chose her freedom over my safety in the end. I loved that he loved and did not falter.

I could hate him for it, but the love ran deeper.

Because I admired him, I realized. For all the insults I'd hurled at him, for all the facets of his character I'd attacked, I admired Prince Evander of Dwellen, and that was something remarkable indeed.

I loved him, and it was infuriating, and I hated him for it.

"Why did you think you needed to change a single thing about you, Blaise?" he asked, affection pouring from his sea-green eyes. He almost let out a frustrated laugh. Almost. "Do you not see yourself? You're perfect the way you are."

Blaise let out a wheezy sob, and her eyes watered over.

I couldn't help the way my head cocked at that. Boisterous, care-free Blaise. Men following her like she was a Fate herself Blaise?

Sure, I'd never thought Blaise was extraordinarily pretty, at least not until she smiled. But if someone would have bet with me on who would venture to Madame LeFleur's with the intent of altering her appearance, they would have owned my father's window-making business by now.

But then I looked closer, looked through the cracks of her expression, and I saw it in the corners of her eyes, heard it in the sound of my memories.

Would you rather fall in love with Evander and get out of your marriage bargain—but you can never be with him? Or would you rather never love him and be stuck married to him for the rest of your life?

Andy has awful taste in women.

At least I have Andy, though.

...fall in love with Evander...but you can never be with him...

My heart stopped.

I heard her answer a second before she opened her mouth.

Evander was eons behind the both of us.

"I love you, Andy," she said.

My heart dropped into my stomach, but Evander only smiled. "I love you too, Blaise. I've always told you, you're my sister."

She shook her head, her eyes somehow both bright and empty. "Not like that."

CHAPTER 55

EVANDER

*T*ime slowed down, reworked itself as my brain tried again to translate what Blaise had just said.

But every time my mind processed and reprocessed her words, it spit out the same result.

"Not like that."

Fates, I was going to be sick.

My hand faltered at her cheek, and before I could recover my composure, she jolted back, rejection soiling her face, her familiar eyes widening.

"Blaise, I don't…"

Her face heated, and she scooted away from me on the floor, wrapping herself in that flimsy burlap. Ellie stood behind me, but I could sense her presence stiffen.

"Please," Blaise said. "You don't have to say it. I know you don't see me that way. You never have."

There was no blame in her voice, no derision. Just numb resignation.

Blaise, little Blaise who I used to toss into the air, sending her flying so Jerad would catch her. I could still hear her giggles when I tickled her, still feel her drool that I'd wiped off my shoulder after she'd fallen asleep on it.

How many times had I tousled her hair, planted a kiss on her forehead, wrapped her up in a hug? All things whose interpretations seemed so obvious to me, so clear.

My face heated with shame. Had I given her the wrong idea, had I gotten so used to wooing the courtesans that I'd taken to bed, that I'd forgotten the line between platonic teasing and flirting?

My stomach churned, guilt piercing through me.

"Blaise, I never meant... I'm so sorry if I..."

She waved me off, though it was a half-hearted gesture. "You never treated me like anything other than a sister."

It wasn't quite relief that leaked into my chest.

My mouth couldn't seem to find words at the moment, but Ellie spoke for me. "You meant to attend the ball. To trick him into falling in love with you by wearing a different face."

There was no judgment in Ellie's tone, but the words stung Blaise all the same. I couldn't tell whether Ellie meant it, but she had that way about her. That way of rebuking that could be so practical, so void of emotion, that it stung all the worse.

Because when she stripped all the anger, all the accusation away, there was nothing left but the truth.

There was no mollifying truth. No watering it down.

Blaise swallowed, grimacing. "No use in denying it, I suppose. Though, that's not how I talked myself into it at the time. I told myself that if I could just talk to you like I was someone else, without you having all the memories of me as a child, I thought maybe you'd realize what we could be. You just..." She took a deep breath. "After Jerad died, you were just so lonely all the time. I could tell you were hurting more than you made out to be. But you wouldn't let me help you, wouldn't let me in. Instead, you turned to them."

Them. The way she pronounced that small, insignificant word made my chest cave in.

Them. Generic. Inconsequential. Unremarkable. Unworthy of being remembered by name.

That was how I'd seen them, though, wasn't it? Just another beautiful female to drink myself to numbness on.

Shame washed over me like a sip of sour wine.

"I knew they weren't making you any happier. You just kept getting more and more…jaded. But not around me, at least not when you knew I was paying attention. I could make you smile. I could do that when they couldn't. They could catch your eye and get into your bed, but I could make you laugh, make you happy. And I thought that would be enough for me, but then the ball was announced, and the idea of you marrying one of those…" She had to swallow to keep herself from a crude word, I was sure of it. "I just thought: here's my last chance. I never intended for it to go this far. My plan was to purchase a potion that would change my appearance for the night, get you to see how much happier you would be married to a friend, rather than one of those shallow females who only wanted you for your title. I planned to tell you before anything happened, I swear it. I just wanted you to see…"

Nausea washed over me at the seduction I might have attempted had things gone according to Blaise's plan, if Cinderella hadn't left early that night. Even if Blaise had been in control as she'd planned to be, she was clearly love-struck, smitten over an ideal of us that didn't exist. Would she have had the self-control to resist, to admit who she truly was, if I had tried to…

My stomach reeled.

It must have shown on my face, because Blaise's expression went empty, like she was trying desperately to shield herself from my disgust. "It was horrible of me."

My mind raced for the evidence to put the pieces of the past together, the moments that should have betrayed Blaise's feelings for me.

The morning after I'd met Cinderella—Fates, Blaise in that psycho's form—Blaise had taken me to the kitchen so I could drown my troubles in pastries.

You wanna tell me what you loved about her?

She'd sounded so different than normal, so uncharacteristically concerned. I'd thought she worried that I'd throw her friendship to the side as soon as we found Cinderella, but that hadn't been all of it, had it? She'd been hurting, wondering what this Cinderella had that she did not.

She hadn't known at the time that she *was* Cinderella.

She'd been hiding behind the suits of armor when I met Ellie. I'd attributed it to her inherent curiosity, but what if there had been more to it? Had her desire to get a glimpse of my betrothed come from jealousy?

Then there was the time she dragged my drunken self back to the castle. But why had she happened across me anyway? Had it simply been a coincidence, or had Blaise been following me?

The next morning, she told me she'd find me a way out of the fae bargain.

And Blaise, the girl who'd despised reading since she was a child, had pored over legal books for hours on end.

It had been Blaise who discovered the ancient law that allowed Ellie's parents to annul the bond.

She'd kept looking even after my efforts had waned.

I'd thought she was doing it for me.

And maybe she was, in her own desperate sort of way that believed the key to my happiness lay with her.

The night I'd carried her back to bed—Fates, I'd *carried* her—what sort of message had that sent? She'd asked me if I loved Ellie, and when I'd responded that I wasn't sure, she'd buried her face in her hands.

There had been a moment when my stomach had lurched, when I'd been horrified that I might have hurt her somehow.

But then she'd bounced right back and been Blaise again, despairing about how I'd had her do all that reading for nothing.

How many times had Blaise donned that carefree mask? How many times should I have noticed the cracks?

I was going to be sick.

Ellie, Fates bless her, cleared her throat and went on with the interrogation like two out of the three of us weren't about to throw up. "So things clearly didn't go as planned. Unless you intentionally requested a potion that would leave you without control of your—well, another's—body during the hours before the full moon meets its apex?"

"Is that when it ends?" Blaise asked. "I'm usually too disoriented when I wake up to notice."

Ellie stared at her, as if to say, *Well, am I going to have to keep asking you the obvious questions, or are you just going to explain what happened?*

I couldn't help but love her for that.

Blaise's voice went dry. "I don't know what happened. I asked the Madame for a potion. She told me her shop was closed, but I suppose she felt bad for me for not being dressed to go to the ball, because she said she might have something and went searching in the back. She came back with a potion, and I paid her, and the next thing I remember, I'm waking up in a ditch in the streets, and the ball is over. I thought she'd scammed me, that she'd just given me a sleeping draft to get me off her back. Besides, I was too upset about missing the ball and my chance to... I didn't have the energy to confront her about it. So I went back to the palace and didn't think about it again until... well, until I woke up covered in blood."

"So we're to surmise that whatever is inside of you isn't the work of a potion, but of a darker magic," Ellie said.

Blaise blanched, and it tugged at my heart. I was so mad at her. So mad I wanted to shake her, but I couldn't imagine what she must be feeling, knowing that she was possessed with some magic psychopath who had a thing for me.

My face must have paled, because Blaise said again, "Please tell me what I did."

Ellie ignored her, pacing the workshop, her slender fingers resting against her chin as she thought. Fates, she was gorgeous when she was thinking. Which was pretty much always. "You were right to research the Queen of Naenden. If anyone will know what's happened to you, it will be her. Maybe she can help."

For the first time all night, hope swelled in Blaise's eyes. There was no forgiveness in Ellie's analytical words, but she wanted to help

Blaise. Sure, that was strategic, in a way. As long as Blaise was possessed, there was a being out there who wanted to take Ellie's life. But still. It was something.

I couldn't help but admire her for it.

It had been worth it, what I'd given up, to keep Ellie Payne under the sun a few decades longer.

She was the kind of celestial being that didn't come around often, a meteor that only showed itself once every few centuries.

That brilliance in Blaise, the one I'd gotten used to being warmed by her entire life, flared back up. She hopped to her feet. "I can go to Naenden. I'll petition the queen, and I'll find a way to get it out of me; I will."

Ellie scanned her over, hesitantly.

"Ellie, I'm so sorry for putting you in danger. I should have told you as soon as I started getting suspicious."

Ellie's stiff back didn't relax; her blank expression didn't change.

But she didn't sneer or turn away either, so there was that.

Blaise whipped around to me. "I'll make it up to you. I promise."

And I believed her.

That made what I had to do so much worse.

"Blaise." Something about the way I said her name must have held a warning in it, because she shuffled, though I could only hear buzzing in my ears. "You're not going to Naenden."

Her mouth hung open. "But I have to get it out."

"I know that. That's why I'll go myself. Inquire on your behalf."

She looked about ready to hug me, so I backed away.

Something inside that child splintered. I could see it in the creasing of her eyes, in the depths of her irises, in the slight gape of her mouth.

"You knowingly put Ellie in danger."

In the corner, Ellie went still as death.

Blaise's mouth worked for something to say. Finally, she found it. "I know that. I'm so sorry. It won't happen again."

I shook my head and exhaled. "No, it won't. I won't hold what happened the night of the ball against you. Nor what happened the

415

first night Cinderella attacked Ellie. But from the moment you woke up soaked in Ellie's blood and kept that information from me, you committed a crime against my betrothed. That's treason, Blaise."

Her mouth sputtered, and something deep inside me cracked. "I'm the heir to the throne. I can't hope to one day be a fair and just ruler if I don't hold my friends to the same standards I expect of everyone else."

Blaise's face was as white as a bleached gravestone. "Are you going to have me executed?"

Fates, the hurt in her eyes made me want to scream. "No, but I will have you tried for your crimes. I'll put in a good word for you, for giving us the information we needed about your possession. For confessing to the truth. I don't expect the sentencing to be as harsh as death; my father was too fond of your father to allow it to come to that. But you will be imprisoned until your trial."

Blaise withered.

She withered, and a part of me died.

"That's probably for the best," she said. "At least she'll be locked up with me. The best way to keep everyone safe."

CHAPTER 56

ELLIE

*M*y father entered the workshop not long after, barging through the doors with one of Mother's rolling pins like he was intending to beat an intruder on the head with it.

"I swear, if you take one more of my Ellie's—"

His face contorted in confusion when he found not just me, but the Prince of Dwellen standing in his workshop.

My father had soundproofed the walls of the workshop years ago at the request of my mother, who couldn't sleep with all the noise I made in the shop late at night. He likely wouldn't have heard the commotion Cinderella made when she attacked me, so he must have woken on his own, seen the workshop light from the window, and come to check on me. It must have been the unfamiliar voices that had him grabbing a makeshift weapon from the kitchen.

"Your Highness," he said, with a slight nod of his head that certainly would not have passed as a bow in court.

Evander bowed in reverence. "Mister Payne."

My father's gaze flickered over to Blaise, who was sobbing silently in the corner. "Do fae collect the tears of mortal women as the secret to their immortality? Because, if so, you owe my Ellie compensation."

My heart warmed even as my cheeks heated with mortification.

Evander crossed his arms behind his back. "Sir—"

My father grunted. "Surely you're more of a gentleman than to bother Ellie in her own home."

Evander sucked in a steadying breath, clearly annoyed. But when he opened his mouth, I spoke instead. "It's okay, Papa. He thought I was in trouble. He only came to make sure I was okay."

My father's eyes narrowed. "And are you okay?"

I swallowed and nodded.

He didn't look convinced, but he at least brought his makeshift bludgeon to his side.

"Mister Payne," Evander said, "if you wouldn't mind calling for the palace guard, we believe we've found the thief responsible for Ellie's stolen property."

There was no anger, no unkindness in his voice, but Blaise let out a shriek of a sob in the corner, one that pierced my heart, despite recalling that she deserved to be punished. Despite reminding myself that she'd put my life in danger on multiple occasions just to spare herself the embarrassment of admitting her feelings for Evander.

My father nodded, then turned toward the workshop door. Before he left, he looked Evander square in the eyes and said, "She's Miss Payne, to you."

Evander swallowed and shuffled uncomfortably, nodding.

After what felt like hours of uncomfortable silence punctuated by Blaise's sniffling, the palace guard arrived and took her away, Evander providing them special commands about where she was to be kept, and under what sort of conditions.

"For you, Your Highness," said one of the guards, handing a piece of parchment to his prince. Evander stole a quick glance at the paper before shoving it into his pocket.

Then they were gone, leaving me alone with the prince.

He stood there, his hands in his pockets, his copper hair falling into his face, his jaw cut, looking as handsome as ever.

He didn't speak.

He didn't take his eyes off me, either.

They typically looked like the sea, a mixture of moss and blue waters, but tonight they blazed green with desire.

Still, he didn't speak.

I realized he was waiting for me.

"You didn't tell me what you gave up." As usual, it came out more like an accusation than I'd meant it.

His throat bobbed, and he tore his gaze away from me, staring up at the ceiling like he was trying to glimpse the stars through the wood and curse me silently. "You didn't ask."

Fates, why was it always like this with us? One of us reaching out to the other, only for the words to come out wrong and to be met with a wall lacking footholds, too slippery to climb.

"You shouldn't have entered into that bond with her." Again, not how I meant to say it. I'd always prided myself on my ability with words, so why, when Evander was around, did everything come out the opposite of how I planned it?

His jaw worked, the only evidence of his temper flaring. "Why can't you just say thank you for once?"

My mind raced back to the glass shop, the fight we'd had then. This was the same one, wasn't it? Him thinking I should be grateful for something I didn't want in the first place. Perhaps it was for the best that he'd be wedding someone else. Let that be the final wedge between us, saving us both from a life of misery, playing out our irreconcilable differences for the rest of my mortal life.

But then again.

Then again.

I hadn't wanted him to, but he had bargained his freedom away to save my life. Twice.

It was hard to tell the difference between shame and gratitude sometimes.

"Thank you," I whispered.

He darted his gaze away from me, his green eyes gleaming.

"I'm sorry," I said. *For what you've given up. For what happened to us.*

A pained smiled flickered on his face. "I'd do it again, if it meant you were safe."

419

My breath hitched before I could catch it, and his ears flicked, his gaze darting to my mouth, to where my breath fogged the air.

He didn't look away.

A moment later, and he'd closed the gap between us. I gasped, backing away until my hips hit the workshop table. He advanced on me, pinning me, his eyes alight with fire.

Heat coursed through me as his gaze dipped to my lips.

"We can't do this," I breathed, my voice ragged and unconvincing.

A sly smile slipped across his face. "On the contrary: you're the only woman I can do this with."

Lightning enveloped me, coursing through my veins and stirring to life every feeling I'd tried so desperately to suppress over the past month.

I shook my head. "You're going to have to marry her come full moon. You were too specific. There's no way out of this."

"Well, then," he said, his gaze drunk on my mouth. "I suppose since you've somehow managed to change me into an honorable male, now's our only chance, isn't it?"

He leaned into me, so close the slim distance between us physically hurt. "You don't understand," I breathed.

He frowned, taking my jaw between his fingers and lifting my gaze to meet his. "Then enlighten me."

"I can't let myself have you, not even for a moment, not even just a kiss, because..." I sucked in a breath. With each word, it was as if another one of my ribs cracked.

"Why not?" His voice was a whisper on the edges of my ear as he buried his face into my hair.

"Because..." Fates, I couldn't do it. Couldn't make myself say it. Why, after all we'd been through, did this feel like the thing that would suffocate me, steal the air from my lungs and be my undoing?

"Ellie." His breath stung at my ear, sending a fire through me, one I wouldn't soon be able to put out. "Why can't you kiss me."

Not a question.

I steadied myself on the table, dizzy now. "Because it'll break me. Because I can't...I can't have you for just a moment. If I'm going to

420

have you, I have to have all of you. Forever. I can't have you then give you to someone else, I just..."

"Why not?"

I pushed him away from me, shoving his chest with such force, the shock of it alone was enough to have him stumbling a few steps back.

He stood there, hands by his sides, looking intoxicated.

I was trembling, and his eyes honed onto my shaking legs. He was back upon me in a moment, though this time, he didn't touch me.

"Why not?" he pushed.

I didn't answer.

"Why. Not."

"Because I love you, okay?"

The words hung in the hot air we shared between us, between his ragged breaths and my short, staccato ones.

He froze, a sly, infuriating grin overtaking his face, and I almost thought he'd tease me, but then he said, "Please let me kiss you, Ellie."

"What? No! I tell you I love you and you...and you..." What was he doing, grinning like a giddy, smug little child?

"I'm afraid I might have omitted a bit of important information earlier."

My heart stopped. "What are you talking about, Evander?"

"You see, I have no intention of marrying anyone but you."

I couldn't breathe. "I saw you make the bargain. I saw you...I heard you..."

He tucked his hand into his pocket, and for a moment I thought it was just another one of his I-don't-care-about-anything stances, but then he whipped out the paper he'd stuffed into his pocket, the one the palace soldier had brought him. "Shall I read it aloud, or should you?"

Apparently, I looked like I was in no position to read anything aloud, because he said, "Very well, then.

I, Evander, Heir and Prince of Dwellen, declare my intent to marry Cinderella and request permission from my father, the King of Dwellen, to do

421

so. By doing so, I transfer all right of requesting who to marry to him, and declare any bargains I make without his permission void."

HE TURNED THE PAPER AROUND, and my breath caught.

IN BIG, gaping letters, in the king's handwriting, the paper clearly stated,

DENIED.

"BUT YOU MADE the bargain with her. How did you do that without dying, knowing it wasn't true?" I asked, not quite ready to believe this was happening.

He rolled up the paper and tucked it into his back pocket. "Because I made my bargain without the knowledge of whether my father had signed this document or not. I had Imogen take it to him in the middle of the night while I rushed here."

"Imogen?"

"She found me right after I woke up. After Cinderella knocked me over the head. She freaked out when Blaise went missing." Well, that explained the blood caked into his hair. I made a mental note to forgive Imogen of all her uncomfortable side glances.

"That seems like quite a risk," I said, half mortified, half delighted.

He shrugged. "Some might even call it rash."

I laughed then, an exasperated, wild laugh that sounded like the drawstrings on my heart going loose.

But then he was close again, and the laugh died on my lips.

"Elynore Payne," Evander said, his eyes dipping to mine before he dropped to his knee before me.

Something cold and metallic and round slipped over my finger, but I couldn't bring myself to look at it. To look at anything but him.

"Please be my wife."

My throat caught, the word stuck in my throat.

His sea-green eyes smiled wide, crinkling around the edges. "If you make me beg, I'll never let you hear the end of it. Not for the rest of your days."

The rest of your days. Not ours. A quiet acknowledgment that he knew the consequences of this decision. That I'd grow old while he stayed young. That I'd return to dust while he outlived me by millennia.

That he knew all this and wanted me, anyway.

Finally, my throat seemed to give way. I broke into a grin. "Okay."

He rolled his eyes. "Okay?"

I nodded.

The smile that broke across his face shattered the last of my self-control, and when he rose and cupped my jaw, bringing my mouth to his, I melted into him.

"That was cruel of you," I whispered, "making me admit I loved you before, while you were blatantly withholding information from me."

"I knew I had one chance, and one chance alone, to get you to admit it."

I could have smacked him.

But I kissed him instead.

CHAPTER 57

ELLIE

I may or may not have rigged the dance cards.

But as it was my wedding, it wasn't as if anyone would say anything about it.

Except for maybe Fin, who was holding the Queen of Naenden's sister like one might grasp a sparkler.

And, oh, did she sparkle.

It wasn't just her dress, golden and glimmering and highlighting the glow of her perfect cheekbones.

It was her smile, practically effervescent. Her warm brown eyes glinting with elation.

Fin's tanned cheeks had flushed.

"Proud of yourself?" my husband asked, sidling up beside me and nudging me with his elbow.

"I'm afraid I don't know what you're talking about."

Evander grinned, ear to ear, and it was a wonder I didn't melt onto the floor.

Evander. My husband.

I wasn't sure I'd ever get used to the way that word hummed in my blood, tugged at the corners of my lips.

"You haven't spoken to me since the ceremony," I mused, sipping on the spiced cider Collins had brewed at my request.

Evander ran his hands through his hair, sending copper tufts sticking out in all directions.

He wore tousled like it was a style. And managed to look good in it, too. It really wasn't fair.

Before my mind could run away with me, launching me into a vision of later tonight when I would be the reason for his disheveled hair, Evander said, "That's because you make me nervous, looking like that. I had to work up the courage to even come over here and speak to you."

He gestured to my gown, which I had to admit was a bit over-whelming to look at. The tailor had fashioned it of white-blue crystal, the ragged gems ranging from pebble to hand-width in size. It was both dazzling and, well, somewhat intimidating. In fact, I'd refrained from wiping my palms on my skirts for fear of slicing my hand.

I sort of loved it.

Imogen had fixed my hair, tying my curls into a simple updo, allowing the thick, shorter strands in the front to drape across my forehead and frame my face.

My heart had given a sad little lurch when she'd applied my paint, but I'd pushed it away.

It didn't do to be morose on one's wedding day.

It had been Evander's idea to hold the wedding tonight, merely a month after the fiasco with Blaise, a mooncycle after he proposed.

Not because he'd wanted to rush into marriage.

No, that side of him had left me stranded in my father's workshop that day, breathless and reeling and so, so happy.

He'd returned three hours later, his father's written blessing in hand.

Then he'd taken my parents aside and spent another three hours convincing them to give us their blessing too.

And then, in true Evander fashion, he'd asked me to marry him.

"You already asked me that," I reminded him.

"No, I know. I mean tonight. Marry me tonight. Even better, marry me right now."

I'd glanced over at my parents, sure they were about to rescind any blessing Evander might have secured, but my father had only let out a bellowing laugh, and my mother, my sure and steadfast mother, looked as though she might swoon.

"What did you say to them?" I hissed.

"That, my dearly betrothed"—he tapped me on the nose, to which I scrunched it up—"is for me to know, and for you to spend the next decade hounding me about."

"We can't get married right now," I whispered.

He blinked, much more innocently than was warranted. "Whysoever not?"

"Because…Because…"

He shot me a look.

I dug my heels in. "Because."

He grinned, then, that look of pure adoration in his eyes threatening to knock me off balance.

I was dizzy. Why couldn't I marry him, again? Surely there was a host of reasons, some pragmatic, some more serious.

My brain couldn't seem to latch onto them.

His stare softened, and he tucked my curls behind my ear. "If you want to wait, I'm not going to pressure you. I'll wait decades if I have to. I don't mind."

I forced a smile to my lips. "Good," I said, though the word fell, thudding to the ground, echoing the sound of my heart. Why did I feel so disappointed? We were still going to get married. Just after we'd planned a wedding, like normal people. "Because we have cakes to order, and dignitaries to invite, and…" I swallowed, then let out a slow exhale. "And honestly, I don't care about any of that. I just want to be your wife. Right now."

Evander had picked me up and twirled me around, and both of my parents had winked, and that had been that.

My father, who apparently had a license to perform wedding ceremonies, had married us in the workshop. We'd waited a few hours, long enough for a messenger to retrieve the queen. The king hadn't bothered to attend.

During the ceremony, a few of my mother's chickens had snuck in and pecked at Evander's ankles.

A few days later, Evander and I had hatched a plan.

Well, it wasn't quite international espionage, but we'd both enjoyed feeling like we were scheming.

I still wasn't quite ready to forgive Blaise for her part in putting my life in danger. It wasn't even just my life, but the lives of the guards Cinderella had killed, lives that could have been spared had Blaise come forward with the truth earlier. Then there was the fact that Cinderella had come to my home, where my parents had thankfully remained asleep in bed.

I shuddered to think what might have happened had my father woken to the commotion, if he'd heard my cries when she etched my face with her knife.

Thankfully, Peck had managed to heal my wounds before they scarred.

Still, that didn't mean I wanted that horrible magic to continue inhabiting Blaise's body.

"Allow me this dance?" Evander asked, extending his hand as the musicians plucked a new song on their lyres.

"How about I let you have the last one?" I winked, and the mischievous look that overcame his face had my toes curling in my shoes.

Not glass slippers, by the way.

With the gentle instruction of my father, I was starting to relearn glassblowing, but I received little help from muscle memory, and I was practically starting from scratch.

Still, I was making progress, and that was enough.

I nodded toward the Queen of Naenden, the true reason I denied his request for a dance. I was too antsy to enjoy the dance anyway, at least until Evander could get some answers.

We'd planned the wedding on the night of a full moon intention-ally, and though I'd been checking the windows all night, and it had yet to crest the horizon, I still couldn't help but feel a shiver racing through my blood at all times.

Blaise was in prison. Locked up. I shouldn't be this nervous, but still.

There was nothing the magic inside her wouldn't do to get to Evander. Three weeks ago, Evander and I raided Madame LeFleur's old shop and found a collection of recipes for love potions. Love perfumes, to be more exact. Each recipe was concocted with a specific target in mind with the intent of "causing obsession directed toward whoever is wearing the potion when the target first scents it."

The one with Evander's name on it had included lilac and rosebuds.

He was a little than more relieved, to say the least. I supposed I would be too if I found out my undying obsession with a psychopath could be blamed on a love potion.

I tried not to bring it up, given he was still sensitive about it. Especially since Blaise had worn it in front of him the night before the third trial. I'd thought at the time that he'd simply found the scent unbearably strong, but I now knew he'd been smelling a love potion made specifically for him. Except that time, it had been a girl he thought of as a sister wearing it. No wonder his nose had curled in disgust.

We hadn't asked Blaise about it, but I liked to think she really had thought she was borrowing it from Imogen. That she'd had no idea it was the dark being inside of her that had stashed the perfume in their room. Imogen hadn't even had the opportunity to deny the perfume was hers, since Blaise had whispered where she'd gotten it.

I'd mostly avoided the topic with Evander, lest I embarrass him, but I hadn't been able to help asking him if Cinderella had forgotten the perfume the night she tried to seduce him.

His tanned cheeks had gone red, and he'd said, "I remember scenting it on her that night. Now that I think about it, every time I smelled it, it was like I would get a burst of...desire for her." He'd coughed uncomfortably. "But El, you have to understand. I missed you so badly, there was no amount of wanting her that was going to make me jeopardize the slim chance I had of getting you back."

I'd found that answer quite satisfactory, indeed.

Evander traced the direction of my gesture to the corner of the ballroom and let out an exasperated huff. "Promise to protect me if the Naenden king gets it into his head that I'm flirting with his wife?"

I shot him a devious grin. "Just make sure you don't flirt with her, or else I might just put some ideas into his head. I hear linen is quite flammable," I said, gesturing toward his suit.

CHAPTER 58

EVANDER

*I*t was with utmost hesitation, and a generous dose of prodding from my beautiful bride, that I approached the Queen of Naenden.

Not that I didn't enjoy her company. Actually, I found her dry personality to be quite refreshing.

But then there was the matter of her husband.

I took a deep breath.

It did nothing to banish the scent of smoke from my nostrils.

Was I imagining things, or were the King of Naenden's gloved hands smoking?

"Good evening, Your Majesties," I said, bowing to the couple who skirted the edges of the dance floor.

Queen Asha gave me a welcoming, lopsided grin.

Her husband did not.

"Prince," he said, eyeing me with suspicion, flecks of amusement in his tone.

Okay, so he could definitely scent me sweating. Great.

"Congratulations on your marriage," said Queen Asha, winking. Or perhaps she was simply blinking. It was difficult to tell given her missing eye. "It seems my brother-in-law didn't do too much damage.

Though I'm starting to wonder what the two of them discussed at the last ball, given both his and my sister's dance cards seemed to have been tampered with."

"Well, you know how those sort of balls go. One always ends up dancing with everyone other than the person they truly want to be dancing with. Anyway, we're grateful you could attend the wedding on such short notice."

"Indeed," the King of Naenden said, lava swirling in his molten eyes. "We'd hardly crossed the threshold of our palace when news arrived that the cancelled wedding hadn't been cancelled after all. We hardly had the chance to wipe the sand from our shoes before having the privilege of trekking right back into the Sahli."

Annoyance pricked at my spine, but before I could spit out a retort, Queen Asha turned to her husband, screwed up her brow, and said, "That's quite a complaint coming from someone who, at one point, planned to send out wedding invitations once every mooncycle."

I tensed, my shoulders knotting, my feet swerving to face the queen, readying to knock her out of the way of the king's oncoming blaze of judgment.

But the corner of the king's mouth just twitched, and he let out a somewhat disarmed chuckle. He glanced down at his tiny wife, and the fire in his eyes seemed to settle into a warm, golden glow. "You make a fair point," he said, tucking his hands behind his back as I tried to keep my jaw from falling off its hinges. Then his gaze returned to me, embers of amusement flickering in the edges of his irises. "It's our greatest pleasure to attend your and Princess Elynore's wedding. I've scraped the corners of my mind, but I simply cannot come up with anything I'd rather be doing with my time."

Queen Asha elbowed him lightly, and his subdued smirk broke into a grin that overtook his entire face.

Fates, the male was good looking. In that unshaven, rugged kind of way that usually had other males (not me, of course) counting how many decades he'd been alive to be able to sport a beard like that.

Not many. Not many at all.

"So," Asha asked, after she'd stifled her giggles. "What's the actual reason for rushing the ceremony…" She gestured to the ballroom, to the dozens of dancers swirling about, "when this is certainly not the first night the two of you have called each other male and wife?"

"I…uh…" My tongue scraped the edge of my mouth, as if it thought it would find an answer there. "How did you know?"

She winked. "Sleuth, remember?"

Kiran let out a huff of air. "Nosy, is what she meant to say."

Asha nodded to my left hand. "Neither of you have taken your gloves off all night. One would think that a happy couple would want to make a display of receiving their marriage tattoos once they entered a fae marriage bargain." She held out her own hand, showing off the inky swirls of flames that snaked from her hand to her wrist. "Unless, of course, the tattoos were already there."

Indeed, the ink on my skin seemed to warm at the queen's mention of it. The etching was a geometric mountain range that marked me as Ellie's. It had appeared as soon as Ellie and I had entered into the marriage bargain, a matching design inking her hand as well.

"Fine. You caught us."

Asha leaned over, peering down my glove as I peeled it away from my skin, just enough for her to glimpse the edges of the tattoo.

The king spoke, his voice low and rumbling. "Which brings us back to Asha's question. What do you want?"

That seemed a bit forward for someone whose wife had come to me seeking information, but whatever. They were right. Initially, I'd intended to travel to Naenden to ask council from Queen Asha regarding Blaise's condition. But even if I could have discovered anything helpful, I'd have to travel all the way back to Dwellen before the information could be of any use. Besides, what if Queen Asha needed to examine Blaise herself? That was already quite a bit to ask of a queen, placing her in a room with a dangerous magical being. Might as well remove the travel barrier.

"Well, since you're already here," I said, to which the king crossed his hands in front of his body this time, squaring his shoulders and looking down upon me like I was the one who hadn't yet passed my first century. "I thought perhaps we both might possess information that would be mutually beneficial."

Queen Asha's expression went stoic, and King Kiran tensed, his ears readjusting, as if to soak in every word.

I wished they wouldn't look like that, like we were talking about the Fate of the realms, or something equally as abhorrent.

I lowered my voice, thankful that Ellie had selected the loudest set of minstrels in town just for this occasion. "Last time we saw one another, you asked about Madame LeFleur's mysterious death. Let's just say we've discovered what happened. Well. Sort of. We know who did it. What we've yet to understand is how."

"Go on," the king drawled, though I thought I sensed a bit of desperation slip through.

"Before I tell you what I know, there's a condition."

"Of course there is," said Kiran, flexing his enormous hands, but Queen Asha absentmindedly slipped her fingers into his, and he calmed.

"The murder happened at the hands of a spirit. A magical parasite of some sort, who took control of a human. If I tell you who she is, I need you to swear not to hurt her."

The king and queen of Naenden exchanged concerned glances, and it was the shadow of fear in their eyes that had the hairs of my arms standing on end.

"I vow not to harm the host," said the King of Naenden. Instantly, almost imperceptibly, the aura of the room shifted, signaling the fae curse had set in.

Asha crinkled her brow and extended her hand. As a human, she was capable of lying, unless she made the bargain directly with a fae. Quickly, I grabbed her outstretched arm. "I will bring no harm to the host should you share all the information you know," she said.

Again, the subtlest of shifts.

Then I told the King and Queen of Naenden everything.

· · ·

"Where are you keeping her?" It was said in a manner of calmness, but Kiran was the type of person where everything that came out of his mouth sounded like a command.

"In the dungeons," I said. "She's watched by a set of trusted guards at all hours."

The king flicked his molten eyes toward the window. "And you said her magic takes over when the moon is full?"

I nodded, following his gaze. The moon still had yet to rise, but it would be any moment now. "I can take you to her."

"Asha?" Kiran's voice was gentle, respectful. Asking for permission before he swept her down into a dungeon with a crazed lunatic. Already, I could tell he didn't want her to go, wanted to keep her as far away from harm as possible.

I couldn't blame him.

But the Queen of Naenden didn't seem to hear him. Her back was pressed against the wall, her fingers digging into the sides of her scarlet dress.

"Asha." The king was at his wife's side in an instant, stroking her hair as she closed her eye, her breathing going ragged.

And then Ellie was at my side, slipping her fingertips into mine. "What happened? Are you ill?" she asked the queen, but Asha made no answer.

Finally, Asha gasped a breath and let out a whisper. "He's upset. Panicking. He wants to warn us."

He?

What in Alondria?

"This way," Ellie said, leaving my side and gently gripping the Queen of Naenden by the arm. She led her through the ballroom doors and into the corridor, informing the guards that the queen was ill and would need her privacy. Kiran and I followed behind, heat and anxiety rolling off the King of Naenden in waves.

The servants had hardly shut the doors behind us when a voice erupted from Asha's lips.

It took me all of one second to realize it was not the Queen of Naenden who spoke.

Is she locked away? the voice demanded, low and horrifying and tantalizing all at the same time.

"Yes, she's locked in a cell in the dungeons."

It is not enough.

The queen's expression was horror-stricken and didn't match the fury that emanated from the voice. She was listening, shocked just as much as the rest of us.

"She's under strict watch. There's no getting out of those cells," I assured her.

She'll find a way. She always finds a way.

Ellie gripped my arm, her hand shaking.

In an instant, Kiran was at his wife's side, holding her steady as she trembled. "Give Asha her voice back, or so help me, I'll—"

Kiran, the voice rumbled, ancient as the dawn of time, and just as weary. It was begging now, pleading with the King of Naenden. *You can't let her escape. She'll come looking for me. She'll come looking for Asha.*

Queen Asha's eye went wide. Fury radiated in heat waves from her husband.

When the King of Naenden's eyes met mine, they were no longer molten.

They were blue as the tip of a flame.

"Where is she?"

"I..." Could I let the king near Blaise in this state? Sure, he had taken a fae vow, bound his life to his promise... But there were ways of breaking a fae bond. With one's life, for example. And the way the temperature in the corridor had spiked when Kiran glimpsed the terror on his wife's face, when he'd heard of the threat to her safety...

I didn't doubt at all that his life was a price he'd gladly pay.

If I let him anywhere near Blaise, he'd kill her.

"We'll take you to her," Ellie said, and I squeezed her hand, desperately trying to communicate with her. Could she not see what I saw? There was death in that male's readied posture. "But it won't do you any good to kill her. Whatever is inside her is ancient, just like whatever is inside you." She nodded toward the queen. "It didn't originate with her, and it won't end with her, either."

I nodded, making sense of Ellie's words. "Just like it didn't end with Madame LeFleur's death," I said, remembering the queen's theory that the magic that inhabited Blaise had once crept within the shopkeeper's body.

Kiran swallowed, but understanding washed over his face. When he spoke, his voice was dry. "Just take me to her."

I opened my mouth to respond, but a door to my left crashed open. Out burst Harold, one of the guards stationed to keep watch over Blaise.

My blood ran cold.

Two words later, and I had a feeling I wouldn't get that last dance with Ellie. At least, not tonight.

"She's gone."

EPILOGUE

BLAISE

I should have known I'd end up here eventually. Rotting in a hole. Though the accommodations Evander made for me in the prison cell aren't exactly shabby.

Evander is kind like that.

I'm pretty sure he threatened the guards within an inch of their life if any of them lays a hand on me, because they keep even their eyes averted.

My cell is simple, like he wants to make a point about this definitely being a punishment for my behavior. The bed is lumpy, and I toss and turn every night until my back is tangled in knots.

If I'm being honest with myself, I sleep the day away, too.

But the cell is clean, and my latrine is changed out three times a day, so it rarely stinks in my cell. And my food, while devoid of pastries and scones, is prepared in an assortment of colors. Like Evander is concerned I'll miss out on key nutrients.

Like I'm a child he's worried won't grow if I don't eat my vegetables.

Andy's been kind to me, even if he hasn't visited. I've no doubt he'll make good on his promise to visit the Queen of Naenden and inquire about the magic that possesses me.

He's nothing if not kind.

It sort of makes it worse.

For the first time in my life, I envy my stepsisters. They're vain and they prattle on about senseless things, so I've never coveted their position. I'd take my stepmother's loathing over her suffocating affection any day.

But my stepsisters are used to being rejected by potential suitors. It's the kind of thing that's bound to happen if you make a habit of throwing yourself at men well above your station, refusing to settle for the sweet farm boys who dote all over you and would happily rescue your family from squalor and raise them to a level of mediocrity.

Apparently, my stepmother considers squalor to be a more reputable position than having her daughters tend pigs like lowly farmhands. So she sics them on counts and nobles and a great many males who might have taken them on as mistresses, but never as wives.

Wives are good for three things:

Status.

Money.

Heirs.

And we have none of it. Who knows, maybe my stepsisters are abundantly fertile, so I take it back. But one out of three isn't exactly passing with flying colors. The no money part, especially.

Well, they have the little I made working at the palace all those years.

Evander has no idea, of course. He would probably have my stepmother's head if he knew.

But she has something over me even Evander cannot fix.

I don't envy the way my stepmother forces my stepsisters to primp and preen and throw themselves at men who will never desire them.

I envy the truth in their words as they comfort one another.

What is Sir Fudgerumple thinking, refusing a beauty like you, Elegance? The man has a wart for a nose, stars above!

It's probably for the best, Chrys. I know Mother can only see his fortune, but I've heard he keeps his mistresses tied up in his cellar. Can you imagine the noise? No, you're better off without him.

My sisters might be horrendous when it comes to character, but they're byproducts of my stepmother's cruelty. It doesn't originate with them. Besides, they have each other.

And they have the kernels of truth they take comfort in—the endless reasons the scoundrels their mother tries to marry them off to would have been a bad match, anyway.

I have no such comfort when it comes to Evander.

At least he'll be with Ellie. At least he'll be happy.

The guards tell me they're to be married tonight.

I'm happy for them. I really am, even if happiness feels more like nausea in this scenario, like having my heart cut into tiny ribbons with the blunt edge of a blade.

At least I hadn't irreparably ruined any hope of them being together the night Evander let me go.

Let *it* go.

That's about the best I can do.

About as positive as I can manage. Given the situation I find myself in, I figure I'm not doing all that badly.

My chest aches, not from the chill of my prison cell, of the frigid air that burns my nostrils and lungs. Apparently, the guards will only bend so far to Evander's will. A fire would benefit not just me, but my prison mates.

I have to admit; I don't mind them suffering.

The first day I arrived, the male in the cell next to me had gone on and on about my breasts.

I'd woken the next morning to his cell empty.

My new neighbor is better, but only because I prefer verbal abuse to some perv undressing me with his eyes. But she's a mercenary who's known for slaughtering the families of her targets, so I don't know that we're on track to becoming the best of friends.

The thought settles like week-old dung in my head.

Best of friends.

I remember saying something like that to Ellie, the day we'd gorged ourselves on pastries in the kitchen.

I'd been joking. Well, my tone had been joking. But anyone who knew me, which wasn't many, would know the crude humor, the jokes, were a barrier, a shield to protect me from my own sincerity.

I'd meant it that day—the part about how easy it had been to become Ellie's friend, to feel close to the woman who didn't turn her nose up at the way I stuffed my mouth full of sweets or find my preferred hobbies unladylike.

Ellie had been my sparring partner, and I'd adored her for it.

She thinks I hate her, that I spent all our stolen moments plotting her demise, but she's wrong.

I'm not even mad at her for it.

The evidence against me is too high a pile to even bother trying to scale. I usually have the energy for that sort of thing, for climbing, but there's not much use when it comes to Ellie.

She's made up her mind about me. And once Ellie's convinced of something, once she's determined a course of action, she's not easily dissuaded.

I'd be lying if I claimed that wasn't something I admired about her.

And it's not as if she's wrong to think what she does. I put her life in danger, allowed my fear of rejection to influence me into thinking I could find a way to keep her safe all on my own.

I can't feel *it* within me; I've about determined that. For a while, I thought I could sense it wriggling in the corners of my mind, groping for control of my body, but now that I'm condemned to this quiet cell in this quiet dungeon in this quiet world, I know I cannot feel it.

If I could, I would've by now.

There's nothing else to distract me, no noise to mask its slithering.

I've tried speaking to it. Either it can't hear, or it doesn't care to answer.

Either way, the end product is the same. Me whispering to myself in my mind, morphing into me whispering to myself aloud, until my guards shift with discomfort, imagining I'm going mad, that I'm talking to myself.

Fates, I hope not.

I've never seen it, of course, the thing that dwells within my mind, that takes over my body and warps it and disfigures it, then smashes it all back together until I'm a bundle of knots and aches.

I hope it's different from me, distinct. The gossip that makes its way across the Sahli desert and through the forests of Avelea all the way to Dwellen reports that a sentient being inhabits the Queen of Naenden. That this being is the one who tells the stories that kept her alive all those nights.

Now, how much of that is informed by the merchant faeries' hatred of humans and wishing to accredit her success to something else, I'm not sure.

I shouldn't allow it to make me hope.

But what am I, if not someone who hopes for improbable things?

Isn't that what got me into this mess to begin with?

A draft crawls into my cell. That usually means someone has opened the door at the top of the staircase that leads to the dungeon.

Even my guard shifts in discomfort.

Footsteps, too loud and frequent and overlapping to belong to one set of feet, clamber down the steps.

I sit up in bed for the first time all day.

So do the other prisoners.

It's pitiful, I know, but it's about the only entertainment we get. If it were up to me, the others and I would play games, word games that don't require pieces or boards. But my fellow prisoners are rarely up for listening to a suggestion that didn't originate between their own two ears.

So here I am, clinging to my cell bars like a convict who's been holed up in here for a lifetime, rather than just a few weeks.

Twenty-eight days, to be precise. There's no window down here in the dungeon, and I like to keep track by counting guard shifts. At least then I can be aware of when it's going to take over my body again.

As the cacophony of footsteps draws near, voices echo through the dungeons.

A female, high-pitched, unsure.

Another, definitely nervous, but less willing to show it.

A woman, lips dripping with the rush of financial gain and opportunity.

I'm not sure whether my heart stops or withers up, deflates.

I return to my bed and crawl back in, tucking myself back into the thin blankets.

"If they ask, I've been stuck in a magical coma for weeks," I mumble to my guard.

He shuffles. "Sorry, miss. Can't lie."

I peek out at his pointed ears, poking out from his head. "Right."

I sit back up, figuring this interaction is going to happen whether I want it to or not—might as well get it over with.

When my stepmother reaches my cell, I meet her upturned nose with a devilish grin. If I'm going to be possessed, I might as well milk it for all it's worth.

My grin must unsettle her, because her mouth drops slightly ajar, but only for half a moment before she recovers her composure.

That's my stepmother's specialty, pretending to have things she doesn't.

That was how she got hold of my father's fortune, doting on his little girl with gifts and toys. She'd stooped to playing with me back then, and my father had practically eaten out of her hand. Not that he loved her romantically—I don't think he ever quite got over my mother. But he was sickly—he always had been—and he wanted me taken care of when he was gone.

He was gone alright, before he and Clarissa reached their first anniversary.

Clarissa purses her lips. "Should've known you'd find yourself in a place like this. You've been trouble since the day I laid eyes on you. It's in your blood, child."

I fight the urge to lunge at the cell door and instead grip my sheets in my fists. It isn't the insults directed at me that bother me; it's the ones about my blood, the implication of the disdain she harbored for my father.

My father.

My sweet, kind father.

What would he think, seeing me like this? What I've become?

Something like guilt and agony roils in my stomach.

Clarissa has a way of doing that, shooting a barb in one direction, and having it land somewhere she'd have never thought to aim.

"Your father would be ashamed of you," she hisses. "Bringing dishonor upon the family."

Alright, so maybe she would think to aim it in that direction.

"Family?" I say, pretending the comment rolled off of my impenetrable skin. "You only like that word when it's convenient to you, Clarissa."

Chrysanthemum, my youngest stepsister, the one about my age, shuffles uncomfortably. She's never been quite as unkind to me as Elegance—yes, that's her real name—her older sister and the spitting image of her mother both in soul and looks. They're both brunette, with austere cheekbones and sharp gray eyes, both stunning in a severe way.

Chrysanthemum is softer, her brown hair slightly lighter, curling at the ends, her eyes blue rather than gray, her lips full and pink, her fair skin lightly freckled.

She's the prettiest of all of us, and I don't resent her for it. Sure, she has the backbone of a glowworm, and growing up, if Elegance decided to torture me, Chrys would be right alongside her in whatever devilish games her sister had come up with to make my life miserable.

But she always tried to make up for it afterward. If they hid the last piece of my favorite puzzle, she'd offer me hers. If they cut up my doll's hair, I'd find one of Chrys's dolls tucked under my bed.

It didn't make me respect her then, the secret gifts, the reparations she attempted to make. It also doesn't make us friends.

But on the spectrum of hate, I despise her far less than her sister.

My guard seems to notice Chrys, too. I can't see his face, but his boots have shifted in her direction, and now he's trembling.

Wait, no.

He'd already been trembling, as soon as we heard them shuffling down the stairs.

I stiffen. Something isn't quite right—it never is, if my stepmother is around—but I can't quite put my finger on what.

It's then that I notice the other woman.

She's cloaked, her hood drawn over her head, so I can only glimpse the lower half of her face. She's pale—not pale like Imogen, whose skin is the color of water after it's been used to soak rice. This woman is as pale as moonlight, as pale as the first frost.

Her lips are pale, too, and she wears no paint.

She stands behind Clarissa and Elegance, and while Clarissa likely interprets this as deference, the hair prickling at the back of my neck tells me she's very, very wrong.

This female fears no one.

She's fae. Even with her ears covered, I can tell by her height, by her perfectly symmetrical lips.

My fingers remain clenched in the sheets, but they're no longer shaking from rage alone.

A scarlet grin slices across my stepmother's face. "Oh, how glad I'll be to be rid of you, my dear."

I fight the urge to scoot back in my bed and instead mirror her smirk. "Seems ungrateful, since my salary is the only thing that kept you fed all these years. Whatever will you do without it?"

Obviously she won't do without. That's why the mysterious fae is here, right? But I know my stepmother well enough to know that taunting is the most direct way to receive information.

"Oh, we won't be doing without anything. Not anymore."

I swallow, but I keep my tone saccharine. "But, dear stepmother. You know no matter what she's offered you, it will be gone before the season is over. When it comes to your girls, *no expense must be spared.*"

I'm pretty proud of my imitation.

Usually, this is the key to inciting my stepmother.

Perhaps that's why I'm so unsettled when she only grins.

"Harold," she nods to my guard, "open it."

I can't help the cackle that escapes my lips. "You think Harold's going to disobey the Heir of Dwellen's personal order and un—"

My words catch in my mouth as the guard slips his hands into his pockets and pulls out an iron ring of keys. "Sorry, miss," he mumbles to me as he slides the key into the lock.

Fear slices through me, severing my bones and tendons and freezing my blood.

She's sold me. Clarissa has finally sold me—to this fae female who refuses to show her full face, whose very presence chills my blood.

I'm not sure what scares me more.

Being sold to a stranger to be and do Fates know what, or that when the moon crests the horizon, I'll no longer be tucked away in my cell.

"Please. Harold. You can't do this. Whatever my stepmother is offering you, she doesn't have it. She depends on my servant's salary. She only pretends to be wealthy."

He shakes his head. "I don't care about Miss Chrysanthemum's dowry, miss. We'll do just fine on my salary, won't we?"

He turns a head and winks at Chrys, who dissolves into her mother's side. She blanches, and for a moment, I think she might vomit.

Oh.

Oh.

I grit my teeth, whirling on my stepmother. "You'd sell your own daughter for a copper?"

If Clarissa is ruffled by my comment, she doesn't show it. "All my Chrysanthemum has ever wanted is a nice male to take care of her, to provide her a warm home in the winter and children at her feet during the Solstice. Now we all can be happy."

"Why not Elegance? She's the oldest," I say, to which my eldest stepsister shuffles, actually shuffles, probably for the first time in her life. I note the weakness and exploit it. "Surely you're not okay with this, with Chrys being sold off to a male she clearly does not want to marry."

Harold clears his throat, but Elegance purses her lips. And from years of knowing the girl, it tells me all I need to know.

She's already tried. She's tried to fight her mother on this, and she failed.

The door creaks open, and something stirs within me, tasting freedom through the cracks.

No, no, no. "How late is it?" I ask, all thoughts second to that one. *How long before it takes over my body?*

"You don't understand. You have to lock me back in."

When my stepfamily shoots me confused looks, I turn to the fae female. "I don't know what my stepmother told you about me, but I assure you, you don't want me. I'm possessed, and when the full moon comes out, which it's about to do, the thing inside me takes over. It will kill you. It'll kill you and everything in its path to get back to the prince. You don't understand—"

"Child, calm yourself," the female says, her voice cool and firm and…gentler, more motherly than I expected from someone trying to purchase a slave. "I am aware of your gift. That is precisely why I've come."

My muscles still, tense like a cat might before it launches on its prey.

Except this time, I sense I might be the little mouse.

I swallow, steeling myself. "I'm not going anywhere with you until you explain what you're here for."

My stepmother scoffs. "You're going with her whether you like it or not, child."

I ignore her, one of my favorite approaches to getting under her skin. She bristles, though this time the slight had not been purposeful. I simply can't tear my eyes off the hooded woman.

"I think you'll like what I have to offer."

I bore my bare feet into the cold stone tiles, tracing my toe into the mortar, but I slip on my favorite mask. The nonchalant one that people so easily seem to believe. "I highly doubt you have anything that would pique my interest. I'm quite content where I am," I say, flourishing toward my jail cell.

The female's pale lips lift at the edges, amused. There, perhaps I can convince her she can take me willingly, if only she tells me what it is she has planned for me.

I have no intention of going with this woman, of course. But I'd rather her not know that until after she reveals what she's planning.

I'm sure she expects me to be grasping for an escape, easy to win over if she dangles my freedom before my gaunt face.

I bet I look like that kind of girl, the scrappy sort always on the lookout for myself.

But Evander put me here for a reason, and he's crossing the world to find me a cure, and so I'll sit here in this cell until he returns to tell me there's no hope.

I'm not sure what I'll do after that. I've tried not to think that far ahead.

"You could possess a power far greater than the one you currently carry," the female says.

I scoff. "Yeah, thirst for power isn't exactly my vice. Sorry."

The female draws her hood, revealing a perfect face with ice-blue eyes, sharp enough to pierce a soul. That's not where my attention fixes, though. My eyes are locked on her bracelet, where a single blood-red jewel dangles.

The sight of it stirs a memory in me, but before I can place it, the female smiles, death on her lips, and she purrs, "My dear, I'm afraid I wasn't speaking to you."

ACKNOWLEDGMENTS

I've been praying for a while now for the ability to do this writing thing full-time. This particular prayer always felt more like a want than a need, which makes it all the more humbling that God saw fit to grant my request.

Jacob, I think you might be spoiling me. I think I might be okay with that. Mom, since you asked, I finally wrote a book where the mother isn't dead or crazy; you're welcome. Dad, thanks for laughing out loud at the jokes in this book. I'm well aware that I'm your least funny child, so it means a lot. Wilson and Maria, thanks for the competition. Karri, your covers are gorgeous and contribute so much to the success of these books. Christine, thanks for putting up with my inability to capitalize appropriately. Alexia, thank you so much for the kind and constructive feedback you provided during the sensitivity read. Rachel, thanks for the generous supply of Jeff Winger references that make reading my beta feedback so enjoyable. Alyssa Dorn, thanks for taking time out of your busy schedule to beta read for me; I don't know what I would do without you spotting the sentences I forgot to delete so I don't spoil the twist for my readers. Morgan Cari, thanks for helping me make sure my characters are lovable and consistent in their development.

To all my lovely readers, I couldn't do this without you.

FREE PREQUEL NOVELLA

Rumors ripple through Alondria of an avenger of the weak, the innocent, the mistreated.

They say he stalks in the shadows, suffocates his victims with the flicker in his eyes. That if you're unfortunate enough to catch him lower his hood, his will be the last face you'll ever see.

Of course, if anyone really knew that for sure, if anyone had ever escaped, they would have known better.

They would have known that the last face my victims ever saw...was a she.

Lydia is used to bringing reproach on the royal family. It's been that way ever since the day the midwife informed her father, the King of Naenden, that his wife had borne not an heir, but a daughter.

What a shame.

With her father dead, Lydia has better things to do than sit around the palace and wait for her spoiled brother to run their kingdom into the ground.

Of course, a princess can't exactly travel alone without earning a *reputation.*

That's fine with Lydia. Because as long as the gossipers stay distracted spreading rumors of her indiscretions, they'll never imagine what she's actually up to.

But when Lydia happens across a petty thief she can't seem to shake, she violates her most sacred rule.

Never make a bargain you can't break.

ABOUT THE AUTHOR

T.A. Lawrence is the author of The Severed Realms, a series of fairytale retellings that feature mystery, danger, romance, and, of course, fae. T.A. Lawrence also writes the middle-grade series The Astoria Chronicles, the story of a girl who frequents a fantasy world through a portal in her neighbor's cotton field. T.A. lives in Alabama with her loving and supportive husband Jacob, who occasionally convinces her to leave the house.

instagram.com/talawrenceauthor
tiktok.com/@talawrencebooks

ALSO BY T.A. LAWRENCE

The Severed Realms

A Word so Fitly Spoken

A Tune to Make Them Follow

A Bond of Broken Glass

A Throne of Blood and Ice (Coming July 2023)

The Astoria Chronicles

The Keeper of the Threshold

The Secret of Atalo